Soul Of Rah

Book Two
of the
Saga Of The Rah

Susan Shepherd

I fled Him, down the nights and down the days;
I fled Him, down the arches of the years;
I fled Him, down the labyrinthine ways
Of my own mind; and in the midst of tears
I hid from Him, and under running laughter.
Up vistaed hopes I sped;
And shot, precipitated,
Adown Titanic glooms of chasmed fears,
From those strong Feet that followed, followed after.
But with unhurrying chase,
And unperturbed pace,
Deliberate speed, majestic instancy,
They beat- and a Voice beat
More instant than the Feet –
"All things betray thee, who betrayest Me'.

Francis Thompson – "The Hound of Heaven" (1889)

CHAPTER 1

"Gah," says Rah, and the dapple colt in the stall beside the crib he lies in lifts its head with a sharp jerk and blows.

"You have awakened him!" cries Cara, looking down into the brilliant blue-green eyes of the Grain God, which in turn look with a child's simple trust into hers.

"Nikolaos!" booms Rush, startling the colt a second time, his voice carrying up and onto the deck, where the Captain of the Palace Guard of Cyrus stands alongside Ramicus of Knossos, discussing their future, now they are the property of Rush the Assassin. But the boy is not startled. He makes a weak attempt to rise to his elbows in the bed of straw, but is unable to lift himself. Cara presses his shoulders back down, cradling his head and settling it back on her lap.

The colt has brought its head over the edge of the crib to nuzzle the boy's hay-colored curls.

"Hali!" croaks Rah, who has not spoken, nor moved, in four days. "This my horse," he tries again, pushing a dry whisper from his parched lips, and lifting a hand to stroke the colt's muzzle.

"That one, and twenty more like him, little cat," says Rush, lifting a hand to wipe the blood from the boy's ear where the lobe has been re-pierced by his rough replacement of the pearl.

"And an earring worth another twenty," muses Tyrus, who has come to stand beside Rush.

"He is awake?" It is Nikolaos, who has not wasted time descending to the hold on a rope ladder but has jumped down into the stable block from the deck above. Ramicus, in the meantime, has circled the deck and is rushing down the wood stairs at the back of the aperture.

"He was," says Rush, unconsciously licking the boy's blood from his finger.

1

"He seems to have fainted again," says Cara, smoothing curls from the boy's forehead.

"He is weak as a kitten," says Enenoch, High Priest of the House of the Sky. "Here, girl." He offers Cara a gourd, which he has found hanging on a nearby water barrel and filled. "See if he will take some."

But it is Nikolaos who, taking the gourd from Cara, lifts the boy's head and pours a few drops of water onto his lips.

"You must drink, Rah." He leans to whisper in the boy's ear. "You must grow strong again. To dance and ride."

Rah's eyes open weakly to regard the Captain. They glitter, gold and green in the sea light pouring into the hold from the canopy above. He gives Nikolaos a fleeting smile, the hint of a dimple pleating his pale cheek. "Fox," he murmurs. "You still watch Rah?" He opens his mouth to the gourd and takes a few swallows.

"We go to Anatolia," continues Nikolaos, a bit light headed now, having been honored with that smile. He speaks only to Rah, though he has an audience of seven.

"Is dance in Anatol-?" responds the boy, looking over Nikolaos' shoulder to the assassin.

"There will be," responds Rush, "when you get there. And your own temple, and dance troupe. Dimius is aboard my own ship sent days ahead of us, along with his company, and your attendants, Pyrus and Aros. As well as the priest, Mochlos, and Ting Ya."

"Ting Ya!" yelps Rah, spitting out a bit of water and attempting once more to rise to his elbows in the straw. "She say-" he begins, but then loses focus, closes his eyes, and nods off a second time.

"This is enough for now," says Cara, petting the boy's golden head. "Please, let him rest." She looks at Rush with something between love and fear. He gives her a dismissive glance.

"You are the last thing he needs to awaken to, woman, for you know as well as I what he will attempt as soon as he can manage to stay awake for more than a few minutes. Get out of that crib. Leave him with Crispo. And you, Captain. He is…" he falters here, his voice breaking, a thing he disguises with a cough. "He is safe from harm with you."

Nikolaos lifts a hand to rest on the assassin's arm. The others watch, not a little amazed. What have these two been through together, that the Captain can be so bold? Who else among them would dare to touch the assassin, least of all to offer him tenderness?

Tyrus has leaned over the crib to tickle Rah's scalp while this exchange is going on, and though apparently asleep, the boy has begun to make his strange, human purr again, a noise that begins somewhere behind his clavicle and rustles in the base of his throat.

"He is fond of your touch, Tyrus," murmurs Cara, smiling at the Bull priest as she slips out of the crib.

"He is fond of gentleness," pipes Crispo, who has been beaming like a noon day sun since the boy first opened his brilliant, sea-colored eyes. "And my cooking!"

Rush has snatched Tyrus' wrist, drawing the man's fingers away from the boy's curls. He looks at the Bull priest with predatory energy in his narrowed eyes. "Let him rest, priest," he says. "All of you," he adds, looking about at the group. "We have no more than a day's sail to Amega. Then my own physicians will care for him." He turns his shoulder, giving them his broad back, "And bring him back to his full strength, or lose their heads."

When he is gone, the group disperses. All but Nikolaos and Crispo, who continue to watch the Grain God sleep, snoring lightly, waking occasionally, accepting a bit of water from the priest or a crumb of bread or dried fruit from the Captain.

He will sleep thus until the Queen's ship reaches Amega, the assassin's compound on the far southeastern shore of Anatolia, and then the cries of wonder from the deck above will bring him to full consciousness, just in time for him to set the land of Hatti on fire.

In an opulently appointed bed chamber and dressing room, on the eastern side of the citadel of Amega, Pyrus and Aros, the Grain God's private attendants, are the first to see the Queen's ship crest the horizon.

"Merciful Mother god, it is the Queen's ship, Pyrus! Look how her canopy glints golden in the sun! They have survived the volcano! Oh, my heart," says Aros, clutching at his breast and dropping to his knees, weeping. "I feel it in my heart, Pyrus, our Sunlight is aboard her!"

Pyrus, always less quick to think the best, leans out of the enormous open casement, his hands pressing the marble sill until he nearly loses his balance and topples out onto the soldier pacing the parapet below. But soon the guesswork is removed from their observations. The shouts of joy, tumultuous whoops and battle cries of victory coming from the compound that surrounds the citadel, is enough to send them both under the mattress of the great bed that is elevated on a platform in the middle of the room. For this is a compound of warriors. The two delicately bred and sheltered Minoans from the House of the Moon have yet to become accustomed to their surroundings. They are in each other's arms, Aros letting out his own weak yelp in reaction to the ferocious baying of the battalion that surrounds them.

It is Pyrus who regains his composure first, extracting himself from his friend's embrace and giving him a maternal shake.

"It is happiness, Aros. They are happy to see that their beloved commander is returned to them, you see? Nothing to fear. We are protected by his good will."

"Protected from wolves by the goodwill of a wolf," whimpers Aros. "I do not know that I shall ever become convinced of my safety here, Pyrus. Oh, my poor Sunlight! How will he survive this place?"

At this, Pyrus must chuckle. "Better to say, 'how will this place survive Rah.'"

Josepha is entertaining her new guest, Ting Ya, in an extraordinary patio garden behind the House of Antaris, when the victory cries of the soldiers from the army compound break the noonday Mediterranean stillness. The patio faces the sea and is cut into the cliffs, offering an extraordinary view of the water, and so, of any vessels heading toward Amega. It is surrounded by waist high stone walls, four feet thick. From the sea, the exterior walls of the patio courtyard reach half way down the cliffs in a sheer drop. Built into these walls is the sign of the bull, the very image of the tattoo that the assassin leaves under the left eye of his victims, flanked by elaborate columns representing the towering strength of the fortress. Behind the courtyard, which is invisible to the sea, the lines of the House of Antaris follow the columns upward toward the top of the cliff. From the sea, it is as if the house is built into the cliffs, an impossible and colossal citadel overlooking all that its king considers his own. But in fact, it is set on a plateau half way up the cliffs, and upon this plateau the armies of Rush the Assassin train and prepare for war.

"He is home, Ting Ya," says Josepha, rising to her feet from her couch, one hand raised to her throat. Her voice is soft and steady, and the light movement of her hand is the only sign that she is relieved at the sighting of the Queen's ship. "He has come home."

Ting Ya has made no effort to rise. She sits patiently on a pillowed settee beside the lady of the house, in the center of the patio, which is deliberately built on a marble platform so that the wife of the assassin need not stand nor approach the wall to see that her husband returns to her. The platform is, at any rate, the only place in the courtyard from which the diminutive Ting Ya can see over the wall. From her own seat, she reaches out with cool fingers to touch Josepha's wrist, and Josepha's mind is interrupted by the image of Rah on his knees before her, naked and weeping over the death of a dingy white cur dog named Hali.

"Jin yu also home," says Ting Ya. And although she has never heard the name, Josepha instantly understands that this is the Asian woman's love word for the boy. Jin yu, in your tongue, means gold in abundance, thinks Josepha, recalling Rah in her own garden in Knossos only a month earlier. How appropriate.

"Yes, Ting Ya, they are both aboard," says Josepha. This is something the two women have shared without discussion from their first meeting. Both are seers, Josepha, by a kind of tactile telepathy, Ting Ya, on perhaps a grander scale, in dreams and visions.

"Now this place fill with light," says Ting Ya, smiling in her mysterious Asian way at her sister seer, "and your husband must face his greatest challenge. For how can such darkness live with such light? Must run from light, like shadow, not able to face what is inside himself."

"Yes, Ting Ya," agrees Josepha. "Now he will run," and internally she thinks, like the rangy black wolf that he is. My love. My love. Now only war will satisfy you.

Along the bright and sunlit hallway of a separate wing of the assassin's citadel, Mochlos the priest walks with Dimius, his dance master. The priest, normally a tall, lean man with excellent posture and a superior bearing, is hunched over, his arms wrapped about his narrow chest, his chin in his hand. He is perhaps one of the only living creatures on the cliff side that is Amega who is not rejoicing at the return of the man of war who established this colony for the sole purpose of training troops for hire. His relationship with the assassin is tenuous at best, and he is not one to forget how quickly such a man can turn. Like his clever peer, Tyrus, he knows he must make himself not only useful, but irreplaceable, if he is to survive life in the service of Rush the Assassin.

"The boy will surely be with him. That man will not have left Crete without our little Grain God," he murmurs, taking long, tigerish strides that only a dancer could match without running beside him.

"Yes, sir. I am sure Rah is aboard," responds Dimius, unable to contain the doubt that has crept into his careful mind these last days. For how is it possible? The boy was kidnapped, perhaps killed. Even Rush could not bring him back from the dead, though he could send the thugs who committed the act swiftly after him to the netherworld. And even if he *had* somehow managed not only to find but to rescue Rah before he was murdered, what of Thera itself? The Queen's ship was on the horizon, yes. But was it without casualties? What must the seas have been like in the wake of that fantastic blast? Even from here, hundreds of miles away, the sound was extraordinary. Pottery shook in the kitchen, although the sea only climbed the cliff a few meters.

Suddenly the priest turns and grasps the dance master by the arm. His fingers are like claws, pressing to the bone.

"I have it, Dimius!" He smiles his crafty smile, a smile Dimius has long known to be dangerous.

"What is it, Master?" responds the dancer, recalling the sting of the priest's reed on his backside and stiffening against his master's touch.

"Without me, without his priest and creator, the boy will lose the soul of Rah, you see? I need only convince the boy of this, and the man will follow. I am the priest of the Moon, ordained servant of his mother, and that is that. Like it or not, I made him. I, and Ananou the Sun Priest, who was no more than an assistant. It is the Moon who rules Rah, her son. I am essential. Essential!"

"But," begins Dimius, his brow wrinkling, for surely there is more to the priest's scheme than this. A man like Rush is not convinced with trivialities.

"I need only convince the boy," repeats Mochlos, smiling his clever smile and saying nothing more. For just how he intends to convince the boy of his power over the soul of the god that inhabits him, he has no desire to share with Dimius, or any other human being.

Far south, along the coast of Canaan, the Queen of Knossos and the Queen of Cyrus have reached the Minoan settlements of Sidon and Arwad. Nanaea will remain here to her last days, her pregnancy, the gift of Ameg, indeed providing her with the daughter she had prayed for, a strong-willed tigress with the heart of a warrior, who will leave home at the age of eighteen summers and follow a Hittite army into Syria, killing dozens of men before her sex is discovered and she is married to her own general, finally settling along the Euphrates River herself during a Hittite reign of Babylon now obscured in history. The household of King Cyrus has settled further north along the seashore and is in mourning, for their queen has returned to madness.

Nanaea's ship, gift to the father of her pregnancy, reaches the harbor beneath the Citadel of Amega under a full moon. It must remain in the harbor until daybreak, when soldiers will row out to meet it and guide it safely into the harbor.

During the night the Grain God of Knossos is awakened by a dream. In it, he sees himself in the blue and gold robes he wore during the dance of the Sun God. He rides in a gilded bucket behind three white chariot chargers. He is no longer a boy, but a man, the dappled colt, no longer a leggy, two year old, but a silver-white stallion. Halix leads the triple horse chariot from the center, flanked on either side by mother and sister. Rah races along a flat plain, flanked by seven other charioteers. He is in the lead, and will maintain it, though the colt's mother, running along on the right, will snap her pastern before the race is ended, and continue running on the shattered bone four more strides before she collapses at the finish line.

Rah awakens to the sound of his own heartbeat in his ears. He is drenched in sweat and weeping. For he has named the mare Ileah, after his twin, and all the heartache of that separation is again upon him. He sits up, and promptly is overcome by a wave of nausea that propels him over the side of the crib to vomit a bit of water and bile, all that his empty stomach has to offer.

Still weeping, and head hanging over the bar of the crib, he feels the smooth flutter of the colt's muzzle at the back of his head. The animal's gentle flehmming is an instant comfort to him. Its lips move like fingers against the side of his neck and to his shoulder like an expert lover and send an electrifying tickle up into his scalp and down to his groin. Rah's halting sobs turn to giggles. He twists to kiss the soft skin between Halix' nostrils where a pink lozenge of flesh peeks through the animal's otherwise grey coat.

"No race, Hali," Rah whispers the promise. "Rah no race Hali."

The colt blows, bumps his chin playfully, returns to its hay. After a moment, Rah slips out of the crib and stretches to find the wood floor with his feet.

He looks about him in the sea-lit dark. The canopy flaps in a mild breeze overhead. Brother Crispo is curled up in a ball on the floor beside the crib, snoring the snore of a fat man. Captain Nikolaos has gone to bed with his new wife, and though Rah cannot know this, he senses it as easily as if he could see into their tiny cabin at the rear of the stable block, slide in between the newlyweds and put his fingers through Cara's tousled hair.

"Ta hah," chuckles Rah. "Fox take Cara. But Cara want Wolf." He shakes his head with a little frown. "And Wolf is love Rah." Carefully, he begins to negotiate a few steps across the floor to the stair. "Wolf is love Rah, Cara is love Wolf," he whispers to himself, taking small, tenuous steps in the near dark. "Fox take Cara." He has found the stair, and begins a slow, dizzy attempt to conquer it. For he is finding his way to the Master's cabin, the direction of which he cannot know, but knows as clearly as he knows that something new has happened to him in his sleep.

"And everyone want Rah," he finishes his private discussion of the fickleness of human desires as he reaches the top of the stair and turns right. "More now," he shakes his head again, almost sadly, with the knowledge. "People so hungry." In a cabin at the fore of the ship, the Master sleeps the light sleep of an assassin. He dreams of Amega, a plateau in the cliffs along the shore of southeastern Anatolia where even the King of Hatti cannot reach him nor dare challenge him. And so, unable to challenge him, the King pays him, pays for his army of foot soldiers and archers and charioteers, the finest and fiercest in all the Kingdom, to wage his wars upon his enemies to the south. Rush knows the King wants the Euphrates and so, Babylon. Has always known it. It is why he established his citadel in the far southeast of the kingdom, ruling land and sea effectively and forcing the King to either hire his army for his assaults on Syria or to face it himself.

Even in his sleep Rush dreams of war, for nothing but war will satisfy him now. Now that desire has made a slave of the Terror of the Aegean.

Rah enters the cabin on a cat's soft feet, his dancer's weightless tread too light to alert even an assassin. He stands over the pallet upon which the Master lies, tottering against the rocking of the vessel like an acrobat on a rope. He looks down, suddenly aware that he has never seen Rush sleeping. It is like viewing a king lying in his sarcophagus, the chiseled features, the neat black beard, the noble brow arranged as if by priests into an expression of supreme sovereignty.

"Handsome Wolf," muses Rah, and reaches to touch the man's cheek with an inquisitive and fearless finger.

His wrist is instantly snatched as in the jaws of a jackal. The assassin's black eyes flash open, flicker over him, then peer beyond him toward the doorway. A look of disbelief crosses the man's face as he looks up at Rah again, squinting into the dark to find the boy's eyes.

"What is it, little cat?" he whispers, releasing the boy's wrist with some reluctance. "Why have you left your bed to come to me?"

Rah totters before him with the movement of the ship. It is clear he is not yet ready to stand, much less to walk and balance on the deck of an anchored vessel.

"Sit down before you fall, boy, and bash that head of yours again," says Rush gruffly, still off balance himself. He has been chasing this creature since he first laid eyes upon him. Never has the boy come to him of his own accord, and the strangeness of this thing is downright disturbing.

"This Wolf is no hurt Rah now," says Rah, moving to plop down on the pallet beside Rush. Seated, he draws his legs up into a half-lotus casually and turns to the assassin as if to a confidante. He peers up into his face under the brush of his golden lashes.

"We go now to war, Wolf? You take Rah?"

"Pah!" Rush must throttle his own laughter. Two things strike him at once. First, that the boy should have somehow guessed that he has been dreaming of war, and then, the absurdity of taking Rah to battle with him.

"So that the Amorites may die laughing?" he says, more to himself than to Rah. But the boy only leans into him conspiratorially.

"No, Wolf, I see Rah. On chariot! Three horse! Three men! So fast! Rah can do this!"

"A three horse chariot? No, little cat. There is no such thing. Not even in Hatti, and we are the best horsemen in the world."

"No, Wolf. *Rah* is best horseman in world. Three horse. Rah can do this. I teach."

Rush can only shake his head, but the vision sticks. He can see it, Rah in the bucket, an archer to his left, a swordsman to his right. And three horses pulling the chariot. "Insane," he murmurs. "Hard enough to get two to run together. Three? How do you train three across? And how attach them to the cart? And three men? No, little cat. You have had a dream, that is all."

"No!" Rah has reached out to snatch the assassin's arm, but his fingers can only close over half the man's massive bicep. Rush looks down at those fingers, fingers made for the sweet gesture and grace of the dance, then back into the boy's angelic face. I would take that hand off at the wrist for that, if it were any other, he thinks. But you, beautiful Rah, have never touched me willingly, and now you do so. How is it that you do not fear your wolf tonight?

But to Rah he says, his voice lowering, "You think you will train this wolf to kill?"

Rah's eyes widen in the dark. He drops his hand from the assassin's arm.

"No train wolf. Train horse," he says carefully. "Wolf know how to kill," he adds, dropping his eyes sheepishly.

Rush squints at him in the dark. The boy is sitting cross-legged at the head of the pallet, which is against the wall of the cabin. Curious, he leans toward him with a quick, aggressive motion and the boy presses back quickly into the wall. Ah, there. That is better, thinks Rush. There is the old Rah. Still, there is no warning burr in his throat, no fear in his eyes, just a soft wrinkle of puzzlement in his brow.

"What do you remember, Rah? Before you fell asleep? Do you remember anything?"

Rah looks down at his hands which now rest in his lap. "I remember I am dance. Bow to King. There is Wolf. Mad Wolf, still mad for Rah spit at him," he looks back up into the assassin's face. "Wolf, he say, 'No say sorry for spit! Bad little cat, make wolf crazy! Wolf heart in chain! I remember."

"And what next, Rah?" presses Rush.

Rah shrugs. "Rah has fit," he says. Then, comically, he leans over his own lap, tipping his head up at Rush, peering into his eyes from beneath. Dimples crease the corners of his mouth. "Wolf is love Rah," he says without conceit, his voice deep from lack of use. "Like meat, Wolf love, hah!" He shrugs again. "Rah do not make wolf love meat! Rah do not make Wolf love Rah." He shrugs again. Suddenly he is pouting. "Hungry," he looks down at the ripple of lean muscle over his empty belly, splays his fingers against it. "Need food."

Rush frowns. Child mind. Dog mind. Mother of the gods, help me. You come to my bed, alone, after what I've done to you? Like meat is right, Rah. If I sit here another moment with you I will make a meal of you.

He lifts himself off the pallet and reaches for Rah's arm. "We will find Crispo. He will know what to feed you." But rather than moving to find the priest he merely bellows where he stands, effectively waking the entire ship with the force of his powerful lungs.

"Crispo!"

After a moment, the thump and lumber of the priest's corpulence can be heard approaching the cabin door.

"Sir?" says the priest softly, opening the aperture to find Rush standing in the center of the swaying room with a tottering Rah.

"Take him back to his bed. Put together something he will eat. Don't overfeed him, hear? I won't have him colic before we reach shore."

"Sir," nods Crispo, shuffling in to herd Rah back to the stable block.

"Crispo!"

"Sir?"

"He came to me on his own," grumbles Rush irritably.

"Yes, sir," responds the priest carefully.

"Go!" he waves the priest away, slamming the door behind him. Then, without provocation, he punches the back of it with a deadly strike, there, just where the boy had been, splitting the finely carve olive wood down to the floor.

CHAPTER 2

In the morning the ship is guided into shore by a small flotilla of military vessels. The assassin disembarks first. Here in Amega he will wear the garments of a military commander, a short, fighting skirt, an exquisite breastplate forged in the settlement's own metalwork mill, and a tall bronze helmet, his usual weaponry strapped to his sides, his waist and ankles. But today he disembarks from the Queen's ship in the white robe of a Minoan Priest of the Dead. Nikolaos, wearing his Cyrian Captain's uniform, walks beside him, in a place of honor to his right. Then the three priests, Tyrus, Enenoch and Crispo, wearing the robes of their houses and carrying Rah between them on a stretcher, and Cara, who also wears the robe of a Priest of the Dead, but with hood up, so that she is completely invisible, then Ramicus and his men, and finally, the eighteen junior priests of the Houses of the Bull and Sky. The horses will be handled by experts now, men assigned to care for the five hundred chariot chargers of the garrison. They will be taken along a narrow path around the side of the cliff to the plateau of Amega behind the citadel. But Rush and the priests, Captain Nikolaos, Cara and Rah are led by a contingent of guards directly into the depths of the fortress and there left in the hands of the assassin's personal household servants.

Upon his arrival in Amega, Nikolaos is first struck by the fact that every man he meets wears the mark of the Tears of the Bull beneath his left eye. Rush, noticing the Captain's amazement, turns to him casually and lifts a brow.

"What is this, Rush? An army of failed assassinations?" quips the Captain, when he has recovered from the shock.

"My forces wear my mark proudly, Captain, as will you, when you realize what good fortune you enjoy by being allowed to wear it and continue breathing at the same time."

"You knew this in Cyrus? That I would work for you?" answers Nikolaos, incredulous.

"Not exactly, Captain. But either way, dead or alive, your arrogance had earned you the mark."

"I see."

"And so it is with all of those here who wear it. Once it is on you, you are either willing to lay your life down for me in battle, or die by my hand."

A tall, lean servant has approached with elegant, light steps from a stair to the group's right. But when he reaches his master, the disciplined manner falters. He lifts his hands as if to take the assassin's in his own, then remembers himself and drops like a rag to the ground in a full body bow.

"Get up, Ham, and take these pests off my hands. You have readied quarters for them?"

"Of course, Master. All is prepared," says Ham, rising to his feet but maintaining downcast eyes. Behind him several more servants, all male, wait obsequiously for instruction.

"I wish to see my wife," breaths Rush, allowing himself an exhausted sigh. "Care for my guests."

"Yes, Sir," says Ham, raising his eyes to his master's an instant and risking a soft smile. "She awaits your arrival in the Master's chambers, Sir."

But Rush will allow himself a bath, a barber and a change of clothing before he goes to his Josepha. For now, he takes Ham and another man aside to speak with privately while the others wait. Then he marches off on his own, without a nod to those he has rescued and whose lives are now his to take or treasure.

"You are to come with me, sir," says the second man to Nikolaos, when Rush is gone. "And you also, madam." He nods to Cara courteously. The two move off behind him, taking the same set of stairs Rush took.

When they are gone, Tyrus and Enenoch are immediately relieved of Rah's stretcher by two strong house servants, and the three priests are led down a hall and up a shallow flight of stairs to a colonnade overlooking a lyceum.

"The Lady has had these wings prepared for the Rah and his temple," says Ham, turning to Tyrus instinctively as the leader of the group, for he knows the man to be Hittite by birth, and this gives him an advantage in Amega. "The High Priest, Mochlos is already here, along with his household. There is room enough for the rest of you, down this wing-" he raises an arm to his right, gesturing to a long hall extending perpendicularly to the one he walks, along the west side of the lyceum, "for you and your staff, Sky Priest, and here "he gestures left down an opposite hall which stretches south, like a claw, into the courtyard where Josepha awaited her husband's return, "for you, Tyrus of Troy."

"I am Hittite, sir," responds Tyrus politely, maintaining a casual smile, although the barb stings. It is clearly a name assigned him by the assassin, and just as clearly one that will stick here in Amega, like or no.

"Beg pardon, sir. But I am to address you so," says Ham, giving Tyrus a small bow of apology.

"And what of the House of the Sun?" It is Crispo, who seemed to have lost his tongue since the company was met at the wharf by dozens of ferocious looking, long-haired men bearing the Tears of the Bull.

"The Master has suggested you should be closer to the kitchens, Sun Priest, as it will be your sole honor to prepare the Rah's meals. You will be given authority over the kitchen in addition to this duty. The kitchen is situated directly below," and here Ham gestures to the floor, "In the wing beneath, which runs along the west of the central courtyard."

At this, the three priests look to one another, Crispo with a look of satisfied superiority on his face, for he has already become indispensable, without trying, simply by virtue of being a priest who is also able to cook.

"What of the boy, Ham?" asks Tyrus now. "You say that the lady has prepared this wing for 'Rah and his temple'. Is Mochlos in charge of him? Or are we all assigned to see to his care?"

"Rah is to have four high priests now, sir," answers Ham calmly. "Moon, which as you know, here is Hatti, is also Sea. Sun, Sky, and Bull, who is master of Earth. All will nurture the Soul of Rah. This is all I know, sir."

"And who is to have authority?" asks Enenoch nervously.

Ham offers the Sky Priest a casual glance. It is almost dismissive. "That would be Mochlos, sir, for he has drawn the god into the host."

"I see," says Tyrus, stroking his beard, eyes narrowing.

"No advantage in that, eh Tyrus of Troy?" whispers Enenoch in his ear after Ham has left them, nodding to Crispo to follow him back downstairs to the kitchens.

"We shall see, Enenoch. Perhaps it is not such a disadvantage to be secondary at the beginning, when it is easy to screw up and anger the assassin, eh? Let us take a back seat and be glad of it. See how Mochlos handles this one."

While the two priests and their staff attempt to settle in their rooms, Rah is carried further down the hall. But a commotion soon draws Tyrus and Enenoch back to the intersection of their respective wings. From their vantage point they can hear the reedy voice of Mochlos rise above the din. Tyrus and Enenoch freeze, still as ghosts, to listen.

"Ah, you see? A slave god cannot be separated from the temple of his birth! It is a miracle he is not dead. Only the swiftness of the magnificent and beneficent Antaris has kept him alive long enough for him to be returned to his priest, so that he may now be restored by appropriate

13

religious ceremony and offerings to the god! Thank our illustrious benefactor, the great Antaris, for his speed in recovering the boy! Assure him that Mochlos of the House of the Moon will do everything that is essential to restore the Soul of Rah in this vessel! Go now, be quick! Send my most humble gratitude to the Master!"

"Well," whispers Enenoch to Tyrus after a moment of silence, which is followed by the quick footsteps of house servants moving toward them from what must be Mochlos' wing. "He has surely set to work making himself essential. But what of us? What good are we if only Mochlos is necessary?"

"Mochlos is a clever man, my friend, but he cannot outsmart the one who has saved us all from Thera, and owns us now. If Mochlos' has one flaw, it is that. He may yet underestimate Rush. And that makes him a fool. If Rush did not believe us to be indispensable would he have brought us here at all? Did he need the weight of twenty more bodies on the Queen's ship? No. I, for one, will be what Rush has decided I will be. A clown? Very good, sir, where are my bells? Hang them from my nose you say? Perfect. I should have thought of it myself. A cook? Where are my ovens that I may bake you your favorite dish? I am a wiz at saucing the human head."

"I don't know how you make jokes at a time like this, Tyrus. Your wit is as dry as my throat."

"Hush. Remove yourself to your quarters until they pass. Then we will visit our fellow cleric."

A few moments later, after the house servants have passed carrying the empty stretcher, Tyrus and Enenoch join together once more to follow the hall to the chambers of Mochlos.

The High Priest of the Moon is standing over a raised pallet, soft with down stuffed linens and strewn with sheep skins and pillows. The little Grain God has been deposited on the bed, but he is not prone. He is sitting up and in the process of folding his legs into his customary full lotus as he regards the priest with haughty eyes.

Paying no attention to the intrusion, Rah continues a conversation that appears to have been one sided from the start.

"No! Rah does not sleep here with this priest! This priest is" and he makes a quick, waving movement with his hand to pantomime the stealth of the vermin he sees in his mind. "Like" he gives up, spits out the word in Greek, "Weasel! He come into Rah bed like weasel, like he is come to take chicken from coop! No! Rah does not stay here! Wolf is kill this weasel for Rah!" And up he springs from the bed, onto his feet, wobbling one instant long enough for Tyrus to leap cross the room and prevent him from crumpling to the fine marble-tiled floor.

"Easy, my little lion," soothes Tyrus, picking Rah up in his arms and re-depositing him onto the fluff and comfort of the outrageously opulent bed. "You can sleep wherever you like, of course! You can have a room in Tyrus' wing, would you like that? We will suggest it to the –" he stops himself, considers his words, "the Master. For now, you will be safe enough here with this-- weasel," he looks at Mochlos who has narrowed his eyes at him until they are slits. "Tyrus is right down the hall. And this bull will come and crush this weasel like a dung beetle if he hears so much as a whimper from the Rah." Tyrus gives Mochlos a deliberate look, raising his brow as if awaiting a challenge. But Mochlos is for once at a disadvantage. He scowls, hands on hips.

"I will not give you the satisfaction, Tyrus. Do not look so smug," he snaps, pursing his narrow lips and taking a moment to mull over the situation. Suddenly his face brightens. "I will put his attendants, with whom he is familiar, in here with him." He shoots Tyrus a grin of one-upmanship. "He will prefer them to you," he adds, and then looks down at Rah. "Am I right, handsome? Would you not prefer to stay here in the care of the House of the Moon amongst your friends? Aros and Pyrus can stay here with you, right here in this room, and coddle you half to death. We will put the dance master, Dimius, in the next. Why, I even have Tuma with me! Does the House of the Bull have a bath master to prepare your sacred baths? Who can care for you better than the House of the Moon, who created you, my little god, eh?" He gives Tyrus a satisfied smile.

Rah has reached up to hold his head, which the priests, arguing over it, cannot know is spinning like a dreidel, and pounding with each word that the priests speak, as if they were thunder claps. "Daah!" he cries in frustration, tears leaking from the tilted tips of his eyes.

"There, are you satisfied, Tyrus? You have upset him. The assassin will have your head!" spits Mochlos. He has no sooner called the master of the house by his most offensive occupation than realizes he has done so, and takes a sharp breath, clapping his own hand over his mouth.

"You had better unlearn *that* habit, sir, else you be relieved of yours!" snaps Enenoch, looking about as if expecting Rush to appear and pounce on them at any moment. "And take ours as well for hearing it!"

But Tyrus has settled himself down beside Rah to put an arm about his shoulder. "Be quiet you idiots, he is not well. Lower your voices. There, my little lion," he says, lifting a hand to Rah's curls to stroke his scalp in gentle circles. "Better now?"

Rah's eyes shudder closed. He leans back against the Bull Priest's hand, pressing it into the wall behind his head, and grunts. "Better," he murmurs.

Tyrus looks up at his friend, Enenoch, who is stroking his chin, brows peaked.

"What do you think, Sky? The boy responds to me, does he not?"

"He does like your hands, Tyrus. You seem to have a spell in them," answers Enenoch thoughtfully.

Mochlos looks from one to the other, then down at the boy. He scowls.

"Pah. *That* will not save you. Anyone can pet a cat," he spits. He lifts his hand to touch the boy's head.

But when he does so, Rah opens his eyes, shoots him an angry glare, and makes a little warning hum in his throat.

"Not anyone, Moon," says Tyrus, smugly.

"No," agrees Enenoch, "Thus far, it is only Tyrus who seems to have any luck with it. Other than the girl, Cara, of course."

"Girls are another matter altogether," chuckles Tyrus. "This one will never complain to have a girl stroke him."

"No," muses Enenoch, failing to enjoy Tyrus' sexual imagery. "This is the fertility slave-god. It is not in his nature to come to man, only to woman. Only that which can be impregnated."

"Just so, the sun may warm a rock," it is Crispo, coming up behind them from the hall. "As the Rah warms us men. But the farmer's fields require him. Without him there is no harvest."

"Yes, as the rain cloud may wet the cliff," responds Enenoch, continuing the Sun Priest's thought. "But brings the crops to life!"

"Just so," smiles Tyrus. "And there is your worth, Sun and Sky. For the Rah requires you to bring forth life." He has stopped stroking Rah's head and has gently laid the boy back down on the down-stuffed bed linen. "And of course, there would be no crop at all if there were no field, no Earth, in which to sew the seed, or Bull to pull the plow," he says confidently.

"And what of me, Tyrus?" snarls Mochlos peevishly. "You seem to have left the boy's creator out of the mix all together."

"Ah, I wish I could, Moon," says Tyrus, turning to him pleasantly enough. "But you are his mother, are you not?"

"He is not so fond of his mother, this little god," says Enenoch.

"That will change," snaps Mochlos. He claps his hands and in a moment a young priest, dressed in the robes of the Moon, makes an appearance and a quick bow at the door of the chamber.

"Bring me that silly fop, Aros, and the face painter. And have two more pallets brought into this room."

"Yes, Holiness," responds the young priest, bowing and turning to do as he is told.

"And Felix-" continues Mochlos, bringing the young man to a halt in the doorway.

"Holiness?"

"Bring me three of our loveliest temple concubines. Young ones."
He turns to glower at Tyrus with a superior grin.

"Yes, Holiness."

"You have concubines with you?" gasps Enenoch.

"The assa--, the Master of Amega ordered me to pack up my entire
household. And so I did. Only the three original wives of Rah were lost, as
is to be expected, when the boy was kidnapped and taken from us, and they
took their own lives."

"He is not well enough for concubines, Moon, you had better take
care," murmurs Crispo. "Give him time to recover his power before you
allow him to deplete himself."

"Nonsense. Whatever makes him happy," says Mochlos flippantly,
marching out of the room.

He is not gone long before the sound of hurried feet approach from
the hall.

"Oh! My Sunlight!" cries Aros, the first to reach the doorway.
Oblivious to the three priests standing about Rah's bed, he immediately
rushes to it, drops to his knees, and takes one of Rah's hands in both of his.
"Sunlight," he coos, and bending to kiss Rah's fingers, he begins to weep
silently.

Pyrus, more cautious, stops at the entry of the room, looks about at
the priests, gives a short bow to each, and then walks up to stand behind
Aros and look down at Rah.

"He is so thin, Aros, I barely recognize him," says the face painter,
reaching over Aros to brush Rah's curls from his forehead.

"He is as lean as a girl of ten summers," answers Aros. "Where is my
beautiful Sunlight, Pyrus? How can he recover?"

"He is strong, Aros. Stronger than any of us expected. He is made of
some fabric beyond our understanding," answers the face painter.

"He is like a young lion," interjects Tyrus. "Nurture it when it is
young, for when it grows to its maturity, you had best have been its mother.
Or it will make a plaything of you."

For a moment there is silence. All five men look down at Rah, who
has pulled his hand away from Aros and turned onto his belly to snore
softly into the downy pillows.

"You two were his attendants, then?" asks Tyrus amiably.

"Yes sir. This is his dresser, Aros. And I am Pyrus, his face painter,"
says Pyrus, taking a longer look at the Bull Priest, whose appearance so
differs from the other two that Pyrus must bite his lip to keep from asking
him a question of his own.

Aros has risen to his feet and turned to look at Tyrus as well, and now
both attendants are staring quite blatantly at the priest.

"Yes, I see you recognize me by my reputation. I am Tyrus, of the House of the Bull," says Tyrus, brushing a hand through the thick locks of black hair that sit upon his shoulders like a helmet. "Thus the rumors. And they are true, to a degree, as are all rumors. I do not shave my entire body, as is the tradition of the Minoan high priest. However I do not completely resemble a yak, as you have been told."

"Your pardon, sir. But your appearance is-" Pyrus falters, "striking."

"I will take that as a compliment, Pyrus." He extends his hand to rest it on the painter's shoulder. "And so begins our friendship. For we have a common purpose."

Tyrus is smiling his most benign and charming smile. Enenoch looks startled, then shakes his head, clucking. "Unbelievable, Tyrus, you think a hundred days ahead of me," he murmurs.

Crispo is looking from the Bull Priest to Enenoch in confusion.

"What are you all conspiring now?" he begins, but is interrupted by the entry of two more men into the chamber. These two are dressed in the simple frocks of palace physicians.

"You will leave the boy to us, now," says the first to enter the room, a tall man of considerable age. His long hair is white, his face leathered and dark, and he is stoop shouldered. But he still has the bearing of a warrior about him, and it is clear by the deep scar across his forehead that he has seen war.

"You are the physicians the Master spoke of," says Tyrus, immediately taking the lead though remaining soft voiced and courteous. He steps away from the bed, opening his hands and gesturing toward Rah. "Well good fortune to you. I myself believe that the Rah is most in need of rest, and the ministrations of his priests, more than doctors to poke and prod and disturb him. But we must follow the Master's will, of course." He makes a move to turn to the doorway, Enenoch following his example. Then he turns abruptly back to the bed, where the two physicians have stopped to stare with some amazement at Rah.

" I assure you," adds Tyrus as if only just thinking of it himself, "he will eat nothing unless this man here," he gestures to Crispo, "has prepared it for him and, as you can see, we cannot afford to let him waste further."

"Thank you, Tyrus," blinks Crispo, unable to come up with a sinister reason for Tyrus' generous comment.

"This is Crispo, High Priest of the House of the Sun, and the Master has just given him absolute authority over the kitchens, and the boy's diet. Take care," he gives the two physicians a sly wink, "not to allow him to ingest anything that has not first been approved by Crispo."

The younger of the two doctors is squinting at Tyrus with some annoyance. But the older man, who is clearly in charge, raises his hand to still him.

"Thank you, Tyrus of Troy. I will remember it, and your-" he gives the priest a cynical scowl, "kind warnings."

"Oh, do not thank me, sir, I only mean to keep my own head here where it does me the most good," says Tyrus flippantly, then waves a hand to Crispo. "Come Brother Sun, let us see what is in the kitchen to be had. I am famished myself, and weary from travel. Let us take some refreshment and then have a nap."

Crispo, reluctant to leave Rah with the physicians, takes an uncertain look over his shoulder at the two men standing like birds of carrion over the boy's bed, then gives them his best frown, a difficult thing for such a jovial face, and follows Tyrus and Enenoch out of the room.

When the priests are gone, the two physicians give each other a worried look, then return their attention to Rah.

"Have you ever seen such a creature, Mehmet?" asks the younger to the older.

"Never," answers the older man, putting his hand to his chin. "This is an aberration of nature. What is it? An ocelot? An ocelot born of a woman?"

"Look at his face, Mehmet. It is as delicate as an Egyptian marble. Is this a boy? Perhaps a hermaphrodite, eh?"

At this the older man gives his junior a withering look. "I should think the Master will have assessed his sex by now. If he says it is a boy, it is a boy. And I, for one, will not go looking for the means in which I may contradict him."

At this, the younger man takes a long breath and a nervous swallow.

"Well, we had better examine him," continues Mehmet after a moment. "We are expected to bring him to perfect health. Open his eye, Sef. Let us see if we can rouse him with the light."

"We are doomed, Mehmet. He is half starved and unconscious," grumbles Sef, who nevertheless does as he is told, carefully bending over the bed to extend a finger toward Rah's closed right eye. With the utmost caution, he lays the flat of his thumb against the boy's cheekbone and pulls the lower lid down.

Rah bats away his hand, startling both men.

"Blessed be the Sun Goddess!" says Mehmet, pushing Sef aside with a gnarled hand and leaning over Rah.

Rah is squinting up at Mehmet with a mixture of confusion and annoyance.

"My gods, look at his eyes, Mehmet!" blurts out Sef, who is peering over the older man's shoulder.

"Hush, you fool," snaps Mehmet.

"Where Tyrus is?" says Rah in Minoan, pulling himself into a seated position on the opulent bed. "Where Crispo? Rah hungry. Need eat." He pantomimes the taking of food as he looks from one man to the other.

"He has the voice of a man," whispers Sef to Mehmet, "but what is he saying?"

"I cannot make it out. He speaks with a cleft tongue, I think," says Mehmet. He attempts to fashion his expression into a smile for Rah. "I am Mehmet, a doctor," he says slowly in Greek, and rests a finger on his own breast. "And this is Sef, my apprentice." He points to the other man. "We are here to examine you now. We must discover your illness," and he moves to touch Rah's shoulder.

But Rah instantly leans away from the man's fingers, lifting his lip in a snarl.

"No touch Rah!" he says, scrambling off the bed and onto his feet. But his brain is not yet as fast as his will. He wobbles, and falls to his knees before either physician can catch him.

"Dear Mother Arriniti," utters Mehmet, falling to his knees as well to keep Rah from striking his head on the marble tiles. "He springs like a deer, but has no strength or balance with which to carry himself. This is the head, Sef. I have seen this in battle." He has begun to examine Rah's scalp beneath the thick froth of his golden curls. Rah has closed his eyes. Now his head rolls back, gifting the two physicians with the countenance of a sleeping angel. He is oblivious to the doctor's fingers. His body crumples, his weight settling harmlessly onto the floor in the man's arms as the doctor examines him.

"This is an injury to the head. The hardest to treat. He could live or die. It is the will of the spirit in him to choose which. We can do nothing but—Ah! Here," he turns to his apprentice. "Feel this. A scar across the back of his head. Barely healed. This is not a recent injury. It has been a month, at least."

Sef has come around his master to touch the raised line at the base of Rah's skull, where his wound from the tomb of Lutarus has nearly healed. He moves his fingers right and left, searching the scalp behind the boy's ears.

"Feel this, Mehmet!" He takes his master's hand and guides it to a depression behind Rah's left ear, the impression left in his infant skull by a mad ride through the air that ended with the abrupt impact of his head against a table edge.

"The skull has been dented. This has happened as a child. An infant. While the skull was still malleable," says Mehmet, settling back on his heels to allow his servant to lift the boy back onto the bed. "It is a wonder he is alive at all." He pushes himself to his feet. "This is a strong will, Sef. This one may live. Let us tell the Master he sleeps peacefully in the care of his priests, and that the best medicine is prayer, and offerings to the god who inhabits him." He nods to himself, considering his own logic. "Yes, let us put this one back on the priests."

With Rah returned to his nest in the downy linens, the two men stand together, hands clasped before them as if in prayer, looking down at the mysterious golden creature upon whom their lives now depend. After a moment of thought, Mehmet shakes his head, weary. "I am an old war horse. An infantry medic. I can clean and dress a wound. I cannot change history."

Sef looks up at his master sharply, then more slowly, returns his eyes to the boy on the pallet.

"Why has the great Antaris taken such an interest in a Minoan slave-god, Mehmet? Why not let him perish, as the gods clearly intended when they wiped out his people? Why bring him here to Amega, to the Hatti, along with his priests? What does this angel know of war? How can he serve such a man of war?"

"You ask too many questions, Sef. You will not live long if you make a habit of questioning the motives of the Master."

"Is it not a physician's duty to ask questions?" responds Sef as the two men move toward the doorway, which is now blocked by several servants who are jockeying to bring two more smaller beds into the room.

"No. It is a physician's duty to answer them," says the older man, taking his apprentice by the arm and leading him around the incoming furniture and out into the hall.

CHAPTER 3

In a great chamber overlooking the courtyard, and situated in a position of complete dominion between the columns of the citadel, Rush the Assassin is taking his wife. Across the sea to the west the sky will remain darkened by the death cloud of the volcano for many months, but here in Amega the sun is high and bright and golden-yellow light pours over the assassin's shoulder into Josepha's eyes from the tall windows. Blinded by it, and by her love for the man who consumes her now like a ravenous wolf, Josepha allows herself to surrender to complete helplessness and thus, know a joy she can only wish for him to know. She slips her small, plump hands over the holsters and weaponry strapped to his sides, presses her palms against the broad muscle-roped plains of his back, and opens her heart to the visions he carries within him.

Where have you been, my love? And what have you seen? Take your Josepha there.

And as she takes the fierce motion of his member into her body, as she releases her spirit to the man who devours her, she sees with the soul's eyes his journey, and feels with the soul's heart, his heart, and finds herself in the Great Hall of Knossos, watching Rah perform the last moments of the Tears of the Moon with talc-smudged cheeks and chicken wings made of torn sleeves. She feels her own heart pound like stampeding hooves, feels her body flush with heat and hunger, feels herself pounce with enormous strength and speed from the dais to take the boy.

"No, my darling, no," murmurs Josepha in her husband's arms, suddenly bursting into tears. "No, no, no, Antaris, no!"

It is enough to bring Rush back to his mind. He pulls away from her, frowning down into her face with some confusion.

"Am I hurting you, Josepha?" A concerned shadow crosses his features.

But Josepha cannot stop herself from weeping. She can only look up at him and shake her head softly.

"You hurt *him*, Antaris," she says, still shaking her head, but bringing her hands up to wipe away her tears.

Now Rush's eyes narrow at his wife with some annoyance. He leans back on an elbow, releasing her entirely. He sits up, throwing his legs over the side of the bed and turning away from her.

"How do you know these things, woman? You see through me as if I were made of glass."

"You cannot break him, Antaris. You cannot. You will put out that light."

"Ah, there it is again," says Rush irritably, reminded once more of Ting Ya's words. And then, accusing, "It is you who are a light, Josepha. You are like a light that follows behind me, piercing through the darkness within me to illuminate my way, so that I may not catch my foot upon the vine I do not see."

Josepha has sat up in the bed as well. She puts her hand on her husband's shoulder, then takes it away and replaces it with a kiss.

"I have never told you anything you did not already know, Antaris."

"No, but you persistently bring to my attention that which I do not choose to see."

There is a moment of silence between them.

"I have told you, my love, that this one will break you," she whispers against his skin finally.

Rush frowns at her over his shoulder. "You are a seer, Josepha," he says. "I should have left you in Egypt."

But Josepha only smiles. "You always take what you need, my love," she answers softly.

Rush gives her a cold look, then allows himself a chuckle. He lowers his head and nods. "My gods, you are brave," he says after a moment.

"Come back to me, Antaris," murmurs Josepha against his shoulder, meaning to invite him back into her embrace. But she has barely uttered the words before her throat closes against a silent sob. "Always come back to me," she whispers, tears slipping down her cheeks.

It is enough to turn the assassin back to her. But this time, the wolf is gentle, and wholly with her. He lays her back against the pillows and nuzzling her neck, sinks into her with something not unlike gentleness.

In a chamber overlooking the practice arena, at the end of the east wing of the citadel, Nikolaos is waking from an afternoon nap. Tucked against his right side, his new wife sleeps soundly, her lips parted and pressed against his breast, her breath tickling his exposed skin.

Well, thinks Nikolaos over her head. You are quite a distraction. And lifting his left hand to stroke back her hair, he considers how he will extract himself from her embrace so that he might check on Rah. But when he begins to slip his body out from under hers, her arm instinctively tightens about his waist in her sleep.

Nikolaos frowns. What was it Rush called her? A burr in his bottom? Suddenly he is back in the City of the Dead and reclining outside Crispo's tomb kitchen taking breakfast with Rush the Assassin, moments before the man would take down a company of renegade palace guards like a woman takes down her wash. He hears himself burst out with a single laugh before he can stifle it.

Cara rouses, lifting her head to smile at him. Then she snuggles more tightly against his chest, even slipping her other arm under him to encircle his waist with a surprisingly strong grip.

"Cara," he says softly, giving her shoulder a squeeze.

"Mmmph," mumbles the girl he only met a half moon ago and is now betrothed to. "Cara, I must check on the boy. I must rise."

But the girl only tightens her hold.

"You are delicious, Captain Nikolaos," she murmurs, giving his breast a kiss.

Enough, thinks the Captain, now fully awake and becoming anxious the way a fox becomes anxious when his escape from the hen house is blocked, though the hen is in his teeth.

"Cara, you must release me, I have an obligation—"

"Oh, pah, Captain. The Grain God is in the citadel of the biggest bastard in the Aegean, and that bastard would walk through fire for him. He is not in need of your protection." She has lifted her head and is smiling into her husband's perturbed face smugly.

"Good gods, woman, are you mad?" whispers Nikolaos in shock. "How can you utter such words under his roof?"

"Where better to utter them than where there is a chance of him hearing them?" she answers pleasantly, finally releasing him to turn onto her side.

"You are no one to scoff at misplaced affection, Cara," answers Nikolaos acerbically. "For you are in love with that 'bastard' yourself, admit it or not."

"Nonsense, Captain, he has married me to *you*, I must love *you* now," responds his wife, poking his chest with a playful finger. "And you me," she adds with a superior grin.

"As my wife, you realize that such insolence can earn you a beating," he sighs half-heartedly, rising from the bed to dress.

"Yes, sir," she says, watching him. "But it is my good fortune that the bastard of whom we speak did not marry me to an animal." And then, with some contrition, she sits up and adds, "I make altogether too much noise, Captain Nikolaos, for my own good. I am a creature of sound. Can you live with it until I learn some manners?"

"Oh, I doubt I will live long enough for that, my dear," says Captain Nikolaos, sitting back on the bed to tie on his sandals and smiling at her over his shoulder.

Early the next morning, before the cock in the courtyard has crowed, a painfully pretty Asian boy wearing a white tunic and loose fitting white leggings, is the first member of the assassin's personal staff to enter the servant's dining area, just off the kitchen on the first floor of the west wing. The boy, who is just seventeen summers, has heard that a priest from the House of the Sun, a man by the name of Crispo, and a nephew of his previous master, the departed High Priest Ananou, has been rescued along with the Grain God of Knossos from the doomed island of Crete by the great Antaris, Assassin of the Aegean, and that this Crispo is now in charge of the citadel kitchens just because he knows how to feed a very particular Blonde.

Leaving his own quarters in the training barracks behind the citadel an hour before his peers will awaken to think of breakfast, Tiko slips out into the dark on a dancer's soft and silent feet. He crosses the empty chariot field and enters the fortress from the servant's access at the north end of the west wing. Four burley guards nod in unison as the boy climbs the cobblestone rise built to sustain the traffic of supply wagons. None question the earliness of the Asian's rising, for the boy from the east, like the sun, is always the first to come to breakfast, so as to be first to enter the gymnasium and prepare for his day. Tiko prepares both mentally and physically, spending a good half hour in meditation before he begins his own routine of stretching exercises. By the time the men assigned to train with him are gathered in the gym, Tiko is ready to face the dark, distrusting faces of his students, who are seasoned men of war and commanders of their own units, with no desire to learn the fighting techniques of this pretty lad from the Far East. Most of them are twice his size and battle-hardened, and are here only because the Master has ordered them to learn what he has to teach them and to take these skills back to their own men.

But this morning Tiko does not intend to go to the gymnasium after breakfast, which he normally takes while milling about in the kitchen underfoot of the dozen cooks who are preparing the first meal of the day for the entire household. This morning he intends to find this Crispo, this nephew of Ananou, and discover where they are keeping Rah, and if possible, to visit his one-time rival in private before he is scolded and expelled by the staff.

For Tiko has heard that Rah is to be nurtured and coddled by not one, but by the four priesthoods of Crete: Sun, Sky, Bull and Moon. And that he is to be made the official slave god of Amega, to whom all must give their respect and love. He has heard that Rush (for despite what he has learned since coming to Amega about the man who built this fortress, in his heart he will always think of Rush as the Aegean Assassin) has plans to go to war with Syria, and to take Babylon for the King of the Hatti. He has learned this from the men he trains, the six commanders of the Armies of Antaris here in Amega. And it is Tiko's plan to participate in this war, not to be left behind with the women. It is Tiko's plan to prove his true worth as a warrior in battle to his beloved master.

And Tiko suspects that his only hope of convincing Rush to take him lies with Rah, with the Blonde, who has his master's heart.

When Tiko arrives in the kitchens this morning he is instantly greeted by a portrait of the very man he hoped to meet. Crispo is wearing the robe of the Priesthood of the Sun, and easy enough to spot. He is surrounded by a dozen cooks, male and female, who are gathered about the central ovens. This is an unusual sight, for normally at this time of day the cooks are only just coming to work themselves, addressing their stations, and preparing to commence their various tasks. But today, the head cook, Haffa, stands with arms crossed over his chest watching a Minoan Sun Priest light the ovens he has been responsible for over a decade. And the junior cooks are standing about in a disorganized assembly, unsure of who it is they are to take orders from.

Tiko leans in the kitchen doorway, his arms crossed over his chest in an unconscious imitation of Haffa, and watches.

"Well, by now you all have heard that a fat Sun priest from Knossos has been assigned dominion over your kitchens," smiles Crispo jovially as he moves from oven to oven with torch in hand, lighting the fires. "And no doubt you have some strong feelings on the subject. You love your head cook, who has done a splendid job managing the extraordinary post of feeding an entire fortress for as long as you can remember. In addition to that, you probably think it a dangerous risk on the part of the Master, to assign a priest," and with this Crispo looks about at his audience and shrugs, "What priest can cook?" and then continues, "and an obvious glutton at that, in charge of a kitchen! Like putting a hog in a potato cellar!" At this there is a twitter of laughter from the junior cooks, although Haffa's face remains hard, like set pudding.

"Why then are you here, sir?" says the demoted head cook, with dangerous impudence. He sets his fists upon his hips, which are not so ample as Crispo's, but nevertheless rather womanly. He looks about at the staff with defiance and waits for Crispo's answer.

"Well, sir," says Crispo, turning to the head cook. "Of course, no one knows the mind of the Master, not you, nor I, nor do I pretend to. But it seems to me," and here he leans toward Haffa and lowers his voice, as if sharing a secret with a close friend, "That since it is I who brought a problem with me, I have been assigned to solve it!"

"He speaks of the Rah," says one of the bread bakers from the back of the cluster of cooks.

"Precisely!" beams Crispo, pointing in the man's direction with the torch. "The boy is a trial to feed, my friends, a trial! And so in his great wisdom, the Master has taken this burden from those he loves, that being you all," Crispo nods at the group, "And you sir," he tips his head respectfully to Haffa, "and assigned the problem to me." Having lit the last of the ovens, Crispo now turns to his audience, takes a weary breath, and smiles a smile that could challenge the morning sun.

"My friends," he says more seriously and quietly to his audience, "I have no desire to disrupt that which is already perfect. I am a priest, and have never run a kitchen for a throng of hungry warriors, though I can prepare a decent soup if pressed to it. And I am familiar enough with your Master and his reputation to know that if I disrupt his kitchen by one hair I will lose my entire head," and here even Haffa must suppress a laugh. "And so, it is my intention to ask you to help me to save my own ample behind. By continuing to do precisely what you have been doing without my interference, so brilliantly. And I will simply set myself up in a small station out of the way of your daily routine, and devote myself solely to preparing meals for the Rah."

There is a chorus of sighs of approval from the junior cooks, who now turn to one another to murmur and nod with relief. Haffa himself has removed his fists from his hips and walked over to Crispo to open his arms and welcome him.

Tiko waits for the pleasantries to die down and for the cooks to move off to their stations. When Crispo is alone, having been offered access to any oven the difficult task of feeding Rah might require, he saunters into the kitchen and begins to shadow the priest.

It does not take long for Crispo to notice that a beautiful Asian boy is following him about, wearing a white tunic and leggings not unlike that of a junior cook, while pilfering a boiled egg here, a handful of dried figs there, and popping the morsels into his mouth with the casual haughtiness of a prince.

Having found the ingredients he requires to put together Rah's breakfast cakes, Crispo now offers the boy a sidelong glance and a wink before he begins mixing batter.

"And what can I do for you, sir?" he says amicably over his shoulder. "Are you friend or foe?"

Tiko, chewing on a bit of spiced lamb sausage he has just dipped in a vat of yogurt behind the dairy chef's back, watches Crispo with a cool dislike in his tip-tilted pearl-black eyes. "You are that old bastard Ananou's nephew. But I did not see you at the House of the Sun," he says giving Crispo's back a poke. "You are House of Sun now, here in Amega, eh?"

Crispo takes another peek over his shoulder at Tiko. He stops mashing the batter, allows his eyes to stroke the boy from crown to toe, then returns to his work.

"I see," he says, then begins spreading his batter onto a floured baking brick. "You were at one time the property of my uncle. And my uncle had a … fascination for you, yes?"

Tiko has narrows his eyes at Crispo. A great embroidered sun, identical to Ananou's, leers at him from the big man's back, bringing back a painful memory of his few weeks in the possession of the Minoan High Priest.

"That old bastard is dead," he spits, throwing what is left of his sausage on the floor. Then, remembering his purpose, he adds more civilly, "You came yesterday on the Queen's ship. The Master took you and two other priests with him off the island when he rescued Blonde. Tell me, priest, where they have put him. No one will tell me, and I must see him!"

"Put who? Ah, so that is your reason for coming to see Brother Crispo this morning. Not a pleasant chat about my uncle. You want to see the Rah! You knew him in Knossos, did you? You were a dancer, then, when you came into my uncle's possession?"

Crispo has pushed his batter laden brick into an oven and has turned his attention to the dairy chef. Over Tiko's shoulder he now shouts, "Young fellow. The white nanny goat that came in yesterday from the ship. Tell me you know where I can find it, that I may live another day! I need its milk, you see, to begin a cheese for the Rah."

"Yes, I saw it come in, sir, she and the white hen," says the dairy chef good-naturedly. "They are in the kitchen yard, in a separate pen. But you have no time to make a cheese for breakfast from her milk."

"True enough, sir, but I must start one," says Crispo, still speaking over Tiko's head and over the din of the kitchen.

"Is she a holy goat, sir?" now asks the dairy chef, looking up from his work to address Crispo. "Or is it only an unblemished goat you need? There are plenty in the barnyard. Most, in fact." Now the man looks up from his own work to call a servant. "Nima, get a bowl of milk from the little white nanny they brought in yesterday, and see if that hen has laid any eggs."

"Yes, sir," answers a boy half Tiko's age before scurrying out of the kitchen with a milking bowl.

"Thank you, sir, I owe you my head," shouts Crispo over Tiko's shoulder.

"In the meantime, will this cheese do, sir? You can see for yourself if you will go to the windows over the grills. The yard is full of white nannies, and lambs as well, and this is theirs."

"You are a scholar, sir. I will pray to the Sun that you die a rich man with many sons."

"Pray that I do not die at all, sir," responds the dairy chef jovially before returning to his churn.

Not a little annoyed at the interruption, Tiko now plants himself under Crispo's nose, legs spread in an imitation of his master's dominant bearing. He crosses his arms once again over his chest.

"You will tell me where Blonde is, priest, or I will cause you no end of trouble with the Master," he says, putting on his fiercest face.

"Yes, I have no doubt that you will, boy. But will you at least tell me your name, so that when my punishment comes, I may curse it?" smiles Crispo, reaching behind Tiko's back for a pot in which to boil Lydia's eggs.

"I am Tiko, sir, and I am assigned by the Master himself the honor of teaching his troops the ancient martial arts of my fathers," says Tiko, ducking sideways out of Crispo's reach, "so that they may use them in battle and destroy his enemies."

"Well I wish I could say it was a pleasure to meet you, Tiko, but I am afraid it is too late for that. Now if you wish to defy your beloved Master's wishes and disturb a sick and sleeping Rah, go and do it, and be out of my way. He is in the wing above, in the hall of the House of the Moon. I would think a clever boy like you might have thought of that yourself. Go and make a nuisance of yourself there, and with any luck, I will be taking my lunch while watching your Master decapitate you in the practice arena."

"Pah," spits Tiko, before grabbing a lemon from a bowl of fresh fruit at Crispo's side and turning to strut out of the kitchen.

It is still dark, with dawn just peaking in his chamber window, when Rah is awakened by the soft puff of Tiko's breath in his ear.

"Wake, you lazy Blonde, it is your old friend, Tiko! Are you so exhausted by the Master's kisses all night that you cannot stand when the sun rises?"

But the old taunt does not have the effect that Tiko is expecting. Rah opens his eyes slowly, turns his head toward Tiko's voice with a moan, and takes a moment to focus on his face.

"China? You come see Rah?" whispers Rah hoarsely. He gives his friend a weak smile. "Good to see you, China." He attempts to rise onto his elbow. "Aros and Pyrus here also. Still sleep."

"Come out into the hall with me, Blonde, We must talk. We must join forces now, else the Master goes to war and leaves us here like women to tend the pigs!"

"I come," says Rah, slipping off the stuffed bedding and finding the floor with his feet. "Head spin, Tiko. Rah has bad fit. Maybe hit head again. Always hit head." He gains his balance and rises to his feet to follow Tiko past his sleeping attendants and out into the hall.

Once there, Tiko pushes him against the wall and whispers into his face, "Listen to me, Blonde. You are the Soul of Rah, now. Four priesthoods to serve you. You know what that means? Never grow up, never be a man. No battle. Is this what you want?"

Too weak to push himself out of Tiko's grip, Rah can only frown and whisper back, "No, China. Rah is teach horse for Wolf. War horse. Wolf has many horse here. Many chariot. Rah is teach horse now. No two horse. Three horse chariot, China, three men. So fast! So strong! Rah can do this!"

"A three man, three horse chariot? You crazy Blonde," says Tiko, shaking his head and releasing Rah's shoulders, leaving Rah to lean against the wall for support. "We heard you played with the Kings horses, we all knew. But what do you know of chariots? This is for warriors! You are just a dancer, Blonde."

"No, China! In Gaul, I am teach horse. Three, maybe five, across. This how I learn jump, China. This how I learn—," he see-saws his hand in front of Tiko's nose for the word.

"Balance," says Tiko impatiently.

"Balance. Stand on back of horse in middle. Long rein. Horse run together. Rah can jump three, five across! So now, men come, take Rah to Cyrus. King of Cyrus, he has chariot. Rah he tell men, no! This horse too strong today! Watch Rah! They see, Rah know horse better. Every day, Rah go down to teach. Soon can use chariot. Easy. But Rah can make three horse run together! Stupid men, this—" he stops to make the outline of a chariot wheel with his arms, "Back, back of feet. Stupid, China. How you can balance like that? Need this-"

"Wheel," says Tiko, watching Rah with piqued interest.

"Wheel! Need wheel under feet! More weight now! More balance! Now can have three men, three horse!"

Tiko has narrowed his eyes at Rah. "You are not so stupid as I thought, Blonde. You are making some sense."

"Need to think like dancer, China," Rah taps Tiko's temple. "This why you see. Wolf does not see."

Now Tiko widens his eyes, then looks down the hall in either direction and lowers his voice to a bare hush. "You have told the Master this, Blonde?"

Rah nods casually. "He say no, cannot do. But-," he leans toward Tiko, hitting his breast with a closed fist. "Rah can do."

Voices down the hall catch Tiko's attention, drawing it away from Rah.

"Come, Blonde, get back into that pile of goose feathers you sleep in." He takes Rah's shoulder and pushes him back toward the door of the chamber. "Master treats you like a favorite concubine, Blonde. Maybe you will give him sons." Shaking his head, he leads Rah back to his bed, then pokes at his stomach, mocking. "You have a womb in there, Blonde? For the Master's seed?"

But Rah only bats Tiko's hand away. Then he sits back down on the edge of the bed and smiles at his old adversary in the dawn light. "Wolf, he is give Rah three concubine already. How many he give you, China?" he whispers, chuckling his dusky chuckle. Then, his attention drawn away from the subject by the growling of his own empty gut, he slips back off the bed. "Rah hungry, China. I find kitchen. Find Crispo. Need to eat."

Tiko looks back over his shoulders at the two sleeping attendants. They are snoring peacefully, unaware that they are about to earn a beating from their own master, Mochlos, by allowing Rah to leave his bed.

"Alright. Let me see that the hall is clear. Then I will show you the way to the kitchen," says Tiko, making no effort to help Rah to his feet or steady him, but leading the way back out the doorway and down to the cooking wing.

Their arrival in the dining room doorway is soon followed by a few sharp intakes of breath, and then a sudden hush over the entire kitchen.

"It is him!" croaks a chicken cleaner near the back door.

"It is the Rah!" cries the butcher at his side, stepping back from the low olive wood table upon which he is dismembering a piglet.

Crispo has looked up from his own work to glance about the kitchen at the startled cooks. Sensing disaster, he wipes his floured hands on an apron he has tied over his frock and steps toward the two boys in the doorway.

"There now! How pleased the Master will be to see you on your feet, Rah! But what brings you down to the kitchen? Do you think Crispo will let you go hungry? Why I will stuff you like a rump roast, my little lamb. I am preparing your breakfast and will have it up to you in a heartbeat. Go back to your chamber or I will be there before you!" He flashes Tiko a furious glare and then returns his attention to Rah and arranges his features into a gentle grin.

But Rah is looking around the kitchen as if he has never seen one. And indeed, never has he seen one so enormous or well-staffed. For the kitchen of Amega feeds not only the occupants of the citadel, but the army of twelve hundred elite fighting men who are barracked around it. Further inland, in the city of Ugarit, the wives of these soldiers, and another five thousand infantrymen and their families, live and work. In this way, the assassin's army is never far from home except when engaged in battle, and so are rewarded not only by the wages and spoils of war during a conflict, but by proximity to their loved ones while in training.

Now Rah looks up at Crispo with widened eyes. "Big kitchen, Crispo. This your kitchen now? Wolf give you this?"

Crispo darts a defiant stare around at the cooks closest to the dining room entrance and Rah's words.

"He speaks of the Master thus?" squeaks a kitchen maid by the door, her hand coming up to her bosom in shock.

"It is his pet name for the great Antaris. They are on such terms," glares Crispo. "See that you do not repeat it." But the girl only shakes her head 'no' at the priest and backs away from Rah, her hand still pressed against her breasts, her eyes huge.

"Can eat now, Crispo? Rah hungry," says Rah, looking over the kitchen maid with some interest before returning his attention to the priest.

At the same time, Tiko is also making ready to go. He whispers something in Rah's ear, then says aloud, "I must go to train the Master's commanders now, Blonde. I will see you later. Maybe we watch the charioteers practice this afternoon, eh?"

"He is not well enough for such activity, boy. Be off now. Go and mind your own business," says Crispo, snapping the bottom of his apron at Tiko. "Be off, or I will flour you and bake you into a loaf."

Allowing himself a devilish grin at Crispo, Tiko departs. As he does, he very nearly careens into Captain Nikolaos, who has come to the kitchen in search of Rah after failing to find him in his own bed.

The cooks have yet to return to their work. They are still staring at Rah with unreserved fascination, and are now doubly distracted by the handsome vision of the Captain, dressed in his Cyrean uniform, and silhouetted in the doorway behind him.

He is in time to catch Rah by the shoulders before he wanders further into the kitchen.

"Bring his tray up immediately," snaps the Captain, turning Rah about gingerly and leading him back through the dining hall.

"Sir," responds Crispo, much relieved that the spectacle that is Rah has been removed from his kitchen, and that he may return to his own task and remind the staff to return to theirs, before twelve hundred hungry soldiers arrive to find that on this, the first day of his employment as head of their kitchen, there is nothing prepared for their breakfast.

"Why must eat in bed, Fox? Rah is good. Rah can eat here with other slave, other servant," says Rah, waving an arm at the expanse of the soldier's dining hall, and looking up at Nikolaos with the kitten-weak, unfocused attention of his first day in Cyrus. And for a moment Nikolaos is utterly distracted. He blinks down into the boy's soft, sea-green eyes and feels the same dizzying pull that nearly took him off his horse the day he rescued him from the Tomb of Lutarus. He catches his breath. So frail you are, Rah, he hears himself thinking. Can you recover, and come back to us as you did in Cyrus? He is unaware that he has stopped in his tracks to turn the boy toward him and lift his chin.

"This is a military compound, Rah. This place will be packed with soldiers in half an hour, hungry men looking for breakfast. You will be trampled, or mauled if they notice you at all. You are safer upstairs in the hands of the priests."

"Where you are stay, Fox? You stay with Rah like before?" He chuckles. "Fox like to watch Rah."

"I must take whatever post Rush chooses for me, Rah. I am his man now," answers the Captain, although the thought of taking a room near Rah delights him. "We will see what the Master's intentions are."

Back in his own chamber, Rah does not return to his bed but, turning to Nikolaos with a mischievous grin and a wink, he instead jumps on Aros, who is flat out on his belly, fast asleep and snoring into his mattress. Rah straddles Aros and slaps his palms over his dresser's eyes as he awakens with a shriek and pushes himself onto his hands, nearly bucking Rah off in doing so. This sends Rah into peals of laughter. Nikolaos can only roll his eyes as Rah tumbles onto the mattress beside his dresser, clutching his sides and fairly howling with mirth.

"You will wake the whole house, Rah!" hisses Nikolaos.

Aros turns his attention from Rah to the strapping young soldier that now towers over him with an irritated expression on his handsome face. Assuming he has done something in his sleep to earn him the wrath of the assassin, and thus a visit from a house guard, he rolls off his bed onto his knees and puts his face and hands to the ground.

"Beg pardon, Officer," he mumbles into the floor as Pyrus lifts himself lightly off his own bed to give the Captain a modest bow.

"Sir," says Pyrus, offering downcast eyes in the universal sign of subordination.

"You two are his attendants, then?" frowns the Captain, looking first from one to the other, and then bending to take Aros by one arm and lift him to his feet.

Rah has settled back on Aros' pallet and is watching with quiet amusement. He says nothing to help his old friends out.

"Y-yes sir. I am his dresser, and," Aros begins.

"I am Pyrus, his face painter. We are of the House of the Moon, sir," says Pyrus, finishing Aros thought.

"Well the boy was down in the kitchens already," responds the Captain, irritably. "You had better learn to sleep light, or else not at all.

This is not Knossos, gentlemen. If he wanders around this compound unattended he will almost certainly come to harm." He gives each a fierce scowl. "He might have run into the soldiers coming to breakfast."

After an awkward moment, Rah giggles again. He points at Aros. "Aros, he think Rah is Wolf, come to bite him! Maybe I tell Wolf come bite Aros!"

"Well, I am glad to see you in such high spirits, Sunlight, after your ordeal, even if it is at my expense," pouts the wounded Aros.

Suddenly Rah is on his feet. "You do not know Fox! You think Fox from Amega? Fox from Cyrus. This Fox, he is Captain of Cyrus. Captain Nikolaos. He save Rah from tomb! Rah maybe die in tomb if Fox does not find Rah!" Then he gives a shrug and lifts his hands in utter befuddlement. "Then Wolf come and tie Fox up like chicken and give him this!" He is pointing to Nikolaos' cheek, and the Tears of the Bull tattoo.

Nikolaos is looking down at Rah with thinning patience.

"You saved him?" blurts Aros, staring at Nikolaos with the fascination of one who has just met his hero.

"Yes, you could say that. Although it is the Master who saved us all in the end, and rescued us from the volcano."

"They say the island of Thera exploded, and sent a column of golden fire like a tongue into the heavens. They say the blast moved the sea," says Pyrus quietly. "They say there is no west now, only east and south. Is it true? Did you see it? Did you see the tongue of fire, Captain Nikolaos?"

"We saw the column of fire you speak of, after the ship settled. We fell into the sea as if the bottom of the world was pulled from beneath us. Then the waters returned and pushed us toward Anatolia with no need of rowers or a sail."

"Fantastic," murmurs Pyrus.

"Surely Crete is gone, and all who remained there," continues Nikolaos, more to himself than to the servants now. "My Queen, my city, all gone." His face has gone grey.

Rah has come to stand beside the Captain.

"Fox have Cara now. New city. New Master. New life. Wolf is take us back to Crete one day. Name city after Fox. City of Nikolaos. Warrior city."

Nikolaos can only look down into the strange, striated blue-green and gold eyes of the Grain God and sigh.

"Is this a vision, Rah? Are you having visions of the future now?" he smiles softly at the boy. "If it was not for you, I too would be no more than ash and bone."

His musing is interrupted by the sound of Crispo huffing down the hall, laden with an enormous breakfast tray. Nikolaos steps back out of the doorway to let him pass as Rah hops onto his own bed, folds himself into a half-lotus and pats his thighs at Crispo.

"Put here. Rah eat. Need to be strong for horse today!"

"Who said anything about a horse?" says Aros to Rah as Crispo lumbers in to set the tray on Rah's lap.

"There is no sense arguing with him. He will have his own way, even here in the Wolf's den, eh, Rah?" responds Nikolaos, watching as Rah attacks the delicacies Crispo has prepared for him like a starved cur.

"You will be sick, eating like that after so many days of fasting," says Pyrus, walking over to Rah to take the tray from him. But he is stopped by Nikolaos.

"Never mind. He will be all will, now, just as he was after his rescue from the tomb. Turned Cyrus inside out. Made a mad Queen sane and drove the rest of us near mad." He pauses, watching Rah pop a whole boiled egg into his mouth and then half a grain cake soaked in honey. "He seems to have an instinct as to how much food he can stuff down before he makes himself ill."

"Did he dance for you in Cyrus?" It is Pyrus, who has turned to look up at the Captain with something nearing camaraderie.

"Brilliantly," responds Nikolaos, who seems to have drifted away again in thought. He shakes his head, as if to rouse himself. "The King's troupe was a dancing bear until he came. Then, somehow," he drifts off again, remembering a boy who seemed to be made of golden light, a boy possessing immeasurable physical grace, who leapt like a cat and landed like air and whose unmatched spirit somehow inspired the King's leaden-footed troupe of ceremony dancers to perform with the same purity of emotion.

Rah has been emptying his tray into his mouth with two hands. "Ta hah!" he laughs through a mouthful of cake. He points at Nikolaos and looks about the room at his friends. "Fox is think Rah cannot dance. Cannot ride horse. He think Rah is little girl, no strong, no fight. Hah! Rah show you, Fox!" Suddenly he shoves the tray off his lap onto the bed and rises, too fast. He stops, wobbles. Reaches for his head. "Head spin," he says, as Aros quickly comes to his side to steady him.

"No horses today, Rah. Please. For Aros. One more day in bed," begs Aros, holding Rah against himself and looking at Nikolaos with soft, pleading eyes.

"Naah!" says Rah, pushing Aros away. "You are big girl, Aros. Should be born girl. Wolf is give Rah all king horse now. We go." He gestures to the Captain to follow him and starts out the door.

"They will eat him alive," murmurs Crispo, flashing a concerned look at Nikolaos.

For a moment, it seems that a shadow has darkened the Captain's face, and a chill washes the room, as if the spirit of the assassin himself has entered it.

"They will die trying," he says, the pupils of his grey eyes sharpened to points. Then he turns to follow Rah, and the short cape of his Cyrian uniform flares theatrically before settling against his sides.

"Such elegance, he has," comments Aros when he is gone.

"That one is like a falcon, sitting prettily on the wrist of the one who brought him, but beware when the falconer sets him hunting," murmurs Pyrus.

Now Aros turns to Crispo, hands on hips. "Why has the assassin not set down a decree here in Amega? That the boy is sacred and cannot be touched? What kind of madness is this?"

But Crispo can only shrug and give him his back as he moves to gather his tray and its contents from Rah's bed.

"I suppose the decree was set down long before we arrived, Aros," says Pyrus. "These are his men. They know him not as the assassin, but as their general. They have fought beside him, seen him in battle. Can you imagine? Do you think any would dare touch what that man risked his own life to have?"

Crispo turns to nod in agreement. "Just so. He does not waste time repeating himself, that man." He moves to the door. "You had better get it right the first time," he adds over his shoulder with a cheery smile.

CHAPTER 4

The stable master of Amega is up at dawn on the morning after Rah's arrival. As usual, he supervises the complicated feeding regime of the horses, as well as their elaborate schooling schedule. Here in Amega, as elsewhere in the land of Hatti, the chariot horse holds a position of nobility. He is a finely trained athlete whose brilliance in battle depends upon his care and preparation in his infancy. He is fed better than most slaves, who are nevertheless treated well in Hatti, and brought up through the ranks like any soldier, first learning to balance and obey the weight of a man, then becoming accustomed to pulling a cart, and finally offered the freedom and honor of the chariot, if he is good enough.

But the twenty prissy Arabians that the Master has brought in from Crete set the stable master's teeth on edge. "Their legs are like those of a stork. How will they take the pounding of speed over rocky terrain? They are nervous and high-spirited. Who will control them in battle? And they can carry almost nothing as compared to a Hatti barb. This is fussy nonsense, waste of my time and a danger to the man who runs them," he scoffs, leaning over his only real confidante, the feed master, who is scooping out varying portions of sweet grain and oat to each animal as he passes their stalls.

"Maybe just here for the Rah to play with," murmurs Ghedi, who is from the land of Punt and the only man in the stable who had any luck approaching the new horses once Ramicus and his men managed to remove them from the ship and release them in a paddock behind the stable block last night. "Fancy beasts, I will say that. Handsome beasts to please a handsome god. Delicate and fine, as they say is the slave-god from Minoa."

"Pah, even you have trouble with them, Ghedi. This boy will be hurt, and then it is *my* head that rolls," scoffs the stable master, slipping his thumbs into his belt. "Waste of everyone's time. But you heard nothing from me about it. I do as I am told. I am a soldier."

"Yes, sir," responds Ghedi dutifully, turning back to the grain wagon he pulls behind him for another scoop of sweet grain. He does so just in time to see the frail silhouette of a wounded angel eclipse the morning light at the end of the aisle of stalls. It is enough to make him drop his empty scoop, which goes clattering to the cobblestone floor and causes the row of horses to jerk their heads from their feed troughs with alarm.

"My gods," whispers the stable master, turning to look in the direction of Ghedi's gaze. "What the hell is it?"

But the angel is tottering toward them. And the sunlight that had turned his halo of curls into a ball of golden light in the doorway has lost him, so that as he approaches them he seems to become incarnate, though as silent as an owl coasting on an evening air current.

When he is still several meters from them the apparition's attention is diverted by the animal in the stall to his left. He turns toward it, approaches the stall, makes a strange, dusky sound in his throat, and says in Greek and in the voice of a man twice his size, "So strong! Look how he is big in chest, Fox, this one will run long, run hard. Good leg, look!"

Standing now in the doorway from which the golden boy seems to have descended from heaven, is a tall and strikingly handsome figure in an elegant uniform.

"That is the one who walked at the right of the Master, yesterday," murmurs Ghedi with appropriate awe.

"Yes," responds the stable master, "And we had better make him welcome." He steps out into the center of the aisle so that both man and boy's attention are drawn to him. Then he makes a strong, soldier's bow, lowering himself to one knee and setting one fist to the ground.

"Sir," he says in a loud voice as he rises. "I am Hagga, the stable master of Amega, and I am at your service."

Immediately the tall figure in the doorway returns the salute of a commander, drawing one arm only across his waist and barely bending at the hip. Then he clears the distance between himself and the two horsemen with a few long strides, passing the golden boy, who has turned back to the horse he has been admiring.

"And I am Nikolaos. Until a week ago, I was Captain of the Palace Guard of Cyrus. As to what my title and function are to be here in Amega, we must await the Master's voice to know it. Until then, I guard the Grain God of Knossos, the Rah, with my life."

"Sir," bows the stable master a second time, and then rising, looks toward Rah for Nikolaos' explanation of the boy's appearance in his stables.

But Nikolaos only turns his head back to the boy himself, as if awaiting Rah's own interjection.

Presently the boy leaves his silent conversation with the chariot horse and turns to the stable master. "Where is Halix?" he asks in Greek, padding past Nikolaos to stand under the stable master's nose.

But the man can only blink awkwardly at the face before him.

"Where is Halix?" asks Rah again with the beginnings of a frown pleating his brows and turning his lips down.

Ghedi has turned from his work to stand beside Hagga. He looks from Rah to Nikolaos to the stable master. Finally, he responds to the boy's question.

"The Arabians that came in yesterday are in a paddock behind the stable, boy. But you cannot approach them like that. You have no protection for your feet. And they are wild. Even I could not draw near them."

"What is wrong with his tongue, Captain?" responds the stable master finally, unable to take his eyes off Rah's face. "I speak Greek, but he chews his words like a man chews jerky."

"He speaks with some difficulty," says Nikolaos, looking down at Rah with affection. "A mark of his epilepsy. He is a true vessel, sir. I have seen him cure the sick, bring rain to a kingdom failing from drought, and," and here he must stop and swallow the thickness that has tightened his throat. "And tame a wolf."

"I go. See Hali," says Rah in Minoan to Nikolaos. Then he turns to continue down the aisle to the back of the stables.

"Gentlemen," nods Nikolaos abruptly to the two horsemen. With another quick salute he takes off after Rah at a near run.

"Finish the feed, Ghedi," says the stable master to his friend, and then he hurries down the aisle after the Captain. "If the boy is hurt in my stable, it is *my* head," he calls over his shoulder.

By mid-afternoon there is an audience of five hundred crowded around the practice arena watching a golden, barefooted angel perform the unthinkable with the untamable.

It is the sorry fate of the feed master, Ghedi, the only other human capable of approaching the trio of animals Rah has chosen to work with without forcefully taking them with a lariat, to serve as a spotter for the boy's antics. Terrified that the boy will fall, or be thrown and trampled by one of the high strung Arabs he handles, Ghedi now stands in the center of the practice field, his long arms dangling uselessly at his sides, praying to a Punt god unknown to the Hatti that the Rah of the lost land of Crete remain undamaged. Meanwhile the stable master stands beside Nikolaos, as well as Ramicus and his five men, who have remained in the service of the stable since their arrival at the assassin's compound.

"He will make your heart stop, sir, and he will fall from time to time, but it is like a jaguar falling from a tree. You cannot hurt him with a fall. And you will not keep him off a horse."

"I will go insane," responds the stable master, who has come to trust Ramicus in a few short hours, and who, despite his protest, is grateful for the words of comfort.

"You will not. You will bear it. And you will still have your head in the morning for he will not come to harm on a horse."

At the moment Rah is balancing on the croup of the colt he calls Halix while leading the other two, the colt's mother and sister, on either side. The trio trot in unison around the edge of the practice field as if harnessed together, with Rah controlling Halix on a long rein and the two mares by lead ropes only. Thus far the boy is having no trouble steering them around the field, and has even bisected it twice at the center, much to Ghedi's unease.

Presently the boy releases the two mares by tossing their leads over their backs. The trio continues to move together, and when the boy tightens the colt's rein all three drop to a walk and then halt squarely. Now Rah slips gently off the back of the colt and approaches his head. He offers the animal a treat from his pocket, a bit of grain cake he pilfered from his breakfast tray that morning, and speaks to the animal. Then he gathers the mares' leads and hands them off to Ghedi.

To his surprise and relief, Ghedi finds the mares relaxed and accepting of his guidance into the stable.

When Rah moves off to find the stable master, Halix follows him, oddly oblivious of the crowd and snuffling his skirt pockets for more treats.

"Rah can make three go." He brings his arms out in front of himself, puts them together, thumbs linked and hands facing downward, and moves the fingers beneath like cantering horses, "Together. You make chariot for three men. Put wheel here," he lifts one bare foot and points to the arch, "under men feet. Center. For balance. Not in back. I show you. Where is men make chariot? I show."

But the stable master can only look to Ramicus helplessly. "What is he saying, Ramicus? He chews his words. Is this Minoan?"

"Of a sort," responds Ramicus. "He says he can make three horses go together, that he needs you to make him a three man chariot with the axle in the center, under the men's feet, for balance."

"Ridiculous," responds the stable master, but he is squinting at Rah with something close to awe. "Who is this boy? Where on earth did he come from? How did he learn to run horses like that? And to balance on the croup! Of a wild animal! This is madness. He will be hurt and then it is *my* head."

By now Captain Nikolaos has come to stand beside Rah. "You had better take him to the chariot maker. He will give you no end of trouble if you do not."

"Bring wheel! Bring here!" says Rah suddenly to Nikolaos. "I show. Where China is?" He turns to shout at the crowd. "China! We show! Need wheel!"

From the center of a group of soldiers standing nearby Tiko suddenly slips through two burley guards. "He wants a chariot wheel," he calls to the stable master in Greek. "Just a wheel. He is an acrobat, sir. Do as he says and I promise you, you will be rewarded."

Rah is grinning from ear to ear at Tiko. "China, you help Rah. We show!"

"Get him a chariot wheel, damn it," says Nikolaos, impatiently. "Or do you drag the bucket over the rocks here in Amega?"

"Sir!" snaps Hagga, not a little stung by the insult. "You there!" He points to two soldiers standing near the entrance to the stable. "Run down to the cart barn and bring me one of those wheels we took off the purple racer yesterday. Hurry!" And the two soldiers hurry off together to find the wheel. After what seems an eternity to the stable master they are spotted coming around the eastern flank of the stable, attempting to negotiate a wheel as tall as themselves and as heavy as two men, over the ground toward Hagga.

"Ah," says Rah, nodding with approval at the monstrosity. "Good. Big! Now Rah show." He walks toward the men as if to take the thing, which is easily capable of crushing him, and roll it the rest of the distance into the practice field himself.

"No, no! Let them handle it boy," says Hagga, flustered. "What in hell is that? I asked for the racer's wheel and you bring me a wheel off a catapult!"

"The racer has been put back together, sir," says one of the men, a bit winded. "The chariot maker suggested this. They were removed yesterday so that the hubs might be recast."

By now the giant wheel has made it into the practice field. The two soldiers who fetched it stand balancing it upright between them, awaiting instruction from Hagga, while Rah comes to stand at the base between them. He takes hold of a spoke over his head as if to climb it.

"Ramicus, I beg you," says Hagga, turning to his new ally.

"He will have it his way, stable master," responds the man from Knossos. And nodding at his own four men to follow him, he advances on Rah.

"This balance. I can do," says Rah, looking up at Ramicus earnestly.

"We will help you, Rah," says Ramicus. "Here now, let Thymus and Kleitos take hold of either side. They will hold it steady while you mount it.

Then Ophos and Eknos will spot you." Then he puts a hand on Rah's shoulder and gives him a pat, lowers his voice and dips his head so that he speaks into Rah's ear. "I know what you're up to, Rah," he says with a wink.

"You help, Ramicus," nods Rah, happy to see his old ally. And, barely waiting for Thymus and Kleitos to take hold of either side of the wheel, he nimbly climbs to the top as a hush of fascination runs through the crowd.

"Oh sweet mother of the gods," murmurs Hagga, bringing his hands to his head.

But before he has had time to turn to see the cause, another hush runs through the crowd, this time beginning on the south side of the practice field, where the back of the citadel of Amega crouches like a great bear with arms outstretched. And as the hush draws toward him, a human wave, beginning also on the south side of the field, folds the entire field of men to their knees in unison.

It is not until every man on the field, all but Kleitos, Thymus and Rah, are down on one knee, one fist in the dirt, that Hagga realizes that it is the Master's approach which has caused the interruption. Quickly, he drops to the ground as well, shivering with dread that the spectacle of the golden boy now balancing on the top of a catapult wheel will surely cost him his head before he is allowed to return to his feet.

"And to die thus," he mumbles, "After all of my years of service to you, Master. Better to have died in a brothel atop a one-eyed whore." His eyes closed tight, teeth grit in anticipation of the blow, Hagga is stunned again when he hears the boy call out to the Master of Amega from the top of the wheel.

"Look, Wolf! Rah is show how make three horse chariot! Look, I show! Thymus, Kleitos, let go wheel!"

And out of the corner of his eye, for he will not raise his head and yet cannot stop himself from looking at what must surely be the disaster that will end his life, the stable master sees the two men step away from the wheel in unison as the boy begins to walk backward like a cat on the top of the enormous circle, driving it easily toward the south end of the practice field, and the Master.

"Holy mother of the gods," whispers Hagga to himself, "He will run the Master over if he does not fall first and crush himself."

But Rah does not fall. He propels the wheel toward the center of the arena, directly at Rush.

"You stop Rah now!" cries Rah in his thick tongued Minoan. "Big wolf," he shouts to the crowd still down on one knee, "Strong, like two!" He grins down from his perch at Rush, dimples flashing. And the big wolf takes hold of the closest rim of the wheel and stabilizes it with a second hand on a spoke.

"What are you up to, little cat?" says the wolf, squinting up at Rah in the bright afternoon sunlight. "You will give my stable master a stroke. Do you not care for him?"

The soldiers have begun to rise to their feet all around the arena. At length, even the stable master musters the courage to do so. Thymus and Kleitos have dashed out after the wheel and now take hold of it again from either side so that Rush can step away. Eknos and Ophos have taken positions on either side of the wheel in case the boy should fall.

"I show you," says Rah to Rush. Then he lifts his arms and makes an elegant bow to his audience, first from one side of the wheel, then the other. The soldiers can only stand in silent awe of the spectacle. Here is a golden angel bowing to them from the top of a catapult wheel while their master and commanding general, the Terror of the Aegean, watches with an expression of amused affection.

"Rah in center," shouts Rah to the crowd in Minoan. "Can drive wheel. No problem. Light. Keep go. But go too far here," he steps forward toward Kleitos, "Or back," he pads backward on the rim toward Thymus, "No good. China! You say!"

At the mention of his name, Tiko now approaches the wheel. His eyes focused on his master, he offers Rush his abrupt Asian bow. "May I interpret for him, sir?"

"By all means, Tiko," responds Rush, as he attempts to maintain a hard expression to hide his mirth. You two are up to something. You are in on this, he thinks to himself. Brothers, you are, like my own sons. And he must catch himself from lifting a hand to pat Tiko's head.

"He says, the axle must be in the center of the bucket, for balance. In front of the men, it pulls the horses off their feet, interferes with their traction. Behind, now their weight interferes with the horses. In the center, the axel takes their weight. Nothing interferes with the speed of the wheel."

"Daah!" cries Rah suddenly, taking a faltering step and bringing his hands to his temples. Instantly Rush is beneath him, arms outstretched. And Eknos, who has made a heroic attempt to reach the same spot and break Rah's fall, is knocked to the ground as they meet, though the collision has no effect on Rush at all. It is a sparrow colliding with a tree. A burst of laughter from the soldiers at the dim-witted Eknos is abruptly curtailed as Rah lowers himself into a sit at the top of the catapult wheel. He lets his legs dangle but holds the rim, though Rush still stands beneath him offering him his arms. Hesitating only a moment, Rah looks down into his master's concerned face.

"Head spin," he says with a lopsided grin, then, in a throaty voice that runs like silk fingers down the assassin's spine, he adds, "Wolf can no catch Rah."

After a moment he collects himself. "Better now," he says, and, pulling his legs up under his haunches to crouch like a gargoyle on the iron rim, he eases into a handstand.

Standing several paces behind Rush, Tiko squints with annoyance at Rah's antics and shakes his head.

"You are so stupid, Blonde," he mutters.

But Rah is supporting himself on only one hand now, balancing above the wheel like a feather standing on its pin in a breeze.

"Now men let go, Ramicus!" calls Rah from his precarious perch.

"Hells bells," mutters Ramicus, but he nods to Thymus and Kleitos to release the wheel.

And as soon as it is done the catapult wheel is in motion, moving backward and away from Rush and the four spotters toward the center of the field, as Rah walks on his hands along the rim as easily as a man might walk across a tiled floor.

"He is not well enough," growls Captain Nikolaos sideways at Hagga. He gives the man a deadly look, as if this were all the stable master's idea, and struts out into the field to stand beside Rush.

"Let me stop him, Sir. He could lose his sense of balance at any moment."

But Rush only flicks him a disregarding look and then continues watching Rah with affectionate awe.

"He has been epileptic his whole life, Captain, or so my physicians tell me this morning. This boy's balance is not in his head. It is in his heart. It is in his soul."

Nikolaos can only look from Rush to Rah and squint with bewilderment.

"I don't understand," he says.

"Nor I, Captain. Nevertheless, behold," says Rush, lifting his open hands to Rah.

At that precise moment Rah launches himself from the top of the wheel, executing a single twisted flip in his descent, then reaches the ground and recovers his feet in a full and elegant bow to his master. Half a second later, the wheel crashes onto the dust with a thud. But Rah is safely out of its reach.

The crowd, which has grown since the display began half an hour earlier and is now nearer a thousand, has erupted with applause and war cries.

When Rah stands, Rush opens his arms to him and the boy steps forward. But his injured brain fails. He wobbles, and nearly stumbles to his knees before Rush can reach him and set him back on his feet.

"No more now, little cat," says Rush softly into the boy's curls as he holds him steady. "You will have your three man chariot, or I will skin the carpenter and make his wife wear his hide for a dress."

"Chariot no for Rah, Wolf," says Rah, peering up into the assassin's face with earnest intensity. "This for Wolf. This for war." He presses the fingers of his right hand together under his left breast, where the priest's golden ring glitters against the sun-brown nipple. "Gift," he says in Greek, "From the heart of Rah."

For a moment Rush can only blink into the blue-green sea that seems to live in Rah's eyes. Then he finds his own balance and turns to the crowd of onlookers.

"This is the True Soul of Rah. You will worship him. You will give him your respect, as I do mine."

And for the second time that morning, the practice arena is a field of wheat under the brilliant noonday sun of Amega, bending for the blade that is the Terror of the Aegean.

CHAPTER 5

Mochlos is scheming. As he looks out over the practice field from the second story window of his private chamber, watching the little dancer he purchased from a trader last spring turn a city of warriors on its ear, he is concocting a plan. In his mind he is in the Great Hall of the Citadel of Amega, surrounded by ten priests from each of the four houses, Moon, Sun, Bull and Sky. He stands at an altar, designed especially for him, made of olive wood and carved and painted in front with the symbol of the Moon Goddess, the triple phases of the moon: first quarter, full, last quarter. At his side is Crispo, representing the House of the Sun. Behind him stand Tyrus and Enenoch, inferior adjuncts of the power of the Moon. Before them, before the altar, stands the boy, in chains. He is blindfolded, and has been beaten with a reed. Beneath the blindfold his face is wet with tears. The vision is unutterably lovely to Mochlos, who has not permitted himself such thoughts for some time, and for a moment the vision is interrupted by a shudder of pleasure that ripples through his bowels and excites his sex. Oh to have you thus, my little slave-god. And the bastard who stole you from me forced to watch, forced to concede that it is necessary.

Now Mochlos imagines Crispo holding a chalice in his right hand. In his left is a packet of powder. The Sun Priest will think the powder symbolic only. But Mochlos has tampered with the packet. He has moistened the powder with a few drops of poison for the boy. If all goes as he expects it will, he will soon have more power than any man in Amega, save the assassin himself.

Mochlos sighs and watches from his perch on the second floor of the Citadel as the little grain dancer he turned into a god performs for the soldiers of Amega and for the Wolf of the Aegean. He gives his own slack belly a pat of satisfaction. I have every right to reclaim him, he thinks to himself. Ameg stole him from me as surely as he stole my House and my freedom. Well, you have let a snake into your den, wolf. I will have him back, and you with him. I will make you see that the boy and I are inseparable, that without me he will die. I, thinks Mochlos chuckling into his nose, and the House of the Moon alone can keep the spirit of Rah in his body. Without us, the Soul of Rah will depart, you see? The boy's body is the host of a god. You must never forget this. Was he not in perfect condition until you interfered? That is because he is a vessel of the House of the Moon, a vessel I prepared and created for the Soul of Rah, and I am the high priest of the Rah, son of the Moon Goddess. The boy knows it himself, does he not? He must be chained at night, fed only that which is blessed by the Moon, and he must dance! He must be whipped by his priest on occasion. You can see how uncontrollable he becomes without it! The Rah will destroy his own vessel! He is a god! He will continue to behave like a god, though he is captured in a boy's body. He cannot understand the limits of the human frame he inhabits! You must allow me, Great Antaris, absolute authority over the care of the boy. You will destroy what I have created by your overindulgence!

Mochlos turns to see a group of junior priests of the Moon standing at his door, hands folded in front of their gowns, heads bowed.

"The carpenter is here, Holiness, to take dimensions and instructions for the altar."

"Very well, show him in, show him in," says the High Priest, unaware that he is a bit angry at being disturbed from his reverie. "And Felix," he adds suddenly, lifting a long, bony finger to his cheek thoughtfully.

"Holiness?" The man looks up timidly.

"Bring me the trunk. The one marked 'A' for apothecary. Wait until I am finished with the carpenter. Then bring it here to me and put it there, at the end of the bed. It was left it in the storage room at the end of the hall, was it not? Bring it here to me."

"Yes, Holiness."

"And have the Sun Priest make me a tray. I have not seen a sweet since I arrived here. Do they have no honey in Amega? No fruit? No delicate cheeses? Oh, for a Minoan wine! What do they sweeten their Meade with, the blood of the enemy? Tell that fat fool, Crispo, that the House of the Moon must have sweets for the Rah. And dainties for its priests. And a good wine. Let us spread our wings a bit, shall we, Felix? Let us behave like the honored guests that we are." And with that he waves away the priests and readies his mind for the chore of designing his new altar. Planting his hands on the sill of his window, he looks out over the practice field to see that the throng of soldiers is on its knees before the beast, their master. And beside the beast, even leaning against his side as the man puts his arm about him, stands the little Grain God of Knossos. *His* creation. *His* Rah. And the beast is bellowing a command at his army, that they should worship the boy, respect the boy, and lay down their lives for the boy.

"Never have you been so vulnerable, Ameg as you have been since you first lay eyes on my little beauty. I have had you by the balls all along and have not known it. But I will take them now." And he smiles a tigerish smile to himself, lifting his fingers from the smooth marble sill and squeezing them into fists to shake at the figure of the assassin out in the practice field. "I will take them now."

It is evening, and he has had a good bath, prepared by Tuma, and a sweet rest in the arms of his three new concubines, Tyla, Hannah and Peek, before Rah finally sees Ting Ya again.

He is asleep with the girls, his golden body lost among a sea of slender brown limbs and opulent bed linens, when he is awakened by Aros and Pyrus.

"The China woman is here for you, Rah," says Pyrus, taking one of the girls by her available arm and pulling her off the bed and onto her feet. "She waits in the priest's sun room. Let the girls go back to their own quarters now. Put some clothes on. Come."

Quickly the girls are made to dress and bustled out of the room, and just as quickly Aros has found a clean skirt for Rah and set him on a stool to brush out his tangled curls, which have grown in the months since he cut them into a fantastic halo for the Dance of the Sun and now twist about his collar in unruly ringlets. But before the two attendants can bring Rah out to meet her, Ting Ya is in the doorway, her face an oval moon of serenity, her mouth curved into a wide smile. She wears a simple unbleached robe that skims the floor, and she stands in the soft lamplight with hands folded demurely and eyes down, as if approaching a temple. Her single braid is draped over one shoulder, the tail reaching for her ankles. She begins a curtsey, but is nearly knocked over when Rah explodes off the stool and leaps across the floor.

"Ting Ya!" he yowls, landing at her feet and wrapping his arms about her legs.

"Jin yu," says Ting Ya softly, stroking his hair. "You make Ting Ya fall, hit head. Then Ting Ya will have fit and be god like you," she smiles down into his upturned face.

"Then Rah is marry Ting Ya," weeps Rah, burying his face into her robe, "Be together always."

"Silly boy," says the Asian slave, stroking Rah's head. "I am too old for you, Rah. How many times I have to tell you? This life, I am too old. Next life, I be too young. Bad karma for marriage. Better friends."

"Always friends," responds Rah, looking up at her through his tears as he rises to his feet. "Stay friends longer."

"You grow, Jin yu. Taller now than when the soldiers took you! But too skinny." She pinches the flesh at his waist. "Ting Ya will make you fat. You still like treats, bad boy?"

Rah frowns, flicking his eyes in the direction of Mochlos' chamber. "I think this priest, he is still not let Rah eat treats from Ting Ya."

Ting Ya can only shake her head sadly. "This priest will not be here, in this life, long if he cannot love Jin yu. He had better be careful. The snake is sly and silent, but he cannot outsmart the wolf. Wolf smell him coming. Take head from behind." She makes her right hand into the jaws of a wolf and snatches the fist she has made with her left. "Then make belt."

But Rah can only give her a puzzled look. He blinks down at her, confused, then smiles, flashing pearl-bright teeth. It seems as if the lamplight has suddenly sparked and the room has lightened. He points north, over her head, toward the stables.

"Rah have horse now, Ting Ya. Twenty horse! Wolf give Rah *all* King's horse. This colt? I name him Halix. Like Hali, you remember? Maybe Hali come back to Rah, come back in horse." He bumps his chest with a fist, as if waking the dog that still lives in his heart.

"Silly boy," laughs Ting Ya. "You cannot make it what you wish." Then she puts a cool palm against the boy's cheek and looks into his eyes. "You must learn to say good-by, Jin yu. Cannot carry the dead with you always. Must not carry ghosts. Do not want to be a haunted man."

All this time, Pyrus and Aros have been watching the two, whom they have never seen together. Now Aros looks to Pyrus, eyebrows lifting with astonishment.

"I did not know they were thus," he whispers to his friend, but Rah's sharp ears catch the dresser's words.

"Hah! You think Rah go only for treat to Ting Ya. You think Rah like baby. Rah is not baby! Rah is never be baby, not even when little boy," he flattens his hand and sets it on the head of an invisible toddler at his knee. "No one is let Rah be baby. Rah must dance to eat. Dance to live. Even when Ileah," and here his voice cracks, as if just breaking for the first time, "Is no live."

Aros can only swallow and look to Pyrus for help. "I didn't mean-" he begins. But it is Ting Ya who interrupts Rah's mood and saves Aros further scolding. She slaps the haunch he has turned to her as he berates his attendant, then shakes a finger at his hurt expression.

"You be good, Jin yu. Do not be cruel to the ones you know love you the best. This man," and she offers her palm to Aros, "He love you more than he love himself. Not so easy to find, this kind of love. Maybe better love than Ileah's, eh? A sister will marry one day, turn her heart to her husband, her babies. Maybe if Ileah live, would be marry, have babies to

49

love. Forget her brother. You do not know. But this man here. He love you. Master of Amega, he love you too, like this one. Ting Ya. She love you too, Jin yu. Many people love you now. You do not have to look behind you for love. Always behind you. It is here now. It is all around you."

Rah's face has fallen at Ting Ya's gentle admonishment. He tucks his chin, even cowers a bit at her words. But as suddenly as the posture of humility appears, it vanishes, as his eyes follow Ting Ya's hand into a pocket of her robe to withdraw a package. She begins to unfold it under his nose, smiling slyly as his pretty eyes grow big with interest and a wide grin ignites his dimples.

"Ting Ya bring Rah favorite treat. I make in Master's private kitchen this morning. Lady Josepha send cook off to market for spices. She tell cook, 'My friend Ting Ya will use this kitchen today, if Janus does not mind.' You should see his face, Jin yu!" She slaps her thigh with her free hand as Rah grabs the parcel of walnut clusters from her. "He walk backward, bow to Ting Ya all way out of kitchen!" she laughs.

Rah pulls apart the package and takes out one of the walnut clusters. He holds it up, examines it, then, apparently satisfied that it is genuine, he opens his mouth to devour it. But he stops abruptly, in mid-bite, and turns to Aros before he does so. "This how Ting Ya make, Aros. More nut, see? Pine too. And almond... paste. What is spice, Ting Ya?" he looks to Ting Ya for support.

"This cinnamon. And some clove, too," says Ting Ya, pointing at the cookie as if one could see the spice. She winks at Aros over Rah's shoulder. "Very special for Rah."

But Rah has turned to Aros to offer him the treat. "You try," he says, with a seductive pout that begs forgiveness.

"Baby, they're for you. You eat them," says Pyrus, giving Aros a look of disapproval as the dresser stretches out his hand to take the offering. "You them, Aros doesn't." He allows his eyes to drop to Aros' ample middle.

"Yes," says Ting Ya. "You try. Learn how to make." She takes a second cluster from the wrap and hands it to Aros, who gives Pyrus a dismissive glare and accepts the treat.

"Mmmm," he murmurs, sinking his teeth into the cookie. "So good."

"Now you show Ting Ya your horse, Jin yu. Come. We walk. I tell you about warrior horse in China. One time, imperial soldier come through village. Ting Ya is little girl, so big," she puts her hand down to her knee. "Father take Ting Ya and brothers to see. So many beautiful horse! Horse wear red and gold, like soldier! Like gods. Brothers afraid, start cry. But Ting Ya not afraid. Run in street to see, run right under horse! And horse, he rear up!" She puts her arms straight up over her head. The warrior's horse is rearing over Rah's head now and Rah is cringing. He is the little girl, Ting Ya. But Ting Ya only laughs. She takes Rah's forearm and turns him casually back through the doorway. As the boy follows, relaxing, she gives Aros one final wink over her shoulder.

"Horse jump over little Ting Ya. Horse, he say, 'Ting Ya! See now. Always be like the turtle, and you will never get hurt. Danger always jump over you! And so Ting Ya stay low. Stay quiet, and slow like turtle. All life, never get hurt."

"She's lovely," says the dresser to the face painter when the pair have gone.

"Yes," responds Pyrus a bit sadly.

"Do you think he means to harm him?" asks Aros, after a moment of silence.

"The priest?" Pyrus has turned to smooth Rah's bed linens. Now he straightens and puts his hands on his hips, considering. "What can he do, here in Amega, living as he is in the mouth of the Wolf."

"Oh, I don't know, Pyrus, but he frightens me. He is too smug, too satisfied with his lot. He has never been a man to share a treasure. I fear," but Aros falters. He cannot speak the words.

"Rush will not allow him to harm Rah, Aros. He would be mad to try. He may be mean, but he is not mad."

"All the same, he is too smug," responds Aros, gathering Rah's laundry for the morning wash.

But in the morning, Rush is gone.

It is Josepha who comes to Nikolaos' chamber after breakfast to advise him that her husband has given him authority over the compound, authority even over his six commanders, and authority over the four high priests, while he is gone.

"But where has he gone? When will he be back?" asks the newly appointed Lieutenant General of Amega.

"I have never known," responds Josepha, looking up into the man's face with candid empathy. "But you will be fine. He would not leave you in command if he did not think you capable." And she gives his arm a reassuring pat before she turns to go, leaving Ham to offer him the heavy package containing his new uniform.

"What does it mean, Nikolaos?" asks Cara when she is gone. "What does he expect of you? His stronghold here has never needed a Lieutenant General before. It has functioned without him all the while he stayed in Crete with his family, masquerading as a shipping merchant."

"That was no masquerade, wife," says Nikolaos, looking over the new uniform Ham has left him to put on. "He will have built this citadel and bought this army of men with the spoils of his business on Crete," he stops to consider, "and of course, with the money he takes as an assassin." He looks up from his examination of a bronze scale vest and a weapons belt that appears to be encrusted in rubies. "But his heart is made for war."

"War, and the Rah," says Cara.

He gives her a considering look. "Perhaps that is my function then. To guard the Rah."

"It would seem so," says Cara, coming to circle her husband's waist from behind and kiss his shoulder. But to herself she is thinking, but what is mine? And as she rests her cheek on his back she repeats the thought to herself alone. What is mine?

Rush has business in the capital. King Hattusilis has sent word to the assassin that he intends to adopt his daughter's son, Mursilis, as his successor above the fierce protestations of his own three worthless sons. He has hired Rush to visit his own offspring, whom he considers unreliable to the point of treason and quite capable of assassinating his grandson in order that one of them might still gain a throne none have earned.

Hattusilis is in Kussara nursing a wound he received in a campaign against Aleppo and the Hurrians in North Syria. And Rush is on his way to Kussara before he visits the king's three sons in Hattusha. The trip will take him the better part of a moon and it is a necessity. Without Mursilis, his own war plans will be frustrated. For Hattusilis has promised the assassin that in payment of his protection of Mursilis he will be granted the honor of leading his push into Syria.

For thirteen days Rush will travel alone across the plateaus and mountains of Anatolia, north to Kussara. He will arrive in time to watch Hattusilis die in his wife's arms, declaring his only daughter's son his successor. He will be taken aside by the Queen and offered a true king's ransom for the death of her eldest step-son, a warning to the other two that their fate will be the same if they make an attempt on Mursilis' life.

By the new moon the Hittite monarchy will be secure, Hattusilis' eldest son will be buried alongside his father, and the reign of Mursilis I will have begun.

But in Amega things are not so orderly.

The normal morning practice schedule has been disturbed by a new addition to the day's events. For on the same morning that Nikolaos discovers Rush has disappeared, his self-appointed charge has created a near panic in the stable. Before Hagga and Ghedi arrive to feed, Rah has grained and hayed his own horses and taken the colt Halix and the two Arab mares out to the arena. By the time the charioteers have begun to arrive to put their horses in driving tack, Rah, with the help of Ramicus and his men, is attempting to jump the three beasts in unison over an obstacle he has constructed from two grain pails and a paddock rail.

Hagga, hearing the commotion outside, runs out in time to see the three animals soaring over the obstacle with Rah balancing on the croup of the center horse. Being green, the trio has taken the one foot fence as if it were three feet high, catapulting Rah into the air. But the boy is unfazed. He diminishes the impulsion by making a feather-light hop and, remaining in unison with the horse even while disconnected from it, he lands again on the animal's croup as a bird might, albeit without the benefit of wings.

The roar of the charioteers, who have left their horses to watch the spectacle, nearly shakes the stable timbers.

"He can do it! He can run three together!" cries Ghedi at Hagga's side, oblivious of his friend's state of horror. "He can drive a chariot thus!"

Pulling himself away from his wife's embrace for the second time in two days, Lieutenant General Nikolaos rushes to his window on the second floor of the citadel when he hears the cheering soldiers. He is only half dressed in his new uniform, but thoughtlessly leans out the portal to observe a red sun rising over the eastern edge of the practice field, exploding in Rah's golden curls as the boy and the trio of horses descend from the jump and round a corner.

"Holy mother of all gods," murmurs Nikolaos, grabbing his sword, his jewel encrusted belt and his helmet before storming out of the bedroom and down the hall.

When Cara reaches the window, Rah is drawing the trio of Arabians to a halt. The morning sunlight has turned his head a strange peach-gold and the animal's dapples silver. Ever the performer, he drops his reins and makes a double somersault off the colt's back. Then he strolls out into the middle of the field and makes a curtain call bow to his audience of charioteers. His heels planted firmly together, he folds himself in two over his golden belt, laying his lustrous curls in the dirt until the cheers die down. He remains motionless until Halix, perturbed by his absence, wanders over to give him an impatient nudge and puts him on his rump.

This elicits a wave of good-natured laughter and more applause.

"Teach us to wage war thus, Rah!" cries a heckler in the crowd. "Who needs a chariot?"

"The master has found us a secret weapon!" cries another.

"Yes! Let the Amorites see him! Thus entranced, we may cut them down like sheep!" cries a third.

"Sweet Rah," whispers Cara from her window. "They will eat you alive, and what will my husband do about it?" Leaning thoughtlessly out of the casement in nothing but a thin sleeping shift, she smiles dreamily down at the field of four hundred handsomely uniformed men. What is this, Mother god? she muses to herself. Only weeks ago it seems I was to be married off to a lummox. Instead kidnapped and sold for a whore, I am rescued by the God of War, and by him married to a prince among men. Now here I stand, I who once believed I would never know love, or the taste of a single hour of fulfillment, nay, a single passionate kiss, here I stand, in the castle of my heart's desire. Here stands Cara, vintner's daughter, girl from Pheistos, deflowered by a pretty soldier and abandoned, thus appointed to be shackled in marriage to a flatulent dim-wit. What changed it all, what turned the ugly course of my life? Was it you, Rah? Are you truly the god of fulfillment, as they say, the true Soul of Rah? Did the priest, in all of his arrogant greed, somehow stumble upon the alchemy necessary to bring the deity of fulfillment into our midst? It seems that all who love you are saved. And everyone touched by you, changed. Modified. Improved. Perfected.

But what is a perfect wolf? Is he better at hunting? Better at killing? More lone? More dangerous and silent? Or just more in love with the moon.

Rush has never been better at hunting, or killing, has never been more dangerous or silent in his coming, than he is on the night he visits the eldest stepson of the widowed Queen of Hatti. But he has also never felt so alone. And love? This wolf is nothing but love, with a great, black, aching heart he bays with each silent breath at the moon he covets and cannot have. I thought I could take you, break you, by force. I am large. I am fierce. You are small. You are grace. Oh, but I thought grace was weak. I have ever been mistaken. For you are like a crystal. Your points are sharp. You pierce me. Your light is blinding. I, who could see in the dark, cannot see when I am in the presence of your light. I thought I could take you by force. Break you. But it is you who have broken me.

Rush stands in a dark corner of the Prince's bedchamber. The Prince is no boy. He is older than Rush, and sleeps with his wife's niece tonight, for he desired her and he takes all that he desires.

Rush stands enwrapped in his black assassin's tunic and leggings and hood. One eye, were it light enough to see it, is exposed yet by the tear the Grain God made when he rose from his sleeping sickness in Cyrus to defend himself from the assassin's kisses. Rush cannot bring himself to mend the tear. He cares not if his victim sees one handsome eye, thick with black lashes and tipped slightly down, as if with some perpetual sadness, before he meets his death. He touches the open hole now and again to remind himself. He is distracted by love, and yet strangely, love has made him even better at what he does, truer to what he is.

Rush approaches the Prince's bed. He looks down at the woman the man has betrayed his kingdom for. She is voluptuous, with large breasts and a tiny waist. Hips like a brood mare. And her face is striking, even in sleep. Sharp-featured and strong. But it is not a face to lose a kingdom for. Indeed, it is not a face even to remember. It is a greedy face, the lips too large, the brows, too thick and sharp. It belies her worldliness. This is a woman who lusts for power, it says. This is a woman who will steal and horde and never be filled.

She is more manly in her features than you, little cat, thinks Rush. No. Not manly. Hard. Jaded. This is beauty without innocence. And what is that? How does he find her attractive? Where is the, what? What is it I am looking for? I look for the face of a wild little cat. I search for your untamed purity.

Without much interest, he slaps one hand over the woman's nose and mouth. The other has snatched both of her wrists to keep her still while she suffocates. He has drawn her off the bed and put a knee between her breasts and a dagger to her throat before the fool Prince can be awakened by her struggling. The Prince continues to snore as Rush leans into the woman's face and whispers, "The king is dead."

His intention is to snap the woman's breastbone in two with his knee. But he is stopped by his own curiosity. Again he asks himself, what does he see in her? How is it that he finds this face worth his father's kingdom, his own life?

He has moved his hand from her mouth as he muses. With his dagger at her throat she is not likely to attempt to scream, and his blade would open her trachea and stop her scream before she finished taking air to propel it if she tried. But the woman is staring up into his mask, into his single exposed eye, with something that is not entirely horror.

"Rush!" she whispers through voluptuous, berry-stained lips. They are the lips of a whore. He looks at them, his brow furrowing under his hood.

"He will pay you twice what that bitch has promised you!"

Her words hit his ears like the thud of the archery's arrow into a cloth practice target. There is no sweetness in the timber of her voice. It is thin, and even so, manly. Demanding of notice even in a whisper. He squints down at her, takes her jaw, turns her face this way and that. Worse in profile, the nose too thick, too long. Where is there delicacy in this face? Perhaps it is her cunt that calls to the Prince, and not her face at all.

Rush releases the woman's wrists and moves his free hand down her body to the hem of her nightdress, then slides his open palm up over her knee, over her inner thigh toward her sex. His hand is slow and hot from exertion. He has had to kill seven guards to enter the Prince's chamber.

Unbelievably, she arches toward him, offering.

"Maybe you want me for yourself, eh? See what he risks his father's kingdom for." She is moving her hips, gyrating. Her pubis reaches for his fingers. "Take," she whispers, confident. "You will want more." She is smiling like a crocodile.

But the words hit Rush like a blow to his heart. And there comes the image, blinding him to her. It is Rah, that first day. Shimmering, shivering, in the clearing where he had carried him to take his head for Cyrus. "For yourself?" the boy had said, his wounded tongue deepening his already dusky voice, his strange, northern lilt turning the Minoan into a pretty song. Oh but you had no intention of giving me what you offered, did you, little cat. You would take a dagger before you let me take you.

Still, here is the Prince of Hatti's mistress, offering her cunt, promising she is worth what the Prince is about to lose for it.

He lets his fingers reach her, stroke her. She is wet, perhaps from sex with the Prince. But no. His fingers can detect her readiness. What monstrosity is this? She is flush with blood. For me. For her assassin.

"You will want more," she says again. Ah, Hatti women. How they lust for power.

His own member has responded to her offer. But this is nothing. He is always heavy with blood when he is hunting. She has mistaken his curiosity for interest, of which he has none.

He hears the Prince roll over toward the place where she lay moments before. He is reaching for her in his sleep and, not finding her, is coming awake.

"Where are you, Sophina?" asks the Prince.

"Betray my presence with a scream, whore, and you will fuck this dagger before you die," snarls Rush into the woman's face, his lips so close to her that the cloth of his mask tickles her nose.

The woman freezes. Still, her face belies her fascination for the monster astride her. There is lust in her eyes. Insatiable greed.

"She is here with me, Prince. Thus she takes your assassin unto herself, as she has taken unto herself the son who would assassinate his own father. The whore does not discriminate. Her love is for power. The currency of the exchange always the same."

The Prince has thrown himself off the opposite side of his bed at the sight of the great, black shape that is Rush rising from the floor on the other. But Rush is quick to leap the distance and take hold of him. He delivers three well placed blows, to the man's temple, chest and liver, then drags him back up onto the bed, moaning and clutching his belly.

As the woman crawls warily back onto the bed to her lover's side, Rush withdraws from them, crossing the room to stand at the window through which he will escape when he is done here. Moonlight touches his shoulder, glints in the lashes of his uncovered eye. He is a sad beast. He tips his head to peer across the night landscape below toward Amega.

From the bed the woman Sophina watches him. Her eyes are calculating. She offers no comfort to the Prince, who sags against her, panting with shock and pain.

Rush crosses his arms and waits for the next utterance from the Prince. It is always the same. In his mind, he has named it 'the song of the assassined' for it is the same chorus, ever the same, his victims sing when they realize who it is who has come to relieve them of the burden of their life.

"Rush," gasps the Prince, whose curious fingers have found that the blood trickling into his eyes originates from the gash Rush's fist has opened on his temple. "I will give you anything you wish. Name your price."

Rush looks over the Prince and his mistress. He takes his time, cocks his head, scanning the woman's body from head to foot. Then he turns away, to peer out of the window into the night, even dipping one powerful shoulder and leaning over the casement to peek at the parapet below, though his arms are still crossed over his chest.

Even now, I can think of nothing but you. Where are you tonight, little cat? Do you sleep in the bed of down I have provided, or have you waited until your attendants sleep and then thrown a skin to the floor, under the window. And do you lie there on your belly, and does the moonlight play with your hair? Or have you scaled the wall of my citadel, you little monkey, to go to the stable and sleep in the hay beside Halix? Have you driven Nikolaos half mad with worry yet? Have you slept with every kitchen maid, every soldier's wife, even my own?

He turns back to the fool on the bed.

"You have nothing I want, Prince."

At this, even despite his injuries, the Prince must let out a panicked chuckle.

"The Prince of Hatti? Has nothing you want?" he squeaks through teeth clenched against the worsening pain in his side. "What of the woman at my side, Rush?" he adds, losing the last vestiges of his composure. "Surely a man like you," and here he allows his eyes to traverse the assassin's broad chest and trim hips, "Can find a use for such a beauty?"

At this the woman's head snaps about to glare at her lover. "You worthless ass!" she hisses at him, shoving him away from her and throwing herself off the bed to rush the door and make her escape.

But a dagger has beaten her to her goal. It thumps the door inches from her nipples, the blade catching in the wood, the golden handle wagging with energy.

"Move again, whore, and I will plant another in your back," mutters Rush as she stares at him with shocked eyes. He nods to the bed. "Return to your Prince."

"What are your intentions for me?" she blinks, clutching her night shift over her breasts, as if with sudden modesty.

"I have none," responds the assassin, walking to the door to take his dagger and replace it in the holster at his ankle. "You are as common as sheep." He has come to stand at the end of the bed.

"Do it then!" cries the Prince suddenly. "Do what you have come to do!"

"Plenty of time," murmurs Rush. Oh, but there again, I was wrong, was I not, little cat? I thought I could break you. Catch you, overwhelm you. Force pleasures on you that you were not made for. But even in my arms you escaped me. Even in my arms! You drive this hunter's heart mad with hunger. Women melt like kittens beneath me. Boys as well, once they can see past their fears. But you? You will not be tamed, will not submit, though you are but a slave, to your master's fondest embrace.

He is hard again. His phallus presses against the cloth of his leggings like a bull in a slaughterhouse pen. But not for this whore, this abomination that calls itself a woman.

"What do you see in her?" he asks the Prince, his hell-deep baritone softened with wonder.

"Wha-?" The Prince is panting through pain that has become so unbearable he can longer keep his eyes on the assassin. His belly has swollen. He is in labor with his own death. For unbeknownst to him, the assassin has already delivered his final blow. He is dying. His liver is torn, and his life leaks out into his abdominal cavity. He is bleeding to death from within.

"*You* tell me then," says the beast that towers at the end of the bed to the woman. "What do you have to offer a Prince? Or any man."

"Can you not see for yourself?" snaps Sophina, sensing his weakness and growing foolish with pride and fear. She tips her chin at him, accusing. "They say you brought a beautiful boy back from Crete. They say you risked your life to have him. Rush, the Assassin, risking his life for a boy. There is your answer. Any man who is man enough to desire a woman can see why a king would give his life to have *me*."

"No," responds Rush dreamily, and failing to take her bait. "Nikolaos would have left you in the tomb." He is talking to himself as he moves from the end of the bed to her side. He takes her arm and pulls her once again off the mattress to peer into her face. "You are ugly with greed. Ugly with pride. You are more crocodile than woman. It is he," and here he nods to the dying Prince still slumped and groaning on the bed, "who fails to be a man by finding womanhood in you."

"You beast!" cries Sophina, who has never known an insult. She raises her hand to strike his masked face, thinks better of it, lets it settle beside her.

Now he has pushed her into the wall at the head of the bed. He presses her there and tilts his head at her. After a moment of examination, he bends, inhumanly slow, to breathe against her mouth, and she is instantly relaxed in his arms. She slides her hungry hands up over his biceps, his shoulders, as if feeling for the power there. She presses her lips against the fabric of his mask, searching for his mouth under the cloth.

"Rush," she whispers, her voice dank with lust.

He draws his head back, pushes her away, pinning her by her shoulders to the wall, not to take her, but to keep her from finding his mouth.

"Why are you so easy, woman?" he murmurs.

"Easy? Hah! You fool. Do you think I have no wiles? I tortured him. I made him beg for it for months!"

"And yet you are easy," says Rush. And releasing her he turns to leave. A breeze from the window caresses his back, calling him. He is lonely for the night, and for the moon.

Sophina is shaking with excitement but also with rage. The assassin has released her! She may live! And yet here before her, wrapped in black muslin, is true power, ultimate strength. Here is death itself. And death has denied her! Propelled by the thrill of his insults, and by the heat of his body which, a moment before, promised to fill her emptiness, she flings herself at him. She claws for purchase at the cloth covering his back.

"Leave me, woman," he says, giving her the mildest shove. She falters on her feet, then rushes at him again.

"No! I will have you, Rush. You will see. You will want me! We are alike, you and I. Do not deny it."

"That is a hellish thought," responds the assassin, opening one hand against her belly, so that for an instant, the heat of his palm warms her womb. But he is merely thrusting her onto her back on the bed in order that he might escape her.

And escape her he does, through the open window and into the night, where he will sleep alone under a full moon.

CHAPTER 6

Rah has returned to the citadel, hungry for his supper after a day with his horses, when he hears his old dance instructor, Dimius, talking loudly with Akbar in the Great Hall.

Forgetting his growling stomach, Rah runs down the hall toward the sound. He skates to a stop on the marble floor of the Master's entrance to the lyceum, and is greeted by the sight of the dance troupe of the House of the Moon, pausing in practice as their two instructors bicker over a bit of footwork.

"Rah!" cries Dimius, stepping forward and opening his arms as Akbar halts his rebuttal and echoes the boy's name.

"Dimius!" Rah has leapt over the stone seats meant for the Master and his wife and launched himself off the dais and into his old instructor's embrace. After a moment, Dimius reluctantly releases him so that Akbar can have his turn.

The dancers have stopped what they are doing in mid-step and now come to twitter and flap about Rah like birds at a feed trough on a winter morning.

"You are frail, Rah. Where is your flesh? What have you been through these last weeks? We believed we would never see you again. You must tell us," smiles Dimius. And taking him again from Akbar to bury his grin in Rah's cherry blossom curls he adds, "You must tell us your story."

This sends a flutter of excitement through the dancers, for they know as well as Dimius that the dance master has laid down a challenge. Unable to express his tale adequately in words, Rah will be forced to recreate his trial in dance.

True to his nature, Rah pulls himself away from Dimius and looks about at the troupe. His face has become a theatre, and the theatre is dark.

The troupe waits, murmuring and giggling with anticipation for the houselights that are his eyes to light the stage of his face.

"I tell you!" cries Rah then, and suddenly his iridescent eyes are filled with dread. He skates backward out of the knot of dancers, flips himself back up on the dais like a leopard returning to its nest in the trees, and opens his arms.

"This how Rah is take from House of Moon!" he shouts to his audience, and he sweeps his arm back, gesturing to the empty stage behind him, and steps aside to introduce his story.

Then, parting an invisible curtain, he enters his stage.

"Go to see Ting Ya," he tells his audience, and he is strolling across the dais, which has become the Bridge Road. His exaggerated walk is easy, bouncing, even silly. His arms swing at his sides, his eyes scan the trees above for life. His mouth is pressed into a silent whistle, for his wounded tongue will not allow the sound. Turning at the end of the dais he continues his innocent stroll by returning to center stage. He pantomimes his leap over the cemetery wall using the master's stone throne as an obstacle. The leap is relaxed, the landing light. But suddenly, his composure is gone. He is pointing over the dancer's heads, horror on his face.

And the dancers look behind themselves in unison, taking in their breath.

"Ting Ya! Man from Cyrus! He take!" and suddenly he is Lutarus, puffed with importance. His knife pressing the invisible Ting Ya to his chest, he growls the awful words. "We take *you*, Rah of Knossos, or-" and his Lutarus has drawn the edge of his sword across Ting Ya's throat, "we kill this woman!" His audience gasps.

Now Rah leaves his Lutarus behind. He returns to the edge of the dais and points back to the spot where the man and his prisoner stood. He is a judge accusing a criminal.

"This man want war with Knossos! This man, he from Cyrus. He think, I take Rah, I make war!"

Returning to center stage and his own character, Rah is dragged off by the palace guards of Cyrus. He kicks and bites, but cannot free himself from his captors. Back at the far right edge of the dais, he is flung by invisible hands down to the floor. He falls, face first, onto his chest and hands. But this is not enough. He must yet be thrown into the tomb. He topples down the stone steps that lead to the floor of the lyceum on the far right side of the dais. He has conveniently staged his pantomime so that these stairs might represent the Tomb of Lutarus.

His audience is hushed. Some of the girls are standing with their hands over their mouths, others are sniffling back tears and wiping the corners of their eyes, smearing their black stage liner. Dimius is standing stiffly beside Akbar swallowing the ball of emotion that has hardened in his throat.

At the bottom of the steps, Rah curls his body into a fetal ball. He is shivering, whimpering. He is no longer human. Has he hurt himself pantomiming his fall? One of the male dancers steps forward, meaning to go to him, but Dimius takes his arm, gives him a sharp look, shakes his head, 'no.'

And Rah is on his feet. Quick as a cat, he has leap back onto the dais to narrate. He points to the spot where he left himself shivering in the tomb.

"This men, they put Rah in tomb, tie up like chicken! Three day. No food. No water. Rah is sick. Fever. Maybe die!" He looks over his audience for sympathy. The girls are all in tears. The men are clenching their fists and jaws with fury burning in their painted eyes.

"Then this Nikolaos?" And he is pointing at the ceiling, toward the upper rooms of the citadel where the newly appointed Lieutenant General of Amega now resides. "He come. On horse!" And Rah is riding a horse, tall and smart. "He find Rah," he jumps off his horse, falls to his knees, picks up the dying Rah with a lover's tenderness. "Take to Cyrus."

Still on his knees but dropping his Rah like so much rubbish, he looks at Dimius proudly. "This how Rah is take from House of Moon to Cyrus."

But Dimius shakes his head, looks about at the others, lifts his hands and shrugs. "But how were you then restored to us, Rah? How did the assassin claim you from Cyrus? You have not finished the story!"

Rah pouts a moment, drawing himself back to his feet.

"I think too much to tell now. But maybe," he looks over the dance master's head at his troupe, a mischievous twinkle in his eyes. Smiles are peeking out from behind the two instructors. The dancers are nodding and whispering amongst themselves, their excitement building.

Dimius looks to Akbar, who responds by giving his shoulder a shove and bursting out, "Hah!"

"What you think, Dimius?" grins Rah, lifting his chin and settling his hands on his hips.

"I think you need to come back to us, Rah, for without you we are nothing. Just another troupe. Give up those damned horses and give us back our lead dancer. And let us tell the Story of the Rah to all the world!"

"You think Wolf is let Rah dance again, Dimius? You think he is let Rah go other city, tell story of Rah?" muses Rah, biting his lip.

"I think he will let Rah do whatever Rah wants to do," says Dimius. "Come back to us, Rah. Give us the story. I will put it to dance. When the Master returns, we will perform it for him."

"Have you not forgotten to consult your own master on such a matter, Dimius?"

It is the reedy voice of the High Priest, Mochlos, who has been watching Rah from the archway at the far west end of the lyceum.

Dimius jerks around at the sound, the old fear of his master melting his bowels. He quickly salutes the priest with a drop to the ground, gesturing for the entire troupe to do the same. Only Rah remains standing, his hands still resting on his hips, his eyes leveled at the priest with dangerous insolence.

Mochlos is moving toward the group like a tiger walking among deer. The troupe remain on their knees, faces down, as he scans their heads, then flicks his eyes up to Rah, who remains on the dais.

"You had better offer your priest respect, little slave god. Do not forget that it was I who made you, and I can as easily unmake you. You host the soul of Rah, whom I ushered into your body. If I dispatch him, you die."

Rah is staring at the priest with disbelieving eyes as he speaks these words.

"What you say, priest? You hurt Rah, Wolf is kill you. Is kill you hard!" he fairly barks from his perch. The dancers are beginning to raise their heads, so unbelievable is what they are hearing. Forgetting the priest's temper, most of them are now watching the exchange from their knees, though ready to bury their heads in their thighs at the slightest provocation.

"Oh, I hardly think that your 'Wolf' will believe that my prayers are powerful enough to put his little treasure back into the world of the dead. He is a practical man, and does not believe in priests. He only brought us here so that you might be worshiped and adored to his satisfaction. But power? He would not have killed Ananou if he believed in it. For Ananou was there at your creation, Rah. He was essential. Nothing can put you back together again if I take you apart, you and your god. You see?"

By now Rah has begun to look about at the others, at Dimius and Akbar and his troupe, with growing concern. But no one is brave enough to comfort him, not even his dance master, who is among the few who have maintained a bowed head.

"This true, Dimius? Priest can do this?" asks Rah.

But Dimius does not respond. He bows even lower as the high priest shuffles toward him to take him by his hair and pull his face up.

"Answer him, Dimius," Mochlos orders.

Terrified, Dimius responds with the words he knows his master desires to hear, "It is true, Rah."

"Good boy," murmurs Mochlos, bending to put the words into the dance master's ear, and then shoving his face back toward the ground.

"Now come down from your tree, little leopard, and offer your creator some respect. Then we will discuss this idea of performing a dance for the Master of Amega, one that could take you, and therefore me, out of the compound. Perhaps to the capital. Such a thing is not without merit. It is quite a delightful idea, in fact. But first, show me that you understand me. Come down here and give your priest a kiss."

But Rah remains on the dais, fists clenched. "I am no kiss this priest. I am hate this priest," he says.

"I do not ask you to love me. But if you do not show your priest respect, then your priest will think that you are not the true Rah, for the god loves his priest. And if you are not the true Rah, then you are an imposter. A demon. And it will be my responsibility to destroy you. This was the fate of two others before you, whose hearts I carved out of their bodies on Mount Ida when they failed to keep the winter back, and thus prove they housed the soul of Rah."

"Wolf is no let priest kill Rah! Wolf is kill priest!" cries Rah then, leaping off the dais to stand under Mochlos' nose and, fists still clenched at his sides, offer him his fiercest scowl.

"No. He will not let me take you to the mountain. But I can destroy you just the same. I can chase the life that the god has given you from your body. I can do it with prayer. The slave boy you were is dead. If whatever animates you now is sent back to where it came, be it demon or god, you will die."

"How you can do this?" whisper's Rah, uncomprehending.

"Do you wish to test my powers over you?" asks the priest, raising an eyebrow and slipping his left hand into the pocket of his robe surreptitiously to capture a minute bit of the opiate powder he has been hiding there in a tiny vial onto the tip of his waxed index finger. Then with unexpected quickness, he snatches Rah's right wrist and lays that finger against the pulse there. "On your knees, little golden one," says Mochlos, his fingers pinching the flesh at Rah's wrist.

And suddenly Rah is on his knees, dropping to them as in a fall, rather than a bow of submission.

"Uh, head spin," says Rah, falling on his hands as the priest releases his wrist.

"Yes, and it will spin until you are flung from it, demon! For I am he who ushered you into this body, and I can expel you just as easily!"

With this, Mochlos looks about at the audience of dancers. His piercing black eyes scan them for dissention but find none. With a nod of satisfaction he gives Dimius a kick, knocking him off his knees and onto his side in the sand.

"You are all still the property of the House of the Moon. Do not forget it. Now get up and come with me, dance master, and we will discuss this idea of yours. You too, Akbar. The rest of you may go and take your supper."

But as the troupe begins to rise cautiously to their feet, there is hesitation among them. They circle Rah, who is still on his hands and knees and moaning. When two of the male dancers move to help him to his feet, Mochlos turns irritably and shoves them back away from the boy.

"Leave him!" he snaps, and the two dancers back away, cowed.

"But we cannot leave him thus, Master. He is ill!" exclaims Dimius.

"It will pass," says the priest, more considerately. And then, looking around the group he adds, "It is a warning only. A warning to you all. Heed it."

But when Mochlos and the others are gone, it does not pass. Rah remains on his hands and knees, struggling against a tidal wave of nausea and dizzying illusion until his epileptic mind finds sanctuary in his illness. He suffers a violent seizure, and is not found until Nikolaos, returning from an afternoon of practice with his new Hittite sword, passes the lyceum and happens to glance in, only to discover the white and yellow stillness that is Rah lying on the sand floor by the dais.

"Rah!" His worst fears upon him, Nikolaos shouts for the guards to bring word to the Master's wife that the Rah has fallen back into the sleep that ever seeks to take him into the realm of the gods and away from them forever. Then he drops to his knees at the boy's side, finds a faint pulse at his throat, and with considerable relief, takes him up into his arms and carries him toward the Lady's courtyard.

By the time he has arrived, Josepha and Ting Ya are there, awaiting him. A soft couch has been added to the seating in the middle of the raised yard, and Rah is deposited on it with exquisite care by the Lieutenant General of Amega.

"What has happened to him, Lieutenant," asks Josepha softly as she kneels at the boy's side and brushes back his hair from his forehead. But she does not have to wait for Nikolaos to answer. She is standing before the priest, Mochlos, her fists clenched in rage. He has threatened her with death. Yes. He can do it. He can expel the spirit of Rah from her body. The boy she was no longer exists. She will be an empty skin. The priest has snatched her by her wrist. She feels waxy fingers press her pulse. He is demanding homage. You are yet mine, he says. You will obey and love me.

Now she is on her knees, overcome by nausea and dizziness. Her head spins! Her balance is gone. She cannot endure it. No more! No more! Her mind escapes, her body begins to spasm.

"Lady Josepha!" It is the Lieutenant. He has lifted her to her feet. He is shaking her by her shoulders.

"He has poisoned him," she murmurs weakly, coming out of the trance and looking up into the man's strange, grey eyes.

"Who? Who has poisoned him?" responds Nikolaos who will only later wonder why he trusted her word so implicitly.

"The priest. The High Priest, Mochlos." She has turned back to look down at Rah, for the boy is stirring. "He has threatened him with death. That he will expel the god from his body. Unless he defers to him in all things," and she is on her knees again, stroking the boy's curls as he begins to awaken. From her knees she looks up at Nikolaos. "And who is to say? Perhaps it is true."

"I will kill him myself," says Nikolaos, offering Josepha a short bow and then turning to go and execute his decision. His hand is already on the hilt of his new sword.

"Lieutenant." It is Ting Ya. She has been standing apart from the scene, but now steps forward to place a hand on Josepha's shoulder and look up at the retreating Nikolaos.

"Madam?"

"This boy, he believe. You kill priest. Maybe then this boy, he die. Maybe he believe he cannot live without priest."

"Madam, the man is a traitor. And I am Lieutenant General of Amega. If I let a traitor live, I will forfeit my own head when the Master returns."

"Forfeit head if boy die because priest die also, Lieutenant," answers Ting Ya, nodding with certainty.

"That is ridiculous. Why, should he die of a belief?" snaps the Lieutenant before thinking better his curt address of an honored guest in the house of the assassin.

"Every man live and die what he believe, Lieutenant," answers Ting Ya without hesitation.

By now Rah has begun to come fully awake. His eyes widen with the sight of Josepha at his side. He has but to utter her name, and the wife of the Master of Amega has instantly encased him in her arms.

"Sweet Rah," she murmurs against his hair and holding him tight. "How I have longed for you."

"Rah have fit," says Rah in explanation, accepting her embrace but not returning it.

"We are here, Rah. No one can hurt you," says Josepha, taking hold of him by his shoulders so that he must look into her face. But Rah is subdued. He does not hold her gaze, but puts his eyes to the floor.

"I have lingered long enough," murmurs Nikolaos, turning a second time to go.

"No, Lieutenant," says Josepha. "I fear Ting Ya may be right." Then, seeing the alarm on the man's face, she adds, "I will take responsibility for the decision, Nikolaos."

"Allow me at least to throw him into prison then, where he can do no more harm, and have no access to the boy."

But Josepha's eyes have drifted over his head. Releasing Rah's shoulders she says, "No." And then she does an unexpected thing. Leaving Rah to Ting Ya, she rises to her feet and takes Nikolaos by the arm, drawing him away.

When she has removed him from Rah's hearing, to the wall overlooking the sea and the cliffs below, she looks up at him calmly, a smile pulling at the sides of her mouth.

Nikolaos looks down at the serene and queenly countenance of the wife of the assassin and for a moment he is back in Cyrus, looking down at his own queen, Media.

"Nikolaos, you have been devoted to Rah since you first lay eyes upon him. I trust your heart is genuine. And I know you will keep him safe or die trying. But you are a clever man. I think you must know that there is more to their relationship, this boy and his priest, than can be explained in the natural world. They are linked, whether in mind only, or in spirit. What if Ting Ya is right? If you put the priest in prison, the boy may grow ill, even die."

Then giving the Lieutenant's arm a playful squeeze she adds, "Come now, Lieutenant, we can outsmart a man who thinks he still owns what my husband has stolen from him."

Nikolaos snaps erect at her boldness. It takes him a moment to recover and ask, "What do you suggest, Lady? You have tied my hands."

"Nothing is decided in Amega without the final word of the Master of Amega, Lieutenant. I suggest we do nothing. But when my husband returns I think you might discuss with him the possibility of safeguarding Rah's life by naming a successor to the High Priest. I myself have always thought," continues the assassin's wife, smiling, "that the Moon, being a goddess, would prefer a high priestess to a priest."

"Do you have someone in mind, Madam?" asks Nikolaos, narrowing his eyes.

"I do. I am thinking of your wife, sir."

"And how will this plan protect the Rah from the priest in the meantime?"

"Lieutenant, a city is made of its rumors. Rah is in far less danger than you think. Let us allow human nature to take her course. The servants will talk. The three other priests have the power to discipline their peer if they choose to do so."

"Pah, what will a priest do?" scoffs Nikolaos and then looks down into the Lady of Amega's eyes with sudden understanding. "You are thinking of Tyrus, the Bull Priest."

"He is a very opportunistic man, Nikolaos. It would do you well to learn his history. Any survivor of Knossos can tell it to you if you will but ask."

"And you believe he will use this incident to his advantage."

"A fighting bull may trim his horns, put on a yoke and pull a plow to save his hide from the butcher in lean times, but he is still, beneath, a fighting bull."

"I understand he is Hittite."

"And as a boy, captured by the Greeks and enslaved. And yet he became the Bull Priest of Knossos."

"And when the Master returns?" asks Nikolaos, turning away from his hostess to allow his eyes to drift out across the sea toward Crete. "What of Mochlos then?"

"I fear he may well come to some swift and unfortunate end as a result of his own arrogance. Therefore it is imperative that the rumor of your wife becoming his successor has already spread, and that Rah has heard it. Then Rah will come to no harm."

"But it will seem to all that I myself have spread this rumor, and impudently, behind the Master's back while he is away, to draw power to myself. There could be a mutiny, and I the target of assassination in his absence."

At this Josepha can only raise her hand to her mouth to stop herself from laughing out loud. Her soft brown eyes twinkling, she looks up at Nikolaos indulgently and answers, "You are a delightfully innocent man, Lieutenant. Tell me, you have met the six commanders of Amega, and many of the highest ranking men in the compound. Ferocious warriors, to be sure. These are the boldest fighting men in all of the Aegean. Now, tell me, which one do you suppose is courageous enough to assassinate the man my husband put in charge?"

Blinking foolishly, Nikolaos drops his gaze to the floor. "No, I suppose I have nothing to fear in that regard. But I do not understand how you can allow Rah to return to the priest's care. He is clearly frightened of the man." Nikolaos looks back to the couch, where Rah has pulled himself into a full lotus as he listens, head bowed, to Ting Ya's soft voice. "I cannot bear his discomfort."

"Leave that to me, sir. Rah must know nothing of our plan. He must maintain his belief that the priest holds power over him. Thus, his belief in the magic of his incarnation is also secured. He must believe in the ceremony of the succession, in order that he might be freed from the priest's hold over him."

Nikolaos has been listening to Josepha with growing wonder. When she is finished, he is peering at her with something closer to awe. "You are brilliant, Madam. You care for the boy's mind like a mother cares for a newborn."

Smiling, Josepha places a plump, delicate finger on the Lieutenant's forearm. "We are mind first, Lieutenant. His is damaged, but oh, so beautifully pure. It is as if the mind and the soul are one in him. Now come, Lieutenant, let us dine together tonight. I am lonely for my husband, and Ting Ya has left me to take the boy back to his quarters, as you see."

"Madam, I am honored," says Nikolaos, making a deep bow from the hip, and then offering her his arm to escort her to the Master's dining room, where he will meet the twin cubs of Antaris for the first time.

CHAPTER 7

"I heard it only this morning from Crispo. He hears everything in the kitchens, you know. It's like a brothel down there."

Enenoch is pacing back and forth in the hall of the Bull. He is waiting for Tyrus to make himself decent, so that he might enter his bedroom chamber and speak in private of the rumor that has had him at his wit's end all morning. He has heard from Crispo that Mochlos has charged the citadel's carpenter with the task of making the House of the Moon an elaborate altar, to be installed in the north quarter of the lyceum for the express purpose of conducting ceremonies designed to underscore his singular importance in the holy preservation of the Rah.

What is more, he has heard from the same source that the priest has frightened his dancer master half to death with the threat that he is magically capable of dismissing the Soul of Rah from his slave god if he so chooses. In fact, he proved it last night! Though it is anyone's guess how he accomplished such a thing.

Tyrus is in bed with a concubine from the House of the Moon when Enenoch comes barging in to wake him with the news. The concubine is taking her life in her hands to be with Tyrus, for it is a capital offense for a temple concubine to lie with any mortal man. All temple concubines are devoted to their own slave god, and there is only one slave god in Amega. With very little to do, and starved of the company of men, it was an easy matter for her to fall for the virile charms of the Bull Priest, whose eye she caught not long after he arrived in the citadel. One lazy afternoon, under the pretense of visiting Rah, whom he knew full well was off playing with his horses, Tyrus found her returning from the baths with a group of temple maidens. He quickly separated her from the group by sliding his fingers gently down her arm as she passed and taking her hand when she slowed to ask him what he thought he was doing. Holding her firmly by her wrist until the other magpies had rounded a corner and forgotten her, he then drew her close, and, finding her willing, kissed her. As she melted in his arms he whispered in her ear, "Maiden of the Moon, come lie with the Bull tonight."

They had been carrying on a secret dalliance ever since.

Now the concubine is gathering herself into decency as Tyrus leisurely pulls on a robe and pulls back the beaded screen to let Enenoch finish his tirade in the privacy of his bed chamber. But the Sky Priest, being of an entirely different nature than his friend, first enters and then, seeing the bouncing breasts of the concubine straining into a bustier, quickly turns to the wall in embarrassment. He remains there, in a haughty silence, while Tyrus gives his lover a goodbye kiss and then pats her now-decent rump as she scurries, giggling, through the beaded doorway.

"Your virgin eyes are safe, Sky. Come. Sit on the couch there, and tell me all that you have to tell." With that, Tyrus moves to his vanity to settle on a stool and brush out his leonine locks, occasionally glancing at Enenoch in the mirror as his story progresses.

When Enenoch is finished, Tyrus turns away from the mirror and sets his brush down on the vanity.

"Well. It is poison, plain and simple. A trick our Mochlos has used with success in the past and will no doubt continue to use until he is undone by it." With this he picks his brush back up, reaching to give his gleaming black mantle of hair one more stroke. The brush midway to his crown, he suddenly slams the bone handle down on the marble top of the vanity, causing Enenoch to jump at the cracking sound.

Tyrus' eyes are riveted to their own image in the mirror. They seem to have turned coal black, near as black as the eyes of the assassin.

After a moment of cold silence, he inquires softly, "Is he well today? On his feet, eating, playing with his horses?"

"He is on his feet. He eats. He has been at the stable all morning. But well? Is the Sun well when he is overshadowed by a thunder cloud? I cannot say that he is well. His light is dimmed."

"Then I will burn that cloud from the sky," responds Tyrus, still glaring at his own reflection in the mirror, though his lids are at half-mast as he calculates. And then, just as suddenly as his anger flared, it is extinguished, and replaced with a broad smile. He turns on his stool, takes his friend's arm and gives it a painful squeeze as he announces, "Sky, this is the opportunity we have been looking for."

"I hardly think that I would be inclined to take advantage of any opportunity that came to me as a result of the Rah's distress," responds Enenoch peevishly, pressing his lips together in annoyance and pulling his arm out of his friend's strong fingers with a jerk.

"We cannot always choose how an opportunity may come our way, my friend. The High Priest of the Moon is playing a dirty game of dice. Like it or not, we are in the game. I, for one, am perfectly capable of beating him at it."

"What do you suggest, Tyrus?" asks Enenoch, looking nervously to the beaded curtain and then back at his friend.

Rising to his feet, Tyrus takes an elaborately embroidered sash from the side of the mirror and begins to wind it about his priest's robe in the loops that will form the waistband of his garment.

"To begin, we must demand from the carpenter two equally grand altars, one for the Bull God, to be installed at the south end of the lyceum, one for the Sky, to be installed at the west end. And we will inform Crispo to do the same. North, south, east and west. Equal powers to each temple. Mochlos will learn of it almost immediately, of course, and be furious."

"He will make the boy ill again, Tyrus, we cannot risk it!"

"No. He will not. He will not dare. He will see his little trick has been discovered by one who made his fortune on a poison. Was it not I who fed the yew branch to the bull? I will inform the new Lieutenant General, that Nikolaos of Cyrus, whom the assassin trusts, that the boy's disease is a sign of imbalance in his spirit. That the Moon has been too strong an influence for too long. What happens to the crops if there is night and no day? What happens to the sea, if there is not but the full? The boy is an acrobat without equilibrium. It is no wonder he grows ill. He is in need of the stabilizing forces of the Bull, the Sun and the Sky. And of a Moon that can wax and wane. A feminine Moon. I will use Mochlos' arrogant attempt to gain sole control of Rah against him, and to our advantage. When I am done, we will have equal or greater importance, and Mochlos' house will be governed by a woman."

"A woman? It is an interesting idea, Tyrus, I must say. I have never understood why the House of a Goddess would be headed by a priest and not a priestess," muses Enenoch, stroking the point of his chin reflectively.

"Because Mochlos is a clever bastard. That is why, Sky. You are a charmingly wholesome cleric. I wonder you managed to avoid your own demise in this cutthroat business."

"I trust you have someone in mind?" whispers Enenoch then, looking to the curtain for eavesdroppers.

"I do. But the choice will not be mine. Thus my decision to inform the fine and newly married Lieutenant General of our dire circumstances."

"The girl, Cara! Yes! She *is* perfect, isn't she. Sweet and constant, yet bold and insistent in her own way, like the moon herself. You think to whisper these concerns in the Lieutenant's ear, and suggest his wife. A remarkable plan, Tyrus. But let us not leave our friend Crispo out of the picture. He is a good man, and a great improvement over Ananou. I am the first to admit, the Sky is nothing without the Sun."

Tyrus pats his nervous friend's shoulder and turns him to the beaded doorway.

"You are a superstitious man, Enenoch, but superstition is our bread and butter. I defer to your wisdom in religious matters. I myself believe only in determination."

"He is also a damned good cook," murmurs Enenoch as the two duck through the beaded doorway and head down to the kitchens, where the High Priest of the Sun will have prepared his two peers a traditional mid-morning Minoan repast.

While Tyrus and Enenoch enjoy their breakfasts, Rah wanders the citadel in search of Tiko. Unaware that his one-time rival is in the soldier's training gym this morning, and on the far western edge of the compound, he has roamed through the fortress, single mindedly determined to access his friend's superior mind for a solution to his new dilemma.

"China is know how to smart this priest," he grumbles over and over to himself as he barges into room after empty room, or startles house servants in the middle of their chores. It is not until he finds the Master's private gym, on the eastern flank of the fortress much as it was in his house in Knossos, that Rah's internal diatribe is interrupted. Then, before he has lifted his eyes to see what is coming at him, the Master's twins have tackled him to the ground like lion cubs.

"Rah! Why have you not come to see us until now!" shouts Philip, who is first to see the golden boy in the archway, and has taken him to the ground by driving his shoulders into his midsection. He quickly straddles his middle while his brother pins the dancer's arms over his head.

"Where have they been hiding you!" cries Quintus into his face, looking down into the boy's sea-green eyes from above.

"Naah!" says Rah, struggling vainly against the combined might of the assassin's twins. They have grown in the months since Rah last fought his way out from under the two of them in their home gym in Knossos, and he no longer has the strength to wrestle away from them.

"Where is the feather I tied to your collar, Rah? Did you lose it when they kidnapped you?" says Quintus, paying no attention to Rah's furious attempts to reach his forearms with his teeth.

"Oh who cares about a feather, Quintus!" snaps Philip at his brother with a sharp look. Then he returns his attention to his squirming prisoner.

"Did they torture you? We heard they bound you and buried you in a tomb. We heard papa found you and saved you and killed them all!" says Philip, who has learned to listen to the soldiers carefully at practice, for it is the only way he can discover and catalogue his father's exploits.

"Leave... me....go!" snarls Rah, panting with exertion and anger. "Must find Tiko!" He makes an attempt to nip Philip's chin but the boy is too quick and pulls away just in time. Rah's teeth snap the air. His eyes flash but begin to fill with tears.

"What is wrong with you, Rah?" says Quintus, squinting down at Rah with sudden concern. "Why are you so cranky with us? Do you no longer love us?"

"I will make him laugh!" announces Philip, and he begins to attack Rah's sides with his fingers. "I will tickle him until he says he loves us!"

"Naah...stop... please!" cries Rah, who is dreadfully susceptible to tickling and almost immediately feels the urge to vomit.

"Zhi!"

In an instant the two cubs have released Rah and are on their feet, arms dangling at their sides, heads bowed so low that their hair covers their faces.

"What are you doing in your father's gym? This is the house of a great warrior, not a nursery. You dishonor yourselves, and your teacher," says Tiko, who stands in the archway of the gym. He snaps his own head low with shame to underscore his sincerity.

The two boys lift their eyes to see their teacher's head bowed. Mortified, they look at each other and then drop their chins again in misery.

"Forgive us, Sensei. But we have not seen the Rah since the day our father gave him back to that stupid priest!" begins Philip.

"Who beat him and drowned him-" continues Quintus, gaining steam.

"And should be boiled in fish oil and plucked like a chicken!" finishes Philip.

"Spare me your excuses!" snaps Tiko, stepping toward them. As he does, they lower their heads again. Even so, they are considerably taller than their compact Asian tutor, who barely reaches their chins.

"And never again disgrace this gym by playing like infants in a sandbox. Now go down to the baths, make yourselves presentable. Your mother wishes to take her midday meal with her sons today."

Both boys bow together in unison at their teacher and turn to go.

"After your lunch," Tiko continues, causing them to halt abruptly in their tracks, "I will take you down to the chariot field to watch Rah."

"Yes!" Cry the twins in unison.

"We heard he can drive three horses together in full tack now!" exclaims Quintus.

"And that the chariot maker is nearly finished constructing a bucket big enough for three men, with the axle in the center!" says Philip.

"Is it ready? Will he try it out today?" the two shout together.

Tiko is looking to Rah for the answer. His mind elsewhere, Rah now comes to attention and responds.

"Maybe try today," he shrugs. "If ready. Horse is ready. Rah is ready."

Tiko gives him a puzzled look, his dark brows pleating with alarm at Rah's lack of spirit. He nods to the two sons of Antaris.

"Go now. Your mother is in need of your company today." And the boys bow once more in unison before taking off together down the hallway.

Alone with Rah, Tiko sighs, hands on hips. He shakes his head at his old rival, then approaches the dancer and lays his arm gently over his shoulders to draw him into an awkward embrace.

"Stupid priests," he murmurs. "They are all the same." He gives Rah's shoulder a soft squeeze. "And they will all meet the same death as Ananou, I promise you."

"No!" says Rah, stepping back and giving Tiko an imploring look. "Crispo no like this Priest. Tyrus no like this Priest." He drops his eyes. "But Mochlos. You know, China. He own you too."

"Mochlos is a dead man. I tell you, the Master will boil his balls in oil and pluck his eyes while he still lives, Blonde!"

"No, Tiko! If Priest die, maybe Rah die!" says Rah. "He say-"

"I know what he said. It is all over the fortress! Stupid priest," answers Tiko. "You do not believe this nonsense, Blonde. He drugged you, that is all. He drugged you to 'make' you, and he drugged you to scare you. You are the same as you were before the ceremony, Blonde. Same thick, stupid head." He raps Rah's skull with a knuckle. "I knew you then. I know you now. Same. You do not believe this nonsense."

Rah is looking at Tiko with a sad detachment in his eyes.

"You say Rah is no Rah? Still slave? Still boy? No god?"

"You are as much a god as you were when the merchant sold you to the priest, Blonde. You could dance. He made you a god to make himself richer. That is all."

But Rah cannot explain to Tiko what *has* changed since the Dying to the God ceremony. He cannot explain his flight with the doves, nor the booming voice that lifts him through the clouds and across the mountains and the sea to explore what has yet to come. And so he nods his head at his friend, compliant and submissive in the face of Tiko's superior intellect, while thinking in his heart that it is sad that Tiko has no wings.

Later that day, while Rah is making his maiden attempt to tack the Arabians to the first three man chariot in human history, Tyrus is entertaining the citadel carpenter and his assistant. He has made a special effort to befriend the man, and has made sure to have the finest Minoan wine on hand, one of the last of Mochlos' bottles which his lover has lifted from the Moon's temple cellar for him. Crispo has done his best to copy Ting Ya's walnut clusters, and has also provided a lovely spread of fine cheeses, exotic fruits and spiced crisp breads. The repast has been laid out on a simple table in the Bull Priest's sitting room, as if this type of thing were common at the House of the Bull. The carpenter and his assistant, unused to being treated to such sumptuous fair, are all but promising the Bull Priest silver and gold fittings for his altar. As the afternoon wears on and the wine is depleted, the three men become more and more jovial until the slightest quip is a side splitting comedy and brings tears to their eyes. Finally, Tyrus, finishing a hearty laugh, leans over the carpenter's glass and pours the last of the elixir into his cup.

"And the bull, sir," he says casually. "The bull to be affixed to the wall of the lyceum behind the altar, itself must be enormous, the horns made of gold, of course, the eyes, rubies. We must remember that here in the land of Hatti the Bull God is above all gods, for he is war. And I myself being born and raised for war here on this very soil, and honored beyond words to now represent the Bull God in Amega, where live and train the greatest warriors in Hatti, can have nothing less. We must remember that a soldier may kneel before the Moon, the Sky, the Sun, but he must bow before the Bull."

"But the altars, are they not in fact to be installed in order that each House may worship the Rah?" asks the carpenter, still chuckling over the last joke.

"But of course, sir. This is the Master's wish. Yet here in Amega, a city of soldiers, is not the Bull the most important House?"

And so it is that Tyrus is, in the end, able to obtain the most ornate of the four altars to be installed in the lyceum of the citadel, and in so doing, convince the people of Amega of his importance in the worship of the Rah and the prosperity and safety of the city.

It will take months for the altar to be completed, for the bull must be cast in bronze and the horns then plated in gold by the fortresses metal workers, the rubies must be obtained from Egypt and then cut and polished by the jewelers, and the altar itself built from cedar imported from Canaan by the carpenter. But it is only a day later that Mochlos discovers the plans for the thing, and for the altars of the houses of the Sky and Sun.

It is on the sixth day of the week, the Sabbath of the Moon, that Mochlos learns of the altar. He does so when, entering the lyceum with a staff of junior priests to conduct a simple mass to the Moon Goddess, he sees that the carpenter's assistant is measuring the wrong wall.

"Sir, I have instructed your master that the altar of the Moon is to be placed against the north wall, not the south," says Mochlos evenly as he approaches the man, having waved his priests to a halt.

"Yes, Holiness, that is understood. But I am measuring for the altar of the House of the Bull," answers the assistant, frowning at the wall as he does so, for a clearstory at the top of the center of the thing threatens to interfere with the placement of the enormous bronze.

"The-? That Hittite bastard!" Mochlos snarls before realizing where he is and regretting the very breath he took to spout the curse. "Who has given authority for more than one altar in the Great Hall of the Master of Amega?" he continues quickly, hoping his reckless words have gone unnoticed.

But the carpenter's assistant has turned to level a killing gaze at the Minoan priest. A burly youth, his fists now clench at his sides at the insult.

"Words such as these will put a man in his grave in Hatti," is his only response.

"My apologies, sir. It is a damned common expression on Crete, one I have never used until this very day," says the priest, chagrined at his own carelessness, "And one I now deeply regret ever hearing myself, else I would have never picked it up for my own use."

"You are very lucky at your age to have teeth, old man, and good ones," answers the carpenter, spoiling to flatten the priest with one blow. "But I wouldn't mind making myself a new set of dice with them, as mine are worn."

"I tell you it is a damned common expression on Crete and one I have not until now used, nor will I ever again!" cries Mochlos, edging away from the carpenter's assistant and toward his priests, who now mill about waiting for him under the clerestory windows above the north wall of the lyceum.

I must keep my head, thinks Mochlos. I live in dangerous times. If I am not careful I will be but a toy for these Hatti wolves to play with. There is not a sane man among them. Blood thirsty devils, all. Dear Goddess, how is a man of my delicate nature to survive in such a place?

But to the carpenter he offers no further words, but puts his hands together under his chin in an attitude of humility as he backs away. Then, seeing the man scoff and turn back to his dilemma with the south wall, he moves off toward an altar made of a few bricks and a plank, and covered with an embroidered linen, which his priests have set up against the north. There he will spout a few morning prayers to the Moon and when he is finished, go to find his dance master, Dimius, for it clear to him at once that he was mistaken to believe that the power of a high priest lay in an altar. No, it is and has always been his power over the slave god Rah, which has made his fortune. So long as he has the little monkey on a leash, so long as they are inextricably linked, he may as well hold the Master's balls in his hands.

Out on the practice field Rah is harnessing Halix and the two mares to the new, three man chariot. The thing has not been painted or decorated with the emblem of the Army of Amega, a raised shield with an eclipsed moon flanked by two crescent shaped blades. It is a rough wood structure, but has an axel at the center under the driver's feet, and a broad enough platform for three men to stand across and move with freedom.

Rah has conditioned each of the animals separately to drive a cart and has ridden them together in his normal fashion, standing on the back of the center horse which is always Halix. But he has never put the three in tack together in front of as large a cart as the bucket of this new chariot.

He takes his time with the tack, harnessing Halix first, then his mother on his left, and his sister finally on his right. With Ghedi keeping the animals calm he attaches the cart to the horses last. After a few circles about the field with Ghedi leading the trio, Rah dismisses him, and attempts to drive the horses from the bucket.

All is well at first, and Rah is able to push the team up to a controlled trot and then a canter before the bounce of the right wheel over a stone spooks the younger mare and causes the team to panic. With only a bit-less bridle on Halix and no direct control of the two mares, Rah cannot stop them, and it takes several brave horsemen to intercept the animals and keep them from running full tilt toward the stable and into the barn with the chariot still attached. Even so, the team attempts to jump a pile of hay before they are brought to a halt, effectively shattering the wheels of the vehicle and leaving Rah and the bucket resting at the top of the stack.

"This will not work, Rah!" cries Hagga, running up to the wreck. "The filly is too hot and too green. The bucket is brilliant and will carry three men, but a team of two sturdy Hittite animals can pull it. These animals are fancy, high strung nitwits and are for show only. Dance with them if you like, but leave my warriors their war horses!"

Helping the boy out of the debris that was moments ago the prototype of the greatest war vehicle earth would witness until modern times, the stable master checks him for injuries. But Rah is unfazed by the crash. He shakes hay out of his hair like a wet cur shaking droplets from his coat and laughs.

"Hagga is right. She is too green, but-" and he takes Hagga's shoulder and draws him close, "Wolf is like, no? We change. Keep single pole, for two horse. War horse. Three men. One is drive. One is-" and he has dropped to one knee and fired an invisible arrow from a quiver on his back. "And one," he says rising, hefting an invisible javelin to his shoulder. "What you think? Wolf is be very happy with Hagga, then, no? Maybe give him-" and he is swaying his hips and fluffing his hair in a ridiculous pantomime of a concubine.

But Hagga has taken him roughly by the arm in the middle of his frolic. You are too pretty a boy to be playing thus before a stable full of horsemen, he thinks to himself. He gives Rah a shake and a scowl, but Rah only collapses against him, giggling.

"You give Rah-" and he struggles against his own mirth for the word in Greek, "Race chariot, heh? For my horse. For Halix. We fix for three across! We be fast chariot in all this Hatti!"

Hannahannas help me, thinks Hagga, putting his arm around Rah and pulling him away from the wrecked chariot while Ghedi and several charioteers work to keep the Arabs calm and free them from it. I will go insane trying to keep you in one piece. If the Master returns and you have but scraped a knee, it will be *my* head that suffers for it.

But Rah is looking up at the stable master in the brilliant Anatolian sun, looking up at him with eyes that put the noonday sea to shame, and Hagga can only sigh and nod his head.

"Very well, Rah, you may race them if you like. But you must train those beasts of yours to mind you better on the long line before you hitch them to another chariot, you understand me? You let me be the judge when they are ready for it."

"Yes!" agrees Rah. "Hagga is right! Too soon for this mare. Rah do this. But-" he gives the stable master a wink, and tips his head at the chariot barn, "Rah is take purple race chariot!" Sunlight twinkles blue-green in his eyes. He winks again and jabs Hagga with an elbow.

"That is Agrippa's chariot, Rah! You want to make an enemy of the Captain of the First Division? I cannot give you the purple racer. Take it from him yourself!" With this Hagga pulls himself away from Rah and stomps off, throwing up his hands and cursing as he does so.

"The boy will drive me mad!" he grumbles, stomping past Ghedi, who has managed to unhitch the team from the debris and begun to lead them back toward the stable. "He wants Agrippa's racer, Hannahannas help me!"

"Who is this Grippa?" Rah asks the crowd of soldiers who have gathered about his wreck, his brows bunched petulantly. "Must talk this Grippa."

But the soldiers only look to one another with wary eyes and move off.

"Who is this Grippa?" Rah asks Tiko, who has pushed through the departing men with Phillip and Quintus at his heels. "Where this Grippa? Must talk him." Rah plants his fists against his hips and frowns, looking about as if he might find the man standing with a sign saying 'I am Grippa.'

"You cannot have the purple racer, Blonde. It is the property of the Captain of the First Division. Very expensive. Very fine. A man owns his own chariot here in Amega. It cost him a fortune and he will not give it to you to crash into a pile of hay," says Tiko, taking Rah by the arm and drawing him away from the stable. "Enough of your silly showing off for today. You must concentrate on the *three* man. Forget those ridiculous fine-legged ladies of yours. They are no war horses. Hagga will give you any team in the stable to test the three man. We are not here to race. We are here to wage war! Forget the Arabs! Two Hittite ponies will pull the three man and not know the difference. The center axel is brilliant! Now there is room for an archer on the left, a swordsman and shield bearer on the right. The enemy will flee in dread before the cavalry of Amega!" Tiko is fairly shouting with enthusiasm as he leads Rah across the practice field with Philip and Quintus following close behind. But as Tiko draws his friend toward the citadel, Rah continues to turn out of his grip to scan the stable yard for the man who owns the purple racer.

"Where this man is? This Grippa? Why he is not here watch Rah?"

"Agrippa is the First Chariot Division Captain, Rah," laughs Philip, who walks behind Rah, deliberately blocking his view of the stable yard. "He has no time to watch a boy play with fancy show ponies!"

"I heard him tell his men that a three man chariot is as useful as a cow with antlers!" adds Quintus more seriously. "You had better stay out of his way, Rah. He will smash you like a grape."

"He will swat you like a fly," says Philip.

"He is a very serious man," puts in Tiko with a somber tone.

"Who race this purple chariot? Grippa drive?" asks Rah, frowning.

"His son, Keret races it. He is eighteen summers. Agrippa is too big a man to race a chariot. Keret is tall and lean enough. A skilled driver. The best in Amega," answers Philip.

"Oh, forget about the racer! Enough of this talk. This is a child's game, racing," says Tiko, losing his patience with the subject. "We will show the Master the usefulness of the three man, Blonde, you and I, and then he will see we are men of war, and he will take us with him to fight the Amorites!"

But Rah has turned back around to hop on his toes in an attempt to see over the twins' shoulders.

"Rah is no here for war. Three man for Wolf-" he thumps his breast with a fist, "gift from Rah. But," he takes another little hop to peek over Quintus' shoulder, "Rah is compete. Is dancer. Rah is race! When little boy-" he levels his palm at his waist.

"You are still a little boy, Rah," laughs Philip, putting one palm on Rah's head and holding him down so that he cannot hop.

Rah bats his hand away. He gives Philip his fiercest scowl.

"That only makes you prettier, Rah," muses Quintus. He gives his brother's arm a punch. "Stop teasing him, Philip."

"Rah beat any man in Illyria! Little boy," continues Rah angrily and glaring at Philip. "No chariot. Five horse-"

Suddenly he throws himself into the narrow space between Philip and Quintus, manages to plow through them and shouts, "Where this Grippa is!" across the field before they can subdue him. "Rah is race Grippa. Any chariot! Beat any man here!"

There is an eerie silence over the barns.

Then the three boys pull him toward the west entry to the fortress, and to supper.

"I hear he wanted your racer. And told he could not have it, he laid down a challenge. He has the Master's favor. You had better watch your step," says the Captain of the Second Division to the Captain of the First in the horsemen's mess that evening. Finishing his stew with a few slurps he pushes himself back from the table and settles his hands on either side of his bowl. Then he calls over his shoulder to the nearest servant, "More mead here!" and belches loudly.

Despite his table manners, Aleksandus is not an inelegant man. He is tall and straight, with piercing brown eyes under thick grey brows whose bony prominence gives him the fierce and intelligent look of a bird of prey. He is in fact Agrippa's cousin, and the two share the look of eagles. Excepting a marginal difference in height, and the fact that Agrippa is the thicker of the two, they are near identical and often taken for twins.

"Am I to accept a challenge from a girl then? Does the hawk take the challenge of a dove? It is a spoilt boy's brag. A soldier does not acknowledge such nonsense."

"Yet how can Agrippa, Captain of the First Division, refuse? Your men will think you a coward, backing down from a boy. What man refuses a test of his prowess? Only he who expects to lose," responds Aleksandus, putting his cup up in the air for the servant to fill.

"My son will kill the little fool," says Agrippa, pushing his own empty bowl aside and raising his cup for the servant to fill as well. "He will run him off the field and wreck him. Then my son's head will watch the sun go down atop a stake while his body feeds the Master's wolf pit."

"Your son can run a fair race," responds Aleksandus.

"There is nothing unfair about a wreck," answers Agrippa.

"No, not in war, but this is a clean challenge. Speed for speed."

"I cannot take the war out of Keret, Aleksandus," says Agrippa, putting down his empty cup with some force.

"All the same," says Aleksandus, "You cannot back down from a boy, least of all this one. He may be a coddled slave god, but we have all seen him drive that team of sparrows from the back of the colt. I would not have believed it possible had I not seen it with my own eyes."

"Ah, Taru, Lord of the land of Hatti," sighs Agrippa, miserably. "What is Antaris thinking that he brings such a creature into our midst? And then leaves him here for us to nurse him, whilst he goes off to do a man's job. He is testing us. It can only be a test. He is testing our hearts and our loyalty. If we pass his test, the reward will be battle. A plunge into Syria! Well, I for one will not disappoint him. If I have to grow teats, I will not. Very well then. A race. Between a pretty slave god who is best at bathing and smelling sweeter than a concubine's rough, and my son. I bow to thee, Antaris, for I love my master. And I am also fond of my head."

With that, Agrippa shoves himself from the table and picks up his weapons belt, which he has laid on the bench at his side. He straps it with resolute gusto about his hips, takes one last long draught of mead, draining his cup, then offers his company a broad belch. As he turns to saunter from the mess hall, several diligent young charioteers from his company jump from their seats to follow his lead.

Aleksandus rises as well but stands a moment, letting the jostling group of youths exit the hall before he adds to the disorganized din with his own. Agrippa my cousin, he thinks to himself as he binds his weapons belt to his loins, I fear you are mistaken this time. The Master has no motive in this beyond his own greed. He took that boy for himself like a man who finds a pearl in a field takes that pearl and tucks it in his pocket, though he has not stolen it, then defends it to the death, though it is not his. But what does a man do with a stolen pearl? Shaking his head and chuckling, he begins toward the doorway.

Our Master is in love with a Minoan slave god. He hears the words in his head before he can stop them, and instantly looks about aggressively to be sure no one else has discovered his thought. I had best be careful where I voice that notion, he reminds himself, else it become my last.

CHAPTER 8

Rush reaches the plateau of Amega on day twenty-six of his journey. He has eaten only once in three days, having killed a young deer whose misfortune it was to be taking at drink at the same river as a hungry wolf that morning. After a meal and a bath in the river, Rush continues south to the fortress, keeping off the roads and out of sight of any travelers. On the evening of the twenty-sixth day, famished but unwilling to take the time to hunt, he stops at a stream for a drink and another bath. He washes his tunic and leggings in the water and when they are dried, pulls them back on. It is not vanity, but the fact that he chooses to breech his own walls that evening, to sneak into his own fortress and, in all the world, his own well-trained warriors are his only match, and the rank smell of a man who has been two weeks in the field will alert a good guard.

It is after dark when Rush approaches the fortress walls, having slipped unseen through the fields of sheep and goat that feed his men, and then the stable yard itself and the chariot horse barn. He must be wary not only of his guards, but of the animals themselves, for a barn full of snorting, dancing horses is as clear an alert as a war horn to a Hittite horseman. He is a wolf in his own hen house, and he moves in shadow and silence through the stable and across the practice field. He skirts the citadel, circling the rise of the service entry where wagons bring supplies from the city and beyond. He takes a moment to watch his own men moving to and fro before the enormous door, which will lie down across a deep ditch during daylight hours but is pulled up and bolted now. They are well armed and vigilant, and his face is grim under his assassin's hood as he observes their routine, which they do not falter from although they are but foot soldiers without a commander present. They can be trusted to remain vigilant for good reason. Returning home from an assassination in Mittani last year, Rush found a guard resting at his post. He was on his feet and awake, but was not patrolling as he was ordered. Five other guards moved about him, alert and ready to defend the citadel. In the morning, before the cock crowed, the change of guard found all six lined up like geese on a poulterer's table, in the gully under the door. They were trussed and beheaded. The heads were not found for two days, at which time the weapons master, who detected a foul smell coming from the mace cabinet in the sword room, discovered them within. No one questioned their fate, for each head had been divested of its Tear of the Bull tattoo.

Now Rush continues around the service door to the west side of the fortress. He will not scale these walls, for that is impossible, even for him. He will continue past his destination, which is not his own bed but the bed of the Rah in the Hall of the Moon. He will climb down the cliff side, sure footed as any goat, until he finds the entrance to a cave known only to him. The cave will take him under the fortress to a maze of storage rooms most men would be lost in for days. But he will not be lost. He will find his way to a tunnel, barely large enough for him to press himself through, and into the back of the wine cellar. There his thirst, and his mood, will tempt him to spend one last hour in his own company before he wanders up into the west wing.

But it is two hours later that Rush the Assassin is finally standing in the doorway of the Rah's bed chamber. He is pleasantly drunk but his mood has not lifted. He is maudlin and still wrestling with the Prince's choice, and, too, with the thing that has *him* in its grips.

It is silent in the chamber but for Rah's kittenish snore, and the occasional snort of his attendants in their sleep. Rush has brought with him a lamp from the kitchen, as well as an amphora of Minoan wine which he has lifted from his own cellar. He stands in the doorway, a thief in his own house, a man with a stolen pearl, and he watches the lamplight stroke Rah's honey blonde curls. The boy is stretched out on his stomach. His face is pressed against the mattress, his mouth open, his tongue resting between his teeth. He is snoring lightly. There is sufficient lamplight to illuminate his high, tawny cheekbones and his silvery-golden lashes.

"You sleep like the dead, little cat," murmurs Rush, crossing the room finally to settle himself so quietly at the end of Rah's bed that neither attendant nor the boy wake from their slumber. Lifting the jug of wine to his lips he takes a long draught, then places it carefully on the floor. "Would you cry out in fear now, if your wolf woke you?" he whispers in Greek. "Or would your heart leap with delight that your master is home?"

Rush lifts a hand to reach for Rah's curls, then thinks better of it and instead leans gently toward him. Supporting himself with one hand he hovers, his breath at the boy's ear. He sniffs his hair, which is perfumed with holy oils. Hyssop, myrrh and lotus. No cherry blossom? The others are sacred, but the cherry, in his mind, that scent is indelibly married to the boy's innocence. He must be sure to see to it that Tuma has all the supplies he needs to keep his little Grain God perfumed as he is accustomed. Still he breathes deep, taking in the virginal scents of lotus and myrrh. Without thinking, he finds himself nuzzling the back of Rah's curls, careful not to touch the boy's nape and rouse him.

"Have you even noticed I was gone, little cat?"

Rush sighs, leans back to rest against the wall, recalls that he still wears his hood and pulls it off to drop to the floor near the wine jug.

"My wife's longing is like a finger ever poking at my heart, no matter the distance between us. My sons wait in my absence like puppies wait at the door for their master's return. But you," turning back to the still sleeping Rah, he tugs the lambskin coverlet, deliberately exposing the boy's shoulders to the chill night air. "No. Your bruised little brain can love a cur, but not its own Master."

Rah's fingers have begun to search for his retreating coverlet in his sleep. They stretch along his side nearly to his toes, and find the assassin's thigh instead. Rush watches, grimly amused, but makes no move to assist him. Instead, he tugs at the coverlet again. Rah whimpers and squirms as the lambskin descends to the dip above his buttocks. Chuckling, Rush continues his tease by lightly skating the back of his hand along the hollow there. Finally, Rah's brows furrow with petulance in his sleep. With a peevish "guff", he comes awake.

"Wolf," he murmurs through a sleep-thickened tongue, seeing his master lounging at the end of his bed. Squinting in the lamplight irritably he draws himself into a half lotus at the opposing end.

He peers at Rush a moment, holding a hand up to fight the glare of the lamp.

"Wolf back," he declares. He squints at Rush as if waiting for an explanation.

Rush looks at him with sad, drunken eyes.

"Wolf back," he agrees, reaching for the wine jug and stretching out his legs.

"Wolf is kill a king," says Rah then, as if he hears the words from another. "Kill a king for a queen," he adds, tilting his head at Rush as if awaiting the details.

Rush darts a sly eye at him, then takes the last long swig from the amphora. "Have the dead of Minoa taken up residence in that wounded brain of yours, Rah, to tell you my business?"

But Rah makes no answer. It is not until the assassin leans forward again that the boy makes an effort to keep his distance, pulling himself back and watching with some mistrust as Rush digs two fingers into a pocket of his tunic.

"I have brought my little cat a gift," says Rush opening his hand under Rah's nose. In it is a polished emerald the size of a man's thumb. Rah blinks at the stone, then up at his master.

In the lamp light the emerald appears shot with gold.

"Ah, it is as I thought," says Rush softly. Then he takes the stone from his palm and presses it against Rah's forehead, causing the boy to flinch first, then giggle. "In the dark, it is the exact color of your eyes," he murmurs, miserable.

Mirth wrinkles the tilted tips of Rah's blue-green eyes, which compete with the fantastic emerald, putting the weight of a thousand stones on the assassin's heart such that he can barely breathe through the pain. He makes a little groan.

Suddenly Rah snatches his hand and begins prying his fingers open to get at the emerald. Rush watches him struggle to pull the gem from his fist, deliberately making it difficult and chuckling a bit himself at Rah's intense focus on the stone. Finally he releases his fingers, allowing the boy to take it. Rah gives him a mischievous look, then presses the stone between his eyes, making a circle of his thumb and forefinger and holding it from above.

"Now Rah have three eye." He giggles his dark giggle, cocking his head at the assassin playfully.

Rush groans again. The boy's face is even more dizzyingly beautiful with the emerald set between his brows.

"You make Rah, eh-" Rah drops the gem to circle his head with the fingers of both hands.

"A crown?" Rush shakes his head with disbelief. "You would be a king in my kingdom, Rah? And then what would I wear? If you are king?"

"Still this," says Rah, grabbing at the assassin's tunic sleeve. "This what wolf wear." His face turns serious. He looks down for the emerald, which has slipped between his legs. He lifts his seat off the bed with an acrobat's grace and searches the bed clothes beneath his bottom. Finding it, he hands it casually back to Rush. The game is finished.

"Three horse and three man, no good, Wolf. Hagga say no. No Arabian. Like girls. Scare in battle. He say, Rah must use Hatti horse. Battle horse. Need only two." Rush peers at Rah in a moment of confusion, then allows himself a small chuckle.

"I see," he murmurs, watching Rah's face attentively. We have jumped to the subject of the three horse chariot. The gift of Rah.

"But the bucket is good? The axel, in the center, can carry three men?"

"We try tomorrow. Hatti horse. Rah drive. China find two men, one-" and he is pulling an arrow across an invisible bow.

"Archer," offers Rush.

"Archer, yes," responds Rah enthusiastically. "Other this!" And he is holding a heavy shield before him, his arms trembling with the weight of the thing. He offers it to Rush, and releases it gratefully when the assassin, smiling, takes the invisible burden from him and sets it on the bed beside them.

"Shield bearer," says Rush, whispering to Rah conspiratorially. You have tried to lift one yourself, then, he chuckles to himself. "You are not yourself the weight of a proper Hatti shield," he says aloud.

"Is heavy," agrees Rah gravely. And suddenly, the boy's demeanor changes again. His eyes flash up at Rush.

"Rah is race Grippa, Wolf. Rah is need race chariot. No three man. Need fast! Light!" he lifts a hand to flutter like a butterfly before the assassin's eyes.

"Agrippa!"

Rush shakes his head. "You have challenged Agrippa, Rah?"

"Yes! Rah challenge! Rah can beat any man, any horse! No one as fast!"

"And he agreed to it?" is all that Rush can think to say.

"Rah challenge!" says Rah, slapping his chest with an open palm. "Grippa must race!"

A stumble in the chamber adjoining Rah's lifts the assassin's attention from the boy's face.

"Hog shit!" comes the bellow of the High Priest, who, having no night vision at all, has struck his toes against a table leg. His exclamation wakes the two attendants, who jump in their beds. Seeing the Master of Amega reclining on Rah's pallet, Aros lets out a shriek, while Pyrus slaps his back against the wall as if to press himself through it.

In another instant, Mochlos himself is standing in the doorway, hopping on one foot.

"What in hell is- Hoh!" Seeing the assassin in the lamplight, he lurches backward still holding one toe, stumbles over the hem of his own nightdress and falls back on his rump.

Rah bursts out laughing, his delicious giggle trilling up and up like a kit's howl. In the same instant, the faces of Pyrus and Aros go white. Gathering himself off the tile, Mochlos makes a priestly attempt to regain his dignity. He adjusts his nightdress, smooths his bald pate, and clears his throat.

Rush has remained completely still except for the flicker of his eyes from the faces of the two attendants, to Rah, to the expression of sheer fury with which the High Priest greets the boy's laughter. It is a flash only, an indiscretion that is quickly covered with a humble bow to the assassin.

But it is too late. Rah's laughter has died in his throat, his face drained of color.

Rush flicks his eyes from Rah to the priest to the attendants. His breath is shallow. The muscles along his jaw line bunch and release. When the priest looks up, the dark thing in the man's eyes leaps at him, nearly knocking him down a second time.

"Majesty! Mah-! Lord! Master!" stutters Mochlos, bowing again, this time putting his forehead to the floor. "I- I awoke to your lamplight flooding the hall! I thought there was an intruder! I – I came to protect the Rah!"

Rush is peering at the priest with tired hatred, his lids at half-mast. Aros flashes Pyrus a wide-eyed grimace, his breast heaving. Pyrus returns it with a barely perceptible shake of his head, "No."

Rush has missed none of it. He turns his head to Rah, who has dropped his chin submissively and has begun to tremble, though the priest is still on his knees.

Why do you fear him, little cat, though I recline on your bed? thinks Rush, allowing his eyes to skate down Rah's torso to enjoy that tremble. At the same time, a sour suspicion congeals in his heart. He looks back at the priest.

"Get up, fool," he says, "And return to your bed, so that I might reward you for your bravery."

Pyrus flashes another startled look at Aros, swallowing hard.

"Master, I-" begins Mochlos from the floor.

"How many tongues must I take," responds Rush as he turns again to Rah and places a solid palm on his shoulder as if asking the boy the question. Rah looks up into his eyes at the touch. "Can men never learn to silence themselves before I do?" says Rush to Rah, shaking his head.

That is enough to send Mochlos, still on his knees, into a backward crawl out of the doorway and down the hall to his own chamber.

When he is gone, Rush looks to Pyrus and Aros, his hand still resting on Rah's shoulder.

"You must be very afraid for *him* to keep a secret from *me*, dresser," he says, addressing Aros first. "Come here, and sit between us now, if you think my little cat is safer with you than with me."

Aros looks as if he will faint in his bed. Still, he makes a valiant attempt to rise before he falls back on his mattress, trembling.

Pyrus is looking from Aros to Rah as if struggling to make a decision.

"And you, face painter. I had no idea you were so brave. Perhaps you would do well in battle. Perhaps I will take you to the front with me, nail a grip on your back and use you as a shield."

"Sir," manages Pyrus, wincing, but he can press no further words from his lips.

Now Rush returns his attention to Rah.

"Do you not trust your Master, little cat?" he whispers gently to the boy.

Rah looks into his face hopefully, but says nothing.

"You are afraid of the priest, Rah. Tell your master why," says Rush with eerie patience.

"He say," begins Rah. Then he shoots a quick look to the doorway and lowers his voice, leaning toward Rush. "He say-" but his words are caught in his throat. The next word is a grunt. He looks up at Rush pitiably.

Rush tips the boy's chin up, brushing his mouth with the flat of his thumb as if to coax the words from it.

"I will not leave your bed until you speak, Rah, though I am bone weary and long for my own. I will sit with you here until the cock crows. Then I will carry you about the citadel all day until you tell me what has happened between you and the priest in my absence."

Rah swallows, tries again. "Priest, he say, Wolf is no believe Rah," he says.

"Not believe you?" Rush's ears pull back. Now he shoots a ferocious look at the two attendants. This time it is the look of battle, a promise of death.

It is enough to break Aros, who gives his friend a guilty glance and blurts out, "Mochlos can make him sick, Sir. We have seen it. The boy challenged him, and the priest touched him, and sent him into a fit!"

Black ice burns in the assassin's eyes as he turns back to Rah. "Now *you* will tell me," he says, his patience gone. He takes the boy's chin in his hand and presses his fingers into his cheeks, giving his head a little shake.

Rah squeezes his eyes closed to push the words past his thickened tongue. "Priest, he say, 'I make god come to live in this boy. I can make god go. Then boy die. No god. No boy.' Then Rah have fit." He opens his eyes, his face inches from the assassins, and takes a breath.

Rush releases his chin. "A dead priest can hurt no one," he says, making to rise from Rah's bed.

"No!" yelps Rah, slipping off the bed to kneel at the assassin's feet. "Hurt priest, hurt Rah!"

"That remains to be seen," mutters Rush, getting to his feet. But Rah is clutching his ankles, making it impossible for him to take a step without tripping, or else kicking the terrified boy.

"He believes it, Sir," says Pyrus, rising to take Rah by the shoulders and pull him off the floor. "He is certain that what happens to the priest will happen to him also. Thus if you imprison Mochlos-"

"Or punish him in any way-" adds Aros, rising to help Pyrus pull Rah to his feet.

"He will suffer the same," finishes Pyrus.

Rush makes a weary sigh.

"Put him to bed," he says to the two attendants, though Rah is still squirming in their hands. He searches the floor for his hood, slips it under his belt, and picks up the amphora.

"No hurt priest!" begs Rah, wriggling in his attendants' grasp.

"Let him go," says Rush, and Rah instantly throws himself at the assassin's ankles.

This time Rush takes him by one arm, sets him on his feet and holds him there.

"All right, Rah. We will do it your way. We will make the priest comfortable and happy, eh? Perhaps he could use an assistant, so much work for him to do, so much prayer and ceremony." He strokes the boy's curls absently. "Nor is he rich enough. He is a man of expensive tastes. It stands to reason, he is in need of more wealth. Perhaps he would like your emerald for himself. It is quite valuable."

"Yes!" says Rah, looking up into the assassin's face optimistically. "Give priest this stone! Then he forgive Rah! No punish for laugh."

Pyrus and Aros are looking at one another, puzzled.

"I shall go and give it to him now," says Rush. "If you promise me you will go back to bed and sleep like a dead little cat. Agreed?"

"Agree!" says Rah, breathing with relief and obediently climbing back onto his bed and pulling at his coverlet.

"Like a dead little cat," says Rush, leaning over to tousle Rah's hair with affectionate patience.

But when he spins about to head for Mochlos' bed, Aros and Pyrus shrink back, for they are privy in that instant to the blackening fury in his eyes.

Mochlos has been lying in his bed and fighting an urge to eliminate his bowels there for a quarter of an hour when he senses the presence of the assassin in his room.

Despite his straining to hear the man come in, it is not sound or light that informs him of his presence, but a heavy dread, heavier even than the one that has been melting his guts. When suddenly he becomes aware, as if by some internal alarm unattached to his physical senses, that he is not alone in his room, he makes a sharp intake of breath and exclaims, "Uhh!"

"You are learning, priest," growls Rush from the corner of the room opposite the door. How long has he been there, waiting to pounce? thinks Mochlos, throwing himself off his bed and against the far wall. He could have slit my throat already, and here I lie, holding my shit to save the bed linens. Very well then, I am a dead man. I must attempt at least to die with dignity. I will hold my tongue as well as my shit for there is no reasoning with this beast. He will only cut it out for me and put it gods know where if I do not.

"Ahg," sighs Rush then, coming forward. And it is only by the approach of that deep sigh in the dark that Mochlos can discern his approach. The man makes no sound, no matter his size, his weight, his presence. And he has put out the lantern he had with him in the boy's chamber. Still, Mochlos does not speak. No. I will not attempt to reason with you. You will only hold my words against me. That is your way. Make a man eat his words, and his tongue, too, if he is not careful. Well I am not going to make matters worse. Lips and rectum tight, he waits.

Silence. How long? What is he doing? Has he left the room?

"The boy fears his maker." It is the assassin's baritone whisper in his left ear.

With a cry of shock, Mochlos attempts to drop to the floor, but he is caught in the man's impossible grip and held against the wall. How did the brute get around the bed so quickly and so quietly? How could I not have known he was coming for me in the stillness? Why do we trust our ears to believe in stillness when a thing like this is amongst us?

"And his maker lusts for his fear," continues Rush, so close that his lips brush the priests cheek.

The priest says nothing, only swallows the bile rising in his throat and threatening to gag him.

"Had I known how to make such a thing," sighs Rush heavily, and the priest can feel the man's sadness curl and tighten about him like an anaconda. Monster. How can you feel sadness? You own the world and everyone you meet. You make meals of us all, thinks Mochlos, trembling weakly.

"Had I known how to make such a thing," persists Rush, "I might have thought myself a god. For who but a god could create such a beauty? Such an unbearable beauty."

The man's emotion is coming off him like a drug. It is as if the energy of his wounded heart is throbbing against the priest's ribs as it does his own. Goddess, I can feel it. I can feel it like heat, like pulsing heat. And for a moment, for just a small instant, Mochlos knows something akin to sympathy for the fiend that holds him in his grip. And even more strangely, he responds with a truth he did not know he could utter.

"I did not make him, Sir," says the priest. "I merely used what I saw in him for my own purpose, much like a man breeds this bull to that cow, and then takes credit for the calf."

"Even so," answers Rush, moving back a bit as if to allow the priest's unlikely honesty space to grow, "Even so, it is you who married the boy to the god, real or imagined it matters not. For now, thinking himself a god, his innocence, his lack of conceit is even more breathtaking. So much so that the dark thing that lives in my soul, at times must bow its head in shame."

"You have no reason for shame," responds Mochlos. What has happened to his tongue? Has he lost control of it all together, now, in his final moments? Perhaps it is true then, that in the presence of one's death one can speak nothing but truth.

"I meant to kill him, and finding myself unable to do so, to take him by force," says Rush, still gripping the priest against the wall but now clearly speaking with head bowed as if in confession to him. "To defile that innocence. To change him. But his illness saved him from me."

"I know not of what you speak," responds the priest, though he is beginning to put the thing together in his mind.

"Now, in my absence, his own maker has threatened to undo the brilliance of his creation. And so the boy is fearful. Afraid that his priest will unmake him. And perhaps it is so. Perhaps the priest can unmake him. Perhaps in his belief, he can unmake himself. I have seen it on the battlefield. A man's belief can save him against impossible odds, impossible wounds. Or kill him with a scratch."

"Lord... Master!" blubbers Mochlos suddenly, still pondering the man's confession, within which he has sensed a weakness he may take advantage of. Yes! He understands now! He has been going about this thing all wrong! The monster wants the boy's heart! Very well. I will be the one to cut it out and give it to him!

Strengthened, the priest whispers in the dark, "I can make him anything you like, Master, anything at all. I can make him docile as a puppy to your...affections." And in the moment of silence that follows, he can feel the man's eyes upon him, though the room is pitch. Yes, there it is. Think on that now, you fiend. Think of the boy coming to you willingly. There is a drug for everything.

But what happens next is utterly unexpected. Sharp nails dig into his cheeks and force his mouth open. Something cold and glass-like is deposited on his tongue, an icy egg. The thing is shoved back toward his throat. It clicks against his molars and the sound somehow informs his brain that this is no egg, this is harder than teeth, and faceted. This is a stone, a gem of some sort. And it is enormous.

"Here is a better plan," responds the assassin. "You will make the boy whole, or you will die."

The egg of glass has been expertly lodged at the top of the priest's throat, blocking his airway. It is held there by a single finger. If he will but release me, I can expel it, is all that the priest can think in this moment.

"Tell me yes or no, priest. Can you do such a thing? Can you assure me, and yourself, that he will never suffer another attack? For if he does, there is no point my feeding a priest and his household, is there? Except to my wolf pit."

Mochlos is nodding "yes" with hysterical enthusiasm. It is the only motion available to him. There is no getting out of the grip of the viper that has him.

"How slowly you learn, and yet you learn, priest," hisses Rush against his ear. And suddenly, he is thrust forward in the air by the front of his nightdress. Tossed like a pillow across the room and onto his own bed. He struggles to take a breath, but discovers with horror that the gem is yet lodged in his throat. Mad with the need for air, he beats at his own breast in vain to force it out.

From behind him comes renewed terror as the anaconda takes him again. Arms of animated iron circle his ribs and squeeze with a short, powerful thrust the last of the air in his lungs through his trachea, forcing the gem to pop from his throat and bounce onto the bed clothes innocently. He gasps for air with heady desire. An unlikely image flickers in his mind. It is the twinkling of the drowning pool just as the assassin pulled him from it for the last time. It is my drowning pool, all over again. Is the beast never satisfied? He falls face first onto the mattress beneath the weight of the assassin, whose hand slips across the sheets in front of his face to find the stone. When he does, he forces it into the priest's outstretched fingers.

"Now you will do as you have promised," says the monster, whose hot breath tickles his ear like a lover's. And Mochlos is dizzy with the combined sensations of terror and titillation.

"I will!" he manages, spitting drool onto the bed. "I can!" And then, "I must!"

"You will use this emerald," says Rush, still breathing in his ear, the hard perfection of his brutish chest still pressed against the priest's back. "It will be his protection from the illness. You will instruct the fortress metalworker to make a kind of crown, one of the tiniest mail, which fits about his forehead and sets the gem between his brows. You understand me?"

"I do," gasps Mochlos. "It is brilliant, Master. Brilliant."

"Between his brows, to complement his eyes," continues Rush, ignoring the priest's flattery. "He has beautiful eyes," he continues softly, lifting himself off the priest.

"See to it that the boy does not suffer another fit, priest. I fear he may not wake from it," adds the assassin. It is with great relief that Mochlos realizes his voice has moved into the hall. But it is not so distant that the priest cannot hear, with chilling confidence, his last words.

"I know that *you* will not."

CHAPTER 9

"Four priesthoods. Four houses for the Grain God, Rah. It is like unto nature, is it not? The Sun to nurture and feed him. The Bull, that is the earth, to hold and comfort him. The Moon to govern him. The Sky to reflect upon him."

Tyrus is giving his first sermon under the pair of iron pegs that now protrude from the south wall of the lyceum to carry the magnificent bronze bull. Today his church is attended only by his own ten priests, and those of the House of the Sky. The House of the Moon is absent, and the House of the Sun, to date yet represented by Crispo alone, is cooking breakfast for the Rah. But house servants and soldiers alike are gathering about the archways into the lyceum on all sides to hear the Bull Priest speak. He is a powerful orator with a smooth, pleasing voice and a striking bearing, and he quickly draws a crowd.

Lieutenant General Nikolaos is on his way to the soldier's practice field when he hears the Bull Priest's oration on the purpose of the four houses of Rah. The priest's mention of the Moon as governor instantly slides a knife of suspicion into his gut and he halts in his tracks at the western archway of the lyceum. He makes a crisp about-face and his short, Cyrian cape, all that he has been allowed to maintain of his palace guard uniform, flutters to settle about his shoulders and gains the priest's attention from his pulpit.

At the sight of the Lieutenant in the archway, Tyrus falters momentarily. Then, turning so that he faces west as if to address Nikolaos personally, he continues what seems a seamless dialogue.

"Now, if the moon should govern too harshly, there are the other three houses to bring the moon to justice. There is the Sun, that in his kind and loving light can yet burn the moon from the sky, denying her the dark in which she makes her plans. There is the ever watchful Sky, with whom the moon must share her glory, and who will not keep her secrets but will warn the people of her misdeeds. And there is the Bull, the House of War, who if he must, can bring that moon down from her heaven and replace her with a kinder heavenly species."

This last has taken the Lieutenant's full attention from his destination in the practice field. He narrows his eyes at Tyrus ominously and pushes his way into the lyceum, knocking several house servants out of his way in doing so.

"Is it your opinion then, priest," shouts Nikolaos across the great hall, "that the High Priest of the Moon has governed Rah too harshly, and is in need of discipline himself?"

"It is my opinion, Sir, that the Moon is a Goddess of mystery and secrets, as is her house! Return to Crete if your heart can bear it. Was it not the intention of the House of the Moon to put the Rah to death, should he fail to hold back the winter? It was only by the Master of Amega's hand that his death was denied her! And it is by the Master's hand that the Houses of the Sun, Sky and Bull have been given equal power over the preservation and worship of Rah! Would I not then be remiss, even treasonous, to deny the truth? That the House of the Moon, and well I know the means, did *poison* the boy to frighten him, and through him, the Master himself, into submission to him?"

"That is a lie, you fiend!"

It is Mochlos, glaring at Tyrus from the eastern archway, his fists clenched in rage.

"It is you who are a traitor to the people of your own country! Did you not fight for the Greeks against them? You accuse me of poison for that was your own method of gain! You fool no one!"

Nikolaos has crossed the floor to stand before the altar of the Bull as Tyrus is speaking. Now he raises a hand to silence Mochlos. He gives the man a withering look, and the priest steps back, cowed.

"You will be watched," says the Lieutenant to Mochlos. "By one who loves the Rah better even than she does her own new husband. You will take the lady, Cara, into the House of the Moon. You will teach her what she must know to please the Goddess and so serve the Rah. You will teach her well, for I will take a finger from your hand each new moon I am not pleased with her progress. The House of the Moon will have a High Priestess, equal in power to its High Priest. Thus, the Moon will have no secrets from me. And thus, should any misfortune come to the Priest, as I believe it well may, yet the Rah will remain unharmed by his affliction, for he will have his priestess. You understand me, priest?"

At this Mochlos, dizzy with rage but not fool enough to speak out against the Lieutenant's injunction, stands speechless in the archway of the lyceum. Clenching and unclenching his fists, he shoots Tyrus a hateful glare, which the Bull Priest returns with a wry smile.

"I do," spits Mochlos through clenched teeth. "As you say."

"Today," says Lieutenant General Nikolaos, unconsciously adjusting his new sword in its scabbard, which makes a slicing noise that travels up the priest's back to tickle his nape unpleasantly.

"Today," repeats Mochlos, stepping back out of the archway and offering the Lieutenant a careful bow before disappearing down the hall.

That evening, at supper with his wife, Lieutenant General Nikolaos broaches the subject.

"Has the priest, Mochlos, approached you, Cara?"

He has eaten little of his meal, a braised partridge in truffles, and Cara has been careful to keep the conversation light. Her new husband has been in a dark mood since he found the Rah lying in a golden heap in the lyceum and there has been a keen glint of fury in his otherwise kind grey eyes, and a new edge in his demeanor that reminds her, strangely, of the assassin.

"He has indeed, husband. He has invited me, with the utmost civility, to learn the ways of the House of the Moon, on the orders of the very Lieutenant General himself. Of course, I accepted his invitation with equal grace. I will begin tomorrow."

Rising to help the servant clear the plates, Cara is stopped by her husband's hand on her arm. A stern look from him sets her back in her place at table.

"Forgive me, Nikolaos. I cannot seem to remember that I am a lady now."

"Not so unforgivable, considering where you have come from, Cara. But you will have a new hat to wear now, in addition to that of a lady. You are to be High Priestess of the House of the Moon. First Priestess of Rah."

"But why, Nikolaos?" blurts Cara at last, unable to keep her curiosity at bay any longer. For what would possess her own husband to offer her up as high priestess to Rah?

Maintaining his grip on her arm, Nikolaos waits for her to reseat herself before he answers. Then he takes his napkin from his lap and pats his lips. He draws both forearms up to rest on either side of his plate and looks down, his jaw set.

"Because the priest has poisoned Rah," he says finally.

"Poisoned Rah?" She is so shocked she has jumped in her seat, but her husband's hand on her arm keeps her in it. "Well how is it that he is still alive then, Nikolaos? How is it that Mochlos was allowed to take another breath?"

"I can prove nothing. I only know what I know. I need a spy in the House of the Moon, dear wife, and you have the eyes of an owl. Nothing will slip by you."

"I see," says Cara, blinking with the dizzying responsibility that has just been set upon her shoulders. He will remove my head himself, though he is fond of me, she thinks, if I fail him at this.

"You will not fail me, Cara," says Nicholas, turning to her then as if reading her mind. There is affection in his face, but the cold grey storm in his eyes has not passed. Yes, she thinks to herself, you will take my head yourself. My gods, you become more like the assassin every day, husband. And yet did I respect your chivalry when I first met you? Or did I dream of the dead glint in that monster's eyes? A woman wants a powerful man. Handsome and chivalrous, yes, but deadly also. You are becoming all three, Nikolaos. Or perhaps you always were, and only now, in this environment, your true nature shows itself.

"I will do just as you say, Sir. I will watch him. I will inform you if anything at all seems amiss."

"You will do more than that, Cara. You will become High Priestess of the House of the Moon. For I suspect that Mochlos is not long for this world."

After chariot practice that afternoon, Rah returns to the lyceum to find Dimius and his troupe murmuring in a huddle under the pinions the carpenter has bolted to the south wall to carry the bronze bull. As Rah enters the lyceum the troupe turns in unison to him, as if he holds all hope for their safety and salvation in his words.

"You are well, Rah?" asks Dimius, stepping out from the center of the group. His words are tenuous, his face drawn with caution.

"Rah is good, teacher," responds Rah, looking from the dance master's face to those of the dancers. "Wolf back," he adds, moving casually into the midst of his comrades.

"The assassin, he has visited you, Rah?" asks Akbar in a whisper as Rah is swallowed by the troupe.

"Hah. He come. He come to Rah in bed, like he come to kill!" He looks about himself dramatically, and watches the faces all about him grow wide eyed with amazement. "Wolf is kill a king!" he continues, enjoying the audience. "Kill a king for a queen. Now go to war. Rah give wolf three-man chariot. Then wolf he take all of Syria, all the way to River. Babylon. What he like. He take."

"You must not tell the assassin's secrets, Rah," Dimius whispers, looking about the lyceum like a man who has seen a thief take bread and, though hungry himself, cares not to bear the same punishment for witnessing the theft.

"No tell secret. Rah make three-man. Everybody see. Everybody know. You come. See too. Rah is show Wolf how to make, so can better kill-" and with a sudden movement that startles the crowd of dancers, he swings his axe arm left to right. As the dancers jump out of the way the pantomime explodes. He is a warrior, holding the rim of the chariot bucket with his free hand, at war with the Amorites. Several of the dancers gathered around him giggle and clap.

Now Rah returns to the center of the group, his voice a dusky whisper. "Wolf, he give Rah big stone for crown to wear! Like King of Egypt! Same color Rah eye is." He points to his right eye, then opens it wider with two fingers and peers about at his friends through it.

"What color is that, Rah?" chuckles Akbar, and the troupe echoes his chuckle, for Rah's eyes are never the same one day to the next.

"Green!" shouts Rah, annoyed, and looking at his troupe as if they ought to know this. "He say, 'I give my little cat crown to wear, give Rah three eye!' But priest come." Now Rah looks about, over his shoulder, his face turning dark with hatred. "Priest come. He is angry with Rah for be give big jewel from Wolf. So Rah say to Wolf, You give to priest, or he hurt Rah."

"And he gave it to the priest, Rah?" asks Dimius, bewildered.

"Yes. He go. He give to Priest," says Rah, nodding. "I think now priest be good to Rah. Today, he give Rah three more concubine. 'Six' he say, better for Rah. This is good number for god."

Dimius is looking over Rah's head at Akbar, an expression of perplexity on his face. Behind Rah several of the dancers make exaggerated shrugs. One spins her finger against her temple, 'crazy', and Akbar shakes his head.

"The priest has ordered me to choreograph your story, Rah. He intends for us to perform the dance for the assassin and his wife," says Dimius, "to prove that Rah is well cared for in the hands of the House of the Moon." He frowns. "But how can Rah be two places at once? How can Rah train Hatti horses to pull a three-man chariot, and be ready for a performance?"

"This no problem," answers Rah. "In Cyrus, Rah is already make this dance. Before the earth is shaking, Rah is ready. We be ready here, too. Easy. Rah is tell story to troupe. Troupe practice without Rah in morning. Rah is train horse in morning. Then, come back, good bathe with Tuma, six girl now! Ta-hah. Rah be ready dance before supper. Two, three hour maybe with troupe every day. All Rah need."

Dimius can only shake his head, smiling. "Then you must tell us the rest of the story, Rah. How can Akbar and I choreograph the Story of Rah unless we know what happened after the assassin stole you from Cyrus?"

"I show you," says Rah, and moving, as in slow motion, in reverse toward the dais he suddenly launches a series of back flips, the last of which, with inhuman precision, springs him up onto the four foot platform. Then, with a curtain call extension of his arms and a dramatic bow from the hip, he begins to teach the troupe The Story of Rah.

Above his head, in the Hall of the Moon, Mochlos paces like a caged tiger before his north facing window. He is awaiting the arrival of the Lieutenant General's wife, whom he must now train for the priesthood. *His* priesthood. In his hand he holds the emerald like a talisman against the oncoming doom that he knows awaits him. Do they think me a fool? Do they think I do not know that she is to replace me now? They may as well ask me to dig my own grave. As I have, with my very tongue. Well, I have not survived the wrath of Thera only to be cut down here by these Hatti wolves. There is an angle here and I will find it. Perhaps it is in the girl herself, yes? What do I know of this girl? She loves the Rah. And I assume her new husband. What else does she love? What can I gain for her that no one has been able to gain for her? I will act kindly toward her, yes. I will not show my hand. I will observe her. I will learn her heart. For if there is one thing I know of human beings it is that nothing can satisfy them. Though they have riches beyond their own imaginings, though they have every created thing and the heart of their people, still they long. Desire, is it not what makes us like the gods themselves? Unfulfilled desire? This is what is eternal in the human being. Only this. Eternal greed. I will find hers. And then I will use it to my own advantage.

In the mess hall that evening, Keret, the son of Agrippa, is chewing a mouthful of herbed fowl, a rather delicate and palatable thing for a warrior, but common fare now that the silly priest, Crispo, has come to influence a man's kitchen with the tastes of a lady. He swallows the savory meat with miserable determination. Everything has changed since the Master returned from Crete with a boatful of sissies. Everything has changed at the stable since the Grain God of Knossos robbed him of the assassin's favor. For he *was* a favorite. The son of the Captain of the First Division, the finest charioteer in Amega. Now he is little more than a joke.

All week long his peers have been taunting him about the race with the golden slave-god of Knossos. All week he has heard the same jibes, that a man does not take the challenge of a fly, nor the dare of a maiden. That his buns must be burning from the seat he sits in, a hot seat indeed, for if he loses, he is less than a maid, while if he wins by any other means than speed, the Master will have his head on a spike by sundown. And what Hatti charioteer does not use every method of war to win, including wrecking his enemy's chariot? His arms are bruised by the elbows of his fellows, goading him. Even his own brother, Kashka, has joined the fun, though he is but a boy of sixteen and has barely learned to run a couple from a chariot himself.

"You mustn't grieve so, Keret," says his best friend, Lysias. "You take them too seriously. For if they were better men, they would be in your sandals themselves, would they not? Now keep yourself strong and fit and find yourself the two fastest ponies in Amega. Go out to the town if you must. I hear there is a man who lives by the cistern gardens, who has been breeding Hatti mares to an Arabian stud. Perhaps you will find your racers there. There is plenty of time to train them. It will take the chariot maker a month to build the Rah a racer fit to challenge your father's. Take heart. You will win, and then you will show the Master that one good man is worth more than ten pretty gods."

"You are a good friend, Lysias," says Keret, "but the man you speak of is my father's enemy. For he sold him a mare that will not breed. How can I then go back to the same man looking for a team for the race?"

"She will not breed because she is cross and high strung. This is the Arab in her! Put her to the chariot with a milder mare. Then you will see what I am saying. Her spirit will become speed!"

Still scowling, but looking at his friend with renewed hope, Keret, slams a fist down on the table so that his plate of herbed grouse jumps in the air and lands with a clink against his cup. "Wine here!" says Keret over his shoulder to the servant who has been moving about the hall between the tables, filling cups. "You have said it, Lysias. Those high strung ladies are not made for war, but they are light footed and hot. I fear they may outrun a team of Hatti barb. And then I am bested by a pretty slave boy who cannot lift a shield, let alone swing a sword!" His cup filled, Keret takes a swallow of wine and nods, determined now. "You give good counsel, my friend. I will do as you say. This very day I will ask my father for the mare. Tomorrow we will begin to teach her to drive the cart. If I can prove to him she is a racer, he will give me the coin to purchase another."

The next morning Rah is harnessing two war horses to the restored three man chariot just outside the stable doors when Keret and Lysias, along with two grooms, lead a prancing black filly out onto the practice field. Momentarily distracted from his own task by the sight of the filly, who is pawing and snorting nervously, Rah turns from his work to watch as the boys attempt to settle the mare and ease her into her tack.

"This one too strong today," he says after watching for a time. But the group pays him no mind. Leaving his own team for Ghedi to finish harnessing to the three man, he approaches Keret. "Too hot today. Give only hay, no grain, maybe, two, three day, then try," he offers. "This be some Arab this mare. You feed too much grain. No good."

But Keret refuses to turn and so much as acknowledge Rah. He is standing in front of the mare, holding her with a halter and a lead rope and attempting to keep her from gaining enough air to rear. Prancing furiously, the mare takes a sudden step forward onto his booted foot. Then, as Keret's yowls in pain, she backs into the two grooms standing at her right and left haunch. With an explosive speed only Rah can see coming, she cow kicks the man on the right, knocking him to the ground.

"My leg!" he screams. "Aagh, she's busted my leg!"

"Keret has fallen to his knees and lost his grip on the lead at the same instant. As the mare rears over his head Rah steps casually between Agrippa's favored son and the terrified Arabian filly. He snatches her lead in one hand and lifts both his hands up over his head at the same time, mimicking her own striking hooves. Now he is bigger than she, another horse, facing her off, disciplining her. She drops to all fours, backs up, gives him her full attention.

"Te jete ende, vajze," says Rah to the filly in a soft, assuring voice. He has lowered his hands but continues to move forward, directly into her, his eyes fastened to hers. "Te jete ende, goxha vajze, ju jeni te sigurt." Be still, pretty girl, you are safe.

Keret is standing again with the help of Lysias. The man on the ground has managed to hobble to his feet as well with the help of the second groom, his leg apparently not broken.

"Damn," says Keret under his breath. "How do you run such animals as these?" He is speaking to himself, but Rah, who has now turned to give the filly his side, is quick to answer.

"Hatti horse here, so quiet. Good for war. But need lot of grain, yes? Too much for this mare! This Arab mare, she is too hot already! You give too much grain, she is bad girl. Bad girl," he is stroking the mares shoulder with the back of his hand now as he speaks. The mare has lowered her head and stopped prancing. Gingerly, she snuffles Rah's shoulder. "Yes, bad girl," he says softly to her.

Keret has given Lysias a sharp look as he attempts to straighten himself and put his weight on both of his feet. "Haah!" he hisses, "She's broken my little toe, I think."

Rah looks up to regard Keret. "She break foot?" he asks. With the lead rope loose, he has stepped toward the two boys to peer into Keret's face with concern.

Keret blinks, momentarily stunned.

"Break foot?" asks Rah again, looking into Keret's eyes with guileless ease.

"What the hell are you?" blurts Keret. "You've the eyes of a devil!"

Rah frowns at Keret, then looks over to Lysias. "Why he say this? Rah is god, no devil."

But Lysias can only blink at him with the same bewildered expression as his friend.

"Rah train mare for you," says Rah, turning from the boys to take the mare's halter off.

"What the hell?" Keret has lurched forward to grab Rah by the arm and take the mare's lead. "You little sneak, she will bolt! We will never catch her! You see, Lysias, he knows the mare can outrace him!"

"What you mean, out race? Rah race Grippa! Rah race for purple chariot!" yells Rah, pulling himself out of Keret's grip.

"Agrippa is my father. You race *me*," says Keret indignantly. The mare has begun to hop on her forelegs again, threatening to rear.

"You scare her," says Rah, reaching past Keret. With deft fingers, he unclips the lead from the mare's halter. She is instantly off and running down the length of the practice field full tilt, neck arched and tail up.

"What have you done, you little freak! My father will kill me with my own sword! He has paid too much for that mare already, and now she is gone!"

"Pretty girl, no?" says Rah. "Look how she dance. Lot of spirit. Rah catch. Rah train for you." And with that he turns back toward the barn for a bucket of grain.

"I will kill him with my own hands now," says Keret to Lysias, his face red with fury. "I will not wait to wreck him in a race!"

"Think what you do, Keret," says Lysias, settling his hand on his friend's arm. "This is the Master's favorite. Pull a single hair from that mop of his and you are not but a head on a spike, watching the sun set over Amega."

Rah has returned from the barn with the pail. Strolling past Keret and Lysias, he gives the pair a wink and a grin and sets out across the field for the mare.

"He is as like to catch that filly as I am to fly to the sun and return with a goddess," says Keret bitterly.

"Let him go," says Ghedi, who has been watching the scene as he steadies the two Hatti barbs. The ponies have been harnessed together but not yet attached to the three man. "He will do it. And train your mare too, though you are his rival. And still win."

"He only offers to train the mare to sabotage us," says Lysias, scratching the back of his neck as he watches Rah advance toward the mare, who has dropped her head to graze at the far end of the field. At Rah's approach she lifts her head and whinnies. Rah continues moving slowly toward her, rattling the pail of grain.

"What language is that?" asks Keret. "And what is wrong with his tongue? He speaks with a stone in his mouth."

"They say he bit it off in a fit. He is an epileptic. A true vessel," says Ghedi, motioning for his helper to bring up the three man behind his team. Out in the field, Rah has taken the mare by her halter and has begun to lead her back to the barn.

"He has her. Damn," says Lysias. "How is your foot, Keret? Let us go and speak with him."

"The boot saved it, I think. I can move the toe. But I will not go to him. We stay here. Let us see what he has to say."

Half way back across the field, Rah stops to stroke the mare's neck, then her flank, speaking all the while in his strange tongue. After several minutes he turns and calls to Keret, "You come now. Drop rope. Slow, slow."

Keret gives Lysias an irritated look. "Does he think I am an idiot now? Will I approach a hot horse like a bear?" With a 'humph' of annoyance he leaves Lysias and the two grooms and walks out onto the practice field toward Rah.

Upon reaching him he moves to clip the lead rope back onto the mare's halter. She instantly throws back her head, nearly pulling the halter out of Rah's hand as she does so.

"Te jete ende, balerin, te jete end," says Rah to the mare. Be still, dancer, be still. "What her name is?" he asks Keret over his shoulder. The mare has calmed with his words.

"She has not earned a name. A war horse does not earn a name until it has proven itself in battle," responds Keret, looking Rah over curiously as he gentles the mare.

"We give her name," says Rah, turning now to Keret and snatching the lead rope. Taking grain in his free hand, he distracts the filly with it as he clips the lead back on to the halter. Then he turns back to Keret, seizing his arm and pushing him toward the stable.

Taken aback, Keret jerks himself from Rah's grasp and gives him a sour look. Rah blinks at him patiently. After a moment, Keret gives in and moves off in the direction of the barns with Rah at his side. The mare follows without complaint.

"We name her, Cupke. Little girl it mean. I train," says Rah, unfazed by Keret's anger. He gives Keret's arm a friendly punch.

"Do you not know who I am? I am the man you have challenged!" cries Keret loudly, for a crowd of his peers has formed at the entrance to the barn and are watching the exchange. He steps sideways out of Rah's reach, halts, and folds his arms across his chest importantly.

"You are Grippa son?" Rah looks at Keret with greater interest. "How is come you not know how train horse, Grippa son? You are charioteer. Must learn how to train horse first, before can race Rah."

This is more than Keret can bear. Outraged, he grabs the mare's lead out of Rah's hand.

"I *was* training her, you little thief!"

But the mare has begun to snort and to pull on the lead, threatening to rear for the third time.

"You scare her, Grippa son, horse no care how mad you are for Rah. She think you mad for her," says Rah, moving between Keret and the mare and putting his hand on the lead and then up to her muzzle. "Here is Rah, Cupke, fundi tabeles." His back to Keret, he does not see the boy's hands fly to the sides of his head in exasperation.

Lysias has come to meet them. "Everyone is watching," he hisses at his friend as he draws him away from Rah. "Why do you let him put a hand on you, and then take the mare?"

"I let him do nothing! He acts of his own will! You see how he is? He knows I am his competitor yet he says he will train her for me!"

"He means only to sabotage us. Now go take the mare from him."

"I cannot! They are in league already. The little devil has cast a spell on her!"

"Grippa son," calls Rah, coming up behind them. "You take from Rah, now. Quiet. No yell. No big move. You lead in to barn."

"Do it," says Lysias. "Else he will lead her in himself and make an even bigger fool of you."

Defeated, Keret turns to Rah. "What then," he says, petulantly.

"You take here," says Rah, offering him the lead. "Now you say her, 'good girl, pretty girl, Cupke, follow.'"

"Hatti men do not talk to horses," says Keret defiantly.

"This why she scare," nods Rah agreeably. "But now we give name. We talk her, like to woman. We stroke her," he strokes the mare's neck, "like woman." He winks at Keret. "All horse is like woman, even boy horse. All same. Like soft hand, soft talk." Taking Keret's free hand, he opens the fingers to deposit a bit of grain from the pail into his palm. "And gift. Like woman, no?" He looks up into Keret's face quizzically. "Maybe you never have woman, Grippa son?"

"I have had a woman," snaps Keret, and gives Rah his blackest scowl. But he has lifted his hand to the mare's muzzle and let her take the treat.

"You treat same way," says Rah. "You yell, wave hands, big show with woman, she no like. Woman want hear her name over, over. Soft speak, soft touch. Rah have six concubine now. Know what talk about. Women all love Rah. Fight over Rah." He winks at Keret again. "Rah can teach you how be good with women too, Grippa son, if you like."

Fuming, but careful not to make a bigger fool of himself than he already has, Keret leads the mare quietly back to the stable. Behind him, Lysias takes one more, disconcerted look at Rah, then marches off after his friend.

"You give Cupke just hay, few day," calls Rah after the two boys. "Then I help you train. She be good girl. You see."

"He will drive me mad!" Keret says to his friend later that day. "How has the Master not killed him himself by now? He is as thick in the head as a barn door!"

"Perhaps the Master has a use for a horse handler who can put three men in a war chariot," says Lysias, pondering the morning's events over lunch. After leading the mare back into the barn the two boys returned to the practice field to watch Rah work the three man with the two experienced Hatti barbs. The experiment was a success, so much so that by the sound of the midday horn the new Lieutenant General himself was in the bucket, an archer to his left and a swordsman to his right, charging around the practice field stabbing bales of hay wrapped in captured Amorite battle flags.

"You had better not insult Amega's little war god, Keret. Nothing good can come of it."

"How you can call that bit of fluff a war god is a mystery in itself," responds Keret. "This whole compound has gone mad, if you ask me." But he follows his friend's advice when, moments after he has spouted these words, Rah walks into the horsemen's mess in the company of the Asian, Tiko, and, upon spotting him at table, greets him with a brilliant smile and saunters over to slip onto the bench to his right.

"Grippa son! You see Rah three man today? Put wheel good place to balance men, now easy for horse carry three. You think Wolf is like?" And he leaps atop the table, his feet inches from Keret's plate, to pantomime Nikolaos in the bucket.

"Hah! Hahh!" he says, slapping his team's backs with invisible reins. "This archer," he points to his left, "he shoot Amorite charioteer, what is Amorite archer do? Lost rein. Horse, "they take off for home. This man here, with sword, he is kill Amorite footmen same time. Who can fight this army now, with three man in chariot, eh? One three-man take two Amorite chariot and footman easy. Amorite, they all run away, like chicken when wolf is come in hen house." Pleased with himself he looks about at his astonished audience of horsemen who had been taking their midday meal down the length of either side of the table. Then he hops down to the bench and slips in to take the seat on Keret's right.

"Taru help me," mumbles Keret under his breath, and he clenches his fists until his hands are red.

"You see?" asks Rah again, taking a grain cake from the side of Keret's plate of lamb stew and stuffing half of the thing into his mouth as he watches Keret for his answer.

Blind with rage now, Keret attempts to jump to his feet, but unlike Rah, he does not make it past the obstacle of the bench. Slamming his thighs into the underside of the table he sits back down with a plop, his weapons belt clattering.

"What is the matter with you, Keret Agrippa," grins Tiko devilishly from his place at Rah's right. "You lose your horse this morning, and now you cannot rise from table without knocking over my cup. Maybe you need to see the physician. Maybe you are coming down with something, eh?"

"A man does not steal from another man's plate in Amega without losing his hand," says Keret through his teeth in a hiss, but he makes no move to draw his sword.

"Rah cannot eat this," says Rah casually, pointing to Keret's bowl of stew. "You come to Hall of Moon, Grippa son. Crispo he is try to make Rah fat, always he bring Rah food, too much, Rah cannot eat. Give to concubine. How can dance fat? You come, you try. Better food there. Grippa son need good food to race Rah. Need learn to train horse. Rah teach you how to be with woman. You learn how to be with woman, you be better with horse."

By now the mess hall has erupted with laughter at Keret's expense. The boy makes one more attempt to climb out of his seat, giving the other charioteers a ferocious scowl as he does so.

But he is stopped by the shadow of the Master himself looming in the doorway.

Instantly he sits back down. Then, realizing his mistake, throws himself off the bench and on to his knees in a full military bow. The rest of the hall has done the same, all but Rah, who looks about first before slipping off the bench beside Keret and Tiko and mimicking them.

"You have succeeded, little cat," says Rush from the doorway. "You have succeeded once again," he stops only to clear his throat and look around at the room full of bowed heads, "in making me a better man."

There is a sudden jerk of movement, like a wave slapping the beach, as all of the charioteers look up in shock. But Rah has remained still, his chin tucked.

"You will finish your rations. Then you will chose three men from among these and demonstrate to me what you have already proven to the Lieutenant General."

With that, Rush disappears down the hall. A hum of murmuring through the mess is hushed by the falcon-like silhouette of Lieutenant General Nikolaos in the doorway.

"Be silent!" he barks, giving the boys a sharp look. "Resume your meal. When you are finished you will all return to the practice field. There you will begin your instruction in the new three-man chariot. Rah," he says with a note of affection, looking down at the dancer's golden head, "chose your charioteers."

At this, Rah looks up from his knees at Nikolaos. He quickly stands, a broad smile on his face brightening the room like a sunbeam. Tiko has risen to stand beside him, his dark twin. On his left, Keret groans under his breath and attempts to make himself smaller. But it is no use. What he fears comes to pass in an instant.

"This Grippa son, Fox! He is race Rah for purple chariot! Must be good chariot man, no? We make him driver."

A stunned silence, then a murmur of confusion rumbles through the dining hall.

"Good choice, Rah. And who is to be your archer?" asks Nikolaos, his eyes skating from Rah to Keret. He cannot help but to enjoy the boy's expression of sheer misery. That will teach the little cock, he thinks.

Now Rah looks around the dining hall, taking a dramatic breath and stroking an invisible beard like a judge pondering a case.

"I think," he begins, but Tiko has grabbed his arm and is whispering in his ear and pointing to the back of the hall. Rah dips his head to hear Tiko, then looks up with a radiant smile.

"I think, Pelet!" and he has hopped back onto the dining table, his bare and dusty toes tickling the edge of Keret's plate, to point with exaggerated certainty at the far end of the hall. "Pelet good archer. Can kill two pigeon with one arrow!"

This draws a chuckle from Nikolaos. "Another good choice, Rah," he says, nodding and then giving Tiko a wry smile. "And what of your lanceman? Who will bear the lance?"

"No sword?" Rah raises his brows, then whirls an invisible sword through the air.

"No sword. First the distance weapon, the javelin. Then the lance. Then, only when these are spent, does the man on the right take up his sword. In this way, he may take out two drivers before he is left with only his sword in close contact."

Rah looks down at Tiko from his perch on the table. "What you think, China?" he asks his friend.

"The lanceman defends his driver, Rah," say Tiko importantly as the room full of boys on their knees nod in agreement to one another. "He must defend his driver with his life." He looks over at Lysias, whose eyes are now as big as turtle eggs. "No one will defend Keret better than his friend, Lysias."

This brings a whoop of delight from the charioteers. Lysias gulps, and Keret nudges him with an elbow.

"Lysias then," says Rah to Nikolaos, pointing to the boy on his knees. "Friend of Grippa son."

"Good," says Nikolaos from the doorway. "Now finish your meals, and be ready to demonstrate the three-man for your Master in half an hour. Ghedi will have a new team in harness by then."

When the Lieutenant General is gone, Rah steals another grain cake from Keret's plate. This time Keret is silent.

"Now you show Wolf even skinny boy like you can drive three-man!" Rah says happily, his mouth full.

Miserable, Keret swallows a half-chewed chunk of lamb from his stew and answers, "What makes you think I can drive that monstrosity, eh? Why do you pick me? The balance is all wrong. I am not accustomed to it. I have had no time to train. And with a man on either side of me. I shall be hemmed in and unable to guide the team."

"You have defeated yourself already with your mouth," says Tiko, who is sitting beside Rah. "This is what I tell the Master's commanders. I am surprised you have not heard it from your father, who is my student. The mind is the greatest weapon. Negative thinking is like a broken blade. For even in the hand of the most robust and skilled soldier, it is of no use."

"He is right I think, Keret," says Lysias from the other side of the table. "It will do you no good to defeat yourself in your head before the battle. This is an opportunity. You must look at it this way. You need only to guide the team. Pelet and I will do the rest."

"Baah," says Rah, clapping Keret on the back and rising, and spitting cake crumbs at Agrippa's son as he speaks. He passes the flat of his hand before his face and now it is the downcast face of a sad clown. The charioteers who have been watching the exchange chuckle and nod at one another.

"What this face is, China?" Rah is pointing to his own exaggerated expression.

"Sober!" shouts one boy from a seat across the room, and the rest of the boys burst into laughter.

"Serious," says Tiko, rising to his feet. "Come, Blonde, let us be sure that Ghedi has picked a good team and waxed the wheels." He starts for the door. As he does so, Rah leans down to press his mouth against Keret's ear.

"Is OK, Grippa son, you see," he says, patting Keret's shoulder, "Wolf is like."

An hour later Keret, Lysias and Pelet are perched in the bucket of the three-man with two strong Hatti geldings attached. Three more chariots, two-man rigs, face them across the field. Two carry archers, the third, a lanceman. The archers' arrows have been blunted with leather and clay, but the boys are in full battle gear nevertheless. The lancemen carry practice lances and javelins and wooden swords dipped in fresh goat's blood, thus, a 'kill' can be scored.

"Stand little bit back, Grippa son, so can balance better," calls Rah from the ground. "Not like two-man chariot. You see? You tell, China." He has had to shout his instructions, for the field is surrounded by hundreds of soldiers who have been told to attend the demonstration.

"He is telling you to stand above the axle," shouts Tiko above the din. "All three must stand across the axle, else you will be pitched forward or else thrown back. It is the same as riding a horse in a saddle. You must not allow yourself to get in front or behind the motion of the chariot."

"I am not an idiot," snaps Keret. "But it is one thing to say it, another to do."

"No scare, Grippa son. Same as two-horse. Already have balance. Just put feet little back," cries Rah over the sound of the battle horn. Then Keret is slapping the reins against the backs of the two barbs and he is off across the field, the three two-horse teams charging toward him from the opposite side, an archer or lanceman to the left of each driver, the brilliant, early winter sun at their backs.

"He is be good, China, you watch," says Rah optimistically. "Grippa son."

It is clear from the start that the two-men have more speed, more a result of the advantage of their drivers' familiarity with the balance in their bucket than the disadvantage of the extra weight in the three man, which is hardly a thought to the two strong barbs. But though all three two-men reach the center of the field before Keret, it is of little benefit to them, for the driver on the left is hit by Lysias' javelin and the driver to the right is struck by Pelet's arrow before either have had time to fire a shot, taking those two chariots out of the fight. The remaining man in each chariot must now disembark and fight on foot, one with only a bow and quiver of arrows, the other with only a sword, for he lost his lance when the driver lost control of his team and he tumbled out.

The field of soldiers is cheering as Keret plows his team toward his remaining opponent. A fierce competitor, he is known to drive his team headlong into his foe, forcing the weaker man's horses to bolt to one side and overturn the chariot, or else to halt and rear in self-defense, and in either case throw the driver and his archer from the bucket. But his adversary sees this coming and pulls his team to the right, avoiding a wreck but putting himself in direct aim of Pelet's arrow. At the same time his hasty move has thrown his archer off balance. He loses the arrow he was pulling from his quiver, giving Lysias the freedom to tag him with his lance.

The crowd of soldiers surrounding the field roars. The disabled opponent pulls his team to a halt. But Keret, whooping with delight, has taken his rig for a victory lap around the practice field, with Lysias swinging his sword and Pelet holding his bow over his head like a prize.

As they complete their lap, Rush walks toward them, Nikolaos at his side. Keret brings his team to a steaming halt and two stablemen run from the doorway of the barn to take the horses by their headstalls. Keret and his men jump quickly from the bucket and line up before Rush, giving him a crisp military bow in unison.

"What do you think of it, Keret Agrippa? Will it serve you in war?" asks Rush with an unaccustomed smile.

"It will quickly clear the battlefield, Master. The Amorites will flee in terror, for they will soon see that we can disable three chariots with one."

"And you, Lysias? What do you think of having an archer on board to cover you?"

"I am free to aim and thrust, Sir, without concern. My javelin is more accurate, my lance unimpeded," answers Lysias proudly.

"And my arrows are steadier, Lord, for there is greater security in the bucket with the axle directly beneath my feet!" declares Pelet, looking to the two others. "Did you not feel it also?"

"My archer noticed this as well," adds Nikolaos, nodding.

One of the defeated 'Amorite' charioteers has approached and now bows to Rush for permission to speak.

"Although we outnumbered our opponent, we all agree that facing such a creature was nevertheless daunting. Were I to see such an army coming, Lord, it would seem as if I were facing a swarm of three headed monsters!"

"Thus you are the first to try the three-man, Keret," says Rush, "And so, being chosen by Rah to do it, you and your team will train with the device and when you are proficient, you will train my army. But first, you three will travel with me to Hattusha, where we will demonstrate the weapon to King Mursilis himself. Then I will obtain one hundred of his best chariot makers, who will return with me, and I will have an army of one thousand three-man chariots by spring, when all kings go to war. Then we will lead Mursilis' into Syria, take the Euphrates, and defeat Babylon."

"Am I to remain here, Sir," asks Nikolaos then, for he has not been privy to this plan until now, "While you are negotiating with your King in Hattusha?"

"You will. You will guard the Rah," responds Rush. "And perhaps you may see to it I have no surprises waiting for me when I return, this time."

CHAPTER 10

It is mid-afternoon when Rah returns to the Hall of the Moon. Accustomed to finding his concubines waiting in his room for him and ready to accompany him to the baths, he is surprised to find instead that the room is empty. He has turned on his heels and is about to dart down the hall to the baths to join them when he notices Mochlos and another figure, hidden in the robe of a Minoan Priest of the Dead, approaching together from the north end of the hall. Knowing all creatures by movement before any other clue of sight or sound, Rah is quick to identify the figure shrouded in white.

He stops, waits, cautious of the tiger at her side, and tips his head quizzically when she pulls back the hood of her robe and greets him with a quite smile.

"I am come to be your Priestess, Rah," says Cara, and when he fails to answer, she continues, "You are to have both Priest and Priestess of the Moon. It is at the order of the Lieutenant General himself."

"How can have both Priest and Priestess of Moon, Cara? You are marry to Fox, not this Priest."

"In fact," says Mochlos carefully, "It is necessary for her marriage to the Lieutenant to be annulled. For she cannot serve two masters, that is, both a husband and the Rah. Just as a priest may not be married, neither may a priestess. Therefore, she has forsaken her marital bed, with the permission of the Lieutenant General, of course, to devote herself entirely to Rah."

"Is like concubine, now Cara?" asks Rah innocently. "Wolf is no like this," he shakes his head sadly.

"No, Rah, not like a concubine. Like a priest. But a woman. Like a kind and gentle priest who wishes only to serve you. To nurture you. To see to it that you have everything that you need, so that the abundant nature of Rah may live in you and through you without hindrance. So that Amega may prosper."

Cara has stepped forward to speak to Rah, leaving the priest at her back. As she speaks, she lifts the boy's chin. She is yet a bit taller than he, for she is a tall woman, but even so, she sees that he has grown in height since she slipped her arms around him and put him beneath her in the Cemetery of the Ancients what seems now a century ago. It is as Tyrus said, thinks Cara, looking into the cat-like face of the Grain God. The cheekbones are even more exotic, the forehead broader, more intelligent, the chin sharper, the brow less childlike, more that of a young man. It is becoming the face of a young lion. And, she thinks, helpless but to allow her eyes to drift down the perfect line and curve of the golden breast, the nipped waist and leanly muscled abdomen, the body also. You will never be a tall man, Rah, but you will be a beautiful one.

"Shall we begin your lessons in morning prayer, then, Cara?" offers Mochlos from behind her.

"Yes, holiness, and I should like to put them to music if I may. For I have watched the morning prayers of the House of the Moon these past weeks and it is a dull thing indeed for the service of so bright and shining a god. I sing, you know," she turns to smile at the priest with innocent affection.

"Do you, really!" responds Mochlos with as much enthusiasm as he can muster. "Well, that is quite remarkable. You must sing for us then, perhaps this evening!" He has taken her arm and turned her from Rah, whom he gives a curious look over his shoulder. "After supper? Yes we will invite the House of the Sun and Sky. Perhaps the Bull as well, why not? And we will have a little recital. Are you good?"

As they retreat down the hall, Rah hears the patter of a dozen unshod feet and the giggling of half as many teenaged concubines flittering toward him from the opposite direction.

"Rah! We have a surprise for you!" cries Hannah, always the loudest. "Tyla and Peek have learned a new dance! Nephtet has had Tuma set her harp up in the baths! I will play the cymbals and sing."

Rah gives the retreating backs of Mochlos and Cara one last look before turning to gather his wives in open arms.

"Rah has Priestess now!' he says, pulling Peek and Tyla to his sides. The others have gathered about him like chickens beneath the farmer's feet. "Cara, she sing also. Sing to Rah. Lullaby. This how Rah find Cara. She sing lullaby. Rah can hear. Nobody else can hear. Then Wolf he come, save Cara. Save Crispo, too. So can feed Rah. Save everybody." He shrugs, smiling at them, "This priest now. He no like have Cara here. But, what he can do? Wolf want Cara be priestess in House of Moon. Cara be priestess."

"Hold still, Sunlight, you will make a mess of it!" says Aros the next morning as he attempts to cut Rah's curls into the halo of moonlight they were for the Story of the Sun God so many months ago in Knossos.

"It is a mess already, Aros. Where is your mind today? You have cut the top too short now," scolds Pyrus from the opposite side of Rah's stool. He is concocting face paint for the face of the Sun God, and Rah has not let him finish a single pot without grabbing the brush and dunking it into the mix to try the color on the back of his hand and down his arm.

"Cut all off, Aros, make Rah like Mochlos, eh?" says Rah, giving Aros a light punch in his ample belly before grabbing Pyrus' latest mixture and reaching for a clean brush.

"Leave it, Rah, you will look like a peacock-" begins Pyrus.

"Silly thing. You've spent too much time with horses and soldiers, you have. Don't know how to behave indoors anymore," mumbles Aros, batting Rah's shoulder with a limp hand. "Turn around now, let me finish."

"Aros!" says Pyrus suddenly, pointing to the collage of colors Rah has painted on the backs of both his hands and forearms.

"It is not too short, Pyrus," whines Aros, fluffing Rah's curls to prove his point. "It will be just stunning, you will see."

"No, Aros. Look!" says Pyrus again, snatching one of Rah's wrists to lift his forearm up to Aros' face. "Do you see?" For Rah has turned himself into a rainbow from his knuckles to his elbows.

"Well he is a perfect mess, I see that. Now he will need a bath-" responds Aros, pouting a bit.

"No, Aros. Not a mess. A rainbow! Don't you see it? I shall paint his entire body! His face, his arms and legs, rainbows! And you shall make him a costume to match!"

Now Pyrus has Aros' full attention. "Yes! Yes, I see it! And what *is* Rah if not a rainbow? A sign of good fortune, abundant harvest," begins Aros.

Rah has been looking from one to the other. Now he raises both hands over his head at the mirror and investigates his work. He drops them, makes his 'wet cur' shake and fluffs out his curls. His head is a ball of yellow light.

"The cut is good, Aros," murmurs Pyrus, a bit dazzled.

Now Rah flexes his shoulders, which have lost their narrow boyishness in the last month and are beginning to suggest the vision of the man to come. "Put here, too, Pyrus!" he draws two fingers along his neck and down his left bicep.

"Sit," says the face painter. And in a few moments, he has extended the colors from the base of Rah's ears to the tips of his fingers.

"Leg, too," says Rah, standing to give Pyrus the canvas of his thighs and calves.

"I must find the proper silks and ask the mistress' permission to use her seamstress!" says Aros, dabbing a mixture of lemon juice and gelatin onto the palms of his hands and then reaching to stiffen Rah's halo of honey-blonde light.

"Not too much of that, Aros," snaps Pyrus, stoking a thick stripe of Egyptian blue paint down Rah's right leg to his big toe. "You want it to move with him. It is not a helmet."

"It had better not be," says Mochlos from the doorway. "For this band of mail will not conform to a helmet. It is made in such a way as to sit firmly on the head, with a bit of stretch, you see? Ingenious." He is stretching a band made of tiny golden mail between his fingers, as if playing Jacob's Ladder.

"What is it, Sir?" asks Pyrus, mystified.

Mochlos has turned the band over as he moves toward the face painter. The gleam of the obscenely large emerald throws pearls of light across the room.

"It is Rah's crown," says Mochlos, smiling at Rah. "Do you like it, handsome? The Master has commissioned it made to keep you safe from the epilepsy. That is the work of emeralds, you know. To protect one from evil, real or imagined, and from diseases of the brain. Of course, it has not yet been charged. That will require a ceremony, and an experienced High Priest. But let us try it on, shall we? Tonight is the full moon. Tonight we shall draw her down, and charge the stone by the power of the Goddess herself to keep you safe so long as you wear it."

With that Mochlos lifts the band to settle it on Rah's head. It wraps itself tightly about his skull and much of the gold mail is lost in his newly cut curls of the same color. It hides under those curls like a young dragon guarding its treasure, scales shimmering, the jewel eye glinting protectively.

"This priest stone," says Rah meekly. "This is no Rah stone. You take," and he reaches for his head to remove the band.

"NO!" cries Mochlos, slapping his palms down on Rah's head in a clumsy effort to keep him from removing the crown. Withdrawing his hands nervously he looks about, as if waiting for an anaconda to strike from some dark corner. "No, Rah. You must wear it now. I *want* you to wear it. I *demand* that you wear it. You understand? Look here," and he takes Rah's arm and turns him to face his own reflection in the mirror. "Look how handsome. Look how the stone magnifies the colors in your eyes, boy. Who else could wear such a thing without looking a fool? No. It is yours to keep and to wear always. If it could be bolted to your head it would be, but cannot."

"Actually," says Aros, musing at Rah's reflection, I could *weave* it into his hair, Sir, in such a way that it would not pull and pinch, as this mail surely will."

"Do whatever it takes to keep him from losing it, dresser," says Mochlos, giving Aros an interested, if not admiring look. "You are quite a bit more cunning than you appear," he adds, looking Aros up and down. "I wonder I never noticed until lately. I am not one to overlook an asset."

Beaming with the unexpected praise, Aros gives the priest a generous bow. "It will be as if it were a part of him, Holiness, and yet simple enough to remove when he sleeps and bathes."

"Just as you say," responds Mochlos, nodding curtly at the dresser and then losing interest in him. "Now, my little beauty, you will ready yourself for the ritual this evening. No horses today. No food, nor concubines. You must bathe and dress for ceremony. Dresser, you will put him in the Shroud of Rah, the cloth he was born in. Nothing beneath, only his gold."

"What of the earring, sir?" asks Pyrus then coolly. "He did not wear that for the Dying to the God. Indeed, he had not yet acquired it."

"I would not touch that pearl if the Goddess herself charged me to do it. Else I be gagging on it in my bed one night with an ape on my chest," mutters the priest to himself with a sharp look to Pyrus. "Have him ready for me in the lyceum at dusk. You will take a bit of drink for me, Rah, when you arrive. Do not be afraid. You will not lose your limbs, it is not but a pleasant liquor made from the pit of the peach. It will strengthen the spirit of Rah," he says mysteriously before leaving the three to ponder his words.

"This priest stone," says Rah, reaching for his head. "Rah can no wear this. Wolf give to priest."

"Silly thing, did you not hear a word that he said to you? Too stunned by your own reflection, hmm?" says Aros, pulling Rah's hands away from the crown. "Now give it here. I will make a silk lining for it, for this mail will catch and pinch otherwise. I will sew flaxen horse tail to the lining here, here, here and here, you see? Then we can braid the horse hair into your own hair each morning and remove it each night in the same way."

"Otherwise you will pull it from your head in your sleep, lay on it and damage it," says Pyrus, turning Rah's shoulders back to face him and kneeling before him with a brush and a cup of blue-green paint. He begins a second stripe down Rah's left leg.

When Aros has left the room to find what he needs, Pyrus, painting a pale green stripe beside the blue-green one, looks up at his charge. Rah is watching him paint his legs in rainbow colors with the happy curiosity of a child. "This good, Pyrus. You make good rainbow."

"Yes, and when you take flight in *this* costume, Rah, you will be like nothing anyone in Amega, I daresay, nothing anyone anywhere in the Land of Hatti, has ever seen."

"Maybe go to dance for King, Pyrus? Rah must dance for kings." He looks at his reflection in the mirror, remembering.

"Oh, I have no doubt you will be dancing for a king again, Baby. For when the assassin sees this production, when he sees *you*, Rainbow Rah, he will want the world to see you, and to know that you are his."

In Hattusha, King Mursilis is preparing for war with Syria. He has gathered the five armies of his grandfather Hattusilis in the valley and has ordered the whole of Hatti to pay one tenth of their stores of barley, oil, raisins and figs, and one tenth of their flocks of goat and sheep, to provide for the camp, which consists of twenty thousand men, six thousand horses and twenty four hundred chariots. His mother, the only daughter of Hattusilis, is also staying at the King's palace in Hattusha, as is her mother-in-law, the former Queen. Mursilis is a young man, not yet married, with a mind for war only. He is aware that his grandfather, the King, paid a fortune for the services of Rush the Assassin, and that it is this fortune that gained him the throne. His greatest threat, the eldest son of Hattusilis, is dead. The other two have fled Hattusha, believing that their fate would be the same as their brothers if they did not. His dead uncle's lover, the woman, Sophina, has disappeared with them, and his spies tell him that she is now carrying on a liaison with his youngest uncle Ammuna, who has gathered a band of supporters in the foothills. There is sufficient support for the two uncles, for many in Hatti maintain the belief that the throne belongs to the elder son of a dead king, no matter how worthless that heir or treasonous his behavior before his father's death. Ammuna has gathered an army of ten thousand supporters and, with a considerable donation of gold and silver from the Amorite king, a legion of Amorite mercenaries. Mursilis is aware of the insurgence. He has in turn sent word to Rush that Ammuna's pockets are full of Syrian coin and that his assassination would be its own reward: an army prepared for war with their own king, needing only a ferocious, Hatti born legend to steal it, tame it, and then lead it into Syria alongside Mursilis.

And so Mursilis, whose fleet-footed, mounted spies are aware that a contingent of Rush's beastly wolves are on their way to Hattusha with a strange new horse-drawn weapon (for the prototype three-man has been covered so that Amorite spies might not discover its existence first) is preparing himself for a meeting with a man he knows only by legend and hearsay, a man who saved his life by killing his uncle, the rightful king in many Hatti minds. And he is not a little afraid.

For this wolf, the man known as Rush the Assassin, could be friend or foe depending on less than the wind's next direction. And he never makes an equal bargain. He must win, and win, losing nothing. A true hero in the minds of the Hatti people, a true demon in the minds of royals and their families. He is no one's servant but his own, and a king's deal with Rush is as dangerous as a deal with the devil himself.

And so Mursilis paces across the balcony of his grandfather's palace, a young man with much ambition and sufficient intelligence to make his goals a reality, a man devoted to seeing his grandfather's dreams of piercing Syria and taking the Euphrates and Babylon, a man nevertheless shivering with trepidation at the thought of finally meeting his savior, the legend and murdering thief, Rush the Assassin.

His thoughts are interrupted by a servant at the door of his chamber, bowing and stepping aside to allow his grandfather's widow entry into the inner room.

"They still treat her as if she were Queen," mumbles Mursilis to his valet, who has jumped to his feet to shut the beaded curtain between his chamber and his balcony.

"Shall I bring her to you, Lord," he says, hands folded and eyes downcast.

"She will burst through herself if you do not," says King Mursilis, turning to give the former Queen his back as the valet moves to open the curtain.

"Mursilis," she says, pushing open the beads before the valet can do so. "I wonder you treat me so unkindly, though I saved your life and gave you your throne."

"You did neither, Madam," responds the young King, not bothering to turn to greet her. His hands are planted on the parapet as he looks south over the tops of the buildings of Hattusha toward the highway that splits the city in half on a diagonal. It is on this highway, he expects, that Rush the Assassin and his men will approach, and he has barely taken his eyes off it to eat and sleep since he heard the man was coming.

"My dear grandson," says the former Queen, drawing near to place a long-fingered hand on his shoulder. "I most certainly did both. I took my life in my hands and gave near half my fortune away so that you should stand here, rather than your uncle, in your grandfather's stead."

Now Mursilis turns to give his grandfather's widow a black glare. He has his grandfather's eyes, she thinks, black as pitch, and quite merciless. I stand on a precipice between heaven and hell. Were either of his uncles king today, I would be dead already.

"You did what you did to save your own thick hide, Madam," says Mursilis, "and though we be young, nevertheless, do not think us foolish, nor forget who our grandfather was, and *what* he was, and do not think that you hold us to an allegiance because you made the only choice you could to save your own life."

I tamed your grandfather and I shall tame you, thinks the former Queen of Hatti. "We understand each other Mursilis. And so there is no need to bicker. But you will admit that while you stand here, trembling with fear and youthful admiration for the man you are about to meet, your grandfather's Queen has already met him, has already dealt with him and lived. And being both the former Queen and confidant of the great Hattusilis' himself, may yet be of some use to you in this exchange. Indeed, your grandfather had a long relationship with the Terror of the Aegean. And should his widowed Queen come to some harm, it may well be Rush the Assassin who defends her."

With this, Mursilis opens his eyes wide, for it is the one thing he has not considered.

"We should have known you would use our inheritance-" he begins.

"Not yours, Mursilis. But that of your three uncles," she counters.

"To pay for your own neck," continues King Mursilis. But he is cowed now. His teeth set, he turns from her to look back over the city toward the highway. "Is this what you have come to tell us, Mother?"

"I have come to warn you, grandson, not to trifle with the interests of the one who comes."

"He has blackmailed you then?" says Mursilis.

"He is in my service, grandson, for the duration of my natural life. This is a treaty signed before your grandfather's death, and written in blood."

"So we are your puppet," responds Mursilis bitterly.

"Not so, grandson. It is in no Hatti woman's interest to castrate a man. Least of all her king. I merely wish for you to understand that I am to live here, at the palace, comfortably, for the remainder of my days, and that if I die any but a natural death, the same fate will be visited on the King who has not protected me from such a fate."

"And what of government, woman? Will you not then also dictate to me how to rule this people?"

"I have no interest in governing, Mursilis. You will go to war, with whom and when you will, just as your grandfather did. That I am treated with the respect due a widowed queen is sufficient."

Mursilis is silent. As the former Queen turns to leave him, however, she stops in her tracks. Her back to his, she puts this next over her shoulder to him.

"And that from here on, until the king's widow is dead, she remain Queen, and that until her death, no other, not even the King's wife, shall take her place as Queen."

"In this you do me a favor, Mother," responds Mursilis, and his answer causes the Queen to lift her shoulders slightly with surprise. But she does not turn back to him. A moment passes. Then, nodding pleasantly to his valet on her way out she says, "You are indeed your grandfather's heir, Mursilis."

In the valley of Goreme, near the city of Urgup, Agrippa is leading the contingent of men guarding the prototype toward Hattusha. He wears the tall Hittite hat and the breastplate and colors of a general and rides a fine black horse bedecked in finery of similar color. He is surrounded by armed horsemen in military uniform. The covered prototype is surrounded by armed horsemen as well, three deep, informing every spy in the Valley of the Gods of its importance.

The troops Agrippa leads are fine soldiers, some of Amega's best, but Rush is not among them. He has taken to the caves on foot, and is doing his own surveillance.

"Why is Tiko no have wing, Ting Ya?" says Rah. It is a fortnight since the high priest and his new protégé drew down the moon to charge his crown. It is a fortnight, too, since Rush and a detachment of soldiers left Amega with the three horse prototype.

"Tiko is son of sons of war, Jin yu," responds the Asian mystic. She is making honey cakes in the Master's kitchen today while Janus, the cook, looks on with suspicious interest. The cakes require a strange new spice called ginger which fills the kitchen with a heady aroma, like crisp leaves on a winter morning in his homeland north of the Black Sea. Rah is watching Ting Ya from a bench he has pulled in from the house servants' dining area. He leans back on one elbow, his long legs stretched out before him. His head tossed back, the pearl earring beckons, 'come hither and touch', but the emerald in his new crown glints like the edge of a polished sword, warning. The crown is a lizard, coiled tightly around the dancer's head, the scales fairly hissing their counsel. This is the prize of the Assassin! Do not harm, nay, do not lay hand upon him!

"Tiko believe in body," continues Ting Ya. "Think everything he can do, he must do with body. Rah come from light, from spirit. Son of morning only. No mother, father in the body. This why Rah have eyes many colors. See all things. Not just body. Can see spirit also." She looks up from her work to smile at him. "Easy to fly when heart can leave body."

"Rah see spirit of Priest of Dead in cemetery, Ting Ya," confides Rah then. "Many priest. Everybody sleep. Rah wake up. See priest come, they come to Wolf. Maybe talk him. I think they do not know only spirit now. No body. Cannot talk Wolf."

"You will see many spirit, Jin yu. You are spirit god now. Come close to death. Man come close to death he can see many thing. Danger come, Jin yu, now have spirit wings. Now can fly."

All this time Janus has been listening to this strange and barely intelligible conversation while watching the Asian woman chop and mix and shape a stiff batter that smells of ginger and almonds into little cakes. He has become accustomed to the Asian taking over his kitchen now and then and has, despite himself, come to enjoy her interruptions. They are, after all, on the authority of the Lady of the House and there is less than nothing he can do about it except to treat Ting Ya like the welcomed and important guest that she is. But he has also learned that she is special to the Rah, and has earned an intimacy with him that no one else has. So, seated comfortably at the opposite end of Rah's bench, his idle, if floured, hands in his lap (for Ting Ya interrupted his own baking this morning) he watches the Asian mystic arrange her cakes on a stone slab at the central prep table and considers her words.

"Where I come from we believe very much in spirits," he offers, looking down the bench at Rah to see if he has caught the boy's interest. "A person who can talk to spirits of the dead can make quite a living at it for we believe that our ancestors can predict the future, find treasure, even tell us the hour of our own death."

"Why you want to know that?' asks Rah, flicking a suspicious look at Janus. Even so, the cook is a bit dizzied by the glance and takes a moment to respond.

"Should one not wish to know the time and circumstances of one's own death, and thus prepare?"

"How you prepare for death? Time to die, you die. Stupid," murmurs Rah, frowning and looking back to Ting Ya.

"Maybe cook want to make his own funeral feast," smiles Ting Ya, setting the last of her cakes on the baking stone and wiping her hands on her apron. "Maybe he not like way Haffa roast the lamb, hm?" And she winks at Janus.

"Nevertheless, a man who can speak to spirits is a wealthy man where I come from, I can tell you that," says Janus, rising from the bench to fire an oven for the cakes.

"Where come from, Janus?" asks Rah, biting into the peach Ting Ya has just tossed him from a basket by the milk jugs on the floor. He has taken three more bites, all but swallowing the fruit whole, before Janus can answer him.

"I am from the land north of the Black Sea," answers the cook, who has moved around the prep table to bend before an available oven and light it. "I was only twelve summers when I was taken. Learned to cook feeding the armies of the great Hattusilis on their campaign for Troy. That is how the Master found me, many years ago, an army cook, and took me for his own household."

"Wolf, he steal you too, Janus," chuckles Rah. "Wolf he steal people like sheep. Take whatever he want." Rah is licking peach juice from his palm, utterly absorbed in the task, when Janus straightens to give him a scolding look. He is about to tell the boy not to speak of the Master with such disrespect, that they will all suffer for hearing such words, that the walls have ears here in Amega, but he is so struck by the picture of the Grain God, leaning back on his elbow and cleaning his fingers with his tongue, so struck by the electric blue-green twinkle of the boy's gorgeous eyes under those cat-like lashes as he flashes him a glimmer of a grin, that he can only swallow his words and gaze at him.

Rah has popped the peach pit into his mouth now and is sucking on it while fixing the cook with the concentrated stare of a young lion.

"Big thief, this Wolf," he taunts the cook, rolling his eyes to motion to the ceiling, above which the Master's private bedroom chamber lies.

Janus can only gulp. "You mustn't speak-" he begins weakly.

Ting Ya is looking at the stricken cook with a soft smile. She takes the loaded baking stone to the oven and sets it within. When she turns back Rah hops off his bench to round the prep table and put a respectful kiss on her forehead. But his left arm has caught her in an embrace, and as he releases her he tugs her braid twice, hard, then dashes out of the kitchen laughing.

"Bad boy!" cries Ting Ya after him. "Ting Ya is old lady. You play like she is young. You break Ting Ya, who will make you treats, Jin yu?"

But Rah is out of earshot and her words hang in the air like the sweet scent of the ginger in the honey cakes baking in the oven behind her.

In the valley of the Goreme, near the city of Urgup, Rush the Assassin wanders through the eerie landscape of the gods, a plateau within the valley created by volcano thousands of years before the explosion of Thera. Spires of rock rise above his head in rows like the cypress of Rhodes. Caves reach into the earth creating hundreds of channels beneath the surface like wormwood. Strange shelves and dishes, the puff and puddle of cooling molten rock, have created a land whose appearance prompted ancient peoples to name this place the Table of the Gods, and the name has remained to this day. But Rush does not believe in gods, only in survival and conquest. And so he moves through the valley with the cautious determination of a wolf. He is hunting, not beast, but man. And the signs all around him tell him that the man he is hunting is near.

The man he is hunting is Ammuna, the brother of the murdered prince of Hatti. All around him is the evidence left by an Amorite army, an unchallenged army, moving fast toward Hattusha. Rush knows that the newly installed king, Mursilis, is preparing to wage war on the Amorites in Syria, and that this army has been commissioned to attack the King by a lesser man. He knows, too, that it is Ammuna, and not his elder brother, who has the courage to do such a thing, for during the last years of the Great Hattusilis' reign, Rush was very much a party to the politics within the house of Hattusilis.

And so Rush follows the obvious signs of a fast moving army to the foothills of Urgup, and, seeing at dusk what he expects to see from his perch in the hills, a great encampment of men, the tent of a Hittite nobleman west of center, he beds down for the night and waits. When the time is right, he will make his way, like a great black wolf, down the hillside. He will enter the camp, darker than the dark, and take down guard after guard in silence until he stands over the sleeping prince. And then he will take the man, and the army he has prepared against his king, with one blow.

In the encampment of Agrippa and his men, Aleksandus is unable to sleep. It is not the wine he drank before he took to his leather, nor the rocky ground beneath his back. He is an old soldier and is more comfortable in the field than in his own bed at home in Amega. Nor is it the fact that their leader has taken to the hills, a lone wolf abandoning its pack to hunt in solitude. He is neither concerned for Rush's safety nor that of the men who sleep around him. But this mission, to bring the three-horse into what has become enemy territory, is tearing at his breast like a jackal.

Aleksandus has considered waking his cousin, Agrippa, and discussing the sanity of this operation. But what good would it do? To question the plans of the Master is treason and, even if his cousin will not take his head for the crime, he will not change his plans to march into Hattusha disguised as Rush himself while the man he pretends to be attempts to tame the beast that is the insurgence of Ammuna and join him with the thing on a leash.

Aleksandus tosses on his leather, from left to right and back to left. He can hear the horses stomping in the dust outside his tent, as if they, too, understand the implications of this mission. For just as everything can be gained if Rush succeeds, so everything might be lost if he does not. Had I a god to believe in, thinks the old warrior, feeling tired for the first time this evening. And in the hands of his own heartbeat, he drifts off to sleep at last.

CHAPTER 11

In the camp of Ammuna the two surviving treasonous sons of Hattusilis are preparing an ambush against the armies of Mursilis. Their spies have informed them that their nephew has mustered twenty thousand men. All signs suggest that he is awaiting the arrival of the Terror himself, who is moving across the Valley of the Gods toward Hattusha with a small contingent of men and a strange new wheeled weapon covered under a cloth. Ammuna and his brother have spent the last twenty four hours arguing whether it would not be advantageous to ambush Rush first, preventing his new weapon from entering Hattusha where it will be better defended inside a walled city by an army twice the size of their own. But they have been unable to come to an agreement. Now, lying beside his murdered brother's lover, Sophina, Ammuna considers his situation. It was he who argued to ambush Rush in the valley. Ten thousand against a few score was hardly a fight. And yet his brother's warning still buzzes in his head like a swarm of hornets.

"Are you brave enough to face the Assassin, Ammuna? For face him you must, if you are to maintain the loyalty of this army. Half of them are Amorites, paid mercenaries. The other half believe I, and not you, am the rightful king because I sprang from the loins of Hattusilis and entered this world seven minutes before you did. But I do not desire the throne. Would you then send an army to capture Rush and not face him yourself? Will those who believe you deserve to be king still believe? Or will they think that a cowardly third born prince leads them. Nay, leave Rush in the valley. Attack Hattusha in the morning, before the dawn."

Attack the Hatti capital? was Ammuna's response. What *then* of the loyalty of the Hatti men he leads? Did he have the leadership, the charisma, to convince a Hittite army to attack its own capital?

Ammuna tosses in his bed beside his dead brother's lover, the woman Sophina. You are to blame for this, he thinks. If my brother had not deserted his wife to have her niece, Hattusilis would not have disowned him. Then he would yet be alive and I would not be lying here in this godforsaken tent amongst men I can scarcely lead with fear of penalty for desertion, let alone with loyalty.

The woman snorts once in her sleep, then rolls into him. Truly a beautiful body, thinks Ammuna. But even in sleep your face is hard with want, woman. Of what do you dream? Who is it you desire to conquer? For it is surely your desire to conquer men that has brought you to my bed.

Aroused by his own desire for domination, Ammuna reaches for the woman, slipping an arm around her tiny waist and drawing her close. Then, as she awakens, he takes her roughly, heedlessly. It is not a merging, but a struggle, as with a thing to be kept and held at bay.

And Sophina groans, with satisfaction if not pleasure, for by this allegiance she will surely become the next Queen of Hatti.

In the morning, before dawn, two hundred mercenary Amorite foot soldiers and a score of chariots, surround the camp of Agrippa. They descend on the sleeping troop like eagles, setting fire to the tents and releasing the horses. But when they searched the debris they find no sign of human remains. The strange, wheeled weapon is also not in evidence. By noon they have investigated the surrounding hillsides and have given up finding Rush and his band of men, who cannot outrun them without their mounts. It is assumed that Rush and his men somehow anticipated the ambush and retreated back across the Valley of the Gods to hide in the caves. The decision is made to follow them into the valley, surround them, and allow their supplies to run out. Then, when they are weakened by hunger and thirst, they will capture them, killing all but their leader, and return him to the camp of Ammuna.

It was Ammuna's idea to send Amorites, a practical choice, since there is not a Hittite alive who would attempt to ambush Rush, let alone capture him.

While Ammuna's hirelings storm on toward the Valley of the Gods, making as much noise as possible in order to encourage Rush's retreat into that dry and barren region, Agrippa and Aleksandus set up their own ambush in the caves. They are more than familiar with the territory and could easily find sustenance there, but they will have no need of it. From their hiding places they will cut down Ammuna's men like so much barley. Then they will take their animals, their chariots, their weapons and their supplies and, following the signs Rush will have left them, continue on toward the camp of Ammuna.

In the evening of the same day, Rush arises from his den on the hillside and dons his assassin's uniform. He has watched the party of a hundred men and twenty chariots leave camp before dawn and head toward his own men. This much was planned and expected, and he suspects that by now Agrippa and Aleksandus will have slaughtered the half of them and taken the others prisoner, to be indoctrinated into his own killing machine. With no true loyalty save that to their purses, those men will be easy enough to coerce to join him.

It is a black night, the quarter moon and stars hidden by a thick sweep of broiling storm clouds, and it is easy enough for the Terror of the Aegean to enter the camp. He moves without sound, detecting the strategic placement of the first ring of sentries as if he set them to their posts himself. He pierces the throat of the watch on the western side of camp, encountering no further guard until he has found the tent of Ammuna. He moves around the back of the tent, taking down the guards one at a time in perfect silence, his crescent blades all but severing their heads before they can take a breath to shout. Then he steals forward toward the front of the tent to dispatch the two sentinels at the flap like a wolf bringing down pigeons in the snow, silent but for the thump of their bodies in the dirt.

"Sophina? Is that you?"

The man's voice is reedy, uncertain. It is not the voice of a king, not the voice of a man who can lead troops into battle. Rush is quick to put his hand over the man's mouth nevertheless. But he has made one error, one oversight. He did not expect that there should be a woman in the bed also. As he feels her body roll against his thigh, for he now straddles the prince, he flinches, as if a snake has slithered against him. Then, comprehending, he takes her throat with his free hand and pins her to the bed.

"Damn," he snarls.

"Rush!" comes the excited hiss from the woman, although her throat is a slender branch he might break in his fingers.

"Free me, Rush, I will not betray you!" she whispers, for without meaning to he is nonetheless squeezing off the last of her air.

"Damned woman," mutters Rush then, for it was not his intention to kill the prince, but with both hands engaged, one of these two must die else he himself be discovered, and his unnecessary murder of the woman Sophina would hardly advance the proposal he is about to offer Ammuna's army.

With callous apathy he takes his hand off Ammuna's face and returns it with a blow to the man's temple before the prince can restore the air in his lungs and shout for his guard, who are at any rate slumped in a neat line around the perimeter of his tent.

Sophina flinches from the blow that skates past her face with such speed and force as to create a draft and puff her hair out over the pillow.

She brings her hands up to her throat to tug at the impossible weight there. Finding that effort fruitless, she slides her palms slowly up the assassin's arm, then down the front of his tunic and beneath it with viper-like patience. It is his turn to flinch, for she has put her warm palms against his midsection, and has found with disconcerting feminine courage, his naked humanity.

Without thinking he eases off her throat, blinking behind the assassin's mask with momentary bewilderment.

"Free me, Rush," whispers Sophina, rising now beneath the lessening weight of his hand. One of her hands remains under his tunic, moving now with delicious boldness over his abdomen as if admiring the muscle there, then slinking toward his chest to press long fingers through the star of hair. Still he cannot think. Distracted, he allows her other hand to slip over his. She pushes it, from her throat down onto her breast. Her nipple is high and tight and tickles his palm. "Take what kings will give kingdoms for. Beautiful thief, take me. You know that I want you."

Her hips have risen to press her naked pubis against his thigh.

"Damned woman," growls Rush, but he has lost his senses. He shoves the unconscious prince off the side of the mattress, frees himself, and attacks Sophina with the hunger of his unquenched curiosity pounding in his veins.

In the early hours of the next morning, the trussed and naked prince will be found by the third guard tied upside down to one of the posts at the front of his own tent. But for the most of the night, he will hear his lover's moans and squeals from within his tent, where he lies bound and gagged on the floor at the foot of his own bed.

"You must enter by the front gate," says Aleksandus to his cousin Agrippa two days later. It is a clear morning, and the contingent of near a hundred men have crossed the Valley of the Gods at last and come to the foothills of Urgup. He has brought his horse up short, causing the band of men behind him to do the same. Sighing, he looks to his cousin, who cuts quite a figure in the garb of the General himself astride a nervous black stallion. He knows that spies from the armies of Ammuna will surely have observed their progress, that is, if Ammuna is still leading the camp, which is unlikely. On the other hand if Rush is in charge twice as many spies, Hittites who know the country, will be crawling over the area like worker ants, as if their lives depend upon the security of the region, which they of course do. So attempting to approach the camp of ten thousand with less than a hundred by any other means than the front gate is pointless.

"Ammuna is guarding the Master's latrine, cousin," he continues, "and his worthless brother is doing his laundry. There is naught but allies amongst the throng we approach. The Hittite men are learning to fight like men, and the Amorites are learning to love the Hittite legend who now commands them. Let us not waste the Master's time, else we will be made an example of. He does not tire of example making."

With a wry smile, Agrippa, turns to his cousin. "Very well, Aleksandus," he answers, then turns about in his saddle to signal the men to follow him around to the right toward the front gate of the camp.

But Aleksandus has put his hand out to catch his arm. "Do you intend to approach in the garb of a Hittite general, Agrippa? The Master has surely not bothered to inform them that he disguised you as himself, and someone may think it impertinent and look for a reward by cutting you down with an arrow before you are able to explain yourself."

With a brittle smirk, Agrippa unstraps and hands his breastplate and helmet to a foot soldier, then raises his hand again to signal his men to follow him into the jaws of the Army of Ammuna.

In camp, Rush is reclining at table with Ammuna's generals when the news that his men are at the front gate reaches him.

"Take their horses from them and provide for them. Pitch tents alongside my own for the men from Amega, for they will lead their company into Hattusha. You, in turn," he nods to the men at table with him, "will lead your Hatti troops back into the city, leaving the Amorites here in camp. Remember that you are my army now, and though I will leave you with Mursilis, you will remain mine. And when I return, we will return to finish these Amorite weasels and march into Syria."

"And what of the woman, Sophina," says the man to his left. Though a Hittite, one of five generals who deserted Mursilis to back the younger twin of King Hattusilis, and well versed in the legends of the Terror, he has been making his displeasure with the assassin's liaison with Sophina known, if cautiously, since Rush's unscheduled arrival.

"She is already dispatched to Amega," responds Rush, eyeing the man with a glimmer of curiosity. "With a letter explaining her station."

"And just what *is* her station?" counters the general, causing the other four to take in their breath at his daring.

Now Rush is smiling, not a comforting thing. He takes his time in answering, removing his gold and silver handled dagger from his ankle holster and testing the blade with his thumb.

The impertinent general's eyes have widened at the sight of the famous blade as he awaits the answer.

"A good question, Darius," says Rush finally, his baritone rumble fairly shaking the cups on the table. "She has been quite a problem here in Hatti, has she not? And will no doubt continue to be one. A problem to the royalty, and to the loyal. And you are a loyal man, stupid perhaps, but loyal.

You are mine now, and you do not wish to see the Terror of the Aegean's command compromised by a good fuck."

"Sir," says the man then, bowing his head in submission. "I did not mean," he begins.

"Lie to me, General, and I will eat your raw tongue while you watch," responds Rush, his smile fading.

"I meant as you say, Sir," says the General, correcting himself.

"Let it be known among you," says Rush, returning his dagger in its holster and looking over his new generals with uncompromising authority, "that the whore, Sophina, is no longer an issue in the land of the Hatti. She is in the possession of the Terror of the Aegean now. From here forth, any man, be he lord, prince or be he king, who lets a woman overcome his senses and compromise his nation, will be personally executed by me. Then, with his disembodied limbs will I beat that bitch to the point of death before I assign her the lowest station in the barracks brothel of Amega."

Looking about at his new generals, Rush raises an eyebrow, as if offering anyone of differing opinion to speak.

"They wear them out quickly there," he adds, "and one as fine as Sophina will not last long."

Four days later, while Agrippa and Aleksandus lead the once renegade generals of Ammuna into Hattusha, Rush the Assassin is roaming the streets of the city gathering information. He has learned the Queen mother is residing in the palace, in the wing opposite the King's. He has learned, too, that Mursilis has gathered the five armies of his grandfather in the valley and has ordered the whole of Hatti to pay one tenth of their stores of barley, oil, raisins and figs, and one tenth of their flocks of goat and sheep, to provide for the camp, which consists of twenty thousand men, six thousand horses and twenty four hundred chariots.

Much of this information is not new to him. Mursilis himself had sent him word of his desire to take the Euphrates, and indicated to him that he was gathering his grandfather's armies at Hattusha. But the words of a newly ensconced, and clearly ambitious, young king meant little to Rush. Nor would he leave the task of sniffing out the truth to spies. Ever a lone wolf, Rush has taken the guise of a sandal merchant from neighboring Alaca, peddling his wares from the back of a donkey. From the servant entrance to the palace he has learned that Mursilis has taken his grandfather's suite of rooms, as is to be expected. Young fool, thinks Rush that evening, having himself taken a room at an inn near the gates of the city. Your uncle was just assassinated, you have made a deal with the devil, and yet you take not the slightest precaution against your own murder. You have much to learn, Mursilis. Alas your grandfather taught you little of politics, though you have inherited his drive to conquer. We will see what use you can be to me.

When the third guard is changing with the second that evening, Rush slips into the palace. He does not use the main portico, nor does he attempt to breach the servant's entry, nor the supply portals. He knows the place, having visited it on many previous occasions, both as the man, and as the mask. Tonight he descends into the cellars from a little known doorway, which until his own recent need for it, had been bolted from the inside and forgotten. It was he who unbolted it from within on his last visit to Hattusha, and now it is his private key to the palace.

Within twenty minutes of his breach of the palace Rush is entertaining Mursilis with the end of his dagger.

"It would be a simple thing for me to make a fool of the new king of Hatti," he murmurs, with the rumble of a bear, into the young royal's ear. "I need only carve the Tear into your cheek, just here," and he sets the point against the youth's left cheekbone. "Then you are the Assassin's whore, and all know why you carry his mark."

"W-what is it you wish, Rush? I have given you information that has secured you ten thousand fighting men, and I have offered you to join me in Syria. I have offered you my friendship and my faith. How can it be that we are now enemies?" says the King, heaving for air beneath the weight of the monstrous forearm on his chest.

"I wish for us to understand one another, pup," responds Rush, sliding the flat of the dagger across the King's face like a barber with a razor, "for you are barely more than a youth, without a full beard, a whelp," continues Rush, brushing the flat of his thumb across the King's chin. "Tell me, who else could your information have been of any value to? Save me, save the one man who could de-ball the cowardly git who led them, and put them on a leash in a single morning?"

"N-no one," responds the weakening King. "No one could."

"And what is the friendship and faith of a whelp to the Wolf of Hatti, hmm?" Rush has taken the king's chin in his hand and now gives it a little shake, a tremendous insult, had the two been on their feet, but such as it is, all the King can think of now is whether or not he will black out for lack of air before this one-sided conversation has ended itself.

Suddenly the anaconda that has been squeezing his chest is gone. In the pitch dark, the King can see nothing, save the glint of the legendary crescent palm blades dancing over his head like a pair of silver butterflies.

"Aaugh!" he chokes, ducking under his covers.

There is only an explosive hiss in answer, and it takes him a moment to recover what dignity he has left and to realize Rush is laughing the silent laugh of an assassin. He pulls the sheet off his head and looks up to find that the butterflies are gone, but in their place is the head of a mummy wrapped in black death clothes, and it is nose to nose with him.

"Aaugh!" he chokes again, but there is no time to duck back under the covers. His open mouth is met with a circle of rags, and then the insistent lips and tongue of an amorous assassin.

The kiss lasts long enough to leave him winded.

Then the mouth is gone, replaced by a bear-sized palm.

"Now we are lovers, you and I, Mursilis, in bed together until you displease me. And this I do for love of your grandfather more than you. For he asked me to make a man of you, and so I shall. Tomorrow I shall enter the city in public, riding a black stallion and accompanied by the five generals of Ammuna, my own contingent from Amega, and a new weapon, which I will display for you as soon as you can find three chariot teams brave enough to challenge it. For this will be a live demonstration, no props, but real blades, real arrows and real javelins."

"As you say," stutters the King, nodding furiously.

"Then you will provide me with one hundred of your best chariot makers, and with provisions for my return to Amega with the prototype. My army of ten thousand you will provide for while my own men train them. And in the spring, when kings go to war, you and I will meet at the plateau of Amega and join forces. I will meet you with an arsenal of these new weapons, and with men trained to use them in battle. And you and I will pierce Syria and take the Euphrates. But first you will show me what kind of king you will make for Hattusha and if you are worthy of your grandfather's throne. For with me tomorrow I bring you a gift, one I would much prefer to open myself."

"What is that, Lord?" asks the confused king.

"The head of Ammuna, still attached and functioning," answers Rush casually.

"And what would you have me do to my uncle, Sir, but imprison him? Can I behead my own flesh?" responds the horrified king, for it is a capital offense for anyone, even a king, to kill a member of the royal family, and yet it is vividly clear to him that Rush intends more for the traitor than mere imprisonment.

"I leave that decision to you," says Rush, smiling behind his mask. "For now. Take care how you make it, little king." He gives Mursilis a fatherly chuck under the chin.

"You ask of me the impossible," moans the King as Rush withdraws his weight from the bed.

But the assassin is already gone, and the King finds himself somehow both relieved and saddened that his childhood hero has come and gone without his ever discovering his face.

"But I will see him tomorrow," says the King aloud to the dark. "Tomorrow he will enter the city atop a black horse, and then I will know the face of the assassin at last."

The following day, at the height of noon, Rush watches from the roof of the inn as Agrippa enters the city astride a black stallion. The prototype follows, still under covers, and is surrounded by his own men from Amega as well as the five generals of Ammuna's ten thousand. This is both prudent and strategic. For in a sense, though they enter Hattusha appearing to be allies of Amega, thus impressing the populace with the might of Rush's following, the generals have in fact been kidnapped. Further, back in the camp of Ammuna, the Amorites mercenaries are lost without their generals, and the Hittite insurgents have been warned to obey Aleksandus and his officers lest their leaders be returned to them headless.

Keret, Lysias and Pelet ride alongside the prototype on their own mounts, dressed in the colors of Amega. They will demonstrate the three-man against three teams in two-man Hatti chariots in the city center, a field just north of the palace designed for celebration and military ceremony. Agrippa will play the part of Rush as long as he is in Hattusha, thus, Rush will retain his anonymity. Agrippa will remain behind with the troops of Ammuna, training them with his own officers to fight not like men but like lions. Then, in the spring, he will take them, along with Mursilis' twenty thousand, to the plateau of Amega to meet up with the assassin's elite fighting troops and newly trained charioteers, who will spearhead their campaign into Syria.

Rush watches the demonstration from the rooftop. It will be a bloody battle, wildly prejudiced against his own men, not only because there are three against one, but because, although the prototype carries a third man, it is nevertheless built for speed also. It is lightweight and maneuverable, but it can be pierced or wrecked more easily than the heavier Hatti chariot. Thanks to Rah, who scoffed at the iron dressings on the Hatti two-man and insisted that anything that could be made of lighter material be made so. My little cat, thinks Rush absently, reminded again of the boy's fantastic and inherent physical lightness and balance. It is like you, is it not? You have made yourself into a chariot, into a war machine for your wolf. Light, balanced, yet strong. Utterly unpredictable. And Keret and his team have had weeks to practice. They will not fail me. *You* will not fail me, little cat. I have put my faith in you.

Out on the demonstration field the Hatti charioteers have lined up to face Keret's team. These are men, not boys, for the Hatti way is strength not speed. But speed and agility will mean something in a moment. They are about to get an education, thinks Rush, and he leans back against the wall of the guard booth atop the inn roof, his long peddler's tunic blending into the white wall, his hood pulled over his black hair.

And the battle horn sounds.

All four chariots take off toward the center. But Keret's team bolts into action faster. The three boys have not compromised the speed of the vehicle, and their combined weight is little more than that of two strong Hatti warriors in full armor. Keret's team wears helmet and breastplate only. Pelet's arrow is already against his bow and Lysias' javelin is lifted. The lightweight vehicle is stable, the position of the axel giving the boy's the advantage of superior balance in flight. The Hatti teams have yet to reach the quarter line when Pelet lets fly his first arrow, taking the center charioteer in the throat with deadly accuracy.

With no driver, the horses veer away from the oncoming fury that is the three-man, throwing the archer out of the bucket. Lysias launches his javelin, cutting down the archer in the chariot to the left just as the center chariot, driverless, dives pell-mell into the chariot on the right. Wheels collide and lock, creating chaos for the driver on the right and his bowman. Pelet launches another arrow, this one putting out the driver's eye. The man lets go his rein and grabs at the shaft, which is lodged in his eye socket.

Two Hatti chariots are disabled, the third is naught more than a man and a team of horses. Keret has won, but the demonstration is not over. Agrippa's son turns the team with remarkable precision and agility and launches an attack on the last manned chariot. The heavy Hatti vehicle cannot outrace him and he is soon close enough for Lysias to put his lance in the man's back.

The crowd of onlookers are momentarily silent. Then, with a raised arm, the King, who has been watching the demonstration from the parapet of his palace, signals his approval. The crowd cheers. Keret is making his victory lap, the two surviving enemy archers on their knees in a position of surrender in the center of the demonstration field. Agrippa has come forward, on horseback, along with the five generals of Ammuna. The crowd, believing Agrippa to be Rush, goes wild, but is silenced and brought to its knees when the King raises both arms over his head, then lowers them to rest on the parapet wall.

"Behold the gift of the Wolf of the Aegean to the new and rightful king of the Hatti! A gift of war against the enemies of the Hatti people, and the greater gift of his allegiance!"

Now the crowd is on its feet again, roaring. Soon enough, the demonstration field will be filled with revelers. There will be food and dancing, and a great deal of Hatti mead. Young Keret Agrippa will be the darling of the people of Hattusha, and will get an education about Hattushan women. I must bring my sons to the city soon, thinks Rush. They are old enough.

With the silent ease of a bird of prey Rush descends from his perch on the roof. Over the back wall, across a garden, into the empty stable where travelers' transport animals are cared for while their masters visit the city, he moves without notice, for once, during daylight hours. Everyone is at the demonstration. Even the servants and slaves have left their posts to lay eyes on the legend, the legend that is stealing a fine colt from the inn, probably a nobleman's, with which to travel swiftly back to Amega.

Rush removes the sack of provisions he has stashed within the grain bin and drops it in a corner of the colt's stall. Quickly he tacks up the animal, which snorts and paws with indignant annoyance at the huge stranger's quick, domineering manner.

"I've no time to coddle a spoilt colt," murmurs the assassin, having fitted the bridle over the animals head and adjusted the bit to his liking. "You will carry me swiftly and safely today, else you will be my meal this evening." Absently his eyes roam over the animal's flank and buttock.

The colt has settled at these words. It seems to look at him with a mixture of alarm and respect.

"I see we understand one another," smiles Rush, staring into the colt's eye. He pauses a moment for emphasis, then leads the animal out the back of the stable and mounts with only a minor disagreement from the colt. Then the two trot unnoticed through the city gate and southward toward Amega.

CHAPTER 12

Less than a fortnight later Sophina of Hattusha arrives at the gates of Amega atop a tall, mustard-colored ass. In the hands of the soldier on her right is the sealed letter of the Assassin. She knows its contents, having been well instructed of the fate designed for her by the Wolf of the Aegean on the morning he handed her over to his own two men, two horsemen from the troop who overtook Ammuna's hundred in the Valley of the Gods. But she is not discouraged. On the contrary, Sophina holds her shapely bosom high this morning, though she is filthy from many days of travel. For within her womb the seed of her victory has taken root. She has missed her menses, and it is not the long, brutal ride on the ass over rough country that has caused this. For she is familiar with pregnancy, though not with birth. An unwanted child, aborted by a witch in Alessa in its fifth month is her educator. That time, only days after missing her menses, she began experiencing the most awful nausea, as if a snake had lodged itself in her gut. It was a boy, the child of a relative of the king, a nobleman, whose birth would have ended her chances forever of securing the Queenship.

But this child, this is a gift. This child, male or female, will save her from the fate that the assassin intended for her. This child, if male, could very well secure her the man she wants more than any other. The Assassin.

At the draw gate of the fortress of Amega the man to her right, the man called Peleshet, raises his shield, upon which is painted the eclipsed moon flanked by two crescent shaped blades which is the emblem of the City of the Assassin. Shouting above, and the gate is quickly lowered. Then a heavily-armed guard of a dozen long-haired Hatti warriors march out to swarm the three who wait for permission to enter. They would be terrifying in themselves were she not a Hatti herself, but what she is not prepared for, what does skate a nervous finger down her spine, is the tattoo of the Tears which each and every one of them wears under his left eye. Sophina swallows, momentarily unconvinced of her pregnancy. The thought flies through her mind that if she is not pregnant, or if her pregnancy is not believed to be that of the assassin, she will be consigned to the barracks brothel. And though she is no virgin, and came to the attention of the manicured nobility of Hattusha early in her life, the men she is accustomed to servicing are bureaucrats. These, these are wolves. I am out of my depth, she thinks, and then, just as swiftly, I am surely carrying their leader's child. They will not dare to touch me.

Peleshet has dismounted to hand the sealed letter to a man who is, by the look of him, slim and quick, a fortress runner.

"Bring it immediately to the Lieutenant General," he says, then turns to lift her off the ass. By the time her feet have found the ground the animal is being led away.

"Wait!" she cries, "My things!" For the sack of her personal items have been tied to the back of the animal's saddle.

"Leave them with me," says Peleshet with some authority, and a man quickly unties the bundle and tosses it to him. He lifts it to his shoulder and turns to follow the others across the gate. When the company has crossed over it into the fortress, the thing is drawn back up on huge pulleys to close with a deafening bang.

Sophina follows Peleshet in silence, the other man who accompanied her to Amega having disappeared amongst the guardsmen at the gate.

Presently he steps back, ushering her into a room on their right. It is sparsely furnished, but there is a large desk at the center with an iron chair behind. On the walls hang rows of Amegan shields and breastplates.

Peleshet tosses the sack at Sophina's feet.

"Will you leave me, then?" she says, attempting not to whimper. He has been unreadable throughout their journey, but he is at least familiar.

"I have no say in the matter," responds her guard enigmatically. No sooner has he said it than a tall, striking man in the dress of a high ranking soldier strides into the room. His grey eyes looking her over with suspicious curiosity, he settles himself behind the desk, planting his forearms before him.

"It is the Master's orders that you are to be taken to the barracks brothel, madam," says the man with the piercing eyes. "To serve his army," he adds.

Is that a squint of discomfort with my fate I see cross that handsome brow? thinks Sophina, instantly hoping for an alliance.

"Sir," says Sophina, smoothing the front of her traveling smock with a diminutive hand. It is a common habit of hers, for it accentuates her high and generous bust while calling attention to her tiny waist. "I have been on the back of an ass for nearly two weeks. Since then I have discovered that I..." and here she hesitates for effect.

"You-?" responds Nikolaos.

"I believe I am with child, Sir," says Sophina, dropping her eyes modestly.

Silence. She peeks at the man behind the desk. He is giving her the look of a man who has found a snake under his bed but has nothing with which to hack its head off.

"His child, Sir," she says, looking directly and daringly into those stabbing grey eyes.

"His? What nonsense," barks the Lieutenant impatiently, and then slams his fists on the desk and jumps to his feet, "What are you saying, woman?"

Now Sophina glances shyly at Peleshet. See here a maiden ashamed to continue her story in the presence of a second man. But the Lieutenant isn't biting for it. He, too, glances at Peleshet, but only to offer him a frown of common annoyance. Very well then, thinks Sophina, and pushes on.

"I was in bed with the prince when he entered his tent, Sir. He struck the prince and trussed him, then took me." There, she has said it. Now decide, handsome, if you will take a risk dishonoring, indeed endangering, the mother of the child of the Terror. You may survive if you postpone my doom, but you will surely lose your head if I am telling the truth, yet you send me to it.

The Lieutenant General has reseated himself in the iron chair behind the cedar desk. He is peering at her with a most calculating look. It pierces her brain like a lamp in the dark. It searches what and where she does not wish to expose. Sophina drops her gaze first, a thing which surprises her. He searches for himself in me. This thought shocks her even more than the first.

"You will be housed with the servants in the Masters quarters," says the Lieutenant General. Her heart leaps. Ahah! I have him! But when she raises her eyes she sees a thing in his face that makes her bones shake. He is not intimidated. He is hiding a wily smile by looking down to consider an unopened scroll on the desk. He fingers the ribbon that holds it in a cylinder while nodding toward the door at Peleshet.

"Take her there now. Advise Ham of her... situation. Put her in the woman's wing."

"Am I to share rooms then with the Master's slaves?" spits Sophina in disbelief.

But the Lieutenant General is finished with her. Peleshet has taken her by the arm, picked up her sack and drawn her firmly, though not unkindly, out the door.

When they are gone, Lieutenant General Nikolaos tosses the scroll, a list of weaponry confiscated from a raid on an Amorite camp two days earlier, across the desk unopened. Then he rises and takes a shorter route toward the Master's suite of rooms, where he expects he will find Josepha at her loom.

Rah is dreaming.

There is a sickness coming. A plague. It came with the enemies of the Wolf, from Syria. No one knows of this sickness, no one but Rah. The Wolf is gone hunting and Rah has searched the compound for the Fox but he cannot find him. He runs down corridor after corridor, looking for someone to tell, but no one pays him any mind. Soldiers walk past him discussing what he knows he should not hear as if he is invisible. Finally he rounds a corner and sees Ting Ya. She is walking toward him but she has no face.

He cries out to her, but his tongue is thick in his mouth and nothing comes out but an awful cawing. The harder he tries to speak, the louder and uglier the caw.

"Must go to city of lights, Jin yu."

The faceless Ting Ya is speaking to him. It is her voice but it does not come from her. It is in his own head. "Must dance for great King."

Then the thing that is Ting Ya begins to wane, like a candle drowning in its wax. Only her robe remains. It keeps her shape briefly, then flutters to the ground in a heap.

Rah screams, backing away from the hollow thing that he believed was Ting Ya. His scream is a gruesome "Caw-caw!" He flings his arms out to his sides and lo, discovers that he has opened a pair of huge and black wings. Now the fortress opens above his head. He sees the sky and his heart leaps with desire to escape this place. With one powerful thrust of his wings he launches himself high into the air over Amega. Dazzled by his own strength and speed, he lifts himself into the clouds.

Up over the mountains he soars, north and west toward Janus' Black Sea. But instead of a sea, he comes to a strange, pitted landscape of pillowing rock and spires. The place is desolate and dry. Rah struggles to grab the air under his wings and push himself upward and away from the haunted landscape but something is pushing him down. He is losing his ability to fly.

This is the Table of the Gods, says the thundering Voice. Here you will rest. Do not be afraid. I am with you.

"I will die here!" cries Rah in his native tongue, but he is descending into a barren and frozen hell. Down, down, down to the earth he falls, tumbling through the air like a feather loosed from a bird's wing.

"You cannot die," says The Voice, so clear he can hear it in his very soul. "For I am with you. And I am Rah."

Sophina is unpacking her collection of foolish choices when Josepha enters her chamber. The room is little more than a cell, windowless but for a thin slit in one exterior wall that she can barely peek through on tip-toe. It is adjacent to a larger room, a kind of dormitory for the female servants with rows of beds and trunks for personal items at the foot of each. Turning from her array of fine dresses, now stained and wrinkled with travel, she sees at the doorway of her chamber a woman in a servant's shift, small and plump, with doe-brown hair and eyes, and the bearing of a queen. Thinking herself in the presence of a difficult peer (for though not amongst the ladies of the brothel as expected, she has nevertheless been consigned the station of a servant) she raises herself to her full height to challenge the impertinent commoner. With haughty authority, she steps away from the bed and raises an open hand at the mess of clothing upon it.

"These must be washed with care and stretched. I have nothing but these filthy traveling clothes to wear until they are, and when the Master returns, as he no doubt will shortly, he will wish to see me immediately, for I bear him a child."

"Of course," says the woman in the doorway. "And this is no way for the Master's child to be introduced to his father's estate. You will come with me, Sophina, and I will put you in a guest room beside the courtyard. There you will have your own bath, and a servant's room beside to use as a nursery."

She has been smiling a strangely warm, even maternal smile as she speaks, and now opens her arms and steps forward to embrace and kiss the smugly satisfied yet slightly off- balanced Sophina.

"And who are you, then, who has been given the authority to be making these arrangements for me?" asks Sophina, stiffening at the woman's touch, which seems to draw her secrets to the surface of her mind and skin.

"I am the lady of the house, Sophina," answers Josepha with easy grace, and a peculiar new knowing in her eyes. "I am your mistress."

In the lyceum that afternoon, Rah and his troupe are practicing the Dance of the Rainbow God. It is a new scene, a clever story Dimius has created as a vehicle in which to introduce Pyrus' most daring paint yet. For it is not just Rah's face that is painted in this scene, it is his entire body. From the top of his hairline to the tip of his toes he is a rainbow of stripes, strategically widened at the shoulder and thighs, cleverly narrowed at the waist and calves, thus exaggerating Rah's still-boyishly lean form to portray a future hero, a promise of the Rah to come.

"You have made him the man he will be," comments Tyrus, who was passing the western archway when he noticed the troupe crowding around something in the center of the lyceum and chattering excitedly like a flock of birds.

Not to be outdone by paint, Aros has designed a costume for the scene: floor length strips of curling silks attached expertly to Rah's golden collar, wristlets and belt, so that each strip is an extension of the color beneath it.

"Fantastic," nods Enenoch beside Tyrus, his hands unconsciously clutched together at his breast in an attitude of prayer. "He is sunrise and rainbow in one sky."

"Look Tyrus," says Rah, lifting his arms above his head and then sending himself into a graceful spin back and away from the group that crowds him. In motion, the costume appears to explode outward in all directions from his form.

"Now Rah dance for King," he says with certainty.

"What king is this, Rah?" asks Tyrus, giving Enenoch a concerned look. "Has anyone promised you an audience with a king?"

"This king of all Hatti," says Rah, still twirling in and out of his group of dancers as the girls giggle at his antics and the men step back with dramatic bows to make way for him. "Wolf, he is go to great city, go to palace! He go in dark, he take this king. 'You are *mine*!' he say. King he is for Wolf now. Young king. No wife. Rah dance for this king. This king, this city, is for Wolf now. We go, dance for king. Dance for people of Hatti. Then people of Hatti is love Rah. King is love Rah, and Rah is give people of Hatti good crop, good fight, too, in battle. Win everything. This what Rah do. This how is suppose to be."

"He is making it up," says Enenoch with a wistful shake of his head. "He is dreaming of the Palace of Knossos, this is all."

"No!" cries Rah, who has made his way like a dervish to the dais and now leaps upon it. He spreads his arms, and the silk streamers attached to his wristlets flutter and shimmer like rainbow waterfalls. "Rah must dance for king! When Wolf come back, we dance for Wolf. Wolf like. Then he bring Rah to king!"

At that moment a movement under the archway attracts Rah's attention. It is a woman in a lady's dress, her bosom all but toppling from the low neckline, her sharp black eyes fixed on him. Startled, he jumps from the dais into the crowd of dancers and so, out of her sight.

"Who this is?" he murmurs to Dimius. "This bad woman."

"I believe she is the Master's new concubine," responds Dimius, who has heard it from a servant in the Master's wing that a haughty noblewoman from Hattusha is now staying in one of the guest rooms in the Master's quarters and claims she is pregnant with his child.

"Wolf, he take this woman concubine?" says Rah, looking at Dimius with distress. "Why she is dress for lady. This no lady. Josepha lady."

"It is Lady Josepha who has asked that we treat her with the respect one would give a lady," responds Dimius, looking to Tyrus, for his position as High Priest of the Bull gives him authority to greet the 'lady' first.

Tyrus has put a heavy hand on Dimius' narrow shoulder to draw him close. "Then so we shall," he whispers with a wink, and moves out of the crowd to approach the intruder.

"Greetings, Madam," booms Tyrus when he has extracted himself from the assembly of dancers beneath the dais. "I am Tyrus, Bull Priest. And this," he nods to Enenoch, who is as ever one step beside and behind him, "Is Enenoch, Sky Priest. Welcome to Amega. May you prosper here, as all do under the protection of the Terror of the Aegean."

Forced to address him as an equal as a result of his eloquent greeting, Sophina steps forward and gives Tyrus a light curtsy. Then she raises her sharp eyes and approaches the group.

"I am Sophina of Hattusha. And I trust by now my standing here in the Master's house has been explained to all who serve him," she counters.

"It has," responds Tyrus with a bit of a glimmer in his eye and a quick sweep of his gaze down the woman's bodice to her belly.

Sophina stiffens at the hidden insult, then attempts to ignore Tyrus and to peek around him.

"And what sort of creature did I spy from across the hall, all painted in colors like a peacock and with a shock of yellow hair like a sun upon its head?" she says, deliberately moving around the Bull Priest and into the crowd so that the dancers must step back and away from her, for her train is long and encrusted with stones and none dare to tread upon it. As the sea of dancers parts, her vision reaches the colorful shore of Rah's body. Transfixed, she allows her gaze to rake him, up and down. Then she steps toward him, her persistent stare directed into his face now, until she is sufficiently close to stop in her tracks and take in her breath.

"Gods," she says, "What is *this*?"

At her daring approach Rah has stepped back, as if to hide in the crowd, an annoyed scowl furrowing his brow. Now he is trapped, surrounded by dancers, his back against the dais. A barely perceptible whir rumbles in his throat.

"This is the Grain God of Knossos," says Tyrus, "This is the Rah."

"Knossos is no more, and yet you say this is the God of Knossos. What, is this a god of tragedy then?" says Sophina, still staring aggressively into Rah's eyes. "Who has brought him here? Or has he dropped from the clouds himself?"

"The Terror himself has brought him here, and us also, myself and three other priestly houses, to worship him," says Tyrus, coming up behind

Sophina to speak into her ear. "Be careful, Sophina of Hattusha," he adds in an even tone, "He is the Master's favorite."

At this, Sophina's head snaps round to regard Tyrus. "Favorite?" she huffs, and she rakes a haughty gaze down Rah's body once more before making a dramatic turn, her train momentarily hobbling her. "I see," says Sophina, lifting her shoulders proudly. "Well, I am the Master's favorite now." And with that she lifts her skirts, shakes out her train, and makes for the hall.

When she is gone the crowd of dancers huddles protectively around Rah, chattering like gulls.

"What sort of nonsense is this?" dares Enenoch at Tyrus' shoulder. "She is a scorpion. How can he have given her favor over the Rah, Tyrus?"

"She is indeed a scorpion, Sky," says Tyrus, pushing aside a few dancers with uncharacteristic force to get at Rah. "A thing to be crushed underfoot, not taken into one's bed." He has reached Rah, who is making every attempt to extract himself from the group of dancers and flee. His flight is impeded by Tyrus, who takes him by the arm, smudging the paint there.

"Would you run off and play with your horses now?" smiles Tyrus, leading Rah out of the group of performers. "Without a care as to the stir you would cause in this costume amongst all of those ferocious Hatti warriors?"

"Let go, Tyrus," says Rah, scowling at the Bull Priest's hand on his arm.

But Tyrus is indifferent to his protests. He draws him away from the crowd and across the lyceum to the western archway.

Out in the hall he pulls Rah aside and puts him against the wall. Rah squirms in his grip, pouting fiercely.

"I go to Hali," he says, refusing to look Tyrus in the eyes. "Leave go, Tyrus."

"Not until I have spoken to you, Rah, and put you at ease," says Tyrus. "You will break your neck in the mood you are in."

As Rah gives up struggling, Tyrus relaxes his grip on the boy's arms.

"Do not allow yourself to be distracted, thus, Rah. This is not the conduct of a fine lady. She has been looking for her rival amongst the concubines, or else in the Lady of the House herself. She has found her opponent is not a woman, but a god. She has nothing with which to compete with you, and she is furious."

"Well put," says Enenoch, who has followed the two out of the lyceum. He nods with assurance at Rah. "You have nothing to fear, Rah. It is *she* who is afraid of *you*, for you are not concubine or wife to unseat, and her feminine wiles cannot usurp your place. She sees an impossible rival. Do not let her defeat you with talk. You are the Master's favorite.

Indeed you hold his heart. This is a scorpion," he spits these words in the direction of Sophina's exit. "She is nothing."

"She is not nothing," corrects Tyrus grimly. "She has managed to become pregnant by the assassin."

At this Rah lifts his head as if struck. His eyes widen at Tyrus. "This woman, she is have Wolf...?" He makes his arms into a cradle and rocks an invisible babe.

"So she says," answers Tyrus, "And so she has told the Lieutenant General, every servant she comes upon, even the Lady Josepha herself."

Subdued, Rah drops his chin. "She is no like Rah. Maybe now Wolf he is no like Rah." He looks up at Tyrus with a sad grin, pointing to his own temple. "Concubine sometime change man. No more dance today, Tyrus. Rah understand. Go to bath." He smears the paint on his chest as if attempting to remove it like clothing and Tyrus must grab his wrists to stop him from smudging the fine silken trailers that fall from his wristlets.

"Aros has worked hard on your costume, Rah. Do not destroy it in an instant," says Tyrus with kindhearted concern.

"No," says Rah, giving him a quick, sheepish look and pulling his hands away from his body. "Aros love Rah. I take off. Then bath, Tyrus." And he has slipped out of the Bull priest's reach and turned to march down the hall toward the stairs to the baths, dutifully holding his arms away from his sides to protect the silks.

"Mischief," mutters Enenoch. "That woman is mischief."

"She has put out his light," responds Tyrus, stroking his beard. "I wonder," he continues thoughtfully after a moment, putting an arm over Enenoch's shoulder and drawing him off toward the kitchens to find Crispo, "What can the Terror of the Aegean do to the snake that has wormed its way into his house? The snake in whose womb his offspring grows? An interesting puzzle, eh, Sky?"

"And one that for once even you, Tyrus, have no answer for," answers Enenoch. "Who knows? Perhaps he will chop off her head and sacrifice the babe to the Storm God."

"I think not," says Tyrus, patting Enenoch on the back. "For there is only room for one god in Amega, now, and that one desires no sacrifice, but only that he be the pleasure of everyone who comes to know him."

CHAPTER 13

On the Table of the Gods the colt, unaccustomed to such a hard and heavy rider, and spooked by the barren and bizarre landscape, the shadows lurching from every spire of rock, the whipping winter wind and the rustle of dried bones left by jackals and birds of carrion, rears full up with such a suddenness that, unable to balance forward again with the weight of the assassin on its back, a weight with no intention of releasing its hold, it topples back and down upon its rider. Then, ridded finally of its kidnapper, it draws itself to its feet and dashes off, back toward the valley, toward the lush greenery of the lowlands, taking saddle and pack with it, and leaving Rush to walk the remainder of the journey home, with no provisions save his blades, which are ever holstered to his sides and ankles.

"We will meet again," mutters Rush, rising stiffly from the hard ground and looking about to see if any of his provisions might have fallen from the horse when he did. But no, there is nothing. Not even a gourd in which to capture water, and this is a hard country and will take several days on foot to traverse.

"And then you will make me a good meal."

Four hours later it is dusk, and he is roasting a rabbit over an open fire at the mouth of a cave. The night is coming, and it is clear and cold. He can count the stars, for there is no moon. His mind wanders, back toward Hattusha, to the demonstration of Rah's three-man chariot, then forward, to Amega, and to what awaits him there.

Are you up to some mischief, little cat? What have you in store for your Wolf, eh? Have you decided that you must dance for kings? Visit the ancients? Die on a mountaintop at the hands of a priest? Or are you content to play with your concubines and your horses. Must I cut your priest's head off when I return or can he behave himself long enough to train you a priestess? And what of the woman, Sophina. Why do I suspect that I am not finished disciplining that bitch-in-heat? Has she lay eyes upon you yet, Rah? What does a Hatti woman, one who has turned the heads of princes, do in the presence of such masculine beauty? Will she tear out her eyes in shame when she sees yours? Will she grind ash into her the tresses she is so proud of when she observes the halo of light that is your golden head? What knee does not yearn to bend at the sight of you? Only that which is too stiff with pride to bend at all.

With no blanket, nor extra clothing to punch into a pillow on this cool winter evening, Rush can only allow himself fragments of sleep, rising every hour to keep a fire going. In the morning he rises before the dawn, finds a pigeon in a snare he has laid, and cooks the meat for breakfast. Then he begins the long walk home.

That same morning, the High Priest Mochlos is in the lyceum with a handful of his priests and the woman, Cara. Over his shoulder, on the south wall, is the abominable bull that Tyrus has had commissioned and hung in honor of the Bull God, the god of war, the Hatti's most beloved deity. The thing is enormous, cast bronze with horns made of gold, and the eyes, rubies. It stands like a great challenger, facing north, in a pose of attack, its furious head down, its front leg lifted as if it is about to paw the ground, its nostrils flared, its ruby eyes sparkling with the heat of battle. It is truly magnificent, Mochlos must admit. Had I artisans like this in Knossos, what a palace I might have lived in, thinks the priest wistfully. But what a silly thought. We had the very best artists in Knossos. But the assassin took the best of the best for himself and brought them here. This man here would have been fried like a turnip now if he hadn't. Alas, Tyrus has a god who lends himself to such renderings. What is the moon? A circle? Hardly inspiring.

And then, out of the corner of his eye, his attention is caught by the golden vision of Rah standing quietly in the western archway. Rah, no longer the pretty boy he made a god last summer, but a handsome youth, a bit taller, a bit more well-formed even than then. He is developing the characteristics of a man, thinks Mochlos, but a man so beautifully formed as to make a maiden weep in shame. Why do I concern myself with this silly bronze bull? Can Rush love a bull, or a bronze? But this, this is a creature to crush cities for. And he is still mine, for it is my magic that protects him from himself with that fabulous crown he wears.

Satisfied, Mochlos gives the ferocious bull a sneer and opens his arms to his own god.

"There is my creation! God of the harvest. Good morning, handsome, you are just in time for your own offering. Will you not join us today and welcome your new priestess to our house with your presence at her first offering ceremony?"

But Rah does not leave the archway. Something is troubling him today, thinks Mochlos. There is mischief about, and it affects him. What has changed? Is it the woman, Sophina? The slippery viper who claims to bear the assassin's seed? In a flash of recognition, Mochlos' eyes widen with understanding. Holding one hand out to Cara to warn her off, he whispers, "A moment, Madam," and approaches Rah with hands folded together at his breast.

"Is there something troubling you, handsome?" he offers sweetly when he reaches him.

Rah is looking at him with a mixture of suspicion, distaste and hope. Then he drops his gaze, takes one of those pretty little panting breaths of his, and says, "When Rah in Knossos, priest he say Rah is must go to City of Dead. Bring gift for dead. Where City of Dead is in Amega, Priest? Rah is must go."

Ah, thinks Mochlos, here is the very mark of my hand in this creation. Yes, that is the rule you must follow now, or risk offending the host god. Very good. And when the assassin returns, here he will see my brush stroke in this wizardry that is Rah. But only if I perpetuate the need.

"Yes, Rah, but the City of the Dead is in Knossos, buried under a foot of ash, no doubt. We cannot go there. Not even the Master of Amega would dare to tread that earth, still hot from the molten breath of Thera, not until all of Crete has cooled. But there is a place of the dead in every city," and here he turns slightly away from the boy and strokes his breast with greedy fingers, "And so Amega must have one. I have not heard of it. You must investigate. You must learn this from the soldiers. Or perhaps Tiko. Yes! Tiko will know. He is a smart boy, isn't he. He will have heard of it. But Rah, you cannot leave the compound without the Master's permission. None of us can, least of all you, whom he loves."

"Wolf is no here," mumbles Rah, before turning on his bare heels to pad down the hall toward the practice arena.

When he is gone, Mochlos wipes his damp palms against his vestments before returning to Cara. He is not half way to his altar when he feels the heat of a pair of jealous eyes upon his back.

"You are the one who made him," she says, accusing. Her voice is dark, sultry, but immodest. It is unknown to him. The woman, Sophina.

"You are quick to find what you are looking for, Madam," returns Mochlos, turning with the grin of a tiger on his lips. "What else do you know about me?"

She crosses the floor with determined steps. She dresses for harlotry, thinks the priest. Her face is painted like the Egyptians. Probably as plain as a mouse under all that theatre paint. He reaches to take her hand, though he is repelled by it instantly. It is the narrow, needle-fingered claw of a bird. With considerable self-discipline, he bends to kiss her knuckles.

"The Master has impeccable taste," he says, delighting in the lie.

She is unsettled by his gracious reception. Looking over his shoulder she finds Cara, and changes gears.

"Who is this?" she asks him.

She speaks to me as if I am a servant, thinks Mochlos. Aggressive little bitch. I will see you put to rights. But to her he answers, lifting a hand to offer her to greet Cara, "This is Cara of Pheistos, former wife of the Lieutenant General, whom I am training to be High Priestess of the House of the Moon. You have not met?"

"We have not," says Sophina, giving Cara a raking glance but no salutation. "Nor do I wish to." She turns her piercing eyes back to him. "I wish to see the Rah," she says suddenly, with as much authority as a king.

Lots of drama from this one, thinks Mochlos, unimpressed. Well, let us give her a bit of what she is looking for, that she may not be too suspicious of our willingness to please her. She knows that she has made an enemy of me by proclaiming herself, and not my creation, the Master's favorite. I must not make this too easy for her.

"But Madam, the Rah is out in the practice fields with the charioteers of Amega. Surely you do not wish to walk out there," he nods to the archway, "into that sea of masculine...zeal. You are liable to... come to harm." Oh the understatement, how he delights in it! It is all he can do to chew the inside of his cheek and keep from laughing out loud.

"I do not intend to," says Sophina, confidently. "I will see him when he returns to the fortress. Send him to me in my chambers."

This elicits an unexpected burst of mirth from Mochlos. He puts his hand on his chest to stop himself and takes a breath. "My word, woman, do you think I can send the living Rah to the chambers of the Master's concubine? Are you so quick to have me parted from my head?"

"Then I will visit him in yours," snaps Sophina. "Though what you think I might do with a girlish youth is beyond my imagination. I am a Hatti woman, priest. And I have known the Wolf of the Aegean. I question you do not know the difference."

"I do not care what you question, girl," snarls Mochlos then, showing his teeth at last. "You think to come here, to that wolf's den, and dominate his pack. But see here, his queen is your mistress. You would do better to take advice from her demeanor, than to attempt to gain control of his heart by being the common, power-hungry bitch that you are. Do you not wonder how such a woman can have gained all the world with a soft voice and a gentle hand?"

"She is a foreigner, and a weakling. She is no match for me. He needs a Hattushan queen, a woman who can appreciate him," responds Sophina dismissively. She turns her shoulder to him and sets to leave.

"You are not fit to make her bed, let alone to lie in it," Mochlos hears himself grumble, surprising himself by his ire at her disrespect for Josepha. Then he notices that a pair of ladies-in-waiting have been listening to this exchange from the archway.

Well, that will get back to the Master, I suspect. But how long have they been eavesdropping I wonder?

Sophina has turned to the archway just in time to see the two women as well. For an instant, she stops in her tracks, her back tightening. Then she lifts her skirt and moves toward them, giving them a fierce look as she exits the lyceum. The two put their heads together, murmuring, before they, too, move off in the direction of the Lady's chamber.

"Where City of Dead is, Tiko?" asks Rah that afternoon in the soldier's mess. Crispo sends his meals there now for if he does not, Rah will forget to eat at all and simply steal bread and cheese from the plates of whomever he sits beside. Today he has not touched the tray sent over from the house kitchen, however. Two unleavened cakes, neatly buttered and topped with freshly made goat's cheese sit forlornly beside an aromatic fish stew, and even his dessert of sauced pears in yogurt does not gain his interest.

"No City of Dead in Amega, Blonde," answers Tiko, who has set to his own meal of roast mutton with enthusiasm. "This is a Cretan tradition, this cleaning of the bones. There is nothing like it here. The dead are burnt on a pyre, the greater the man, the bigger the fire. Now where I come from, our ancestors are honored properly. They are buried alongside one another, father and son, the wives beneath. Then the living can visit and leave gifts, and burn incense, so that the dead might also remember the living and entreat the gods to watch over them and bring them prosperity."

"No City of Dead?" blinks Rah. "How can Rah visit dead, bring sacrifice to dead if no city? God be angry with Rah. This no good. Need find City."

"You are a thick head, Blonde," answers Tiko, rapping his knuckles against Rah's temple. "How many times do I have to tell you, you are the same boy you always were, not a god. Same thick headed Blonde." And he gives Rah his back to turn to the archer sitting beside him. "Good shooting today, Heth. You have a sharp eye and a steady hand. Maybe I teach you some Chinese hand-to-hand, heh?"

But the man sitting on the other side of Rah, a burly youth who works the catapults, lifts his cup to summon for more mead with one fist while punching Rah's arm lightly with the other.

"There is a city of the dead alright," he whispers into Rah's curls as the servant fills his cup. "It's up in the north, about three days travel on foot. But don't expect anyone to mention it. No one but me. They're all superstitious ninnies. Think the place is haunted and evil and all. I been there," he adds, taking a swig of wine.

"You take Rah," says Rah, jumping to his feet and grabbing the man's arm in a vain attempt to draw him up with him. "Rah must bring gift to dead. You take."

"Whoa, little god! It is not my business to escort deities to their appointed rounds!" responds the man, pulling his arm from Rah's grasp. "Besides, no one has given you permission to go anywhere. Far as I can see, you train horses and design war chariots for the Master. That's your business. Not making expeditions to the Valley of the Gods."

But he has raised his voice and all eyes are upon him. A hush has come over the table and all down its length men have turned to hear what is being said.

"No one speaks of the Table of the Gods," says Heth then.

"Didn't say nothing about the Table. Just the valley is all," responds the catapult man.

"If you speak of the dead, you speak of the Table," says another man from across the room.

"They eat the dead there!" blurts a youngster, newly arrived from the village of Amega and still unsure of himself. He has jumped to his feet and now looks about the room excitedly. "They say that there are thousands of bones in those caves, bones of the enemy, bones of slaves, bones of those with no families to offer a proper pyre. They bring them to the Table, and let the gods eat their remains!"

"Wolves is eating them, is all," responds the catapult man. "Jackals, vultures, vermin."

"No!" shouts the youth, now quite full of himself, for he has the full attention of the entire mess hall. "A wolf will not eat what it has not killed or seen killed. A vulture will not venture down a hole to find a meal. The bodies are thrown down into the caves. But men have returned from the Table who have seen those bones lined up, like soldiers, as if they'd been counted and laid out in formation for battle. They say at night, when the moon is full, you can hear them howling their war cry! And woe to any Hittite soldier who is lost in the caves of the Table! For when night falls the enemy's ghosts come back to life looking for vengeance. They take up their mortal bones and regroup in battle formation. But do not expect to die like a man, slain by sword or arrow or javelin. These soldiers have no weapons save the teeth in their skulls. And so they will eat a man alive!"

The mess hall is still. The boy's last words ring against the mud brick walls like bells. For a moment, no one moves nor speaks, no one but Rah, who is looking down at Tiko with determined fury.

"Why you no tell Rah this, China?" he says.

"It is all nonsense, Blonde. A baby's ghost story. The dead of Amega are burned on the outskirts of town, and that is that. What is it to you what the Master does with the corpses of his enemies?"

"Why you call this place 'Table of Gods?'" Rah looks to Heth over Tiko's shoulder.

"When a soldier dies honorably in battle, even an enemy, he becomes a god. That is why it is called the Table of the Gods," responds Heth.

"This place where god eats. Rah must go, bring gift. No gift, god is angry. Bring plague. Maybe too late already," says Rah, more to himself than to the others, and he has turned and left the mess hall to make what it will of his proclamation.

"What is he saying," says Heth at Tiko's shoulder. "What is this about a plague?"

Now the men in the mess are murmuring among themselves, the volume of their private discussions growing louder and louder. Finally, Tiko must rise to his feet and raise his arms at his sides to gain the attention of the disorder that Rah has left him to deal with.

"Enough! That is enough now! You all know that the Rah is…peculiar. It is difficult enough to understand what he is saying when he is making sense!" And at this he gets a few chuckles. "But today he is full of dreams of the glory of Knossos. He is afflicted by sadness for his lost kingdom. Take no notice of it and tomorrow he will be right again. He is as changeable as the weather. He is not an oracle!"

This has settled the men down a bit. There is more murmuring and nodding amongst them, even some more chuckling. But Heth takes Tiko's arm as he sits to finish his mutton.

"What is all this about a plague, teacher," he says under the rumble of the other voices. "This is no trivial thing, to predict a plague. What if there is some truth to what he says? Perhaps we should bring this to the attention of the Lieutenant General."

"And what do you think he will do, archer? Ride out to the Table himself, with the Rah tucked under one arm and a wagon full of gold and silver for the grave robbers to plunder? You are not so level headed as I thought. You are not ready for training for the martial arts." And pushing away from the table, Tiko gives Heth's shoulder a shove and walks off in search of Rah.

But Rah is not out in the Arab's paddock behind the stables talking to Hali as he expected. Nor is he in the lyceum, practicing with his dancers. Very well then, thinks Tiko, he has gone to the baths to seek solace from his concubines. I will not disturb him there. Agitated, he trots off instead to find Ting Ya.

When Sophina finds Rah later that afternoon it is in the guest wing of the fortress. She has just stepped out of her own chamber when Rah rounds the corner of the adjacent corridor, on his way to Ting Ya's room, which is at the end of the hall she occupies. Recalling his reaction to her earlier in the lyceum, she quickly ducks back into her room, fearing she will frighten him away before she has had a chance to put him in his place. When he is just past her door she steps out. Now you are trapped you little rat, she thinks, but her overconfidence is momentarily extinguished when the youth turns at the sound of her door opening, his fantastic eyes as iridescent as the magnificent emerald that winks at her from his forehead.

"I will to speak with you a moment, here in my chamber," says Sophina, lifting her chin and gesturing for him to precede her into her room.

"What is lady want Rah? Rah is no slave, make lady bed," says Rah, scowling and backing away from Sophina's open arms.

"You will do as I say," sneers Sophina, drawing closer now in order to whisper, "Or I shall scream and tell whomever comes to my rescue that you were forcing yourself on me, you little animal." She has advanced to the point that she can poke his chest with the manicured nail of her index finger. Having done so, she is momentarily diverted from her attack by the jewelry piercing Rah's chest, the thick golden ring around his neck, the gold belt. So much gold, she thinks, and then cannot help but brush her nail across his breast to touch the piercing. Skin like a new lamb's belly. And golden like apricots are golden at harvest time. Sophina purses her lips, furious with her own observations. She withdraws her finger reluctantly and points to her chamber, looking to and fro down the hall to be sure that this exchange has not been noticed by the ever curious eyes of the fortress servants.

Rah has made no motion to obey her command. He looks at her with fear-bright eyes and flinches at her touch. He shakes his head, 'no,' which only serves to call her attention back to the emerald between his brows.

"Oh you will learn to obey me, slave-god. And to fear me. I carry your Master's babe. Now think, if you have a brain to do it, what will become of you if he suspects that you attempted to defile that seed with your own, eh? I will see to it that you are skinned and fried in your own blood!"

Rah's brilliant eyes have been fixed on hers, but suddenly he lifts his head, hearing with his uncanny hearing footsteps rounding the corner at the far end of the hall. Seeing him distracted Sophina grabs his wrist and quickly pulls him off balance and into her chamber just as Tiko turns the corner.

She is quick to shut the door behind him and throw the latch.

Rah faces an opulent bed, a bed fit for a king visiting his favorite concubine. Momentarily lost in an ugly memory of his visits to Queen Nanaea somewhere long ago, he makes a miserable sound in his chest. Annoyed, Sophina sets her hands on her hips and waits for him to turn to her. His back is beautiful enough to set her teeth on edge, but when he turns, light from a row of western windows illuminates his torso, delineating the perfect musculature of his chest and abdomen. He tenses, holding his hands in fists like a small child readying to cry or tantrum, but this only serves to flex the long muscles of his arms, defining each group and bunching his dancer's shoulders.

"You are quite an exotic thing, aren't you? Where did they find you? Pick you out of some barbarian nest up north no doubt. They say they are all yellow-haired up there. Is that what fascinates him so? Well you don't impress me, slave-god. I will find excuse to mar your beauty, and then I will have you and your priests routed from this place like the infestation that you are."

She has come up to stand face to face with him. Rah, slightly taller than her, looks down into her eyes with unabashed hatred. It is enough to send her fury over the edge. She slaps him, hard across his cheek, cutting a thin line in his left cheekbone. Blood beads along the cut.

"There, not so pretty now, are you," she snarls. "Do not dare raise your eyes to mine again, slave-god. Next time I shall put that eye out." And opening her hand under his nose she reveals the clever weapon that has cut him, the sharpened prongs of an inverted ring, one that must once have held a large jewel, glints from her palm.

"Hatti women do not travel without defenses," she smiles.

Rah has not raised his eyes to hers again. His face remains turned away from her in the direction of her slap. He squints, a chastened cur awaiting another blow.

"Say something," says Sophina, tapping his chin with a fingernail. "You speak like a fool. But you are not mute. What is the matter with your tongue, eh? Did someone cut it out for you? Someone got there before me?" She attempts to pinch his mouth open with two fingers, but Rah pulls his face from her grasp, growling. Instantly she backhands him across the right cheek, raising three more welts there.

"How will you explain these now, slave-god? Will you tell your priests I pulled you into my chamber to abuse you? No, I think not. You and I have a secret now, and if you fail to obey me that secret will have you skinned alive."

"What is lady want Rah?" says Rah softly, gritting his teeth against her touch. For without thinking Sophina is running her fingers down the crease of his breast to his abdomen, measuring the silk of his skin there against her own.

"Not what you think, slave. For that is all you are to me, a pretty slave boy. One who has somehow managed to steal the heart of the most powerful man in all of Hatti. You are an obstacle. Well I have surmounted greater obstacles than you to get what I want. I will surmount you as well. Do not think you will maintain the Master's favor with your wiles. You will stay clear of him from now on, you understand? He is mine. If I learn that you have been in his bed I will make good my threat to have you skinned!"

"Rah is no concubine to Wolf!" shouts Rah, slapping her hand away and glaring at her freely and with fury. She raises her hand again and he steps backward so quickly that he loses his balance and falls on his back onto the bed.

"Rah is Grain God. Rah bring rain. Dance for king," he continues, subdued. "Make god happy so bring all good thing to people. Rah is no concubine," he repeats dully, and looking away.

A rustling of skirts coming down the hall takes Sophina's attention. And Rah quickly slips off the bed and out of her reach.

"Shall I cry for help?" hisses Sophina.

"No cry," says Rah, still keeping his eyes averted. He is panting in little, circular pants and perspiration is collecting at his throat, pooling to slip down the perfect crease of his breast.

"When I am through with you, you will have eyes to match your tongue," spits Sophina, moving toward him. "Now get out. Confine yourself to the priest's wing and the stables."

"Rah must dance," begins Rah, inching toward the door.

"No more dance. Stay out of the lyceum. Stay out of his sight. You understand me?"

Nodding, defeated, Rah pulls the latch and escapes.

"What has happened to your face, Rah?" asks Aros that evening. "You look as if you'd been in a fight with a cat!"

"Two cats," chuckles Pyrus from his bed in Rah's room. "No matter, Aros, the paint will hide it. He's probably taken a fall, or had some stones fly into his face from the chariot horses hooves."

"Is that it, Sunlight?" asks Aros, getting up from his own mattress to look Rah over. 'Has Tuma seen them?" But Rah only turns away, throwing himself down on his bed face first and covering his head with a pillow.

"Tuma see, Aros. Leave be," he mumbles from beneath it.

"No more catfights, Rah," says Pyrus, turning over on his own mattress to settle himself for the night. "If the Master comes home to find that face of yours marred, he will find more than one way to skin the cat who scratched you."

In the morning, the Master is returned. Waking Josepha in the early dawn, he has slipped into bed beside her and pulled her toward him to spoon her without a word. A kiss, then a stroke of teeth along her neck to her ear and a wolfish growl tell her that her sleep has been disrupted by the one who owns her heart, and not some monstrous intruder.

"My darling," she whispers, twisting to kiss his beard.

After sufficient nuzzling, she interrupts his lovemaking to let him know what he must know.

"The woman, Sophina," she begins.

"Not a good subject to raise just now, Josepha," murmurs Rush, pulling her buttocks against his belly and licking her ear.

Giggling, Josepha tries again. "I am sorry, Antaris, but you will be angry with me if I do not tell you."

Drawing himself up on an elbow, Rush frowns, looks down at his wife in the dark and waits.

"She has told Nikolaos that she bears you a child, Antaris. Naturally, he could not send her to the barracks brothel."

After an eerily silent pause, she determines to continue. "She is in the guest wing."

The grinding of teeth above her head breaks the stillness.

"Nikolaos would have put her in with the house servants," he says at last.

"And so he did. I thought it best that your heir be treated with appropriate respect."

"My heirs, whom I have just visited though they do not know it, are your sons, Josepha. And they sleep in the next room. I have no other heirs. Nor will I."

"As you say, Antaris," answers Josepha weakly, for her head is swimming with the implications of what he has just said. "But the child is your babe, nevertheless, and I..." and here her voice cracks with the tears coming.

"Josepha," he answers then, and pulls her head back gently by her hair to bury his face in her neck. Before she can take a breath to continue he covers her mouth with his own, holding her so tightly that she can barely breathe at all. "Josepha what grace you have," he whispers when he has at last released her.

Bringing her hand to his cheek she swallows her tears and responds, "Please, Antaris, for the sake of the babe," and then she adds, "And for mine."

"Do you know what lions do, Josepha? They kill their own male cubs, if the mother is not clever enough to save them. They kill them because they know that they have hatched a rival. I see this in Hattusha and in Kassara. I see it in the families of kings. What do you think this woman is responsible for, this mother of the babe you would protect from its own father, eh? She is responsible for the assassination of the great Hattusilis' son. What do you think of such a viper now? And what do you think that viper will spawn, but more vipers? Whoever the father? How much more so if that father is fierce? This is no matter for you to concern yourself with, wife. If there is a babe, and I very much doubt that there is, but if there is, it will be safe. It will be safe because of your grace, but it will never be an heir to me. And it will live in exile."

"Antaris-"

"This conversation is ended, beloved. Now give yourself to me, forget that it was had, and never again dare return me to it."

In the morning, Rush looks for the boy in the Hall of the Moon, but is told by his attendants, Pyrus and Aros, that he was gone from his bed when they awoke. He checks the baths, but finds only a few Minoan priests washing themselves in preparation for their morning prayers. He interrogates Crispo in the kitchen, sending half the staff into a panic with his presence, for he is never seen in the kitchens, but Crispo informs him that he has not seen Rah since the morning of the previous day, when he came down for his breakfast of Lydia's eggs and the white nanny's milk. Annoyed and not a little alarmed, Rush tries the stables. With his throat in the big man's fist, Hagga admits that he had seen Rah that morning at dawn walking out toward the Arab's paddock. He has not seen him since, and all three Arabs are still out in the field. He has just grained them himself. Shoving Hagga out of his way irritably Rush checks the paddock himself, but the boy is not there. In the soldier's gymnasium he finds Tiko in the middle of a martial arts demonstration with the four remaining commanders of the Armies of Amega. It is from Tiko that he learns of Rah's behavior in the mess hall the day before.

"I have not seen him since, Master," says Tiko, "but I expect that he took his supper with Ting Ya last night as usual. She may know something."

When he returns to the fortress, Rush finds Dimius and his dance troupe chattering excitedly in the middle of the lyceum.

"Where is Rah, Dimius?" booms Rush at the crowd, and the dancers part like stalks of wheat in the wind to expose their dance master. "Should he not be amongst you this morning, teaching his teachers to dance?"

Trembling, Dimius looks about at his troupe, then answers miserably, "We have heard it from the early kitchen staff that he took some food this morning and headed for the stables, Sir. We do not expected him for practice until this afternoon, but-"

"But what Dance Master?" snarls Rush.

"We understand he was upset by something, Sir, and that he has been asking about where the dead are buried in Amega-"

"There are no dead in Amega," responds Rush, turning to go. "He can ask all he likes, the answer will be the same."

"Sir," dares Dimius then, and when Rush looks over his shoulder at him he is standing with clenched fists and a determined look, a stark contrast to his normally submissive expression.

"What is it, Dimius? Must I loose that tongue of yours so that it will talk?"

"The...the woman, Sophina, Sir. She was here the morning after her arrival. She saw him at practice and demanded to know who and what he was. When the Bull priest told her who, and what, and that he was in your great favor, Sir, she told him, and us, in no uncertain terms that she was your favorite now and that there would be no other favorite from here on but she."

Dimius' boldness has drawn a collective sharp intake of breath from the group of dancers. They look from him to Rush to him again with exaggerated trepidation on their painted faces. Some of the girls have even gone so far as to bring a fist to their mouth, elbows raised dramatically, and pretend to bite their knuckles.

Rush's mood lightens with their mischief. He shakes his head, bemused. "Too silly for Amega, the lot of you. And the silliest of all is off looking for a cemetery to visit, that he might appease the god he hosts and bring Amega good fortune. You will tell him, when you see him, Dimius, that he is to report to me immediately. If he does not, I shall come find you personally and take my frustrations out on *you*, you understand?" Then he looks about the group and leans forward, menacing. "You *and* your flock of clowns," he growls, drawing an even larger intake of breath from the dancers.

"The moment I see him, Sir. I shall escort him to you myself if you wish," says Dimius, quickly.

Rush looks the dance master up and down a moment, then nods appreciatively at him as he turns to go. "You are a good man, Dimius. And you love him. Keep nothing from me, and you will continue to enjoy my protection."

"Is that what he calls it?" whispers Akbar to Dimius when the assassin is out of earshot.

"So it would seem," responds Dimius.

"I thought you had gone mad when you dared to tell him what that woman said," continues the choreographer. "It could have gone either way."

"Think what he risked to save Rah from Crete, Akbar," answers Dimius, looking at his friend with patient certainty. "This woman came to Amega on an ass, destined for the barracks brothel, or so the rumor has it."

"But the babe-" begins Akbar.

"Does that man seem to you to be the type that will be governed by a babe?" says Dimius, lifting a brow at Akbar. When the man fails to answer, the dance master turns to his troupe, claps his hands, and shushes them back to practice.

That morning Mochlos the priest visits the kitchens not long after the assassin has made his appearance there.

Two unusual visits in one morning sets the kitchen staff humming with speculation, and Mochlos, hoping to dampen the gossip, quickly pulls a girl off the prep bench near the door and whispers in her ear, pressing something into her palm as he does so. The girl looks down at her hand, pockets the contents, and slips off the bench in search of Crispo, who has left his oven to find fresh eggs in Lydia's laying box, hoping that Rah may yet show up for breakfast.

She returns with the Sun Priest and leads him to Mochlos who still stands uncomfortably in the kitchen doorway. Crispo gives the girl's bottom an innocent pat and gestures for to her to return to her station. Then he approaches the High Priest of the Moon with an expression of suspicious curiosity.

When they are out in the hall and out of earshot of the kitchen staff, Mochlos speaks.

"We have had little to do with one another, Sun, before or after our arrival in this city of warriors. I suppose your uncle did not speak well of me, though we were never enemies. Nevertheless, I must risk asking for your trust."

"It was a common enough thing for the heads of the priestly houses in Knossos to be rivals," responds Crispo, shaking his head sadly. "My uncle and I were hardly on good terms ourselves and he shared little with me in regards to you. I believe I was a disappointment to him, being so opposite to himself in nature." Crispo tucks the eggs he has gathered into his apron pockets so as to give Mochlos his full attention. "But why do you speak of a trust, Moon? What could you possibly wish to trust to a silly priest who spends most of his time in the kitchens with the help?"

"Precisely that," says Mochlos, drawing Crispo aside as two servants with a large, double handled basket of breads, held between them, come out of the kitchen and hurry past toward the officer's dining hall. "You have surely heard by now of this woman, this Sophina of Hattusha, and of her claim that she carries the assassin's babe."

Now it is Crispo's turn to look about and nervously draw Mochlos further down the hall to an alcove. "Please sir, let us not speak of the Master in such terms. You know as well as I that these walls have ears. Nor do I wish to be heard discussing this particular subject. I value my head and my skin also, sir, and you are speaking of a man who is in the habit of parting one from the other faster than the poultry chef can part a chicken."

"Look, Sun, I am as fond of my life as you are yours, but this is a matter of grave importance to the Rah."

Now Crispo flashes Mochlos a look of dread concern and some ire as well. It is a comic look on the face of the Sun Priest, whose countenance is made for gaiety, but Mochlos plows on. Taking a packet from the interior of his left sleeve he grabs the Sun Priest's hand and presses it into the palm. "There are five small vials of powder within. Put one into the woman's breakfast each morning, and on the fifth day, she will miscarry."

Crispo withdraws his hand as if it has been stung. The packet falls to the floor, but Mochlos snatches it up unharmed.

"You are mad! I will not be part of such a scheme!" hisses Crispo, setting both hands on his breast and drawing back. "Say no more and I have heard nothing!"

But Mochlos plows on, undaunted. "She looks to harm him, Crispo. I tell you, she has seen him and she hates him. We must act first. That viper will strike and she will strike quick. And if the Rah is gone, we have no purpose here in Amega. Not I, nor you, nor either Sky nor Bull. We will end up on the boy's funeral pyre I tell you!"

"It is enough to say she wishes to harm him, Moon. I would sooner be skinned myself than to see him come to harm. But what can she do? And how can ... what you suggest... be of any help in the matter? And how can she possible harm Rah? She has no access to him."

Mochlos has pushed Crispo further into the alcove and now peeks out around the corner and down the hall to check for prying ears. When he is satisfied that there are none, he draws Crispo close and continues.

"Have you not heard the rumors? Could it be that I have been kidnapped to live in a country in which kitchen staff are not the most well-informed population in any given house? Do not pretend ignorance, Crispo, you know as well as I do, and I witnessed it myself, that the woman has informed the Rah that she is the assassin's favorite now and that there will be no other. You think that Hattushan snake intends to sit about weaving swaddling dresses for her babe and relying on the paternal instincts of the Terror of the Aegean to save her hide? Rah is her rival, or so she sees it. For in truth her rival is the Lady Josepha, and that woman has *no* rival. I tell you Crispo," mutters Mochlos, reaching for the Sun Priest's hand and re-depositing the packet of poisoned vials into it, "This is an ambitious woman, who seeks to be sole benefactor of the assassin's goodwill. I am bartering with my own head when I tell you, she aims to put an end to the Rah, and to all of us who serve him."

"Then the assassin will make her wish she were never born," says Crispo, frowning.

"That may well be so, and you and I know him well enough to say so. But apparently she does not. My gods, man, she thinks she can outwit the beast!"

"Sir!" hisses Crispo, slapping a floured hand over the Moon Priest's mouth which Mochlos quickly cuffs away, though he snatches hold of the man's wrist.

"Crispo," he says, squeezing the priest's arm in earnest, "I am out of my depth here in this chamber of horrors called Amega. It was bad enough, being kidnapped by the son of Hades and brought here to this den of murderers. But now, now my very life's blood is being threatened. Without the Rah, Crispo, I am a dead man. I see it now. And just as clearly, I see that that Hattushan snake means to destroy me. Nay, to destroy us all."

Grimly, Mochlos releases Crispo's wrist and wipes a bit of flour off his cheek. He looks down at the packet of vials in Crispo's hand and sighs. "I am not a good man, I have never pretended that I was. I love wealth, fine food and clothing, power and position. I have ... certain predilections that some might find offensive. But a man is his nature, is he not? Is it my burden that I am made as I am? Or is it not the offense of the one who made me that I am what I am." Now he reaches for the hand containing the packet and clasps it in both of his. "I know I am not worthy of your trust. What have I ever done to earn the faith of my religious brothers? Nevertheless, I can with all sincerity tell you that I would not have come here to take this risk if I thought that there were any other means of saving my own hide. And that I love my own hide at least is common knowledge. And I swear to you, without the Rah, none of us are worth a damn to the assassin. We will be reminders only, something to be blotted out. At best we will be exiled, back to the charred corpse of Crete perhaps." Again he squeezes Crispo's hand. "Do what you will. I can do nothing more." And he turns to peek out of the alcove and see if it is safe for him to go without being noticed.

"Moon," says Crispo then, putting out a hand to stop him. "I will consult with Bull and Sky. If they agree, I will do it."

"It is but an aborted seed, Sun, she can be no more than a few weeks pregnant. It will appear that she was mistaken, or else lying outright, about her condition. What need is there to bring two more witnesses into it? Had I wished for their opinions I would have consulted them myself."

"What is in it, Moon?" says Crispo, opening his palm to look down at the packet as if considering. "Will it harm the woman, or merely curtail the pregnancy?"

"Herbs, roots. Nothing you could not eat yourself without suffering any ill effects. If she is in fact pregnant, she will have her menses on the fifth day, provided you do exactly as I say. Each morning, put one vial in her breakfast. It must be consumed. She will have no other symptoms, for it merely returns her womanly cycle. Wait another month, it will be of no use at all."

"And if she is not pregnant?"

"It is the same. It will bring on her blood." Mochlos gives Crispo one last pleading look. "It is nothing, Sun. Women use it all the time. I've no doubt she has used it herself in her time."

"Then let us leave it thus," says Crispo, pocketing the packet with certainty. "I must learn for myself in the next day or so if she means the Rah harm. If I discover it is so, the first vial will be in her morning drink two days hence."

"Fair enough," responds Mochlos, nodding. "But may I suggest that if you want to know her intentions, you start by asking the Rah himself? That is, if you can find him?" And with that, Mochlos ducks out of the alcove and scurries off to find Cara.

CHAPTER 14

As it happens it is on the same morning that Rush returns to Amega, Rah disappears and Mochlos schemes to abort Sophina's baby, that Cara returns to her former marital chamber to move her meager possessions into a room across from the High Priest in the Hall of the Moon.

Knowing full well that her husband, from whom she has not as yet been formally divorced, rises at dawn to go to the stables, she has waited until after breakfast to return to collect her things. Upon returning to the Master's wing she calls upon Ham to help her, and is informed that Rush has returned in the night.

The mention of the assassin's name, as always, sends a current of electricity up Cara's spine and temporarily jams her brain. Standing at the foot of her marital bed, a half dozen neatly folded shifts tumble from her arms as Ham rushes to catch them before they hit the floor.

"You are unduly stressed this morning, Madam," says Ham, returning the still folded dresses to her arms and giving her a curious look. "Perhaps you will allow me to gather your things myself and bring them to you in your new quarters."

"No Ham," she answers, embarrassed. "I'm fine." And then she adds sheepishly, "I suppose the dissolution of my marriage is only now hitting me, here in my husband's chamber."

Ham is watching her with one brow tilted. I am too old to lie to, says that brow.

Cara looks up into the man's unreadable face and straightens her back. She takes the bundle of clothing from him and turns away quickly. I wonder, she thinks, how long have you known Ameg? You are older than he by a good many years. Have you been with him since he was a boy? Hah. A boy. Can I imagine him a boy? A youth, lean and strong yet not the brute he is now, beardless, yet with those predatory black eyes, that generous mouth…

"Madam?" It is Ham, interrupting her reverie and looking her over with something not unlike sympathy.

"You don't believe me," she says then, turning to frown up at him. "Am I so transparent, Ham?" she smiles weakly.

"It is a look I have seen before," says Ham softly, "at the mention of his name."

"No doubt on the faces of women mostly," says Cara, bringing a hand to her mouth. I am all mouth, says the running commentator in her head. Will I never remember I am a lady now, and stop speaking to servants as if I am one of them?

"Mostly," says Ham wryly, and at this, Cara allows herself a giggle.

"But not always, Ham?" she ventures.

"Not always," says Ham, his eyes alone smiling.

"I am such a fish," she shakes her head. "Such a fish out of water. All I do well is sing. It is the one thing he has forbidden me to do in his presence! Now I am gifted by my new husband to the House of the Moon for the worship of the Rah. But what do I know about being a priestess? Less than I knew about being a wife."

"You will make a fine priestess, Madam," responds Ham, taking the things she has gathered and putting them in the large basket that two servants have brought in and set before him on the floor.

"How can you say?" she looks at him quizzically.

"There are two things a priest or priestess must have to succeed in the land of the Hatti," says Ham, moving to a dresser to pack the contents. "They are devotion to the god he or she serves, and vigilance. For there is much intrigue in this land and a great love of power."

"Well, then perhaps I *shall* do well. How could anyone who has met him not love Rah? And as to vigilance, I observe too much, I think," Cara answers. She waits until the basket is filled and Ham has waved the two servants away to deposit it in Cara's new room in the Hall of the Moon, then steps close to Ham and whispers, "For instance, I have observed that that Hattushan woman, that Sophina, who claims to carry the… the Master's child, hates Rah, and thinks herself a match for Lady Josepha herself. She said dreadful things, Ham, about Josepha…"

"You are speaking to a servant, Madam!" says Ham sharply, turning to give Cara a warning look and bringing his finger to his lips to shush her as he steps to the doorway and peers out in either direction.

"I know who I am speaking to, Ham," returns Cara when he has turned back to her. Her face set, she steps boldly up to him and hisses in a whisper, "I am speaking to one who loves his master and to one whom I can trust by this very fact. Someone must tell him, Ham! If you had heard her speak of Josepha…"

"I would have kept my own counsel, Madam, as you must. Leave the gossip to the kitchen help and to the laundry. Leave it to the Ladies own help to return it to her."

"But my own husband has assigned me to spy!"

"To report to him what you observe of Mochlos. Not to carry gossip about the Master's new concubine back to him. Do you not see that you will call suspicion upon yourself?"

"How so?"

"A scorned woman," answers Ham gently, "Will always degrade her competition."

That is enough to make Cara's eyes fly open with surprise and embarrassment. She slaps her hand over her mouth, staring dumbly at him, then begins to giggle again.

Ham can only smile and shake his head.

"Competition," repeats Cara, giggling. "I am no one's competition, least of all for the affections of the assassin."

"Nevertheless," says Ham more sternly, "leave the gossip to the help. Tell the Lieutenant General what you observe of the Priest's intentions. And leave the foolish talk of the woman, Sophina, to the help."

"You are a good friend to instruct me so, Ham. And I thank you," says Cara, lifting a few things from the dresser and depositing them into another basket, one small enough for her to carry herself.

Later that morning, Mochlos finds Cara redistributing her things in her new chamber.

"It is rather pleasant, having space of one's own," she says, smiling, as he enters, "after so many months of having none."

"I understand you were kidnapped from your home in Pheistos to be sold for a virgin," responds the priest, folding his arms over his chest and moving to the window to peer out at the activity in the practice arena. The sea of dark, long-haired Hatti warriors is unspoiled by the blonde halo of curls he looks for. "You were rescued by the Master," he continues, "and given to the Lieutenant General aboard ship."

"That is so, Holiness. But before that, I was betrothed to a man in Pheistos. I was the daughter of a vintner there, and had no interest in marriage whatsoever, but desired only to sing." Dreamily, she unfolds a shift, shakes it out and lays it on the bed. "I suppose I will no longer have use of these things."

"And what did you think of the man who rescued you from your fate, Cara? He must have seemed quite a brute to you then. Or did he show up as Ameg the Merchant, as he did so many times in my own household,"

Mochlos gives a dry laugh. "And here I thought he was a dandy. We all did. Who could have imagined I was entertaining the Terror himself in those days?"

"I thought he was the most horrible thing I had ever seen!" says Cara, looking up from her work, as if surprising herself with her own memory. "My gods, he sent me round the corner for a sack, and there in the alley lay a man with a stump for a neck, and holding in his arms a leather bag in which he carried his own head!"

"Typical," mumbles Mochlos, who has been distracted by something he sees happening in the arena.

"But then, one night, waiting for him at an inn in Cyrus," Cara has come to stand beside Mochlos at the window. Down in the practice field the man of whom she speaks stands, his back to the fortress window in which she observes him. Without realizing it she has drawn her hand to her throat and taken in a breath. It is all that Mochlos needs. He looks from the man in the field to the woman beside him and he knows.

"Woman, what would you do to have him?" says Mochlos at her side.

She gapes at him, wide eyed with embarrassment, then looks down at her feet, then back out at the man who has drawn up to a moving chariot and taken the reins of the lead horse, as if utterly oblivious of the danger of doing such a thing. But his commanding presence has subdued the horses. They shift in their tack. Blow. Come to halt.

"Have?" she whispers. "To have such a man is to be his." She looks at Mochlos. "And he will not have me. Thinks me an annoyance and a burden at best."

"Have his heart then," offers Mochlos carefully, taking the woman by the arm and drawing her away from the window. "There is magick for it. Moon magick. His heart could be yours in a single cycle. This is nothing." He shrugs, offering her a gentle smile.

But Cara only pulls her arm from his grasp and steps away, shaking her head. "I would not have what he would not give freely," she answers.

"But it will seem as if it *is* freely given," the High Priest retorts. "Though it may be short lived, nevertheless you will at least have for a time what you never hoped to have at all. And know what it is like to master such a heart-"

"Why would you offer me such a thing, Holiness?" answers Cara, peering at him distrustfully.

But the priest only shrugs again, turning away as if to leave her. "A little insurance, that is all. Do you think I don't know why you have been sent to me? To learn the office of the Priesthood of the Moon? The man hates me. He intends to replace me. Such a spell would be my insurance that you remain loyal to me, and safeguard my position here."

"I want no such spell," says Cara, but she is gazing at Mochlos with obvious curiosity.

"You think I cannot do such a thing?" he asks then, one brow peaked. "Of course I can. But there is a backlash, you know, in any such spell. Today he will desire you, but one day he will hate you, and that hatred will last forever. The spirit will not be enslaved indefinitely, no matter how good the magician, and once it is free, it will never forget its enslavement. No, nor ever forgive."

"Why do you tell me all this, Mochlos? I could take these things back to my husband and have you imprisoned for witchery," says Cara, reluctantly moving from her view of the assassin at the window and stepping toward him, so that she may speak barely above a whisper.

"I am a priest, not a witch," says the High Priest, shrugging with assurance. "Magic is my trade, is it not? And beyond that, I hardly think you will go running back to your husband to tell him that Mochlos saw the lust for the Terror in your eyes and offered you a love spell with which to snare him."

Cara's sharp intake of breath at this ends with a gale of laughter, a laughter she is helpless to contain. She covers her mouth with both hands, then doubles over, exploding into trilling giggles. "Snare him!" she whimpers, breathless, through her fingers, her eyes big as moons. "Like a big, mean grouse!"

At the image of the assassin hanging in a snare, Mochlos bursts out laughing beside her.

After a time he wipes a finger under one eye and says, still chuckling, "Silly woman, what on earth am I going to do with you? I see now, he gave you to me as a punishment in itself."

"There it is," agrees Cara. "And you to me for the same purpose." She pokes his arm.

But Mochlos only shakes his head, attempting with difficulty to frown. "You take me entirely too lightly, my dear. Do you not know I have a reputation for cruelty and calculation?"

"I did not know, Sir. But I thank you for your honesty. I shall be utterly respectful of you from this day forward."

"Please, don't, Cara. You will bore me to death," says Mochlos softly, before leaving the High Priestess-in-training to her chores.

Down on the practice field Rush stops a moving chariot to accost the charioteer. The man quickly jumps down from the bucket and offers him a full military bow as Hagga runs out from the stables to take the reins of the lead horse and lead the chariot away.

"When did you last see the dancer, Mikalya? Was he here at all this morning?" asks the assassin, careful not to allow an edge of concern to creep into his voice.

"Not this morning, Sir. Not since yesterday, at midday meal," answers the young horseman, rising to his feet. He has been following Rah around the stable yard, picking his brain about horsemanship, ever since he witnessed the demonstration of the three-man, and some of his peers have joked that he is utterly smitten by the god-slave. In fact, Mikalya is simply in awe of him and of his horsemanship, the likes of which he has never witnessed in all of his eighteen summers though he has already fought as far west as Troy and as far east as the Tigris.

"And what did you hear him speak of at supper, Mikalya? Anything of interest?" asks Rush quietly. When the boy does not answer immediately he adds, "Be careful, Mikalya, to remember everything, even that which you think may incriminate a friend."

With this warning, Mikalya takes a deep breath and looks down at is hands. Realizing that the assassin has already learned something of this conversation, he searches his memory.

"He was asking where we bury the dead, Sir, here in Amega. Master Tiko told him of the pyres, but he would not be satisfied with that. He became quite panicked that there was no place where he might go to honor the dead, and finally a catapultman--he happened to be sitting beside him--well... he spoke of the Table, Sir. And then all the ghost stories began to fly back and forth and ..."

"And someone mentioned where he might find the Table," finishes Rush.

"I think I recall the catapultman mentioning it, Sir," says Mikalya.

"You have told me all you know?"

"That is all, Sir."

Finally, Rush finds Nikolaos. The Lieutenant General has been in the shield room all morning, the room in which he interviewed Sophina upon her arrival. He is checking inventory, for a large shipment of weaponry-javelin, sword, lance- arrived last night from Hattusha. It is a gift from the King, an offering of friendship and allegiance to the Wolf of the Aegean.

When Nikolaos looks up from his scroll and sees the assassin darkening the doorway he tosses the parchment to the desk and jumps to his feet. He has not seen Rush since the man left with the three-man prototype, his two top commanders and his best charioteer more than a month ago. Now, in the big man's presence again, he finds himself oddly off balance. For the past month he has been given charge of Amega, a compound of highly trained fighting men, warriors that a year earlier he might only have dreamed of commanding at the end of his military career.

He has adapted to the role with surprising ease. But the true Master of Amega has returned home, and suddenly, in an instant, he is but an awestruck youth, cowed by his own fear and respect for the monster in the doorway.

"I have returned home to a house full of blind men, Nikolaos," says Rush, his black eyes unreadable.

"How so, sir?" responds the Lieutenant carefully.

"He has not been seen today, except by the kitchen help, who noticed him take some provisions early this morning," murmurs Rush, more to himself than to the Lieutenant. "His two attendants put him to bed last night, with bruises on his face, and yesterday, in the soldier's mess at noon, he was heard to be asking for the whereabouts of the dead of Amega. His priests have not seen him at all, and his dance troupe tell me that the woman I ordered to the barracks brothel was put up instead in my own wing, where she could inform my wife that she is with child, *my* child. And that this same woman, apparently granted full run of my house by I know not whom, interrupted his practice yesterday dressed like a queen instead of the whore she is, to tell him that she had replaced him in my affection."

"Rah, Sir?" says Lieutenant General Nikolaos weakly.

"You have one hour to find him, Lieutenant. When that hour is up, and he is not in my hands," and here Rush lifts those great bear paws of his and holds them up for the Lieutenant to contemplate, "You will be stripped of your rank."

"Yes, Sir," says Nikolaos.

"You will not find him, Lieutenant, in an hour, nor in a day. He is gone. Gone off into a harsh land, unknown to him, full of wild beasts and bandits. Gone off to find the Table of the Gods so that he might appease the dead and save us all from some imagined plague. Somehow, I know not how, though I left the man I trusted most with his safety in charge, I have lost what is most precious to me. I have lost the Rah, and instead I have a harlot whom I assigned to the barracks brothel, in my guest hall, where she has filled my beloved wife's head with concerns that are not hers. I have lost the Rah, and I have lost the man I trusted him to, leaving me with no Lieutenant General to oversee the fortress while I go in search for him."

"I will find him, Sir. I will follow his tracks to the place you speak of myself. You know I will. You know I will follow him," begins Nikolaos, but he is stopped by a catch in his throat. "Not this time, Captain," says Rush, lapsing eerily back to the title Nikolaos held when he searched for Rah in the catacombs of Cyrus. "This time I go alone. And when I have found and caught him, I will return to the business of war. For I have split the armies of the Hittite deserters and the Amorites who had plotted to take Hattusha, and I have returned the King's generals to Hattusha under the command of Agrippa. The Amorites camp like dumb cattle in the foothills of Urgup. Now I return to Hattusha to gather the King's armies together and crush them. But there is one more person, who knows the Rah better than anyone alive, whom I must speak to before I do so."

But on his way to Ting Ya's chamber at the end of the guest hall, Rush first stops to visit Sophina.

"Rush!" Sophina cries with confident expectation when her door slams open against the stone wall behind it to reveal the man. "You have heard of our babe!" But her ecstasy is curtailed when, as she rushes to the door to embrace him, she finds herself confronted not by equal delight but by the black energy of a panther in a tree above her head.

"Are you not gladdened by the news?" she says then, stepping back to offer him an elegant curtsey and as soft a smile as her strong features can manage.

Rush can only shake his head, his fury dampened by her courage. He finds his lip has curled into something like a smile in answer to her own.

"You are the consummate Hittite woman, Sophina. And I would be lying if I did not admit that I have a fascination for your strength and courage. You have an appetite for power to make an Egyptian queen blush. And if it is true that you have managed to hold my seed, if that womb of yours is as wily and grasping as you are yourself, our son or daughter will indeed be a force to be reckoned with. But I have heirs, Sophina, both here in Amega and in Mycenae. The child you would give me would only be a rival to them."

"Oh, but Rush-" she begins, but is stopped when he steps forward. Casually, even dreamily, he settles his hand against her shoulder, then slips his fingers around the back of her neck, his hand easily enclosing the entire column, and strokes her throat with his thumb.

Careful not to insult what could be an amorous gesture, Sophina stands her ground, looking up into the assassin's face in search of some indication of his affection. But he is not looking at her face. He seems to be lost in thought as he examines the skin along her trachea with the flat of his thumb.

"But you are rude, Sophina, you are without class. You have no grace. You have insulted my household," he begins, speaking so softly that she can barely make out the words. "You have crept into my home like a viper steals into a soldier's bedding when he is out sleeping in the field. His mind is not on vipers. He is ready for tomorrow's battle, perhaps his first. He is intent on war. Nevertheless, there he find himself, in the pitch dark, lying suddenly with a poisonous and uninvited thing in his bedding, a thing that is threatening to take his life right there, in the dark, as he sleeps, denying him even the honor of the killing fields. Do you know what I did with the first such snake I encountered, Sophina? When I was a boy of fourteen? I bit its head off, skewered the monster on a stick and ate the meat. I made a pendant of its skull and a necklace of its skin, which I wore for some time to remind me always that there are such creatures in the world and that one must be ever wary of and ready for them."

"Do not blame me for doing what I did, my love," responds Sophina, "To save myself and to have you. Anything less would have been weakness."

"True," smiles Rush then, putting a bit of pressure on her throat so that she must look up into his face with a bit less pluck. "And most of your foolishness is forgivable. But Sophina, you have insulted the Grain God of Knossos, and chased him from our midst. Do you think you will hold a pregnancy without him?"

"You cannot believe such religious nonsense!" cries Sophina then, her hand reaching up to grasp his wrist and pull his fingers from her throat.

"I have seen it happen, this magic. I have seen cities prosper and fall dependent on the whim of the god whom that slave hosts. And so here is my promise, the same I gave my wife, who pleaded on your child's behalf because it is my child also. You will be under my protection so long as you are carrying my seed, and so long as there is a living child of mine who calls you its mother. But the day you lose that child, you lose also your life, Sophina."

To this she has no response, only the widening of her eyes and the stiffening of her neck in his fingers. He can feel her swallow under his thumb. "And I think that day is not long off, Sophina. You have tread on too many in my absence, so that even I could not protect you from the bed you have made for yourself."

With this, he draws her close, yet by the neck, and, smiling mildly, brings his mouth down on hers. He kisses her as he remembers kissing Rah the day he came upon him on the path to Ting Ya's in the rain. He brings his fingers up and twists them into her hair, pulling back her head, and drives his tongue into her mouth. A taste of what is to come.

Everything is a weapon to a warrior, thinks Rush absently, as Sophina struggles to find an unblocked avenue in which to take a breath.

Then he releases her, dropping her onto her own bed with as little interest as one might have for one's soiled laundry, and strides out of her chamber.

Ting Ya is at her altar. Yesterday, after Rah left her in her chamber, she closed the door behind him quietly and carefully removed the fine silk robe she wore. She replaced it with the simple sack-cloth shift she had worn on Crete, the dress Rah most often saw her in, and she loosed her braid over her shoulders to allow her grey tresses to fall freely to her ankles.

Then she moved to a small alcove in one wall and lit a row of candles, and several sticks of the expensive myrrh incense Josepha gave her in welcome upon her arrival at Amega. There, before her altar, she knelt down on her haunches, Asian style, before a small clay statue of a boy and a dove. It was a piece of art which had been made en mass with the High Priest's money by a local artisan to be distributed in Knossos as a replica of Rah, a kind of house god, not long after the boy arrived at the Villa. It was in her possession only because it had been in the guestroom she was assigned when the house was suddenly ordered to pack up and board the assassin's ship to flee to Anatolia.

Now she understands why it has been left in her custody by the Sun Goddess.

It is time for much prayer and fasting. Rah is in danger, as is all of Amega. And so Ting Ya has donned the clothes of her former life as caretaker of the ancients to pray and to fast before the altar of the Rah. She prays for the boy, and for Josepha's household, and she does not cease until she is interrupted by the thump of the assassin's war-scarred knuckles on her chamber door.

Rush is surprised to see Ting Ya in sack cloth, her hair loosed and wild, when she opens her door to him. He blinks, even steps back a pace, frowning, until the old Asian slave raises her dark eyes calmly up to his and steps back to offer him entry.

"You know something." His first words are hard, demanding. This woman has always been something of an enigma to him, though his wife is fond enough of her for her to be his sister-in-law, and the boy, Rah, has always run to her like a child to its mother.

"Where the Rah go," says Ting Ya with something akin to sympathy, "Great man cannot follow."

"Hogwash," snaps Rush, stunning himself with his own offensiveness. Nevertheless he plunges on. "Not only will I follow him, I will catch him, and then I will give him what he deserves for running. He is still a slave, Ting Ya, as are you. My slaves."

"Yes," says Ting Ya, dropping her eyes then, "Slave never forget she is slave. But," and she turns back to her altar to pick up a bundle of fresh incense and light it. Presently she continues. "Rah, he believe he is god-slave now. Believe he have power to keep all who love him safe. Believe he owe his master this. And so Rah, he go to do his duty for his master. Go to bring gift to the dead. Rah, he love his master now. He say he dream a plague come to Amega, come from enemies of master. Say he must go to bring gift to the dead so that this plague does not come."

"This I have already heard," says Rush, less brusquely. He has noticed the statue of the boy with the dove on the altar and has come up behind

Ting Ya and reached over her shoulder for it. He had seen one at the Palace of Knossos not long before Crete fell. Several of the statues had been distributed amongst the royals by Mochlos as gifts, reminding those in power where their power originated, and that it was Mochlos who had summoned the god to live amongst them, in human form, in the body of a golden slave boy who could tame doves.

"Ting Ya try to tell him, plague already here. Come with this woman from warrior camp. She sick already. She not know. She think she carry master's child."

"What are you saying, Ting Ya" says Rush over her head, and still fingering the statue in his hand absently. "I sent Sophina directly from the camp of Ammuna, in the foothills of Hattusha. There was no plague."

Now the old Asian has turned full round to face him. She barely reaches his chest, nevertheless she stands tall, lifts her eyes to his, and speaks to him with a force that sends the unaccustomed chills of true fear up his spine and into his hairline.

"This man, Ammuna, he is traitor to king. Make deal with enemy to king from east. But this enemy, also his enemy. They trick Ammuna. This mercenary army, it bring plague, too. Smart." She touches her forehead. "Very smart. This plague not in man. Not in woman. This plague start in animal. Enemy keep animal separate until ready."

Rush's eyes have narrowed to slits. His jaw is a fist of clenched muscle.

"The donkey," he whispers through his teeth. "The donkey they sent her to Amega on. And I ordered her sent back here, as a punishment. I brought this on myself. I have brought evil to my own home. It is my own mistake-"

"No," says Ting Ya then, shaking her head. "Cannot think this way. Weak man blame himself. Warrior, he blame enemy."

"I have already waited too long, Ting Ya. The boy is missing, the animal is in my own stable, amongst Amega's finest war horses. They may already be infected."

"No commander greater than his weakest soldier," answers Ting Ya enigmatically. "Some will die. Too late for them. But must fight plague. Fight with fire."

"What of the woman, Ting Ya? Is she infectious?"

"Woman is sick. But plague come from animal. No touch animal, no die."

"I was just with her. She is not sick," responds Rush, but he looks down at his hands with loathing just the same, remembering how he had taken her by the throat, even kissed her, just moments earlier.

"Woman is sick," repeats Ting Ya with certainty, turning back to her altar. "But plague come from animal. No touch animal, no die."

But Rush is already gone to call for Ham, and to order the heavy, elaborately carved door of the guest chamber which the woman Sophina inhabits be barred and nailed shut until she is dead, and everything inside, including her corpse, burned.

CHAPTER 15

Down in the stable yard Hagga is looking for Ghedi. He has not seen him all morning and it is now mid-afternoon. He has checked the chariot horse barn and found nothing amiss. All the horses had been hayed and watered and are munching contentedly in their stalls. He has checked the Arab's paddock and found the same. But no one has seen Ghedi, who is usually happy to help handle the horses at practice out in the arena whenever he has a spare moment to do so, although this job has never been formally assigned to him. It simply became a common practice, after he had been working in the stables for a few months, for the charioteers to ask for him whenever they had a problem with one of the horses or needed an extra man to help tack up an unruly team. But now Ghedi, who has always been reliable, is missing. And something else is disturbing Hagga, for there is something wrong with the donkey that came in with the Hattushan woman five days earlier.

Hagga is not particularly concerned about the donkey. The miserable animal was balky from the start and was in poor weight. At any rate, as a normal precaution against disease, it was put out in a separate paddock, a good distance from the barns, built especially for the purpose of isolating animals coming in from the field. The Hatti had not yet forgotten the plague that had devastated the Anatolian peninsula almost two hundred years earlier, brought to them by their wily eastern enemies by way of infected rams left along major roadways within the kingdom. When the rams were caught and put in with the native farmers' sheep, entire flocks became infected, leading to plague and famine. Although it was eventually discovered that the plague could not typically be passed from human to human, and had completely died out over a hundred fifty years earlier, any good stable keeper to this day nevertheless separates animals coming in from the field from his own beasts for a week or so. By then any illness will make itself known, for infected animals typically die within days, sometimes hours.

Having searched the entire stable block and exterior yards, Hagga at last wanders down to the grain room on the slight chance that Ghedi may have slipped off to take an afternoon snooze on his straw mattress there. It is an unlikely picture, for the feed man is more apt to spend any spare time he might have working with a difficult colt or mending tack, but Hagga is beginning to suspect the worst.

When he opens the door to the little stone chamber the smell that hits him first is enough to set him rocking back on his heels. Has a rat found its way past the barn cats and died in here?

But no. The moan coming from the pallet in the corner of the room, behind the grain bin, is not that of a rat.

"Ghedi? Is that you? What has happened to you?" His mind whirling, Hagga can only think of robbery or some other foul play. But Ghedi has no enemies. Indeed he is loved by peers and betters alike.

"Ghedi?"

Still no response, only silence. Finally, unable to stand the ugly images of his own speculations any further, Hagga pulls a rag from his pocket and, holding it over his nose, steps into the feed room and peeks around the grain bin. What he sees is more terrifying to him than his worst visions. For Ghedi is lying on his mattress, his normally ebony skin gone ashen, his eyes sunken and crusted in puss. His hands and arms are covered with his own vomit, as he has clearly been trying to keep his sickness contained to the mattress upon which he lays.

"Hannahannas, mother of all gods, Ghedi, you are with plague! Why did you come here? You may infect the whole stable!" is all Hagga can think to say to his dying friend. But Ghedi can only draw in a wheezing breath and release a choking cough into the mattress, unable any longer even to lift his hands to his face.

"Taru, King of Heaven, help us, help us all!" cries Hagga then, backing swiftly out of the grain room and slamming the door shut with a terrible thud.

Out in the stable yard, in a paddock situated behind a wall built from the stone and rubble that had to be moved when the field was first cleared, the mustard-colored donkey upon which Sophina of Hattusha road into Amega, lies dead. That morning it failed to come in for its breakfast of grain and water, preferring instead to follow instincts even more ancient than itself, which told it to separate itself from the living during its last hours. As the Mediterranean sun peaked overhead, it wandered down a gulch to the farthest corner of the field and fell behind a tuft of wild grass and flowering shrubs. Minutes later a quartet of turkey vultures came to roost in a nearby acacia tree and wait. They did not wait long. And while it was still warm enough to cause the birds to blink their reptilian eyes against the steam erupting from its belly as they tore into it to feed, a handful of arrogant crows hopped closer, hoping for a portion of the feast.

Rah is wandering.

He has wandered all of his short life and this sense of wandering, this detached, even wild loneliness he experiences, is not a feeling he is unaccustomed to. He awoke early on the morning of Rush's return and was, ironically, bidding farewell to Halix and his Arabs when Rush was rounding the fortress from the west to enter his home from the caves driven into the cliffs beneath it. And so while Rush moved like a demon's shadow through his own cellars, Rah was balancing his perfect and ethereal weight on the paddock fencing to stroke Halix between his ears and murmur a few words of farewell. And as the colt's mother nudged it aside so that she might receive her due from Rah as well, he chuckled softly and pulled her ears, just to annoy her.

"Bad mama, always want to take Rah for herself, eh? Let me say good-by to Hali now."

With the formalities of separation over, Rah hopped down from the fence and reached into the potato sack he had taken from the kitchen that morning and pulled a carrot from it. Turning back to offer Halix one final treat, he was bumped in the cheek by the colt's soft muzzle. He kissed the pink lozenge there and popped the carrot into the animal's mouth, then picked up his sack and headed off. He headed north, toward the mountains, thinking little of what lay ahead for him, but rather remembering only the words of the woman, Sophina, the strike of her claws across his cheek, and the urgent need he felt to flee from her. He was fleeing now, in part to find the burial place of the enemies of Amega and to offer sacrifice, because the House of his Master was in danger. A plague was coming, and only sacrifice to the gods would save them. But he was also fleeing from his Master's new concubine, who had told him that he would be skinned and fried like a grain cake if he dared remain in the presence and in the favor of the Wolf.

By noon, Rah is far from Amega. Crossing the stream in which Rush washed himself and drank before entering his own compound the night he gave Rah the emerald, he, too, stops for a drink, and then cannot help but slip into the water for a swim. It is a hot day despite the time of year and he is refreshed when he finally drags himself back onto the shore. He lies there in the sun, drying off, before drawing himself up and looking about for a clue as to the direction of his goal. To the north and west is a steppe, and beyond, a low mountain range. Above the steppe a crow circles. It takes a few casual flaps and changes direction, north and west again.

"This where spirit live," says Rah to himself. "Crow show Rah."

Rah heads off in the direction the crow flies. He will continue until he reaches the strange, otherworldly landscape of his dream. There he intends to offer the gods of the dead his only possessions: the pearl of great price, and the brilliant green gem in his crown.

Sophina has discovered the truth.

Not five minutes after Rush left her she felt her blood come, in a sudden and unexpected gush, and run down her left thigh into her shoe. At first she is so shocked she just stands where she is, trying to comprehend what has happened and, with the curious irony of the mind, attempting to come up with another alternative that might explain this sensation. Then, finding somehow the courage to lift her skirt, she finds the deadly reality of her body's betrayal slipping down her leg, and she feels herself swoon.

"No. No. No. No," she repeats in a numbing trance as if she could stop the blood with determination alone. She tears off her dress, rushes to the basin and begins wiping herself clean with a soaked linen towel. But the blood is like a torrent. There is no stopping it. It takes her a moment for the first cramp to hit her like an assassin's fist, doubling her over. She was never one to bother herself about her womanly pains and it seems at first that this is no more than her menses. But when the second cramp strikes she is on the floor on her face, and she is in a crumpled and bloody heap when the pounding of hammer and nail at her door brings her out of her frenzied state and back to the present. She raises herself up to one elbow and screams for help. But help does not come. Only the pounding of the hammers continues. Men. Men working at her door. Building something? No. Securing something. Securing the door. Nailing her into the chamber.

Sophina screams in rage and pulls herself to her feet to throw her body against the door.

"You bastard! You bastard!" she shrieks until her throat is raw and the words can no longer be forced through it. But the man she accuses is not there, and even the men working on the other side cannot hear more than the muffled pounding and scraping of her fists and nails on the face of the foot-thick door.

Down the hall, in the Master's chamber, Josepha is drawn to her window overlooking her courtyard and the sea. She is thinking of Sophina and she is thinking of the babe that has been lost. It was alive when she touched the woman the day she came, although no more than a fertilized seed, like a warm egg in a laying box. But the woman was sick. Something had attached itself to her on the journey from the Hattushan battle camp, something was feeding on her, other than the seed of her beloved, and that thing was in her blood now. It would continue to feed there, she knew, until it had consumed its host. She could feel its hot hunger through her finger tips as she closed her arms around the woman and the spark that was her husband's seed. The woman was hungry, yes, eternally hungry and unsatisfied, but the thing that was feeding on her was hungrier, wilier.

This morning, as she lay in her husband's embrace, she felt a different hunger burning inside of him. Different, too, from the usual heat of his ferocious temperament. This was always the same with Antaris before he waged war, this heat. But now there would be a different war than the one he was preparing for. For the Rah has fled, this she had been told by her ladies late that morning. It was all over the compound, how the Master had given orders to find him, and how no one could. He was last seen in the kitchens pilfering food for what surely must be a journey.

"You will find your way, my love," thinks Josepha at the window, looking out to sea in the direction of Crete. "You will find your way. The boy is leading you on. And when you have found the thing that can finally quench that fire in your heart, we will return home to the scorched earth where he was made. May the one God, the true God, the God above all others watch over you and keep you safe, and bring you home to me once more."

Rah is nearing the foothills north of Amega when night falls. The temperature has dropped and he is grateful for the sheepskin he has brought with him, and the woolen robe he stole from the assistant priests' linen room before he left. As dusk settles he finds a hollow beneath a juniper in which to stuff the sheepskin. His bed is quite comfortable, and he allows himself a few mouthfuls of bread and cheese before passing into a dreamless sleep. In the morning he is awakened by a flock of wild guinea fowl that have been roosting in a nearby tree. They noisily descend from their roost with military order, then chase one another about like feathered beetles, lifting their rounded wings out at their sides and running at top speed behind their opponent. Rah watches their antics for a while, then wanders about in search of a nest. It is winter in Anatolia, but oddly mild, the heat of Thera's fury having settled like a blanket on the peninsula north of the Mediterranean. Instinct tells him that the birds might be laying, and he spends some time searching beneath the maquis shrubs nearby, finally disturbing a hen to find a warm clutch of six small eggs beneath her. They are half the size of a chicken's egg, and Rah wastes no time in cracking them over his opened mouth and gulping them raw. Then he continues north, following a small rivulet into a valley between two great mountains. He is oblivious to the Anatolian leopard that, disturbed by his presence in its hunting field, has lost interest in the fowl and has chosen to pursue instead the scent of egg on Rah's fingers.

By noon, Rah has reached the base of the mountains. Above his head no crow breaks the monotony of clouds packed against their southern flanks.

"Rain come," says Rah to himself. "Maybe find cave. This what Wolf is do." And so he continues through the valley, keeping the stream to his right and hugging the base of the mountains in search of shelter for the evening. Behind him the leopard follows, holding back in the ever thickening shrub and wood but easily maintaining pace with Rah. The smell of the guinea egg on the boy's fingers entices it to continue north, well out of its hunting ground, and it is hungrier than it might have been by evening, had it remained home to take a hen during the hour of their hierarchical ascent back into the roosting tree. It keeps pace with Rah and on the oddly injured sounds he makes as he goes. For Rah is muttering to himself as he wanders north, of Sophina and of the plague, of Ting Ya and of the King for whom he will dance, of the Wolf and of the priest and of the City of the Dead on the Table of the Gods where he must sacrifice his gifts to save Amega.

But behind the leopard a lone wolf, a wolf mightier than any leopard, a wolf who is hungrier even than this one, has picked up the trail of a little cat, and of the unfortunate predator who follows him.

CHAPTER 16

By the evening of the same day, the four priesthoods of Rah at Amega have convened in the lyceum. Each house has taken its proper station at the north, south, east and west end of the hall, and each priest has had an opportunity to lead his church in prayer for the safe return of the god-slave. Each house has been instructed to fast and to wear a simple sack cloth robe, not unlike the robes worn by the Priests of the Dead on Crete, until the boy is found. Mochlos has been eyeing Crispo throughout the ceremony, and when the groups break up to return to their own halls, he takes the Sun priest's arm and holds him back until the room has cleared. Then he pushes him off and away from the archway and hisses, "Have you heard what has happened to the woman Sophina?"

"I work in the kitchens, Moon. I could have hardly avoided hearing it if I were deaf… and blind as well," responds Crispo tiredly. "Oh I am not one for fasting," he continues with a bit of a pout on his plump lips. "I will have a devil of a time with it. I don't see the need, do you? What good will it do Rah if we all starve here in the fortress while he is out wandering about in the wilderness? Better we should have a good meal to keep our strength, and offer sacrifices."

"You could do with a bit of fasting, Sun," responds Mochlos, giving the priest's corpulent frame a cursory glance, "but if it is not in your nature, do as you like. As to my house, we will fast. But I must know, did you feed the woman the concoction this morning? Had she already lost the child when the Master locked her away? Or is there some connection here with the plagued donkey in the stable yard? If she rode in on the donkey she is surely diseased. Then it is not our responsibility whether or not she lost the child."

"You needn't worry that the assassin will find you responsible for what he did to Sophina," answers Crispo, giving Mochlos a light shove and heading for the exit. "She had already had her breakfast meal taken up to her chamber when we spoke. And as I told you, it was my intention to speak with the Rah before making a decision. No," and here he turns to give Mochlos a look of knowing caution. "Remember Moon, I was assigned to the Priesthood of the Dead for near six months before we left Knossos. I have perhaps a better first hand recollection of the assassin, and of his ways of dealing with his unfortunate enemies, than any one of you. This is… typical of him. He simply took a precaution, before he left, to insure that the plague would not spread."

"Goddess help me," whispers Mochlos. "Are you saying the woman was not sick? That he nailed her into her chamber to die as a precaution?"

"I am indeed," answers Crispo.

A shiver runs up Mochlos' spine as he notices a head pop around the archway. Cara is waiting for him.

"We are in the possession of a madman," mumbles Mochlos. "A sadistic lunatic."

Crispo gives the High Priest of the Moon a quick glance of surprise, then purses his lips and answers, "He gains no pleasure from what he does, it is all logic to him. Symmetry. For did she not attempt to trap him with a babe? Now she is herself trapped, nailed inside a plush coffin. But do not shed too many tears, Moon. She will surely die of plague before she starves to death. The beast is already dead. And I heard only half an hour ago that a stableman, one who dealt with the same beast when it arrived, was found in the grain room choking on his own vomit. They have sealed him in and set him ablaze."

"Will they not burn down the whole stable then?" asks Mochlos, offering Cara a little nod and a wave of his hand to say he will join her in a moment. She gives him a demure smile and steps back out the archway.

"The room is made of stone, three foot thick. It is vented above. It is a veritable oven." Crispo shakes his head sadly. "Poor man knew what he was doing when he chose such a place to die. He was thinking of the stable, the horses. I understand he was a good man, much beloved of the horsemen."

"Thank the Goddess he made such a choice," swallows Mochlos then, moving toward the exit. "The only thing worse than dying of plague as far as I can tell is dying at the hands of the assassin himself."

Over a rise and down a gulch, Rah continues wandering north along the stream the following morning. He had slept in a recess along the rocky foot of the mountain that night, a crevice just big enough for him to crawl into along with his sheepskin and sack. The leopardess slept in a tree nearby, coming once a stone's throw from his hiding place but not yet daring to take this strange creature, who smelled of cherries and goat cheese and egg and who talked to itself in a strangled rolling growl almost incessantly. She sniffed the footprints made by his sandaled feet, even lay several meters out from the recess for a time, paws stretched out before her, watching him, as if she too had somehow come under the spell of the golden boy from Knossos, the dancing leopard of Crete.

Half a day south, Rush follows the trail Rah has made in his unthinking meandering. There are footprints, of course, in the dry and salty earth, and the outline of his body on the shore of the stream he bathed in, but also evidence of his nest under the juniper as well as the remains of the six guinea egg shells that he breakfasted upon.

"Silly little cat," murmurs Rush, "You are as easy to track as a blind rabbit."

Rush follows his senses, neither pushing too fast nor wasting time, but keeping always to the clues that the earth has left him. It will be long past nightfall before he comes upon his quarry, and when he does, he will have more than a wandering boy and a hungry leopard to deal with. For camped in the rocky hills just north of Rah's path is a band of Amorites spies, men who were forced into service more than chosen for the ambush that was to take the dismembered Hittite army in Hattusha. These men are seasoned soldiers and have fought the Hittites before, when the nation was ruled by the great Hattusilis. They had seen the might and determination of the Hatti in battle and were not convinced that the Amorite plan, to plant a plague animal while befriending the enemy uncles of the new king, would weaken the Hittite defenses. In fact, they had seen enough of this warrior nation to know that the mercenary Amorites might as easily be cutting their own throats by turning against Ammuna just as he readied his troops for an overthrow of Mursilis. The Hatti were not fond of deserters, and less fond of infiltrators. It was more than probable that the two Hittite armies would band together in the last and crush the moles between them. After the assassin had dealt with Ammuna himself and split the Hittite generals and the Amorite mercenaries, sending the generals back to Hattusha with his own men and the strange new weapon, the plan appeared all but foiled. A few Amorite captains, remaining with the mercenary army in the foothills, came up with the idea of sending a small band south to follow the donkey to Amega and spy on the progress of the plague, which was originally meant for Hattusha. Two days earlier these men had seen the smoke lifting from what appeared to be a furnace right in the center of the stable. Horses and fire didn't mix and there was only one explanation.

"They've discovered the plague," argues the oldest and the leader of the band. His name is Kaspir, and he has been an Amorite soldier for most of his life, only returning to service this winter on the promise of a handsome commission that would keep his wife and sixteen children fed for another year. "We can neither go forward nor backward. If we return to our captains with this news we will be part of the massacre of our army. With the Hittite generals back in Hattusha, and under the command of the Great Wolf of the Hatti, we will be crushed like fleas. Let us return to Syria and to our families."

"And what will become of us there? If we are not returning to our camp to fight, then we are deserters," answers Marut, a younger man with no family of his own to return to. There is little in Syria for him but a widowed mother, a small farm and five younger siblings to feed. "We will be impaled. Better to return to die in honorable battle."

"Either way it ends the same," scoffs Kaspir. "We are dead men walking…unless by some miracle we find treasure on our way back to camp."

But the group has only to settle for the night for treasure beyond their imagination to find them. By day's end, Rah is thirsty and tired. He has not seen the crow since the first day and has determined that he must continue in the direction given him by that bird until he sees another. It is dusk when he gives up his rather rapid pace north and wanders down to the stream bed for a drink. There he steps dead into the camp of the Amorite spies, who have bedded down around a fire for the night.

The instant he perceives that he has wandered into a camp, Rah drops his sack and bolts. But Marut is just returning from filling his gourd at the stream himself and the boy careens into him, causing him to drop it. Marut's first impression is that a young girl has wandered into camp from a local village and is now fleeing the advances of the three men he left in camp. He tackles the boy and quickly brings him to the ground, only to discover that the maiden he is attempting to pin has the strength of a wildcat. As he turns his head to call to his companions for help Rah twists much as he did under the lethal weight of the assassin the day Hali died. He sinks his incisors into the man's forearm.

"Mother of the gods, Inanna, she bit me!" yelps Marut, tearing his arm from Rah's teeth and turning him over in the same instant. "What the-?"

By now Wadin and Lar have roused from their beds to grab Rah's arms and feet as he continues to wrestle with Marut. Finally pinned, Rah nevertheless continues to writhe beneath the three men, snarling and snapping at whichever of their appendages might be close enough for him to reach. The men, though, are too stunned to notice. They stare down at the golden-haired boy whose eyes match the brilliance of the emerald between his brows and whistle in unison.

"It is a boy," says Marut stupidly.

"No, Marut," gasps Lar, looking down into Rah's eyes as he pins the boy's wrists above his head. "This is no boy. This is a god-slave!"

"And a damned important one at that," adds Wadin, who has released Rah's ankles so that he might crawl beside Marut and get a better look. "Will you take a look at that stone!"

Rah has given up trying to buck Marut off him and is lying still, glaring at each man in turn, a growl burring deep in his throat.

"No one lets god-slaves wander about in the wilderness like this," says Kaspir. "Nor do the Hatti keep them." He has come to stand over Rah's head, hands on hips, as he appraises their prize. "This is a Minoan slave-god, or I am a harem girl."

"How could you know such a thing, sir? Have you seen one before?" asks Lar innocently enough. He is but twenty six summers but has fought all over Syria and as far south as Egypt. Still, he has never been to Crete, and rumor has it that the island is no more, blown away by a volcano somewhere in the middle of the Great Sea.

"I have not," answers Kaspir patiently. "But I have heard enough stories to know that the Minoan's chain their slaves by the waist," and here he opens Rah's robe to reveal the golden belt around his hips, "the god-slaves in gold, and that the Minoans are fond of exotics and procure them from all around the world."

"This one must be from the Sky King's mountain! It is as if he were dipped in gold! And look at those eyes! Are they not the jewels in Inanna's tiara?" gapes Lar.

"Get off him, man, and put him upright," orders Kaspir now, slapping Marut on the back of his head and dislodging his hat. As Rah is forced to his feet he makes one more, wild attempt to twist and jump free of the grasp of the men holding him. He succeeds in knocking Wadin over and nearly bolting off, but Marut, the biggest man in the group, tackles him to the ground a second time. Rah lets out a strangled cry of rage and frustration. This time he is on his belly, and his mouth is filled with sand. He begins a high pitched warble that careens over the arid land, south, toward the ear of the wolf who tracks him. Marut slaps a calloused palm over his mouth to stop the noise and hauls him to his feet, pinning his wrists behind and turning him toward Kaspir.

"What shall we do with him, sir? He must be worth a fortune in ransom," he puffs, for his struggle with the boy has taken a good bit of wind out of him.

"No doubt, but I am a soldier, not a thief and a blackmailer. Besides, punishment for kidnapping a slave is worse than for desertion. And I have no desire to be planked and left for the ravens to eat. I prefer being hacked in half with my own battle axe."

"Wolf is kill you!" cries Rah suddenly in Minoan, having spit enough sand from his parched mouth to form the words. But they are barely audible to the soldiers, who can only blink in amazement that the strange, gilded creature they have captured has wits to speak at all.

"Give him a drink, idiot," says Kaspir to Wadin, who has returned to his feet and now goes off toward the fire to find his water gourd. When he returns, Kaspir takes the gourd and hands it to Rah, nodding to Marut to release his wrists so that he might take it. Rah looks at the thing suspiciously for a moment, then glares back up at Kaspir.

"No take," he says.

Frowning but maintaining his patience, Kaspir takes the gourd and drinks from it. Then he hands it again to Rah, who acquiesces. He takes a mouthful of water, swishing it through his teeth, and spits it at Kaspir's sandaled feet. Lar and Wadin look at one another with wide-eyed shock. Such a thing should cost a man his ear. But Kaspir only frowns down at his splashed feet and shakes his head.

"Now speak again, little fellow. What is this language, eh? This is not the language of the Hatti. Nor is it Egyptian."

"Leave go!" says Rah now, in what he has learned of his master's language in his months at the fortress. He yanks his left arm from Marut's grasp. "Rah must go to Table of God! Leave sacrifice! Save Amega! You are stupid, enemy of Wolf! Wolf is kill you!"

"Is he saying Wolf, Captain? This is Hatti!" gasps Marut. "Oh, goddess, Inanna, does he speak of the Wolf of the Aegean? The Wolf himself? We are ghosts! Twice dead!"

"Who owns you, boy," says Kaspir to Rah then, making a good show of composure in front of the others. "Speak in the Hatti tongue, if you can, for I understand a good deal."

"Wolf is assassin, stupid man," spits Rah. "He is kill you, you touch Rah. He kill everybody touch Rah." Now Rah has boldly shoved Marut away from him and stepped up under Kaspir's nose. He fixes him with a blue-green stare to make the oceans weep and plants his hands on his hips, defiant. Kaspir is momentarily dazzled by the combination of the emerald glittering in the campfire light and the fantastic compliment of those pretty eyes. He steps back, certain he has no interest in touching this god-slave, who has just informed him that the very Terror himself, will deal with him if he does. He swallows, looks about at his companions, who continue to look to him for leadership. He brings his hand up to his beard and rubs his mouth as if in thought. In truth, he hasn't a thought in his head. Sensing his distress, Rah lowers his lids to half-mast and steps toward him again. He lifts his chin at Kaspir.

"You touch Rah. You see," he says with brutal confidence. "This one," and he tosses his head back toward Marut, "He touch Rah. No good. Now he die. I see assassin kill three men for Rah," and he snaps his fingers under Kaspir's nose, "Like this, so fast. Bad way to die. He like to take off head-"

"Enough, enough little fellow!" blurts Kaspir now, for there is no horror greater to an Amorite than the loss of one's head, as this will cause him to wander forever in the nether world searching for but never finding it. "No one is going to touch you, I assure you. We are at your service, are we not, men?" And he raises his hands to the others for support.

"From this day forth!" nods Lar in enthusiastic agreement.

"Most absolutely, little god. Upon my life!" sings Wadin behind him.

But Marut is looking from one to the other in a near panic. "What is to become of me? For I have indeed touched him!"

Rah looks back at him. "Maybe Rah no tell Wolf. Maybe," he says. "You come with Rah, north. We find Table of God. All enemy of Wolf sleep here. Rah sacrifice to dead. Then plague no come. Wolf is safe. Josepha safe. Hali safe." With this last his eyes drift south toward the stables of Amega. He sighs, bumps his chest with a fist.

"He is saying that the Wolf has sent him to make a sacrifice to the dead," says Wadin, nodding to the others.

"We can all hear," snaps Marut sullenly, for all four men have at one time or another learned enough of their enemy's language to be useful spies. "And everyone knows that the Terror has slaughtered thousands of us in battle and that those unfortunate enough to be officers on the day they die are thrown into the Valley of the Gods at Goreme. It is a dreadful, haunted place. Those men are decapitated and forever separated from their heads. They wander in eternal darkness in search of them. We cannot go there. They say that when the moon is full the headless corpses of the dead officers come to life to eat the living."

"Yes!" says Rah, pointing at Marut. "This what Tiko say. This where Rah must go!"

"The devil with that," frowns Wadin. "You go on yourself, little slave-god. You've no need of us. You've your own magic to protect you."

"No," says Rah seriously. Then he looks at each man in turn, fixing one and then the other with his brilliant stare. When they are still and watching, he takes a dramatic, sad breath and points to the emerald in his crown. "This stone. Keep Rah safe. Rah must give to dead. Save Amega."

"You are sent to sacrifice yourself then, little fellow?" says Kaspir, looking at Rah with a bit of wonder.

"No," says Rah, shaking his head emphatically. "Wolf is no let Rah go. Wolf go north to bring three man to king. Make good war with enemy. Then bad woman she come, tell Rah, you go! No more Rah! Wolf love woman now, no more Rah! So Rah is go. Crow say go north. Big voice. Say go follow crow. Give sacrifice to dead."

"Could it be that he has run away, Kaspir?" wonders Marut now. "That he has taken it upon himself to make a sacrifice to the dead at Goreme? Perhaps he is a prophet! Perhaps even now the Terror has returned home to find that he is missing, and is in pursuit!"

"Thrice dead, we are," mumbles Wadin miserably.

"But we could serve him!" cries Lar suddenly. "If we serve the servant of the Wolf- "

"Then we serve the Wolf," finishes Kaspir.

"What is this he is saying about a woman?" pipes Lar. "And a crow?"

"It is no matter," responds Kaspir. "These are the ghost voices of a prophet. One cannot expect to decipher them." He steps toward Rah, makes a military bow. It is an ugly thing to the Grain God, an abrupt, aggressive chop at the waistline, so that the sharp tip of Kaspir's hat very nearly pokes him in the chest. Rah draws back with a dancer's grace. The entire exchange has become a chance to perform and he is adding drama at random, as if the sudden happenstance of an audience is too great a treat for him to resist. When Kaspir raises his eyes, Rah gives him a heart-stopping smile and bows back, but his bow is the bow that stopped the blade of the assassin. Kaspir, Marut and Wadin blink stupidly as the boy lays his glossy curls in the grey sand, drawing his arms back to sweep the ground with the backs of his hands. Lar gasps. All three men have stepped away from the boy, as if a puff of heavenly wind, created by the grace of the movement, must sent their simple mortal flesh back on its heels.

Marut gulps. "Do you think the Wolf will not simply assume we have stolen him and part us from our heads first, before we have had time to explain why four Amorite soldiers are in possession of his god-slave?"

"We had better talk fast when he comes," agrees Wadin, "And in our sleep, for he is fond of the night."

"Here then, little god," says Kaspir, who has moved to pick up Rah's sack of provisions and the sheepskin that fell to the sand from the mouth of the sack when he dropped it.

"You come and sleep by the fire with us tonight. We will guard you, for there are beasts out here who know nothing of the Wolf of Hatti. You, Wadin, you will keep the first watch. Lar, you the second. Marut the third. I will take the dawn."

"Why me the first watch?" shudders Wadin. "He is like the wind, is Rush. By the time it is here you are choking in the dust of it. He will beat the dawn. Let me sleep through my death."

"I will take the first!" spouts Lar, taking Rah's sheepskin from Kaspir and putting it over the boy's shoulders, for the sun has set and the night has become chill. Rah turns to give Lar a scowl and takes the skin from him.

"For who has seen him and lived long enough to know it?" continues Lar, unfazed by Rah's annoyance. "Better to see the Wolf of Hatti and then to die at his blade with that reward!"

"You no touch," says Rah, smoothing the sheepskin against his chest with one hand. "No touch." He looks around at the others dangerously. "Or Wolf is come and-" and here he draws a finger under his jaw. He makes a little hiss, the blade opening his throat. "Take head off."

"No one is going to touch you," says Kaspir hurriedly while giving Lar a scowl of his own. "And Wadin will take the first watch."

"Inanna help us," murmurs Marut as the group moves back to the fire to settle as best they can for the night.

An hour later, while Rah sleeps in contented safety by the fire and Wadin shivers with his back against a tree a few meters from the others, the leopardess sniffs the ground, tongue lolling, where Rah stood in sandaled feet as the soldiers interrogated him. She sniffs, pants, raises her head as if to catch the greater portion of the scent that she follows. Then she lies down on the spot, stretching out her paws before her, and finally rolling over and over on her back to take it up into her fur. When she is finished she shakes herself and moves off to jump into the tree behind Wadin's head, so silently that he does not look up when the leaves shiver in the branches above. A bird perhaps, an owl landing in the tree after a hunt, or a rodent. An hour later Wadin will awaken Lar to take his place, and the leopardess will watch with little interest in the two rank-smelling men, for her nose is attuned to egg yolk and cherries, and her eye to the golden head of the growling boy she has followed so far from her hunting ground.

Rush reaches the encampment not long after Lar leaves his post at the tree to wake Marut to take his place. He has increased his pace since he discovered the leopard's footprints following the boy's, and all day he has been edgy with excitement. For either the animal has taken Rah, in which case he will come on the scene in time to rescue the boy and engage it in combat (he is already picturing its skin hanging on the wall over his marital bed) or he will catch up with it yet in the act of stalking Rah, in which case he will put his gold-handled dagger in her back before she knows that her fine coat is prey to a greater beast than she. In that case he will give her hide to Aros to make a costume for the dancer, and order Dimius to create a dance in which to tell the story of the Grain God's rescue.

But for now the one thing he will not do is consider the thought that Rah is already dead, that his fine flesh has become a sweet meal for a hungry cat. For each time he approaches the thought his mind goes black with dread, a dread he has never known, has never had to face. It is like falling off a dark cliff, or like losing his way home, though he knows that his household is in danger and yet he is confounded and unable to reach them to save them. More and more these days this feeling has begun to burrow its way into his brain. It is like a tape worm that feeds on what is there and makes more of itself until it would consume its host. It began when the China woman foretold of the plague, a plague that he himself brought to his own house, and of the boy's flight from Amega to a place, how did she put it? 'Where the Rah go, great man cannot follow.'

I will follow you to the edge of the world, little cat, thinks Rush. And when I find you I will beat you to within an inch of your life. But no, I would not harm that face, that form. Nor would I break that spirit. Better to chain you in golden chains, force you to wear a thousand emeralds to match your eyes. Better to compel you to dance for me. Dance for me again, little cat. Dance in this leopard's skin and Pyrus will paint your face to match. Spit at me, bite me, growl and snap. Only do not come to harm.

Do not go where I cannot follow.

And so the woman's words haunt him through the day and on into the night until he hears the rustling and murmur of men changing guard in the camp of the Amorite spies, and moves silently back into the brush to watch and to wait.

"Come Marut, it is your watch," whispers Lar, shaking his friend's beefy shoulder. Marut snorts, slaps away his hand, rolls to his other side.

"Akh, you are a devil to wake," grumbles Lar, stepping back to poke the man between his shoulders with a toe, for it is not uncommon for Marut to wake in a rage and strike a man before he has fully come to his senses.

But tonight Marut only slaps at his foot and pulls his wool up over his shoulder. "Take the third watch for me tonight, Lar, and I will take yours tomorrow," he says.

"I do not expect there will be a watch tomorrow. Let me sleep tonight for it may be my last," answers Lar. He looks off into the dark brush. "To hell with it, we may as well both sleep." And he moves off to his own leather to settle down for the remainder of the night.

It is not long before both men are snoring.

It is near morning when the leopardess leaves her tree. Unaware that a greater hunter than herself has taken note that her footprints lead toward the very tree against which the Amorite watch was kept until the last imbecile failed to wake the next, she descends from her perch at last sometime before dawn. Rush has not moved from his own hiding place, a copse on the opposite side of the camp. But when the animal moves toward the boy sleeping by the fire he pulls his favorite and best balanced blade, the silver and gold Minoan dagger, and readies to set it between her shoulder blades.

What he does not anticipate is that she will slink toward Rah from an unexpected angle, so that she is not clearly visible to him, the glare of the dying fire and the bodies of two other men obscuring his target. When he sees her again what he sees sets his mind reeling. It is not possible. Is the boy already dead? Is this his corpse he spies? Have these men abused him unto death and now this cat intends to drag his limp body away with her into the brush?

For the leopardess is sniffing the boy's hair, panting like a mother cat who recognizes its own young after a long separation. Her mouth is wide, her tongue lolling. This instant seems to last forever, and is only interrupted by the sound of the boy coming awake, no doubt from the rank scent and heat of the big cat's breath on his cheek.

"Gah!" says Rah, and the sound brings Rush to his senses and sends him forward from his hiding place to a clearing at the edge of the camp. In an instant he has sent the blade spinning over the Grain God's head and into the leopard's back.

Like a top she whirls, snarling, rolling, clawing and biting the thing that is embedded in her shoulder. Rah has drawn back but is frozen now watching the great cat thrash in the sandy dirt inches from where he lays. The sound of the animal's agony has awakened the men around the campfire and all stare as if struck by a bolt of lightning at the big cat writhing in battle with the blade of the assassin. Then the dark horror standing at the edge of the campsite steps forward and Lar cries out to the others, pointing , "The Wolf!"

Like the prince of Tartarus himself, Rush stands wrapped in black muslin from head to foot, one-eyed, feet splayed, crescent blades drawn at his sides to finish off the cat. But before he moves, Rah cries out, "NO!" and throws himself at the blade embedded in the animal's shoulder, plucking it from her hide and hurling it back at the feet of the assassin.

"No kill!" he yelps, rising to his feet and backing away from the black hell at the edge of the brush. By now the cat has taken off into the maquis. Rah is staring boldly at the shadow that is the assassin, to the utter amazement of the four Amorite spies lying paralyzed with fear at the sight of the dreaded Terror.

"You no kill," says Rah levelly to the hulking black horror. His cloak has fallen open and he is panting like the leopardess, fists clenched, poised for flight.

"You would be dead a dozen times if it were not for my blade, you little fool," responds the demon. He speaks Hittite, and the voice is hell-deep but strangely tempered. It is an astonishing thing to see, this queerly softened monster, his own black breast heaving with fury, for he has been distracted from his purpose and has lost the cat, his dark voice modulated as if in fear of spooking the boy.

But Rah has begun to back away. He has put the fire between Rush and himself and is moving toward a clearing between Kaspir and Marut.

"Take him, fool!' shouts Kaspir to the other. And Marut is on his feet just as Rah springs between them and shoots like a deer toward freedom. But it is too late. Marut has caught his foot and tripped him. Rah falls to his knees, twists, slashing at Marut with the nails of his right hand, snarling into the man's face. Marut draws back in time to avoid Rah's snapping teeth. He lets go of Rah's leg and the boy is on his feet and gone, like the leopard, into the darkness beyond the fire.

All this Rush observes from where he stands.

"You will not catch him in the dark," he says at last, though Marut has stumbled off into the bush after the boy.

Kaspir is looking up at him with awe.

"Do you address me, sir?" he says finally.

"You are Amorites," answers Rush. "Get to your feet."

All three men scramble to their feet then, heads bowed, shoulders lax. A moment later Marut returns from the brush.

"I cannot find him, sir," he says meekly to Rush, his eyes to the ground. He has come to join his brothers by the fire. "I meant to catch him for you."

"We all meant to catch him for you, sir, and to keep him safe," continues Wadin. "For we knew he must be of great value, sir, a Minoan slave-god. And being that he was not far from the Fortress of the Terror... that is, Amega when we caught him, that he must be yours."

"He is quite beautiful, sir," adds Lar stupidly.

Rush has said nothing. Finally, he stoops to pick up his blade, the gold-handled dagger that the boy tossed at his feet. He flicks it through the air lightly, catches it, returns it to the holster at his heel.

"You are the officer in charge," he nods to Kaspir, who takes in a sharp breath at his words but can find none of his own in answer.

"Well?" says Rush, squinting at him with his exposed eye before turning to kick sand into the fire. "Fools," he continues, and with a few annoyed stomps kills the remaining glow. "A fire, out here. It draws the jackals. Are you brainless?"

"We are-" begins Kaspir, finally finding his voice.

"You are spies," grunts Rush, moving to pick up Rah's sack and search through the contents. There is not much left but a heel of dark bread, a small round of cheese and a few handfuls of hazelnuts. "You followed the woman and the donkey to see that your master's work was done. Now you think you will bribe me for your lives with what is my own. You snatched the boy to save your hides. Now I will make your hides into saddles."

He has turned back to the group in time to see Kaspir fall to his knees before him.

"No, Master! We meant no harm nor theft! We hoped only to serve the Great Wolf of the Hatti, by serving his servant, sir!"

"Amorite dung, get to your feet!" barks Rush, annoyed at the name his enemies have given him. But as Kaspir stumbles to his legs he kicks him full in the chest, knocking the wind from his lungs and throwing him back down to his buttocks several meters from him. Kaspir makes a second attempt to rise to his feet only to be pinned by the skirt of his tunic to the ground between his legs. This time he stays where he is, panting like a winded dog, his hands laced over his genitals.

"Now you will work for me," says Rush, coming forward to stand over the terrified Kaspir. "You will spy for me, against your own. Amorite filth. You are like weasels in the hen house. And so I will allow weasels to be weasels. You will return to your captain and tell him that Amega is in a panic, that the horses are dying in the fields and that my standards have been taken down and replaced with plague flags."

"Yes, sir! We will leave immediately! This is genius-" begins Kaspir. But he has not finished his statement before his words are stopped by a second dagger, which has somehow cut the chin strap of his helmet just below his left ear without opening his throat.

"You speak to the general of the Armies of Amega, worm," growls Rush irritably. "Address me again as an equal and I will make a wineskin of your bladder." The assassin has tossed Rah's sack, into which he has stuffed the boy's sheepskin, at Marut. The man grabs at the airborne duffle while ducking at the same time, as if he expects it to be accompanied by another flying weapon.

"Vermin. You live because I have stamped out the plague your brothers sent to me and to my family. And so now I will send you, a plague of lies, back to your brothers. Fail to tell them precisely what I have instructed you to tell, and I will hunt you down and teach you how long it can take a man to die a tortured death, in a way you have never heard of nor could imagine."

"You ...you are sending us back to the camp of the Amorites then?" asks Wadin, who has until now been unable to press words past his tongue to speak.

"For now you will remain with me," answers Rush, "Do you think I do not know you are less trustworthy than jackals? We will catch the boy, and then we will cross the plateau and I will see that you return to your captain with my own eyes. I will watch, and I will know by his reaction if you have done as you have been told. Now pack. What is not on your backs in the time it takes me to track his direction will stay here."

A hazy morning sun has breached the horizon by the time Rush has convinced himself that the leopardess has turned south and has left a blood trail in that direction. He has also discovered that Rah has continued north, toward the pass and the plateau. He is in fact on the correct path to the Table of the Gods, which is just as well in the assassin's mind, for it must be crossed if he is to return to the Amorite camp to plant these spies.

Further north, Rah is no longer wandering. At sunrise he spotted a pair of crows over the pass in the mountains and he has determined to follow their lead. Wrapping his robe tightly about him, for it grows chill as he continues north, he fights his desire to stop in search of food. He has forgotten the leopard, forgotten even the wolf, for he is intent on delivering his sacrifice before the woman and the plague she has brought take hold of Amega.

CHAPTER 17

Captain Nikolaos stands at the window of his marital chamber looking out across the practice fields of Amega toward the tree line and the mountains beyond. Out in the farthest pasture from the stables is a bonfire, one that he himself ordered. It is the corpse of the unlucky donkey that carried the woman Sophina into the compound. Being thrown atop the burning donkey is the tack it rode in with. From where he stands, he cannot smell the flesh of the donkey roasting like a sin offering to the gods. But he can smell flesh roasting nevertheless. The smell is not that of donkey, nor of pig, though it is not unlike pig. It is human flesh, and it is coming on a breeze from the window of a guestroom down the hall. Bits of charred linen and other unsettling flotsam waft past him as he stands by his open window.

At least it did not take you long to die, he thinks, remembering the proud and ambitious creature that turned his own ambitions to ashes not long after she did her own. Within three days, the smell of death seeping down the hall was all the evidence he needed that the predictions of the China woman were accurate, and he ordered, with some satisfaction, that the door be opened and the woman's corpse be set on fire along with all of her belongings. The fortress is itself fireproof, being built of brick and stone. Once the fire died, the room would be thoroughly cleansed and returned to its original purpose.

As for the man, Ghedi, there had been a proper funeral once his burnt remains had been collected from the grain room. He had been loved by many, and it would not have been wise for the Lieutenant General left in command to fail to give him a decent and honorable Amegan burial, which amounted to the remnants of his pyre being taken out into the bay and released into the waters.

"Like Crete," thinks Nikolaos out loud, looking west toward the island. "What is left of you, Caphtor, land of the sun? And where are you, my Queen? Should I not have remained with you? What am I now, but a useless shell, demoted to captain? Captain of the palace guard of a dead city... of a Queen lost."

For though Rush demoted him to his former rank in their last moments together, he made no provision for his fate, neither informing the remaining commanders of the relegation nor stripping Nikolaos of his new uniform and jewel encrusted belt.

"He means only to shame me in my own eyes," thinks Nikolaos out loud, "Knowing that I am enough like him to care little of the judgments of others. And so now I may yet give orders, imitating what I was until his return, or else slink like a rat into its hole and watch the world crumble, hoping that I might feed on the debris that is left. Well I am no rat, Rush, though you think that I am."

And turning from the window he takes his fine new Amegan sword from the sheath at his belt and lays it down on his bed, just there in the center, between his side and that which had been Cara's, as if to remind himself of what he has already sacrificed for Rah. He unfastens the jeweled belt from his hips, lays it down on Cara's side like a sleeping bride. He takes a moment to compose himself, then moves to the dresser, opens it, finds the short Grecian weapon and simple leather belt he brought with him from Crete.

"You have a head or two left in you," he murmurs. Slipping the weapon into the holster at his waist to replace the Amegan sword, the sword of Lieutenant General, he draws in a single determined breath, grits his teeth, and strides out of his room to find Ramicus.

"They are kept in the pit, sir," says Ramicus, choking a bit on a mouthful of pheasant when the faces of Thymus and Kleitos on the opposite side of the table cause him to turn to see who has just cast a shadow over his noonday meal.

"Pit? What pit? Who keeps dogs in a pit?" snaps Nikolaos. He is looking down the table now, peering with keen grey eyes at the other men, addressing the question to the entire room.

"Well sir," answers Mikalya, the young charioteer from Troy who was one of the last men Rush spoke with before he left, "It is not for a horseman to know the keeping of war dogs, but the two men who came in with the woman,, that is, Peleshet and Mammut, they were quarantined out by the pit until today. I heard this from Hagga himself," he adds, nodding at the others at table. "They can take you there if you must go."

"Where are these men now, Mikalya," asks Nikolaos more gently. He had forgotten that he, himself, had ordered Peleshet and his man Mammut to be quarantined moments after he learned of the plague. In his distress over his own demotion, he had forgotten them entirely, and only now breathes a sigh of relief that both have survived. Hearty men, he thinks, putting his plan together in his mind as he leans over Thymus to press Mikalya for more information. But it is Thymus who answers him.

"Them two, they come back to the soldiers' barracks yesterday. I run into them at dinner. Well, hell, sir, I thought they might need a drink after all they been through. Went into town for a few. I'd imagine they might be sleeping it off, sir, as neither of them was much good at drinking."

"Why go to town when there is good wine in the cellar here?" asks Nikolaos foolishly.

"They make an alcohol of potato in Hatti, sir," pipes in Kleitos. "Not allowed here in the compound. Get your fool head cut off for drinking it, too," he adds, kicking Thymus under the table and giving him a sharp look.

"Potato?" Nikolaos squints, swallows.

"Awful stuff," agrees Kleitos. "I prefer wine myself."

"Very well, get back to your meal," answers Nikolaos, shaking his head in thought. "And there will be no more drinking from hence forth," he adds, turning to the door. "For we are going to battle."

When he is gone, the men at table stare dumbly at his retreating back. Then a cacophony of voices rise in speculation. "Battle? Battle in winter? On what front? Does he mean to engage the Amorites on their own ground in winter? On whose authority does he command such a thing?" Nevertheless, each is secretly excited by the prospect. They had thought that they would have to wait until spring, when kings go to war. But now it seems that the planting of the plague animal has provoked the assassin to move Amega ahead of the anticipated season, thus enjoying the luxury of a surprise attack. And who knows? Perhaps he intends to take Babylon and so control the Euphrates. By day's end, the entire compound, and much of the town, will be on fire with anticipation.

But Nikolaos is unaware of this. He turns his back on the soldiers he has confronted for information in the mess, and strides purposefully toward the soldier's barracks. When he arrives he awakens the guard at the open doorway, who is taking an unscheduled snooze in the noonday sun, by booting him onto his side and sending him face first into the dirt.

"Bring me Peleshet and Mammut," orders Nikolaos. "Let me catch you asleep at your post again, and you shall awaken to your head falling into your lap." And he settles his sword in its scabbard, making a slicing noise as he does so, and strides past. The man scrambles to his feet and rushes past him down the hall to duck into the sleeping quarters and awaken the two he is looking for.

"Sir," says Peleshet, stepping out of the sleeping quarters as he pulls his tunic over his head to make a curt bow. "You wish to see me?"

"I am told you are well, Peleshet," responds Nikolaos, less irritably. "Did you fall ill, or have no symptom of the illness?"

"I was spared, my lord," responds the other, turning to see that his own man, Mammut, has joined him. "As was my man."

"Very good," responds Nikolaos. "I understand you were quarantined out by the 'pit'."

"That is correct, sir," answers Peleshet. "In the handler's barracks. About a mile west of the compound. The Master keeps the dogs of war out there. Their handlers ride out daily to feed them, work with them and so on. But the barracks is empty in winter. Handlers only live out there in the spring to train the pups."

"But why there, Peleshet? Was there nowhere else in Amega you might have been quarantined?"

"I myself am a handler, sir. As is Mammut. It saved handlers riding out daily."

"How many animals are there out there, Peleshet?"

"Close to two hundred sir."

"And you know them? You can recognize one from the other?"

"Absolutely, sir."

"Then you know the two that Rush himself keeps with him when he is home."

"I should say so, sir," responds Peleshet keenly. "They are the largest and fiercest of all the dogs. They take no orders from any but the Master himself. He is the only one that can handle them, sir. But when he is not at the compound, he keeps them with the others out at the pit."

"Listen carefully, Peleshet. You will have three horses ready in half an hour. You will take me to the pit. You and Mammut."

"Sir?"

"We are releasing the Master's two."

"But I cannot handle them, sir! No one can! They will take off, to track the Master!"

"Exactly. Him, and the Grain God he follows."

An hour later, Nikolaos, Peleshet and Mammut stand at the edge of a manmade enclosure, dug twelve feet down into the rock and several hundred feet in circumference. A stair, cut into the side of the rock face of the pit, leads down to the sand floor. Rows of kennels, made of iron rods mounted in brick, separate the animals into groups of five and six. Each kennel is equipped with a shelter at the back and a clever plumbing system branches off from a fissure in the rock at the far end of the pit, and feeds a trough which passes through the floor of each kennel.

"Two men can care for all of these animals?" asks Nikolaos as the men descend the stairs.

"A man brings a wagon load of rabbit or grouse each day," answers Peleshet, "but it is up to us handlers to feed and to clean the pens. Water is no issue. That irrigation pipe feeds off an underground stream."

"And where are the Master's two?" asks Nikolaos as the men halt at the bottom of the stair. He is shouting at the top of his lungs now, for the noise of the dogs barking in anticipation of a meal is deafening.

"Right here, sir," says Peleshet, pointing to the two monsters in the closest pen.

Steadying himself, Nikolaos approaches the cage. As Peleshet reaches out to stop him, he puts up a warning hand and shakes his head, 'no' at the man.

"They know me!" he shouts over the wild snarling of the two enormous beasts. "I walked for miles in their company with the Master!"

Peleshet gives Nikolaos a look of concern, then nods and steps back, placing himself behind the iron gate that opens back and away from the stair. He motions to Mammut to join him.

Warily Nikolaos offers the dogs the back of his hand to sniff through the bars. Their recognition is immediate and astounding. Their vicious snarls have turned to yelps of pleasure and their hurling attacks against the bars to leaps of joy. Smiling with relief, Nikolaos unbolts the gate and frees them.

The two monsters snuffle at his ankles, knees, even his sex. Then one picks up another scent along the ground and barks with even greater joy. His companion immediately leaves Nikolaos to sniff alongside his brother, and Nikolaos watches as the pair trot toward the stair and then ascend step by step, sniff along the edges, tails wagging.

"They have found him, sir. They will track him now, to the ends of the earth if need be."

"Let us hope he is not that far gone, Peleshet," answers Nikolaos, his voice booming over the din. "Now you two will follow the dogs. And when you have found their master, you will inform him that Captain Nikolaos means to stage the army of Amega south of Hattusha, on the heels of the Amorites, and that he awaits his Master's orders to engage them in battle."

Peleshet looks to his man, Mammut, with wide eyed surprise. But there is no time to inquire, nor would he dare inquire, why the Lieutenant General of Amega has referred to himself as Captain Nikolaos. And Peleshet is a good man. He nods to Nikolaos, then makes a proper military bow and heads for the stair. He and Mammut will follow the dogs on horseback, and deliver the message exactly as ordered.

Rah has nearly reached the mountain pass by evening. He has been taking water from the stream, which he has continued to follow in the direction of the crows. He has had nothing to eat, save a few wild grapes, and is weary by the time the sun begins to set behind the mountains to his west. Somewhere in his memory he struggles with the familiarity of the sensation of the tongue of the leopardess against his cheek, her meaty breath on his neck. The memory has pulled him back down a long chain of memories to a time when such a sensation was comfort and safety to him in a motherless and unprotected place. The place is calling to him now. Come to me, it says, for in me there is rest and peace. In me there are no burdens. In me there is no plague, no hungering Wolf, no woman Sophina. As he sinks further and further down this chain of recall, he continues his gradual climb through the dwindling vegetation. He sniffs the air like a hound and struggles with his ability to think in any spoken language. His thoughts begin to come in pictures now, in the recall of sounds and sensations and smells. A goal remains in his mind to reach the place of the dead, but he has lost the ability to imagine it in words. He is looking for a memory, a cemetery of burial mounds on the northwestern face of a mountain, each with an exterior stair descending to the chambers within. He is looking for the cemetery of the ancients that Ting Ya tended on Mount Ida, and his purpose for reaching this place has become blurred. Perhaps Ting Ya is there, waiting for him with honeyed walnut clusters, her soft, Asian voice full of reassurance. Perhaps she will offer his gifts to the dead for him, not the doves of Galateo, but the emerald and the pearl he wears now, the gifts from the Wolf, fitting penance for the sins of the Wolf against the dead who have sent the plague to Amega. Yet all of this comes to him not in words but in pictures. His ability to speak and to think in human language, always so tenuous, is gone, licked away by the rough tongue of a leopardess on his face. He knows as if by instinct that he must make reparation for the sins of the Wolf. He must do this to protect those he loves, that is Josepha, Ting Ya, Aros and Pyrus, Tuma and Tyla, Peek, Hannah and Nephtet. And most of all Halix and the mares. But once this is accomplished he will return to the wilderness to find the leopardess, his mother.

On the fifth day of his journey, Rah makes it through the pass in the mountains and spots a pair of turkey vultures circling above a plain. These are not the crows he is looking for, but to his warped brain they are more significant even than those. The crows, with their sharp looks and arrogant cawing were intelligent teachers, guides. These creatures, with their awful, wrinkled heads and their long, square wings, the feathers of which splay like black fingers pointing the way to the dead, are evidence that he has reached his destination. As if in confirmation, the spring Rah has been following has disappeared under an outcropping of low rock to his right and the landscape has dried to a salty dust. Ahead of him is a plateau, a strange terrain of pooling rock and eerie spires. It is winter, but the explosion on Thera has ushered arid air over the Anatolian peninsula and, except at night, it is barely cooler than early spring. Rah understands none of this. For him, this is the landscape of his dream. This is where the voice of the God, Rah, spoke to him, telling him that this is the Table of the Gods, and that here he might rest.

With only a priest's cloak for comfort, Rah finds a recess in a wall of rock in which to make his bed for the night. But he is unable to sleep. The moon is near the full and as dark approaches the terrain about him becomes sinister. Eerie elongated shadows reach at him from the stalagmites that twist upward from the rocky ground. Now and then he hears the low moan or hoot of some wild animal. Perhaps an owl. Perhaps a fox or a jackal. More and more startled by every noise, fear begins to set his mind racing with ugly images of bear and wolf, snake and scorpion. At last, unable to rest where he is, Rah struggles to his feet, draws his cloak tightly about his shoulders, and begins to wander about in the moonlight, starting at shadows and making his own animal sounds in unconscious unison with those around him.

The moon is nearly down when Rah returns to his hole in the rocks. Exhausted, he passes into a dreamless sleep sitting up, his arms wrapped about his legs, his head on his knees. He is awakened by a scuttling noise near the edge of the niche he has crawled into, followed by a low howl out over the mountains to the west, and then the distinct but far away sound of marching feet somewhere to the north, on the rock floor of the Table.

Rah sits bolt upright, then slams himself against the furthest recess of his niche. Still as the rock he hugs he listens, his eyes squeezed shut, his ears pricked to hear the breath of a lizard, the undulation of a viper. For a moment, there is nothing. Then, another lone howl, deep and dark as the Scandinavian wood where he was born. Immediately following the howl, an unutterable silence, and then the stamping of feet in unison echoes through the air. This time it is clearer, closer, and coming toward him, as if an army of feet has followed him up the rise and is now making its way to his hiding place in the rocks.

Rah struggles to hold himself still against the back of his tiny cave. But his instinct to run is too great. As the marching feet advance toward his hole, he loses his battle with his nature. He races from his little den in the rocks, intending to head north, away from the sound of those feet, but he has only taken a few steps in that direction when he realizes that the noise is all around him. He hears it rising from the pass in the mountains, but also before him, further north, where the table of rock drops off to a valley and wilderness beyond. He hears the stamping feet to his left and to his right, above and below. He whirls about, looking for soldiers to appear from the deepening darkness in every direction. He spins and spins as the noise grows louder, clapping his hands over his ears and letting out his own howl of terror.

It is the warbling cry of a wounded animal, and it lifts up into the air and across the rocky plateau of the Table to the ears of the Wolf of Hatti.

Rush has not slept for two nights when he hears the sound that is unique to Rah lifting over the rocky landscape. He has reached the southern edge of the Table, the Amorite spies he has taken into his custody following wearily but determinedly behind him. Earlier that evening Lar, the youngest of the group, fell to his knees and then to his face in the dirt with exhaustion. Rush stopped only long enough to pull him to his feet and back hand him with a blow that might in itself have broken his neck, into a prickle bush.

"You have feet now to walk upon. See that you keep on them, or lose them," he snarled in the man's terrified face. Then he turned to continue up the trail. There was no means of tracking Rah in the dark, except by instinct. Surprised that he had not come upon him yet, surprised that the boy was still moving, he continued up the narrow pass through the mountains. It was the most obvious route once night fell, for any other direction would either lead him across the stream, which was unlikely, up the inhospitable slope of a mountain, or back down the trail toward Amega. So Rush continued north, occasionally breaking his own enforced silence with his deliberations.

"The little fool has managed to find the Table. By what means, I wonder, is he led? Nuisance. Should have left him on Caphtor, left him to be disemboweled by that chicken-livered priest. So fond of sacrifice to the dead, he is."

None of the Amorites dared respond, of course. They kept pace with the hulking shadow of the assassin as best they could, pulling each other along at times, slapping one another in the head when any seemed to be failing or about to fall to their knees.

Suddenly they began to climb the rocky pass, losing the sound of the stream behind them.

Just as suddenly the assassin turned to address them.

"You will camp here. Make no fire. Make no mistake. I will hunt you like grouse and hang you from your feet in the trees if you are not here when I return."

"You have our word, sir," responded Kaspir.

"The word of a spy is like the liver of a coddle fish. Nevertheless, I will take your word tonight, with your liver as ransom," grumbles Rush as he snatches Rah's sack from Marut and turns to disappear into the darkness.

No one dares move nor drop to their weary knees in relief until the shadow of the Terror's immense shoulders, and the barely perceptible sound of his steps, have been gone for near five minutes. Then Wadin turns to Kaspir to ask, "What do you suppose will happen when we tell our commanders back at camp that Amega is in ruin?"

"Perhaps they will assume that they can take Kussara, or Hattusha, now that the compound of the Terror has been compromised," answers Kaspir, shaking his head miserably. "Our brothers are doomed, as are we. But what can we do but obey him? Should we attempt to reach camp ahead of him to alert them, he will catch us like pigeons in a snare and have our hearts for breakfast that very morning."

CHAPTER 18

Having sent Peleshet and Mammut after the dogs on horseback, with orders to inform the assassin of his plan, Nikolaos returns to the fortress. He calls the four remaining commanders into the shield room and gives them their orders. Then he makes his way to the Hall of the Moon. He finds Cara first, unexpectedly, coming down the hall with two priestly attendants. She is clothed entirely in the garb of the priesthood of the Moon and her head is covered. But he recognizes her by her height, her gait, and by her sudden halt as she lifts her hooded head in surprise at finding him here.

"My Lord," she says, bowing neatly, for a priestess is nevertheless the servant of the house and city in which she is kept.

"Cara," says Nikolaos with a gentleness he has not heard in his own voice for some days. "Where is the priest, Mochlos?"

"He is in the lyceum, my Lord, with the others. They pray and fast for the safe return of the Rah."

"Go and get him for me, Cara. Tell him Nikolaos has need of his services. Bring him back here, to his own chamber. Do it immediately."

"Sir," says Cara, bowing curtly again and then dismissing the two attendant priests with her hand and moving past Nikolaos to find and collect Mochlos. Alone in the Hall of the Moon, Nikolaos wanders, peering into one room after another until he comes upon the Grain God's attendant, Aros, in a large and sunny chamber with three beds, two against the hall wall on either side of the doorway, and a larger, handsomely pillowed couch against the far wall. In one corner is an open trunk filled with colorful silk costumes. The attendant himself is holding an elaborate headdress in his hands. The thing is made of green and purple peacock feathers which splay out in an enormous fan around a mesh headband.

"Your excellence!" gasps Aros when he looks up to see whose tall and elegant form has blocked the doorway. He drops the piece on the pile of costumes and makes a quick, servant's bow.

"It is alright, Aros," responds Nikolaos, coming forward to stand beside him at the open trunk. He picks up the headpiece carefully, turning it to and fro, examining it.

"He has worn this in Knossos?" he muses, flicking his grey eyes at the dresser.

"No sir. This one has just been made. I designed it myself, for his... for the performance we had expected to put on for the Master."

"A performance? Here in Amega?" Nikolaos gives him a curious look.

"Yes, sir. It was to be the Story of Rah, god of abundant harvest. Rah was to play himself, and within the story all of his previous dances were to be performed. Then his face painter, Pyrus, accidentally came up with a new costume. A rainbow! Well, they are all accidental in the end I suppose. For it is more often than not by accident that we create our costumes, Pyrus and I. At any rate, this was to be the headdress of the rainbow. Is it not fantastic? And Rah, painted head to toe in rainbow colors, stripes twisting about his limbs and reaching his extremities. And a costume of silks of every color, well here it is, just here." Aros has leaned over the trunk in his enthusiasm to show the man he still believes to be the Lieutenant General of Amega the fabulous silken strips that together make up the costume of the Rainbow Rah.

"But I suppose there will be no use for them now," adds Aros dejectedly, as he carefully sets the pieces back on the pile of costumes in the trunk.

"Do not be so sure of that, dresser," comments Nikolaos. Before Aros can respond, footsteps hurrying down the hall toward them take his attention. He has turned and is facing the door with an air of authority by the time the shaven head of Mochlos appears and bows in the crisp light.

"You had planned a dance, then, priest, a dance for the Master. The story of the Rah," he says to the priest with cool curiosity. Mochlos flashes a look at Aros, who can only blink back at him and swallow. When he returns his eyes to Nikolaos he collects the presence of mind to offer him an appropriate bow, then answers, "We had planned it, yes, Master Lieutenant. The boy was fixed on in. And as you know, he will have his way in the end."

"Yes, I suppose he will," responds Nikolaos, reminiscing with some affection. "Well, you have a few days left while the troops are preparing for battle. I suggest you apply all of your skills, and all of your prayers, toward a successful outcome, priest. Because you will be joining us."

"I! ... well this is... What are you saying?" blurts Mochlos in shock.

"Oh yes, priest. You, and your dancers. You will follow behind the troops. We go to the foothills of Urgup, to camp on the hindquarters of the enemy. The Master will attack from the north. From Hattusha. I have sent men to overtake him and advise him that we are coming to support him from the south. When he returns orders to do so, we will launch an attack, crushing the army of the Amorites between us like grapes in a press."

"But what need have you of my services, Lieutenant? I am but a priest. My duties to the Rah can be performed here in safety. And what good are dancers in a battle of titans?"

"You are a priest, yes. And you made the Rah. But you are also skilled with poisons, are you not? Will you deny it and kneel to whet my sword here and now?" answers Nikolaos, stepping forward ominously and sharpening his gaze to talons.

"No sir. I will not!" responds Mochlos, for once at a loss for further words. My dear gods! He is as dreadful as the other, he thinks, dropping his eyes and folding his hands before him in submission. "I am you servant, of course."

"And well you should know it by now, priest, for if it were not for the Rah himself, I would have used you for target practice in the killing fields the day you poisoned the Grain God."

Now Mochlos loses what he has managed to collect of his composure and looks up into Nikolaos' piercing glare with wide-eyed terror. He sees the knowledge of his misdeed in the man's pale eyes, reaching for him, and he is a rat looking up at the talons of an eagle that has descended on silent wings until the very last moment. It is too late, he thinks. He has me. But Nikolaos merely gives him a shove, pushing him back into the hall wall.

"Poison can be of use in battle, priest. Now we will see just how skilled you are at your craft. As for the dancers, they are for the comfort of the Rah, when he is found. And he had better be found, priest, or I will think your prayers are futile. Tricksters and deceivers, just like their master. I will hold you personally responsible for his safety, so pray hard, priest. Pray hard."

"Yes sir. I understand you exactly," answers Mochlos. Bowing formally, he takes a step to his right. But Nikolaos' sword is already at his throat before he has had time to make his escape.

"Cara will stay here at the fortress," he says quietly.

"Of course," answers Mochlos quickly, with a look of surprise on his face.

"You understand that if she were for any reason at all to … take ill, during her tenure with you, for that, too, I will hold you personally responsible."

"Excellence," responds Mochlos now, with a bit of an edge to his voice and a lowering of his lids with a touch of resentment. "I need no instruction as to the care of the High Priestess in training. I am in fact quite fond of her and would be myself inclined to 'encourage' anyone to 'take ill' who thought to harm her."

That is enough to raise Nikolaos' brow and to return his sword in its scabbard.

"I see. Very well, then. You have your instructions. Prepare yourself and your dancers for travel."

"Sir," bows Mochlos, a bit more stiffly than before, and he edges from the younger man's grasp and, straightening his shoulders, makes his way back down the hall.

"Will I go also, Excellence?" It is Aros, who has come from Rah's chamber to peek down the hall at the retreating priest.

"You, and the painter. And all of these," Nikolaos waves a hand at the trunk of costumes against the far wall of Rah's room, "personalities as well. For I believe there will be need of them in Hattusha."

"Yes sir!" answers Aros with as much relief as gladness. And when Nikolaos has disappeared down the hall, he turns in the other direction to find Pyrus.

Rah has lost his way.

He has spun and spun, round and round in the dark, trying in vain to keep the sound of the ghostly marching feet in front of him. But in every direction he turns he is confronted with silence, and the tramping feet are behind him, ever approaching, and in his damaged mind headless soldiers threaten to appear out of the gloom to grab at him and to tear at him and to pull him into pieces and attempt to satisfy their eternal hunger by stuffing his flesh into the holes where their heads once sat upon their shoulders. Finally, dizzy and exhausted, he collapses to his knees, burying his own head under his arms but still howling like a terrified animal.

In the dark that sound is the only mark Rush has to shoot for. But the boy has wandered far from the pass, among the looming stalagmites that stand like sentinels all along the floor of the Table. Rush must feel his way to the sound, much as he did in the pitch darkness of the labyrinth of Cyrus, listening and intuiting the boy's hiding place under the palace. And so he follows the reverberating howl with the cunning of a wolf, sifting the echoes from the warbling agony that issues from the throat of the boy himself. If I call to him, he will only run, thinks the Wolf. He is here, but he is not in this world. It is the same as in the Hall of the Kings of Cyrus. I will recover his body, and I will consider how to recover his mind later.

But when he finds himself on an open plate of rock, Rah's pathetic yowling strikes his ear directly, unconfused by the distortion of surrounding echoes. Then his extraordinary night vision discerns the pale head of the Grain God from the volcanic debris around him as the boy crouches in a fetal ball, his head tucked under his arms so that his elbows form a kind of cross, and the sight is more horrible to him than the sight of the boy's drug induced palsy on the day he was made. That day the grotesque display could be accounted for by poisons fed to him by the priest. But here on the Table in the shadowed darkness what is most disturbing to him is that Rah is under no other influence than that of his own panic, and of remembered pain. He is lost within himself, and even the strength and protection of the assassin cannot soothe him.

He is gone mad, thinks Rush. His mind is gone, somewhere that I cannot follow, just as the China woman foretold.

Rush moves to the take the boy up in his arms and throw him over his shoulder, knowing full well that his back will suffer for it and be covered in nip marks and welts in the morning. But his footfalls break the cycle of Rah's screams and the Grain God looks up from his terrors in time to see him coming. To Rah, the assassin is the worst of his fears come true. The tramping feet of the ghost army have stilled as if in respect, perhaps in awe, of the one who put them in their graves, but the towering, black-wrapped, one- eyed monster that bends to take him is worse even than these. Rah lets out a high pitched human shriek and attempts to rise and to flee. He is successful only in giving the assassin a better opportunity to tackle him.

And once again, Rush is pinning a wildcat under his superior weight, and patiently gripping and releasing, gripping and releasing the boy to allow him to exhaust his physical strength.

In time, his patience pays off, and Rah stills. The two lie, one atop the other, panting in the salt dust that covers the Table, Rah's back against the cool, smooth volcanic rock floor, his breath coming in rhythmic puffs against the assassin's shoulder.

"Enough, now, little cat," pants Rush into the boy's curls in his gentlest voice. "I must take you with me. I've no time to return you to Amega."

But Rah only squirms against the man's impossible strength and weight, then gives a little growl of frustration.

"You understand me well enough, though you may not speak it," says Rush, lifting himself off the boy and pulling him to his feet. Then he takes his jaw in his hand and gives it a shake. "Now you will come with me, on foot, or else I will carry you, eh?" and he bends as if to hoist Rah onto his shoulder, at which the boy skips back, staring at him distrustfully, but he consents to step around the assassin and to submit to his goading as he is urged back across the eerie landscape of the ancient volcanic plateau toward the pass.

"You would have died up here, little fool," mumbles Rush behind his back. "There is no water but that which issues from the cracks in the ceiling of certain caves, caves you would have never found. And what is it you were howling at, eh? Was anyone hurting you? Or did you see the specters of the armies of my enemies? Well they are but ghosts now, and no harm to anyone. And if it is their heads they want, they will have to look for them back in their own country, for I have sent them there. There at the head of the Euphrates where their brothers are most likely to camp on their way into the land of the Hatti, that they might consider their futures before they cross my borders."

Presently Rah stops in his tracks, for there is a light ahead, the light of a campfire. He makes a warble in his throat, looks back at Rush for assurance.

"Idiots. It is only the Amorite spies. Cloth-eared and hogshit-brained." Rush pulls Rah back by the hood of his cloak and hands him his sack. He points to the light ahead. "They have made a fire. Go and sleep, little cat. Here is your lambskin. There is no army visible nor invisible that can harm you whilst you are in my possession." He gives Rah's curls a rough pat and shoves him forward. As Rah greedily takes the sack and pulls the skin from it, Rush walks soundlessly into camp, pulls a burning branch from the infant fire and throws it onto Kaspir's sleeping form. The man awakens, screams, brushes the branch away and rolls onto his belly to put out the flare that has taken hold of his tunic.

"Dimwits," mutters Rush, kicking dirt onto the remaining flames. "A nation of greedy dimwits, and I shall take your Babylon before I close my eyes to death, not because I want her, but because you are weak and deserve that she be taken from you." He seems to be talking to himself and it is only with considerable effort that Kaspir is able to make out his words. Assuming there is instruction or condemnation for him in them, he sits up and offers in perfect Hittite, "I beg your pardon, Master?"

"Did I not tell you it would draw the jackals?" answers Rush with disgust. But his attention is drawn away from Kaspir when a rustling in the brush interrupts him. Before Kaspir can draw his next breath Rush has sprung into the maquis in the direction of the noise. A bearlike human roar, then the screech of a wild animal, and silence.

The sun is up when Rush returns with the skin of the leopardess hanging from his belt.

He walks quite directly and deliberately to where Rah is lying and drops it on the boy's head.

Rah awakens beneath the bloody skin, yelps, scrambles out from beneath it and stares at it, panting. He looks from the skin, quite obviously leopard, to Rush, back to the skin. His fine chest is heaving.

"You killed her!" shouts Marut, looking about at the others. "He killed her with his bare hands!"

"Not hands," says Rush, still staring obstinately down at Rah, who meets his eyes with his own hateful glare. "These," and he pulls the crescent blades from his sides. The malicious weapons glitter in the morning sun.

Rah is burring at him from a seated position on the ground.

"Say something, damnit," says Rush to him suddenly. "Where is your anger, eh?" He steps toward the boy, slipping the blades back into their holsters under his arms.

Rah lifts his lip in a trembling snarl. His eyes are cool emeralds. They glitter like the stone he wears between them but he makes no human sound, offers no sapient challenge to the black bear that rears over him.

Rush bends to leer at the boy malevolently. "You will wear that skin for me, little leopard," he growls, his own eye hard and cold as black marble. Then he turns to begin packing his leather and gear. The others follow his lead without question, and Rah rises to his feet but makes no attempt to pack. It is Marut who takes Rah's sack and stuffs the boy's lambskin bed into it. Rah watches him do so, then raises his hands as if to take it from him.

"It's alright, little god, Marut can carry two," says the big man gently.

Rah makes no response, only holds the man's gaze a moment. He blinks and the sun goes down, thinks Marut, lifting the sack over his shoulder to lie against his own. Then the men are hurrying to keep up with Rush, who has already disappeared up the pass, and to maintain his humbling pace across the Table of the Gods.

In the camp of the Amorites, the remaining mercenary legion awaits with lessening hope the return of the Hatti defectors. Since the mass exodus of the Hittite army back to Hattusha under the command of the assassin, the integrity of the Amorite army has begun to disintegrate. The leadership is in constant flux, for shortly after the spies were sent to Amega one captain killed another over a game of dice, leaving twenty-five hundred men unmanaged. No one stepped up to take his place, for the mercenaries were governed by their backers in Syria, wealthy businessmen mostly who had an investment in closing down the Hittite grip on the Aegean trade routes. Captains were selected and installed based on nepotism, and no mercenary being paid by kingpins in Syria had any interest in taking on more responsibility than he was being paid for. With one captain dead the remaining bands became more unruly and self-interested even than before, and gambling and fighting to break the boredom became commonplace. By the time Rush and his little band of Amorite spies reached the Valley of the Gods, an entire company of men had deserted. The Amorites were down to a little over eight thousand men, twelve hundred horses and a few hundred chariots.

In Hattusha, circumstances were quite different. The five generals had been skewered. Ammuna lay in prison, and Aleksandus and Agrippa, along with the men they had brought with them from Amega, were put up in the palace. The renegade army, subdued by the example made of their generals, were sent into the valley to join the King's own twenty thousand. Mursilis, still believing Agrippa to be the Terror, waited for the assassin to bring up the question of Ammuna's fate, but the man never broached the subject. He seemed a different character altogether from the anaconda that had awakened him in the middle of the night weeks earlier to choke him with a kiss, then order him to watch the new three-man chariot demonstrated in the morning and then send one hundred of his best chariot makers back with him to Amega to produce the weapon in mass. Three days ago the man Mursilis believed to be the assassin left with the hundred chariot makers, leaving his trusted commander, Aleksandus, in charge of keeping an eye on Mursilis. Of course that was not how it was presented to the King. He was told that Aleksandus would remain behind to protect the throne, a personal guardian in case the Amorites attacked Hattusha. But Mursilis, even at his tender age, was not fooled by this nod to his nobility. He knew that Aleksandus would be cataloging his decisions from here on in and reporting them to the Terror, and that what he did with Ammuna would be the first test of his worthiness to keep the throne.

And so Mursilis paced and fretted and eventually, grudgingly, went to his grandfather's wife, the Queen, Tawan Anna, for her advice. After all, she had met the man, was even under his protection. She must have some clue as to what he meant for Mursilis to do with his uncle.

When Mursilis invites the Queen back to his private chamber she is neither surprised nor smug that he should do so. She merely greets him with a royal's grace and waits for him to sit before she does so herself.

"How can I be of help to the grandson of my King?" asks the Queen with, despite her years, the uncompromised deportment that won her the status she holds.

Hesitating only briefly, Mursilis levels his gaze at his grandfather's widow with refreshed bitterness and answers curtly, "The assassin is testing me."

"Of course he is, my Lord. We would expect no less," answers Tawan Anna, smiling gently.

"Do you use the royal 'we' madam? Or do you tell me that my grandfather assigned him this undertaking in addition to the job of securing your protection?" answers Mursilis. But of course, Tawan Anna makes no answer. At last he releases her gaze and, clenching his teeth, looks down at his own left hand which grips and releases the gilt armrests of his chair with rhythmic tension. Upon his middle finger the king's seal, imbedded in his grandfather's sacred ring, cautions him to maintain his composure with the only person who may be able to help him now.

"The man you speak of is assigned nothing by any but himself, Mursilis," says the Queen carefully. "But he loved your grandfather. And he loves Anatolia. And he will not leave a fool in power here long."

"Of this I am aware, Mother," answers Mursilis with strained respect. "Let us then stay to the matter at hand. He has left me with a riddle, a riddle I must solve or lose my throne."

"Ah," answers Tawan Anna, nodding knowingly. "What to do with Ammuna."

Mursilis' eyes flash wide then drop back to his own left hand, the hand upon which rests the power to kill, to maim, to exile or to imprison for life his uncle. But it is too late. Tawan Anna has seen the look of respect and awe in his eye, respect and awe of her, the widow of the great Hattusilis. It is about time, thinks the Queen. Do you think I earned the love of the man who made a nation, nay, an empire, from a band of goat herds and bandits, simply by opening my legs?

"Send him back to the Amorites, my King. Send him back to his father's enemies, the killers from Syria whom he chose to lead in battle against you," she answers, leaning forward in her chair with calm and guileless certainty.

"Am I that much a fool to you, Tawan Anna, that you can even suggest such a thing with a genuine face?" responds Mursilis.

"I do not need to tell you this, my King. Understand that I could as easily let you make your own decision. But you have tested those already, have you not? Hang him, and offend the thousands of soldiers who followed him, believing that the King must be the son, and not the grandson, of the reigning king. Imprison him and you offend the people, for you offend your own blood and the blood of your grandfather by imprisoning a royal longer than it takes to make a bold decision. And exile? A Hatti prince? A more dishonorable death than hanging. No, you have considered all of the possibilities, save the one that will suit the station of the criminal, and the symmetry of the assassin's mind."

"Send Ammuna back to lead the army that camps in the foothills like a panther lying in wait? Give the beast back its brain? You want me skinned alive and hung in a tree for all of Hattusha to see, by the very man who took him out of the Amorite camp to bring him here for judgment?"

"Think like a king, Mursilis, and not like a common soldier. You have a people to govern. Send him back, with any man who desires to follow him. Whoever remains with you will have been forced to give you their allegiance once and for all. Those who desert you will have done so in public also, and will be bound by their decision. Then you will truly have a people who love you and will lay down their lives for you, for you are their choice."

"But I could lose every man who followed Ammuna! Near ten thousand of them. Not Amorite mercenaries, but Hatti warriors!" the King hisses, leaning over the arm of his chair toward the Queen like a true confidant suddenly.

"How many more thousands will Ammuna need to have the courage to face the assassin?" answers the Queen moderately.

"You think he will fight for Hattusha?" whispers Mursilis, blinking.

"He has always owned Hattusha," answers the Queen. "He will fight for what is his. He will slice through the traitors like a scythe through young wheat. Then he will lead you into Babylon."

Mursilis slowly sits back in his chair and, regarding his grandfather's widow with reopened eyes, he strokes what will one day become an exceptionally handsome beard.

"You are a convincing creature, Tawan Anna. But if you are wrong-"

"I have not reached the age of a dowager as Queen and survived your grandfather's temper by being wrong, my King. You cannot leave Ammuna in prison until the assassin returns. You must make a decision in order to secure your right to rule. And you cannot exile a Hatti prince. You cannot punish a royal with death for you will turn the people against you. Only one option remains. Send him back to the Amorites. He and all who wish to follow him. Let them chose their king, and once they have chosen, let them die honorably and in battle. Then you have extracted the traitors from your midst, quashed an internal rebellion, and destroyed your enemies all with one verdict."

"There is one other option," muses Mursilis, watching the Queen slyly.

"And that is?"

"I could let the people chose."

He has barely said it before the Queen throws back her head and laughs. The sound is soft but scornful. He waits with renewed irritation for her to finish.

"Only if you wish to convince the Terror that the Hatti need no king at all, and can govern themselves, like the Sumerians of Gilgamesh!"

Lowering his lids at her with annoyance, Mursilis nevertheless allows the Queen a nod of respect. Then he rises from his seat.

"I will do as you say, Tawan Anna. There is something diabolical about the plan that my heart senses will please the man."

"It is the fact that you give Ammuna and his band back to him on the battlefield, where he may kill them himself without mercy."

Now it is Mursilis' turn to laugh. Then he offers her his hand, and she rises.

"There is one other thing, Mursilis," she says suddenly as she draws close to him, still grasping his hand. But as his brows darken in anticipation of her words, she purses her lips and turns away, releasing her grip.

"Tell me." It is an order. But the Queen only shakes her turned head.

"No. If I tell you what he wishes you to discover for yourself, I myself will incur his wrath. And I am not willing to do that, Mursilis. Not even if you were my own son."

But when she has left him, King Mursilis himself is smiling. He is returning, he thinks. In daylight he was not what I expected. More refined in features, more temperate in nature than I might have expected from the thing that settled on my chest that night and spoke to me as if I were no more than a boy to be chastised. And his voice, there was something missing in his voice. That night it was like a voice from the underworld. And in the day, a commander, yes, but not a man who could command the armies of Tartarus. He has disguised himself, thinks Mursilis. He is playing a role. One day I will see the man beneath the disguise, perhaps beside me in battle. Then I will truly be acquainted with the Wolf of Hatti.

Crossing the Table of the Gods in the morning light and in the company of the assassin and four armed men, Rah is complacent, even meek. He walks beside Marut as if the two had become fast friends since the man offered to carry his bag. Now and then he lifts his eyes to search the man's face as if looking for a sign of friendship, or at least comfort, and Marut cannot help but return his gaze. The two gradually drift back behind Lar and Wadin, who are the youngest and fittest and most able to maintain the assassin's pace. A conversation of sorts develops between them in time, though it is not in words. Rah occasionally stops at a sound that Marut cannot hear and the big man must take his arm and draw him on, nodding forward at the broad back of the Wolf, then giving Rah a frown and a shake of his head. If I lose you again I will pay dearly for it, he is thinks to himself, and the boy's blue-green gaze wanders back to him, quizzical and empathetic. At last the assassin stops at the mouth of a cave in the rocks, and Rah takes a handful of Marut's tunic from behind, tugs it, and pantomimes a thirsty man drinking.

"There is running water in this one," says the assassin, turning to catch the tail end of Rah's pantomime. He gives the boy a sour look. "We will fill our gourds here."

The assassin makes a torch of a strip of poplar bark stuffed with tinder and lights it with flint and a bit of iron. Then he leads the men into the cave. They have travelled a quarter mile, following the bright glow of the assassin's torch, before he stops them, holding the fire over his head. In the silence the trickling of water from a fissure in the rock somewhere within a tunnel running perpendicular to the one they travel can be heard.

Rah has drawn up against Marut and begun to make a warbling growl in his throat.

"Keep him here with you," says Rush to Marut. Then he nods at Kaspir. "Take their gourds, Captain. You and these two will follow me."

As Rush begins a slightly upward climb into the passage toward the sound of the water, Kaspir gives the other men a look of surprise behind his back. "Captain?" he mouths in Amorite, then shrugs and follows the assassin's fading torchlight.

At the bottom of the passage, Marut drops his sack and sits on it. "Do my ears deceive me, or have I just heard the Wolf of the Hatti give our Kaspir a commission?" he murmurs to Rah, whom he can no longer see but can still hear, panting lightly beside him in the dark.

"He is fond of killing Amorite captains. I think I will wish to remain a footman in his army. What do you think, little god? How does one remain safe in the company of the lord of the underworld? You have done it. Tell me your secret."

But Rah makes no reply but for a steady and barely perceptible burring in his throat.

"You are a strange one," mutters Marut. "What sort of god-slave are you, eh? Are you a sun slave? You certainly look the part. Or sea? Yes, those eyes of yours. Where did he find you, I wonder. Not in the dark. Not in a cave. On a mountain, more like, or in a cloud. You are from the north or I a serving girl. They say they are pale as ghosts up there and fierce as lions. But now you are his. Now we are all his. Inanna help us."

By now Rush and the others have filled their gourds and are approaching. Marut straightens his back and stands against the cave wall at attention as Rush steps out of the passage into the main chamber with the torch. He gives the two an unreadable look and walks past them, handing Rah a gourd of fresh water as he does so. The boy takes it, gulps down several mouthfuls from the open end, then allows Marut to take it from him and tie it to his own weapons belt. The two follow behind Kaspir, leaving Wadin and Lar to take up the rear.

Outside the sun is blinding, the place itself utterly bizarre in the daylight. It is as if they walk still within a cave yet under a blue sky in harsh morning light. The stalagmites and hardened puddles of volcanic rock that terrified Rah in the dark appear like giants frozen in time, or like pillars of salt.

"Here is your army," says Rush, nodding about him. It is impossible to know if he speaks to Rah, and to his experience of the place in the pitch dark the night before, or if he speaks to Kaspir and the others. No one dares answer him, and he continues north over the volcanic plateau, making it almost impossible for the Amorites to keep pace.

After a time Marut drops back to whisper to Wadin, "What did you see?" For Wadin and the others have been marching with grim faces since their emergence from the passage in the cave with Rush.

"Speak not to me of it for I will tell you nothing," answers Wadin in Amorite. "Only be grateful that he allowed you to remain behind with the boy."

"But there were no skulls!" whispers Lar, stopping Wadin to grasp his arm. "Only the bodies, lined up like, like cords of wood, one atop the other! Surely that was not the only place to find water! He wanted us to see it! Wanted us to know," and he stops short as Wadin pulls his arm from his grasp and shoves him away.

"Speak not to me of it!" he hisses, nodding at the fast retreating back of the assassin. Then he hurries to catch up with Kaspir, who has remained doggedly on Rush's heels.

An hour later they are descending into a valley. At first the terrain is barren, but as they continue their slow climb down the steep slope the maquis returns, then marshy grasses and brush as if some watercourse feeds the vegetation. Rush continues north and west, and only after several more hours does he stop at the edge of a stream.

"This will lead us to the river," he says, gesturing for the others to rest. They fall to their knees, dropping their packs and plunging their faces into the icy water. Rush is removing his garments when a splash brings his head up. Rah has stripped and jumped into the stream further down the valley where it has widened. He dives under, surfaces, shakes himself like a wet dog, then plunges under again. Rush watches, intrigued. The boy is under water for over a minute. When he surfaces again he has with him a fish the length of his forearm. He sets the animal firmly in his teeth and swims to shore, dropping it at Rush's feet.

Rush is looking at him with unveiled wonder.

"What in hell are you?" he murmurs, lifting Rah's face with his hand. The boy looks up into his eye with a strange new defiance. His silvery-blond lashes sparkle with droplets of water, cooling his eyes to turquoise.

Rush fights the urge to back hand him to the ground. How do you strike such a face? he wonders to himself. It is like striking the face of God. All of the old urges have returned to him in one searing instant. His spine tightens. How good it would feel to whip you, boy, to hear you yelp in pain. I cannot tolerate your beauty. You are like the meat of a man's horse after days in the battle with no food. The senses delight, but the stomach is in revolt. And the heart breaks. The meat is seasoned with the man's own tears, for the horse took him into battle, remained his loyal slave even to the end, giving itself as a meal that his master might live. So it would be to take you. I would hurt myself even more than I would hurt you, and I would lose you.

Rah is glaring up at him with the whisper of a smile in his aquamarine eyes. Then he turns and dives back into the stream. He disappears under water for less than a minute and returns with two more fish, neither as large as the first, one in either hand.

"Mother Inanna," murmurs Kaspir at Rush's side. "He is like a bear that can snatch fish out of the water with his teeth."

"He is like a little leopard," Rush corrects him. "A beautiful little cat that will not be told what to do, but will now and then, when it suits her, allow you to stroke her." He has removed his hood along with his tunic and is now standing in black leggings several feet from the shore of the stream. He watches with unchecked amazement as the boy returns to him with the prize of two wriggling fish. Looking from Rush to Kaspir, Rah drops the fish at the assassin's feet and then puts his fingers together and stuffs them into his mouth, as if he were taking up a pinch of boiled barley or millet and feeding himself.

"He has lost his speech," says Rush, who seems to have taken Kaspir into his confidence, at least for the time being.

"On the Table," responds Kaspir, nodding knowingly.

"No," answers Rush. "This is because of the leopardess."

"He is angry with you for killing her for him, sir?" asks Kaspir carefully.

"He eats fish," says the assassin suddenly, ignoring Kaspir's question. "Have your cook make a fire now and smoke the meat over it for him. Cook it well, I won't have him wormy because an Amorite cannot cook a fish properly."

"Wadin will cook them for him, sir."

"Boil the water for drinking also. This is Anatolia, and the wilderness can be treacherous."

"Just as you say, sir," answers Kaspir, taking up the three fish and turning to Wadin, who is sitting on his pack, heaving.

"Make a fire and cook these well for the god slave of the great Wolf of Hatti."

Rush makes a quiet frown at the Amorite title, but he is soon distracted by Rah, who has begun a strange crouching movement along the edge of the stream toward the wider northern bank.

"What is he up to now, I wonder," murmurs Rush to himself, but when the men rise to see what has caught the boy's attention, he raises a fist, the universal sign of a commander for his troops to come to halt.

Rah is crouching further and further along the edge of the stream, picking bits of greenery as he does so. Presently the head and shoulder of a beast appears from a copse of trees not far from the bank. Rah is making cooing noises, now looking over his shoulder at the animal, now dropping his head and ripping at the greenery in his hand with his own teeth. As

Rush and the others watch in amazement, a colt in full Hatti tack steps out of the copse toward the boy. Running its muzzle along the ground it approaches Rah at a near trot, stopping short just an arm's length away.

"A loose horse!" whispers Marut, who has come to stand at Kaspir's side. "A sign of a battle nearby!"

"No," answers Rush in a far more sinister hiss. "It is the beast that threw me. I took it in Hattusha myself." Slapping the fish from Wadin's hands he adds, "And it owes me a meal." The assassin steps forward and strides toward Rah, whose back is to him. He has taken the colt's broken reins and is standing now, cooing and petting the beast between its eyes.

"That is my animal, little cat. Come, bring it here to me," says Rush in a voice that attempts to be reassuring. In fact, it is no more reassuring than the hiss of an enormous snake, and it startles both Rah and the colt, who backs away, straining at the rein Rah holds as the assassin approaches.

Rush has covered half the distance between them when Rah takes a step toward the colt's shoulder, his left hand now twisted into the animal's mane.

"Do not dare it!" growls Rush, but it is too late. The boy has launched himself into the saddle with one catlike spring. The colt backs off the reins, rearing, but is unable to lose the fantastic acrobat that seats him now. Rah takes up the reins and turns the animal quickly in a circle, kicking its sides and driving it into its bridle. The animal settles, finds its senses, and submits to his direction. He turns it toward the stream, plunges into it and crosses before Rush can reach the spot where he mounted. Then he is off at a gallop, racing north, in the direction the colt most desires for it is headed home to Hattusha.

"I will chase you through Tartarus!" bellows Rush at the retreating pair.

But Rah is out of range of his voice before he has finished his words.

CHAPTER 19

In the fortress of the Terror at Amega, Ting Ya prays to the ancients before her altar in the alcove of her room. She has taken no food for four days and drinks only boiled water which has been steeped with the essence of a certain plant leaf that she has brought with her from Crete. It is an act of purification, for Ting Ya knows that it is only the purification of the world that will keep the Rah within it. And the purification of the world begins with the self.

Now and then she rises from the small woven rug before her altar and walks to her window which overlooks the Lady Josepha's courtyard. Over the stone walls she can see the Great Sea stretching west toward Crete. She does not allow herself to imagine the once green and golden land of the Minoans covered in ash, but looks up to the sky and considers the birds of the sea, who continue their daily lives in peace as if the country she for so long called her home has not been turned to a dust and ember hell. Now and then, looking out her window, she sees Josepha seated on her couch in the courtyard, but the lady is not looking out to sea. Usually she has her box of jewelry tools in her lap and she is fashioning some trinket. But today she is not distracting herself with jewelry making. Today Josepha is not alone. With her is the handsome one, the one who has watched over the Rah from the beginning, saving him from the bad men who stole him from Knossos, from death itself, and finally, from the ferocious hunger of the Wolf.

Returning to her altar, Ting Ya kneels, deepening her prayers and her commitment to her fast. She believes in these things, but is wise enough to know that sometimes these things use the world of men to express their power. And today she is happy to know that the handsome one has come to inform the mistress of the house that he is taking the warriors of Amega north to fight for the sake of the Rah. He will take the priests of the Rah with him, and his dancers, and as much that is familiar and comforting to the god slave to draw him back into the world of men. She knows these things because she knows that a man cannot change what he is, and that this man is a like a Shang warrior, who would gladly prefer to give his life for his emperor and god, than live in the aftermath of his death.

Outside, Nikolaos is discussing his plans with Josepha. The lady of the house has listened quietly to his report, her hands folded in her lap, her eyes tracing the exotic tiled patterns on her patio floor.

Only when he is finished does she lift them to meet his own.

"You know you need not come to me, Nikolaos, for permission. Neither can I give it to you. You say that he has discharged you from your duties as Lieutenant General and returned to you your former rank of Captain of the Palace Guard of Cyrus. Who then, is your queen? Or to whom do you owe your allegiance? And why do you come to me?"

The words themselves are challenging but the tone of them is gentle, even conciliatory. Nikolaos blinks at them, confused, then drops her gaze and looks down at his hands.

"Need I say it for you, Captain Nikolaos? Have you not always, since the moment you first lay eyes upon him, been in your own heart sworn and committed to defend and preserve the Rah? And what were your Queens last orders to you, shall I guess? Are you a man who would sneak away on his own whim when the earth was caving in and her city falling into ruin, leaving her to fend for herself? Or did you come to her, as you come to me now, looking for permission to follow the pledge already burning in your heart. You have your orders, Captain Nikolaos. They have not changed."

"You are a remarkable woman, Josepha. I have been in the presence of queens with less bearing, and of kings with less wisdom."

"You have not been in the presence of the King whose wisdom instructs me, Captain Nikolaos," answers Josepha mysteriously. "All others are shadows, or else parts of Him."

"I will do my duty, madam, as you say. I will follow through with the promise I made to Media in the last days of Crete. And that is to guard the Grain God with my life. I have now an army at my disposal. I will not leave you defenseless, but take the half."

"As you say, Captain," responds Josepha, rising so that he may do so as well. "May the favor of the Most High be with you."

In the evening, Nikolaos is interrupted in the Commanders' Mess by an excited and determined Tiko, who has learned from the two commanders who have been chosen to remain behind that only half of the warriors of Amega will be leaving for Hattusha in the morning.

"You must take me also, sir. I can be of service to you when you find the Rah. A boy understands a boy. "

"We were all boys once, Tiko. And I would not have one of the Master's favorites come to harm because I brought him into battle when he was assigned to instruct his soldiers here in Amega. You will stay. And you will be satisfied to stay for it is your Lord and Master who leaves you behind to teach his sons and to guard his home."

"Of course," responds Tiko a bit sheepishly now. "A good warrior does what his commander tells him. I will teach his sons. And I will guard his home with my life." Tiko puts a fist to his chest for emphasis, bows his deep, Asian bow, and withdraws. And for a moment Nikolaos sees himself in the boy and smiles. I, too, thought that the best thing a man could do was to go to war for his sovereign. But it was all self-centered and vain glory that I chased, admiration and prestige. Such a heart comes to know that the self is not the center of the soul, but that the soul is fed and given life by something outside of itself, like an umbilical cord feeds the fetus. Then personal glory and reputation become as nothing. It is the thing that feeds, the thing that sustains the heart that is the thing that we must strive to humble ourselves to serve. It is not a king, nor a human master, nor a people nor a nation nor a land, it is the source of life, of harvest and abundance. And I believe that the boy, Rah, is the incarnation of that source, come to visit, to lift us to better understand what is worth preserving.

Two days after Rah has escaped on the lost colt at the mouth of the river, Agrippa and his original score of men, with the hundred chariot makers from Hattusha, meet Rush and the four Amorite spies on their journey north over the plateau. They come in carts and in chariots, on mules and in wagons. Agrippa has taken the three-man prototype as well as Keret, Lysias and Pelet back with him to Amega in order to recreate the chariot to the specifications of the three boys who know it best. He is, of course, unaware that Rah is missing, but when he is questioned by the assassin it becomes clear to him what has happened in Amega since he left and that the boy has been lost.

"I took a dark colt in Hattusha to speed my return to Amega," Rush tells him. "But the animal threw me as we approached the Table. The boy caught the stray beast at the head of the river, in full tack and with my provision pack still fastened to its saddle. He leapt upon it and headed north along the bank. I fear he will wander into the Amorite camp," confides Rush to his first commander.

"We spotted a cloaked rider on a dark horse galloping north yesterday, Sir. He was indeed headed straight for the foothills, where the Amorites remained camped in some disarray. We assumed he was a spy or else a messenger. He was traveling too fast for any of us to have a hope of intercepting him."

"If the boy is taken, he will be recognized as a precious god slave, just as he was by these fools," Rush waves a distracted hand at his Amorite captives. "Then he will be held to ransom their own lives." He strokes his beard, a single motion, then turns to Kaspir.

Kaspir has been watching from the campfire over which Wadin is roasting the triplet of grouse the assassin returned to camp with this morning, as if the barren plateau they now travel were teaming with them. In fact, Kaspir has not seen a living creature since they veered north from the river shortly after Rah's escape until this man, Agrippa, appeared wearing the dress of a Hittite general: the short fighting skirt, the elaborate and intricately hammered breastplate, the tall hat and jewel encrusted weapons belt. Rush himself is still in his black assassin's tunic and leggings, his head alone exposed, his mask tucked into his belt. His braid reaches his hip. His own weapons, the strange array of hand to hand blades, are strapped to his ankles and ribs. For Kaspir, it is as if he were privy to a conversation in hell, the Wolf of the Hatti contracting the very prince of Tartarus himself, only with roles reversed.

"What are your orders, Master?" he hears the man called Agrippa ask solemnly.

"You will return to Amega, commander. You will set these carpenters to the task of building me an army of three-man war chariots. My plans to take Babylon in the spring have not changed. Build them precisely as the Rah instructed."

"You have it on my honor, Sir," answers Agrippa. "But if I may ask, what are your intentions for these?" and he nods at Kaspir and the others.

Gods help us! thinks Kaspir. He is asking if he might take us back with him to Amega for a military execution!

"These will do my bidding, Agrippa. They will be of excellent service to me in the days to come, or else I will wear a very thick human coat upon my return to Amega, made of their collective skins."

"Yes, Sir," bows Agrippa, and upon rising gives Kaspir the look a wardog gives a prisoner its handler has denied it the pleasure of finishing off in battle.

When the men from Amega have left with the Hattushian chariot makers, Rush calls Kaspir to his side. His heart beating so loudly in his ears that he can barely hear, Kaspir rises from the fire and stands before his new master.

"How may I be of service to the Great Wolf of the Hatti?" he asks, still unaware that the Amorite title irritates Rush like a burr between the pads of his paw.

"It is time for you to prove yourself, Captain Kaspir," he says, a curious smile turning his generous lips. The grin, on such a face, sends hot cramps through Kaspir's bowel. He struggles to maintain his dignity and answers, "My life is yours, Master."

"Indeed it is, Captain," says Rush, and with the suddenness of an attack he takes Kaspir in a bearlike embrace, ignoring the man's "Huughh!" of surprise, and kisses him full on the mouth.

"Take your men and return to your captain. Amega is burning. The household of the Wolf has fled on ships, south to Canaan. Messengers on horseback fly north to Hattusha to inform the Wolf that his home is ablaze, his soldiers have defected in fear of the plague."

"But they will have seen this man, wearing the garb of the great General of Amega, moving south from Hattusha with this band of men and materials. They will believe it is you!" cries Kaspir, still shaken by that ferocious kiss, but trying desperately to be helpful and to show where his loyalty now stands.

"And will tell you so, and ask you if you have seen the man. To which you will reply that you have, and that a lone horseman, traveling north at a gallop, intercepted him, no doubt telling him of the fall of Amega."

Now Rush has turned to put his arm over Kaspir's shoulders and to pull him close in the confident embrace of a friend. His beard is close enough to Kaspir's face that the hairs of each, his black as pitch and Kaspir's salt-and-peppered, mingle. The heat of another cramp deep in his bowel nearly puts the old Amorite warrior on his knees.

"I will know what you do and what you do not do, Amorite dog. You will follow my orders precisely. Not one word more, not one less. Keep the mouths of these fleas of yours closed," he nods to the others, "and when we meet again, we will meet as friends to celebrate the death of your comrades. You and I, we will share a pint of Hatti mead, and I will make you one of my own." He gives the man a squeeze, and Kaspir feels a strange popping in his shoulder which will give him pain for days to come, reminding of this pact.

"You honor me, Master, and I will not betray you. No, never! Upon my head!" Kaspir manages to pant above the pain.

"Upon your head, indeed, little Amorite dog. Now go and take your fleas with you. I have no further use for them."

"But the boy, Sir," dares Kaspir, "Would you not have Marut and Lar, at least, remain with you, to help you to find and capture him?"

"He is already caught, Captain. For the horse he rides returns him to Hattusha, where he will be recognized by my own men who remain in the city to guard a king I myself put upon the throne."

"I see, Sir," answers Kaspir dumbly.

"And if you were to return to the Amorite camp without these three fleas you hope to leave with me, what then? What will you tell your captain has happened to them? Add nothing to my story, Captain Kaspir. And leave nothing out. Else I will add and take away as well when next I see you."

Not quite sure what this new threat might entail, Kaspir offers Rush a brisk bow and turns to address the other three.

"Pack, all of you. We head for Urgup to do our new master's bidding," he barks. The men jump to their feet, Wadin dropping the skewered birds to burn in the fire.

"After they have eaten, Captain," Rush clarifies, closing his eyes with impatience.

Twelve miles north a young lieutenant from the Amorite camp has spotted a hooded rider on a dark horse galloping toward Hattusha. He runs to his commander, interrupting him in the act of relieving himself in the latrine pit, and tells his tale. A rider in the white robes of a priest is galloping north on a dark horse, alone and fast as lightening, toward Hattusha. He has never seen anyone ride so fast. And in the wind created by the rider's own speed, the hood fell back revealing a head of pale yellow light, shining in the sun. Not the head of a man at all, nor any human he had ever laid eyes upon.

The Amorite captain takes his time climbing out of the hole, dug several weeks ago and continually filled to cover the stench of the daily waste of a large and well fed army. He belts his tunic as he reaches the top, grabs the young guard's arm and shakes him.

"You had better be telling the truth, Jibril."

"I have no reason to lie, sir," responds the confident young man. "I have seen a god, racing north on horseback to Hattusha. If we fail to intercept him, his divinity will surely favor the city and we will be crushed."

"Go to the stables. Take the fastest horse in camp. Take Reh-kabil's chariot racer. Take another man with you, and do not return without the god!"

Jibril needs no further urging to commence the mission he hoped would be his the moment he lay eyes on the golden-headed god, surely racing north from Amega, from the city of the Wolf himself. I will be the first! He thinks to himself. I will catch him and once we have Amega's god, we have Amega! Then I will return to Syria and be hailed a champion. I will win much recognition and live to be a rich old man.

With great haste, Jibril takes the racer from under the noonday stable-man's drunk and sleeping nose. He has never raced a chariot but he is a decent enough horseman and tacks the animal up in his own saddle and bit and mounts the animal quickly. On his way out of the compound he passes the tents of his own unit of one hundred. He shouts from his mount, "Tell Semal to find a fast horse and to follow me! I go to capture the god of Amega, who gallops north as if on wind to the city! We must intercept him before he arrives!" Then he is racing north, urging the fleet-footed racer to a heady speed in the direction in which he last saw the golden-headed god.

Despite his appearance of galloping without cease toward Hattusha, Rah has been pacing the colt carefully all day. He has only asked his mount for its top speed in open places, careful to consider the animal's hooves on the dry and rocky ground, and the stamina of its fine legs and heart as well, and he has taken frequent breaks, bringing the colt down to a trot for several minutes to cool and then stopping to rest, water and graze the beast. The pair have become fast friends, for Rah has found a grain pouch within the saddlebag Rush left attached to the animal's back, and while stopping to rest he has offered it handfuls of grain, all the while cooing at the young horse in comforting tones and running his hands along its neck, flank and legs.

"Kollaj, djale te shpejte," says Rah to the colt in a soft, assuring voice. "Kollaj. Ju jane te sigurta." Easy, fast boy. You are safe.

And so Rah and the colt, whom he has named Dashuri, are startled when, having slowed to a trot to rest, they are overtaken by a young man on a horse far above his caliber of horsemanship. In fact, Rah is forced to take Dashuri's reins and pull him round in a circle several times in order to avoid his dashing off after the out-of-control pair, who have passed him and continue in a mad gallop toward Hattusha.

"What this is?" wonders Rah, whose contact with Dashuri has returned to him his speech and his humanity just as water blossoms a rose. "This man, he not ride this horse. This horse, he ride this man." And with that he takes off after the horseman, unsure whether or not Dashuri can catch the animal, who is in full flight, but quite certain that the pair cannot run on at this speed forever and must eventually come to some obstacle or else tire to the point that the fresher horse will eventually be able to pull alongside. And that is all that Rah will need to stop the other.

Back in camp, Semal is roused by a tent mate with the message from Jibril.

"To hell with that. I will not run hell bent for leather toward the enemy and be shot down by an archer's arrow at the city wall. Let him catch his god himself, if he has a means to."

"He has taken Reh-kabil's chariot racer!" cries the other man.

"Pah! Fast yes, ridable, no. He will break his neck on that one," mutters Semal, rolling over on his leather and pulling his cloak up over his head.

Rah is a hundred meters back from Jibril when Reh-kabil's racer loses its footing on a patch of loose rubble and falters, hurling Jibril over its neck and onto the rocky ground on his back. The horse regains its feet and trots off matter-of-factly, as if the whole thing were not but a misunderstanding between friends. *Surely you did not mean to think I would allow you to ride me like a pack animal? I, Reh-kabil's finest racer? I am a chariot horse. I do not support the weight of a fool on my back. I take a man into battle in a bucket, and that is that!*

Rah trots up to the fallen man, his hood down, his platinum curls blazing in the noonday sun that burns behind him. His face is in shadow.

"This horse, she is too strong today. No ride this horse. I catch." And he is hopping off Dashuri and moving in the direction of Reh-kabil's mare, Dashuri following like a dog.

"What kind of thing is this?" says Jibril out loud, though to himself. "He speaks gibberish! This is no earthly language." And he pushes himself to his feet and begins to follow Rah toward the racer. But his advance causes the animal to throw its head up from the patch of vegetation it has found and bolt.

"No," whispers Rah, turning in the sunlight as Jibril catches up to him. "You let Rah. You scare her."

But Jibril can understand none of it, only that the god has the eyes of a seraph and the face of an Egyptian goddess. He blinks, shading his eyes from the sun so as to better see the vision but the vision is gone. The boy has turned and now walks with casual ease toward the spooked horse, cooing in his strange tongue, and holding out his open hand to the beast.

Reh-kabil's racer blows. *Well, it is about time someone offered me a treat.* She trots over to his extended fingers and nibbles at the grain in his palm.

"What the hell are you?" whispers Jibril, who is walking so close behind Dashuri that he is swatted in the face as the horse switches his tail in a greeting to the other animal.

"Pah," spits Jibril, and then, "Watch out, she is hard to handle. She has been known to let a man close in on her and then turn and kick him in the head as she gallops off. Wicked animal."

He shakes his head.

"Te jete ende, goxha vajze," says Rah to the mare. *Be still, pretty girl.* Then he rubs her head and takes her rein. "You ride Dashuri. Rah ride this one now," he says turning to give Jibril a smile to make a king faint. Then he runs a hand down the mare's neck, gives her withers a scratch and hops up into the tack. "You ride Dashuri," he says again to Jibril, nodding to the colt, who has come up to the racer to snuffle and sniff her shoulder. But the racer will have none of it. I am too good for you, peasant colt, she says, turning to give him her haunch with a switching tail.

"You get on or she kick you," says Rah, nodding again at Dashuri. "She is come in heat, this one. You keep Dashuri away or she kick you both."

Shaking his head with confusion at the gibberish, Jibril turns and mounts the colt. Well, at least now I can take him back to camp, he thinks, and taps Dashuri's flank to move him up to the racer. He expects to take the mare's reins and lead the boy back to his captain. He has no sooner come up alongside her, however, than the mare has turned and let fly a good solid hoof into the colt's chest.

"You stupid!" cries Rah, allowing the mare to distance herself from the colt before he turns her to face Jibril. The colt is prancing gaily now. He has had a whiff of her scent and is quickly losing his mind.

"These two cannot run together. You go ahead. I follow," says Rah.

But Jibril has lost control of Dashuri. The colt, determined to get more acquainted with the mare, pins its ears and rears full up with such a suddenness that Jibril's weight topples it back and down upon its rider. Ridded of the nuisance on his back, Dashuri blunders forward with unearned confidence, prancing toward Rah and the mare and switching his tail with excitement.

"You learn, Dashuri. She is no ready for you," says Rah, giving the mare her will. The racer screams, cutting the air with a sound only a mare can make, and strikes at the colt with her right foreleg. But the colt is undaunted, and more enflamed with desire than ever. He prances forward, neck arched, tail soaring. Look, now, how handsome I am! And I am yours, my hot-tempered beauty!

His insolence is more than the mare can bear. Buffoon! She screams, whirling to plant both of her hind hooves in his shoulder.

Rah has managed to remain onboard, and only barely. Now he kicks the mare forward, trotting a good distance from Dashuri, who has had the wind knocked out of him and is limping off to find some fodder in which he can drop his head and hide his shame.

"Maybe lame now," says Rah to the man on the ground who is only now coming to his feet and rubbing his sore buttock. "Now maybe you walk."

But Jibril can understand none of it. He raises a fist at Dashuri, who pays him no mind, then begins limping toward Rah.

"I must take you back to camp with me, little god. Now do not make it come to blows. Dismount and come here to me. We can both ride the mare back."

"What is this language he speak?" says Rah to Reh-kabil's racer. But the racer only snorts. You have a light hand and I can barely feel you on my back. You I will carry. Let us leave this fool here in the wilderness and return to camp where I may pasture with my sisters.

"Nice mare," says Rah, walking the racer carefully toward Jibril. "She is fast, fast, eh? Too much horse for you. I take her. Dashuri he know she kick him now. He is be good. You take Dashuri." He nods again at the colt, who is wandering not far away looking for greenery in the dry soil.

Jibril follows Rah's nod toward the colt. He purses his lips, then gives his buttock cheek one more comforting rub and stomps toward Dashuri.

"Soft, soft! You scare him now!" says Rah. But Dashuri has had enough. When the man takes his rein this time he is contrite. He gives Jibril no difficulty as he mounts him, only pays his leg and hand no mind as the young Amorite attempts to turn him about to return to his own camp.

He is a hostage on the back of the colt. Rah is trotting away north on the mare and Dashuri is determined to keep up with her, though he has learned enough respect to stay clear of her kicks.

I am on my way to Hattusha, thinks Jibril, his head reeling with this new turn of events. I am going to walk right into Hattusha with the Wolf of the Hatti's slave god! But somehow, he is not as disturbed by this strange happenstance as he should be. He is mesmerized by Rah and, as the day lengthens, only takes his eyes off the halo of cornsilk curls ahead of him when the watchtowers of the city of Hattusha appear and then the grand and sprawling fortress of white stone that is the city wall, gleaming in the distance like polished marble.

"Two day, maybe," says Rah turning about in his saddle to see what is going on with the colt and his new rider. Dashuri is trotting along at a safe distance from the racer's hind end, but clearly in control of the ride. Jibril is a passenger only. Dashuri pays his tight rein no heed and prances and snorts with unbound enthusiasm.

"Ta-hah, he want to mount her. Yes, Dashuri? You want this girl? She is not ready for you, she is kick you again, you try. Be good boy, we wait. When she is ready you, Rah is give her to you. Good match. Make fine baby!" He flicks his eyes at Jibril, who is looking at him over the ears of the prancing colt with unabashed amazement, for the boy is riding the mare as if she were no more difficult to handle than a plow horse.

"What is your name?" Rah says to the Amorite in Hittite.

Jibril, who has learned some Hittite in camp, responds, "I am Jibril," cautiously.

"Ah! Jibril! Good name. We go to Hattusha, Jibril, so Rah can dance for king!"

"Dance for-?" but now Jibril understands. The god is sent from Amega to dance for success in battle. If he can dance like he can ride, thinks Jibril, Babylon is lost.

"We go," continues Rah, turning back in his saddle to scratch the mare on her wither and give her a pat. "You be okay, Jibril. I tell King Wolf is own me. I tell King Jibril is give Rah nice mare from enemy camp. Gift to Rah. Friend of Rah. You be okay."

CHAPTER 20

Kaspir and his men are packed and about to depart from Rush to descend into the valley and approach their Amorite captain with the news of Amega's fall, when the hell dogs of the Assassin burst from the brush to attack them.

Marut's thigh is caught in one of the animal's jaws, seconds from having his femoral artery opened, and Lar is on the ground, pinned by the throat by the other, when the booming baritone of the Wolf rings out over their heads, "Hup, hup!"

The dogs instantly release their victims and bound across the ground. They leap to their master's chest, wriggling and wagging and slobbering like pups. Wadin has taken his battle axe in hand, Marut is reaching for his crotch, looking for a wound, and Lar is coughing and rising to his feet, when Rush says, as if to himself, "Down," and the dogs are on their bellies at his feet, still wagging with unabashed delight that they are reunited with their alpha, but subdued and admonished.

"Inanna," breathes Kaspir, who also has his battle axe out. "I thought they were bear."

"Wolves are not bad enough?" cries Marut, still feeling his thigh and crotch to see that all is as it was before the beast attacked him.

"Mother of the gods, Inanna, they are his!" cries Wadin, who now drops his axe to the ground and falls to his knees in the exhaustion that follows a shock.

"Surrender," says Rush to the dogs, paying the men no mind, and the dogs have leapt to their feet to trot about the terrified group, sniffing and wagging. They are content with the others but Kaspir, who has not dropped his axe, disturbs them and so they both sit, as if on command, before him, jaws dripping vicious and victorious canine smiles. They are growling low in their throats, so low that only Kaspir can hear the threat behind the smiles.

"Drop that weapon, Captain, or meet your death," says Rush quietly.

Kaspir drops his axe, knees shaking. Just as he does so, the larger of the two beasts barks at him happily, causing him to step back in fright, then turns to its master, wagging.

"Assu suwanna," says Rush. Good dog. And then, "Hup, hup!" and the two animals are at his heel again, awaiting their orders.

"Take up your weapons and depart," says Rush to the men, and, breathing sighs of relief, the four Amorite spies gather themselves and start down the valley toward the Amorite camp.

Moments later, Rush hears the expected pounding of a couplet of horses approaching from the south. He waits for Peleshet and Mammut to appear, dismount, and drop to their knees in full military bows, their horses standing at a halt behind them, having been trained to "ground tie" wherever their reins are dropped.

"Master," pants Peleshet, his right fist closed against his breast in deference to his sovereign, and waits for permission to impart his message.

"Speak man," says Rush, one hand on the hilt of his battle sword.

"Captain Nikolaos," and here Peleshet cannot help but look up into his master's eyes. "Captain Nikolaos wishes to inform you, sir, that he is staging the Army of Amega south of Hattusha, on the heels of the Amorites, and that he awaits his Master's orders to engage them in battle."

"Hah!" barks Rush, raising his gaze to heaven. "Is that so," he shakes his head. "Clever fox. Clever pup. And so now you will return to Captain Nikolaos with these words, Peleshet. Hear them well. Tell him he is to take my left flank, around to the west. We will let them decamp and move to attack Hattusha. Then we will come up behind them. It matters not their number. We will determine who is in charge, if anyone. Tell him always to stay on my left flank. Understood?"

"Understood, Master," answers Peleshet, unaware that the assassin's words echo those he told Nikolaos outside Crispo's kitchen tomb in the cemetery on Mount Ida the day the renegade palace guards of Knossos came to pillage the priesthood.

"And remind him, Peleshet," Rush begins, as the two men turn to mount their horses.

"Remind him, Sir?" asks Peleshet, turning his mount to face the assassin.

"Remind him, that though I am an army unto myself, yet we together remain an alliance."

"Sir," nods Peleshet, and then kicks his gelding's flank and takes off to deliver his message to Amega.

At the head of the Euphrates, at the very borders of the Amorite kingdom, an army of twenty thousand are encamped, awaiting their Amorite commander's orders to enter the land of the Hittites. They have had word from messengers on horseback riding out of the land of the Hatti like black moths flying up from a stagnant place that Amega has fallen to a plague. With the wolf who guarded the borders of the enemy gone, the King of the Amorites has amassed his personal army along his own borders to be sent into Anatolia. They will join with the mercenaries and Ammuna and take Hattusha, which now has an army of thirty thousand at her disposal but a young and inexperienced king, no more than a boy, really, in charge.

But the King of the Amorites is unaware that his army is in disarray. For at the mouth of the river is a ravine and a cave, and within the cave are stacked the heads of a thousand Amorite officers, their embroidered command insignia's stuffed into their rotting jaws. Now the Amorite army is in disorder. Some have deserted, others simply refused to go on, to step foot into the land of the Wolf. These, of course, have been impaled on their own javelins or hacked to pieces with their own battle axes. This has quelled full rebellion, but has done nothing to embolden the Amorite men, whose greatest fear is that of being separated from their own heads in the afterlife, to wander forever in search of that which has been taken.

This morning, in what will become in the millennia to come, early February, the message has come from the King to push forward into Anatolia, that the scare tactics of the villain, Antaris, will not defeat the great Amorite empire before it has even begun its push into the land of the Hatti.

And so the Amorites decamp and begin their restless and wary march into Hittite territory. It will take them three weeks to make the journey that it took the messengers, riding like the wind on their finest animals, only fourteen days to complete. In the meantime the Wolf they so fear is making his way to Hattusha himself, disguised as a sandal merchant and carrying with him little more than his assassin's attire in a sack. His wardogs trot alongside him, keeping to the brush when there is brush, maintaining a distance when there is no vegetation to conceal themselves in.

In the valley of Goreme, at the foothills of Urgup, Ammuna, released into the wilderness by a posse of Hattushan palace guards, has found his way by foot into the Amorite camp. The greeting he receives is not the greeting of an army for its lost general. Ammuna has arrived alone, stumbling on worn sandals in the dirt and covered with a fine silt from his wandering in the dust that is the Anatolian winter. He makes it to the gates, parched and exhausted, and is abused severely by the guards there until he can convince them that he is indeed the dead Hittite king's own son. His brother has made no attempt to lead the mercenary Amorite army since Ammuna's exodus with Agrippa and the generals of Hattusha and he is of little help now, having realized that, as the only remaining Hittite in camp, he is a pawn to be kept for barter at best, and a plaything for drunken soldiers to dismember on an otherwise quiet evening at worst. He makes no attempt to defend his brother, not even after he has been brought in by the chief officers to identify the man.

"Is this then, your brother, Ammuna, third born son of Hattusilis? This dog that wanders about in the wilderness with naught but a peasant's robe and an empty water gourd?"

"It is," answers the other, looking from his brother to the leading official with some embarrassment.

"What has happened to you, Ammuna?" says the official then, standing up to walk around the prince with distaste. "How is it that you have kept your head, and been returned to us? Is this some peace offering? Or is it a Hatti trick, meant to lead us to believe that the Hatti have honor and will not kill their own princes?" He looks to his compatriots, who nod and stroke their beards in agreement.

"I know not why I have been spared, Iamhad, only that I was taken from the dungeon under the palace, under guard, and thrown out of the gates of the city with not but the garments on my back. But I will tell you this. It is a high crime for anyone, be he Hittite or foreigner, to kill a Hittite prince. Even a member of his own family cannot do so without facing a trial by the people of Hatti."

The veiled threat in his words is not lost on Iamhad, who puts his hands on his hips and barks a single "Hah!" but looks back at his cronies with a frown of apprehension.

"Mayhaps they return you so that you can lead us into battle against them. Mayhaps they desire to crush you in battle, and thus the people can have no contention against their new king, that he killed his own uncle like a common thief. What say you to this, Ammuna?" asks the Amorite commander.

"I say you speak wisely, Iamhad, wisely indeed. And thus do I not still have value to you? For if this is their belief, you may use me as a decoy, a prop. Send me forth with a battalion, east and north around the city. Let them believe that I lead the Amorite army in its entirety. Then you may take the less guarded western wall, and we will cut them off and starve them out! Then you will have your Hattusha!"

"You always were a traitor to your own people, Ammuna, I will say that for you. But a traitor is a traitor. And you know that if we split our army into two, the Wolf of the Hatti will eat the half whilst his pawn, that boy Mursilis, will take the other. And yet without desiring to do so you speak well. For we have had word from our spies that Amega is burning.

While you were planning to use Syria to take the throne, we were planning to take all of Anatolia. The ass upon which the woman Sophina was sent to Amega was a plague animal. Now the compound of the assassin is burning and the Wolf and his clan have escaped on his ships to Canaan to live amongst the Philistines he so loves. And so we are free to march on Hattusha, free to surround her and to take her, free to cut her off from the river and starve her out. But I will not give you the east, but take that myself. You will lead a battalion around and over the mountainous western flank and attack that wall by surprise whilst I take the river, cutting off supplies into the city." Iamhad puts his hands on his battle belt and puffs his chest, pointing the tip of his oiled and braided beard at Ammuna. "I needn't tell you that if you fail me, you and your brother will be returned to your nephew in pieces."

Ammuna is looking at his brother in shock. "Is it true? That Sophina was sent on a plague animal into Amega? And that Amega is burning?"

"I was here myself when their spies entered camp, brother. They fell upon their knees and swore on their lives and on the lives of their families. It appears to be true."

"Sophina is dead," whispers Ammuna, looking from his brother to Iamhad. "What have I left to live for? Be it as you say, Iamhad. And may that murderous devil, Antaris, watch everything he loves turn to ash."

And so Ammuna, garbed in the battle dress of a Hatti general, is sent with one third of the Amorite army north and west into the mountains. He is separated from his brother, who is now no more than a hostage, though he needs no greater motivation to play his role than the unruly army around him, led in reality by a group of Amorite officers hidden within the ranks.

In Hattusha, Aleksandus has learned from his own spies that the army of the Amorites has split and is set to confront the city on two sides. The city is walled on all but the north side, which opens to the river. Steep mountains and sheer cliffs make her unavailable to the north and west, but to the south and east the land opens to a valley, beyond which are the plains of central Anatolia. It is at the southeastern edge of the plains that the Table of the Gods, the strange chimneys, caves and spires of volcanic rock left by a forgotten volcano the size of Thera centuries earlier, serve the Wolf of the Hatti as a burial ground for his enemies' headless corpses.

Aleksandus has sent orders to the Hattushan troops staged in the valley to spread across the eastern perimeter of the walled city. The ten thousand who followed Ammuna now make up the front guard, along with their generals. They will give their lives first, if lives are to be lost. Another battalion is set along the southern wall, and a third is sent to guard the northern approach to the river.

Rah has followed his instincts north across the plains, maintaining the direction in which Dashuri first took him, now and then resting the animals and allowing them to graze and drink at a stream. Jibril has made no further effort to return Rah to his own commander. After two days in the boy's company, he has forgotten his captain, forgotten his orders, forgotten his countrymen. He is fascinated by the sheer beauty of the creature he meant to capture and now follows, himself captured in the spell that is Rah. Finding himself eagerly listening for every chewed and half-swallowed word that emanates from the boy's lips, though he can barely understand the language of the Hatti and the husky and broken voice coming from such a light and lovely face is almost too distracting in itself to allow him to bother with the meaning of the sounds, he hangs on every noise Rah makes. Even the growls and snarls he sometimes emits in his sleep are a point of fascination for the Amorite youth, and having been awoken by them once, he now finds it difficult to sleep for fear of missing another of the god's bad dreams.

On the morning of their second day in each other's company, Rah rouses Jibril with a poke in the chest. Awakening to the blue-green eyes beneath the fantastic emerald crown, fastened in a halo of pale curls through which the sunlight gaily glows, Jibril can only blink and wonder if he is not himself still dreaming.

"Up. Up, Jibril. Today we meet King. Today we go Hattusha!" smiles Rah, his dimples electrifying his countenance like the lighting of a hundred candles in a golden temple.

"Jibril is hungry, little god. We have not eaten in two days. Let us hunt and find some food first," answers the young Amorite tiredly, but yet unable to take his eyes from Rah. How like a young lion he is, he thinks. But with eyes to rival the bluest skies. This is a sun god, surely. This one can make the heavens cry with his retreat.

"No eat, Jibril. Eat in city. Eat with King. Then we feast. Take Dashuri. Follow Rah." And he has handed the youth from Syria Dashuri's reins and turned to hop with casual grace onto the back of the hot-tempered racer before Jibril can argue further.

"Where is your saddle, little god? She will put you on the ground!" cries Jibril, realizing as he catches up a safe distance from Reh-Kabil's racer that the boy is riding bareback.

"No saddle, Jibril. She like leg. Better talk her with leg. You see," and he has spun the animal in a pirouette on her haunch from his seat, his rein loose and knotted against her wither. "She like talk from Rah leg. She is no drop Rah," says the boy casually, smiling at Jibril over the racer's silvery head.

By mid-morning, the pair are trotting up to the southern wall of the city of Hattusha, having taken the Merchant's Road straight through the valley between the staging grounds of the split Amorite armies. Scouts on either side of the approach report to their commanders that the rider who was seen racing toward Hattusha is now in the company of one of their own men.

"But I sent the man to bring him back to camp!" swears Jibril's captain under questioning. His words are useless.

"Why was I not informed that a god slave from Amega was riding toward Hattusha? I would have sent an entire brigade after him!" cries the captain's commander. "Now he is too close to the city to capture, and has one of our own men following him like a goat, who can be tortured for information."

The captain is impaled against a tree on his own weapon.

Over the southern wall of the city, archers have noticed the approach of a pair of horsemen and have sent word to their commanders.

"Perhaps they come with a message from the Amorites, Sir," offers the senior officer of the Army of Hattusha to Aleksandus.

"Or bring us plague, or come to offer a false surrender and then attack from the north," responds Aleksandus casually. "Bring them to the gate, no further, and I will speak to them from the wall." And a posse of six riders leave the city to meet the two and escort them to the gate.

From the wall, Aleksandus looks down at the approaching figures. One is small, cloaked in a dirty white robe with a cowl hood covering his head. He rides a fine-boned chariot racer bareback, a thing he finds oddly reminiscent of someone he cannot quite bring to mind. The other is clearly an Amorite, dressed in the battle garments of his tribe, but riding a dark young colt far too fine to be a battle horse.

"What is this nonsense?" says Aleksandus from the parapets, looking to the Hattushan general whose troops he has taken under his command to guard the south wall. "These are not enemies, but only wandering fools! Send a man out to greet them. Tell them that Aleksandus of Amega has command of the city, and that they must go elsewhere, whoever they may be. This city is staged for battle and I cannot allow any movement, by man or animal, in or out."

But when the posse approaches, Rah jumps from the racer, who stops short in its tracks as if tied to the spot where its reins have hit the ground. He runs to greet the men, and as he runs, the hood of his cloak falls back from his head.

Aleksandus, watching from the parapet, freezes in shock.

"Taru, God of War, it is the Rah of Knossos! It is the Master's favorite!"

By now Rah, ever the performer, has thrown his cloak from his shoulders and dropped into the bow to which the assassin would always owe his heart's captivity.

"Take him!" shouts Aleksandus from the city wall. "Bring him here to me! Do not harm a hair of that golden head else I lose my own!" he cries, straining to lean over the battlements to be heard several hundred meters away.

The posse that has galloped out to meet the travelers now stops in a cloud of dust. The lead man dismounts to stand before Rah. Jibril has been forgotten. He sits astride Dashuri, who hops gaily on his hind legs, barely aware that he is still under saddle. We are home! We are home in Hattusha! Let us race into the city where I may find my stall and my grain waiting for me as I left it!

Rah rises to his feet. He regards the man who stands before him, a young Hattushan with fine features and a trimmed beard. The man is looking at him with confused respect.

"I am to escort you into the city," he says, unable to take his eyes off Rah's face. "Both of you. Please, mount your animal if you can and follow me, or else mount mine with me and pony the other behind."

"Ta-hah!" chuckles Rah, turning to the racer. "Rah can mount, no problem. I be on her before you are on this one," he challenges, winking at the man. And before the man can turn to his own horse, Rah has hopped lightly back onto Reh-kabil's hot-tempered mare with no more assistance than a fist full of mane at her wither. She takes a few elegant and mincing steps backward, connects with Dashuri, and kicks.

It is all the encouragement Dashuri needs to take over the ride. He explodes, rearing to his full height, drops Jibril in the dust, then takes off like a javelin in the direction of the city walls.

"Agh!" cries the man from Hattusha. For his mount has yanked its rein from his hands and is now galloping off in a cloud of dust after Dashuri.

The racer rears as well, but, unable to lose her rider, is spun in a tight circle until she has calmed.

Before he realizes what is happening, Jibril is pulled up behind Rah and is clinging to his narrow waist for dear life, for the racer is galloping at top speed, with two bareback riders now, toward the city gate, and determined to beat that over-confident colt to the stables.

The man from Hattusha is left where he stands, rubbing his hand where the rein has skinned it, and murmuring to himself, "What in Tartarus *is* he?"

Rush has made his way to the foothills of Urgup. He has watched Iamhad move a battalion of men north and east, clearly with the intention of taking the north river and closing down supply routes into the city. It takes him little thought to come to the correct assumption that Ammuna has been sent, with a smaller battalion, into the rocky and mountainous regions protecting the city's western front.

"Idiot," says Rush to himself, standing on a slope overlooking Iamhad's error. "Now you have lost a third of your army to the terrain. They will do nothing but struggle with the elements, whilst I take you down like a wolf takes a ram who has just done battle with another and is now at his weakest. Fat lot of good it will do you to take the river, without a head."

But the failings of the Amorite commander do little to distract his heart, which remains under the spell of the Grain God of Knossos. He has not seen Rah since the boy escaped him on the colt two weeks earlier and he has thought of little else, for war is easy for a warrior but love is hard. He wonders if the boy has made it to Hattusha, been thrown by the unruly colt, or been cut down by the enemy, taken for a spy or a messenger from Amega. If I catch you myself, little cat, I will beat you to within an inch of your life. But if *they* have hurt you, Rah, then I will take the heart of each man with my own blades. I will cut through them like a lion cuts through a herd of deer and I will skin their leaders and make hollow flags of them to fly over their own borders. Yet nevertheless, I will be as hollow as their skins, for I will have lost what I need most.

Then, pacing like a caged bear, he tears off his outer garments, revealing the assassin beneath. And commanding the dogs to follow, he moves like a wraith down the slope toward the new encampment to deal with Iamhad himself.

Less than a day's journey away, Nikolaos and half the army of Amega, including the two hundred wardogs and their handlers, are moving rapidly north across the plains toward Hattusha. Behind the army, and surrounded by a rear guard, the dance troop of the House of the Moon follows, along with Pyrus and Aros, and of course, the High Priest. The priest has come equipped with his best poisons though he knows not how or why such a thing could be of any value in war.

Having been advised by Peleshet of the assassin's exact words, Nikolaos has staged his troops for a rear battle, expecting with full confidence that the man will somehow send the Amorites pell-mell into their jaws singlehandedly. When that happens, he will be ready for them, and he will be merciless. It is not so much for the City of Hattusha that he fights, although he understands that protecting the city, and therefore the assassin's interests there, is his duty. But somewhere out there in the wilderness north of him, the Rah of Knossos is in danger. He may already be taken by the enemy, perhaps molested and degraded, an impossible beauty made a toy for imperfect men, before he is slaughtered.

And so Captain Nikolaos is thinking like the Wolf he now follows. I will close in on them on all sides. I will annihilate them, then I will send the assassin's army home. And if I do not find you within their midst, Rah of Knossos, I will ride out across these plains, even to Hattusha, to find you. I *will* find you, and return you to your master, *our* master, or die trying.

For two weeks Nikolaos has pushed north, across the Table of the Gods, across the plains of Anatolia, allowing his men no more sleep than he allows himself, a few hours a night, before they are roused to push on. In that time he has visited the priest only once, and then only to assure himself that the man will have what he needs when he needs it.

"For this you should have gone to Tyrus!" blinks the high priest with surprise and not a little self-doubt.

"Find what you need in the land if you have not brought sufficient quantity with you," responds the Captain, leaning dangerously at Mochlos and pulling back his lip to show a perfect row of white teeth.

"As you say, Sir, as you say," responds the priest, his hand splayed on his chest and making a small bow in reluctant obedience. "But this is an enormous thing you ask, I-"

"You will use that clever brain of yours or prove to me you have no need of it," answers the Captain.

"Indeed," says Mochlos, swallowing. "Indeed I will, Sir."

Less than fifty miles away, Rush the Assassin is making his way down a brushy slope toward the camp of the Amorites. The moon is at the half, bright as a lamp in a labyrinth, and he has learned from watching and waiting that the battalion is made up of nine units of one thousand men, with eight hundred horses and half as many chariots and teams. Not an enormous foe, thinks Rush, but the horses will be a problem. Even if Nikolaos had been able to take every able horse in Amega, and every chariot, he would have only half this many. But these fools know nothing of wardogs and like the Egyptians use sight hounds to help them catch an occasional deer to supplement their provisions. They will get an education, but alas, will never return what they learn to their king.

Several hundred miles away the King of the Amorite's army is fearfully crossing the borders of Rush's world, encroaching on his territory, invading his space. They will have passed the unfastened heads of their officers and their spirits will be low, their wills weak, thinks Rush. But an army is an army, and a fearful one is a wild animal. Nevertheless, that is a battle to be won at a later date. For now, we will deal with the scorpion lying in our boots. I will need you for this, Nikolaos. Then, when they are running like cockroaches, pell-mell, across the plains, I will leave you to finish the job and continue to Hattusha to find Rah.

Rush navigates down a rocky gulch at the bottom of the foothills and moves with a panther's stealth toward the stable tent of the Amorites. When he reaches the first guard he slices his throat before the man has noticed the shadow of death approaching him from behind. He lays the body down like a husband lays his bride down on her bridal couch, then moves to the next. Not a single horse has snorted by the time he has cut fifteen men down and left them to sleep in the grass.

Inside Iamhad's tent, the Amorite commander is dreaming of his wife in Mari. She is brushing her hair before a bronze mirror, looking at him over her shoulder with a wisp of a smile on her perfect face. She is his third wife, but his favorite, a girl of only eighteen summers with the body of a goddess and the pleasant temper of a good servant. She is with child, and the soothsayers have told her that the child will be a male, and will grow up to be the image of his father.

The soothsayers have also told her that her husband will not live to see it, but will lose his life in battle with a great black wolf, a wolf who steals souls and leaves them to wander in the wilderness forever.

"Remember what I told you, Iamhad. You will not live to see the child. But I will raise him well, and he will make a name for you all the same."

"I will raise my own son," answers Iamhad, walking over to put his hands on his wife's fine shoulders. And then, overcome with longing for her, he bends to kiss her neck.

And his head takes a blow like a thunderclap.

"Iamhad, filth of Babylon," whispers a voice that is like the voice of God in his left ear, "You come into my country, you and your band of hireling cowards. You think that you will become rich by putting a weakling and a traitor on the Hittite throne. You split an army that is neither skilled enough nor brave enough to take the village of Urgup let alone the walled fortress that is Hattusha. Now I shall make your wives widows." And the blade is in his chest, taking his heart, before he can cry out the name of the beast who has hold of it.

In Hattusha, the king has come down from his own rooms to see for himself the creature that has just ridden through the enemy, past two battalions of his own warriors, a line of highly skilled archers along the south wall, and right under the nose of his highest ranking officer, to enter the palace in a dirty white robe and bare feet.

Mursilis has been informed that the little god-slave is the assassin's favorite. This information came to him from his own man, and then again by a man from Amega, a soldier under the command of Aleksandus, who simply banged on his door as if he were entering an inn, then made a less than adequate bow and looked him dead in the eye to deliver the news.

"He is the Rah, Majesty. He is come from Amega, riding a fine mare he says the man with him has given him, a gift from the Amorites." And then, and surely beneath that thick Amegan beard was the hint of a grin, "He holds the Master's favor."

"But who has given him permission to enter the gates? Who has escorted him to the palace?" asks the befuddled King, too confused and excited by the prospect of seeing this creature who has gained the rank of beloved in the eyes of the Great Wolf of the Hatti to confront the man on his etiquette in speaking to a king.

"No one, Sir. He comes of his own accord," answers the man, his eyes still pinned to the King's as if he spoke to no one more important than a house servant. "That is his way," he adds, appeasing.

"Well, bring him here to me, then," responds the king, looking about for his royal sandals for it has been his habit, since a child, to walk about in his own apartments barefooted.

"I believe he is expecting you in the Great Hall, Sir," responds the man, and now it is as clear as day that his tongue presses his cheek beneath that beard.

"He is exp-?" but Mursilis has had enough. He claps his hand for his valet who, for the first time since the Mursilis took the throne, appears to be missing. He shouts over his shoulder, "Where are my slippers, man?" for he has no idea where to find them in his own wardrobe, having never had to look, and then gives up and follows the man from Amega out of his chamber and down the hall toward the Palace Lyceum.

Downstairs, Rah is entertaining Aleksandus with the kata he learned from Tiko at the House of Ameg in Knossos that past summer. Aleksandus is chuckling, a strange and wonderful thing to see here in Hattusha, where the man has done little but order generals and troops about and growl his reports to the king like a man speaks to a thick-headed youngest son.

"Ha-ha, Rah, this is brilliant. You must show the King how the Hebrew angels fight from the air!"

Rah has come to the end of his little display and has made a very serious and military bow, curls falling over one knee, one fist planted before him. This last bit of foolishness has sent Aleksandus into a paroxysm of laughter.

Rah rises to his feet to offer his Master's second favorite commander the proper bow of a servant. He walks casually up to the great man and gestures in the direction of the palace stables.

"You see this mare, Alek? She so fine, no? I give her to colt, give her to Dashuri. He want her but she is no want him yet. Give a few day. Then she say, 'Ok, Dashuri, you come. We make baby for Rah.'"

"You say this man, this Amorite, Jibril, he came riding out on this fine mare for you, Rah? A present from the Amorites?" asks Aleksandus, throwing an arm over the boy's shoulder and drawing him into a more private conversation.

"Tah! He come ride out on her, but he is no ride her! She is ride him! She is gallop. Pass Dashuri! Rah is have to stop her. Take from Jibril. Give Jibril Dashuri."

"I thought as much. No, they sent him to catch you, little Rah. To catch you and to use you as a hostage. They sent a fool who could not ride what was underneath him and could not catch what was flying before him. So now you are ours, under our protection, here to entertain us whilst we plow through them like so much mulch." With this, Aleksandus looks about for Jibril. "Where is the man you brought in with you?" he says, speaking more to his junior officer than to Rah.

"He has been thrown in the palace dungeon, sir," responds the officer, stepping up to make a quick bow to his new commander.

"Well bring him here to me, we must interrogate him," snaps Aleksandus, the humor in his face turning hard like cooling iron.

"Interrogations are generally handled by the palace guards, sir, in the prison."

"And how many men shall the information pass through before it gets to me, eh?" barks Aleksandus, moving to grab the man by the front of his tunic and shake him. "One thousand men shall be six thousand, and a cavalry of trackers shall be twelve units of twenty by the time I've heard his words!"

"Sir!" jumps the man, backing out of the hall to rush down to the dungeon and demand the Amorite's release into his custody.

By the time he has returned with the man, the King of the Hatti has made it to his throne on the dais in the lyceum. He is staring, transfixed, at Rah, who is executing a series of spins with an invisible partner on the tile floor before him.

"Here is the man, Sir," says the officer, shoving Jibril before Aleksandus at the back of the great room. Jibril can only come to halt before the Hittite commander and drop his head. I am doomed, now. What kind of fool am I, to fall under the spell of a Hatti god? I am better off without this head, that has no brain in it, he thinks.

"Who is this?" asks Mursilis from the throne, gesturing to Jibril. He is looking at Aleksandus over Rah's head, having at last managed to take his eyes off the whirling blonde dervish that has now turned as well to see Jibril enter the hall.

"Hah!" cries Rah, delighted. "This Jibril. Friend of Rah. Where you go, Jibril?"

"Bring him here to me then," says the King as Aleksandus takes the man by the throat of his tunic and drags him before the throne. Once beneath the dais, he tosses the young Amorite like so much garbage to the ground. Rah has come up behind Aleksandus. He is glossy with sweat and panting lightly. He watches with curious indifference as Aleksandus boots the man in his bottom, shoving him onto his face on the tiles.

"Speak up, man," barks Aleksandus, as if Jibril ought to have dared to open his mouth before called upon to do so.

"Yes," echoes the King. "Tell us what is being planned in the Amorite camp. How many troops have you, and how many horses? How many chariots? From which side do you plan to attack? And what has been done with my uncle?"

Jibril has only made it back onto his knees by the time the King has finished firing questions at him. Aleksandus is about to return him to the ground to speak to the Hittite King when Rah moves between them and takes Jibril's elbow, helping him to his feet. He gives Aleksandus a disapproving look and then brushes off Jibril's tunic with a mime's comic timing. Even the King is forced to allow himself a chuckle. He brings his hand to his mouth to suppress his delight at the little god's antics.

"Do you not wish that we should abuse your friend then, Rah?" asks the King gently.

"No hurt Jibril," answers Rah. His words are measured and calm but absolute. He gives the King a firm look. "Friend of Rah," he says, looking into the King's eyes boldly. "Friend of Rah is friend of Wolf, also."

Mursilis cannot help but look to Aleksandus in astonishment.

Aleksandus gives the King a stony silence.

Pursing his lips, Mursilis gestures to Jibril. "Very well then, Rah. Let the man come before us and show that he is indeed a friend of the Great Wolf of the Hatti. Speak, Jibril. Tell us all we need to know."

Rah pushes the shaken Jibril before the King. "Tell, Jibril. Show King." He gives Mursilis his sweetest smile.

"We are fifteen thousand troops and four thousand chariots," answers Jibril, his eyes on the tile floor at his feet though his face is up so that his words are not misheard. "Iamhad is the highest ranking commander, but we are mercenary troops, paid for by the King of Syria. Our loyalty is to our pockets. As to Ammuna, as last I heard he was taken by the Hatti generals into Hattusha. I know not what has happened to him since."

"They cannot take us," says the King then, looking to Aleksandus with confidence. "For we have twenty and six."

"It is not a simple game of numbers, your Highness," responds Aleksandus with something nearing boredom. "These men are hardened fighters, mercenaries. Their chariots and horses are Egyptian. Light, fast, deadly. A city army such as your own could be cut apart by half their own number by such a legion."

"I have the finest army a king's wealth can buy," responds Mursilis. "What is Amorite fighting skill to that of the Hatti? We will remain within the city and wait for them to challenge us. My troops in the valley will protect us."

"You may have the finest army a king's wealth can buy," returns Aleksandus, stepping up to the dais and lowering his voice. "But you are not the seasoned warrior that your grandfather was. You are a boy who does not know when to let a man of war make his tactical decisions….." Then, backing up and raising his voice he adds, "Do you have no interest in knowing on which flank they intend to attack the city, Highness?"

"This fool knows nothing," the King retorts, jabbing his finger in Jibril's direction. "He is a common foot soldier."

"If that is so, what was he doing with a chariot racer under him when he went out to capture the Rah?" asks Aleksandus, who now turns a shoulder to the king to address the young Amorite. "Spit it out, man, or I shall take your tongue," he offers him casually, folding his arms over his breastplate.

"No take Jibril tongue, Alek!" cries Rah, throwing himself at the Amegan commander's feet.

"Too much drama, Rah," answers Aleksandus, taking the boy by the arm and lifting him up to stand at his side. "Speak, dog," he barks gruffly at Jibril.

"I was told only that we were to take the river, Sir!" answers Jibril, looking from Rah to the Hittite commander worriedly. "I believe that the plan was to cut off supplies into the city."

"Ah, a siege, eh?" says Aleksandus, nodding. "But what good is a siege without surrounding all avenues of escape? No, Iamhad is splitting his forces. We must be ready on all sides, especially the least likely, that is, the west."

"The west is a natural barrier," says the King. "No army could make headway from that direction. The mountains and cliff sides would stop them."

"An army, no, but one man, or a team of them, could breech the western wall to assassinate the king and leave the city in a panic," answers Aleksandus, looking up at the King with brows lifted.

"An assassin," murmurs Mursilis.

"Or a band of killers, trained for just such a mission. Therefore we will maintain our troops in the east, guarding the river, whilst we guard the western wall from within with our best men."

"Excellent," nods Mursilis.

"You keep your tongue, today, Amorite dog," says Aleksandus to Jibril then. "Return him to the prison 'til I have had a chance to think what to do with him." He lifts his beard to his officer.

"No, Alek," says Rah, stepping between the officer and the Amorite lieutenant. "Jibril friend of Rah, now. He stay with Rah."

"Pah, he is an Amorite dog and he will be glad to sleep under the palace of the mighty Hattusilis tonight!" answers Aleksandus, once more stepping forward to take Rah under his arm. "Now you come and have dinner with me, Rah, and tell me how you came to be riding into Hattusha when this man spotted you." He has turned Rah from the dais and is leading him away when Mursilis realizes that his authority has once again been ignored.

"Perhaps you would both be so kind as to dine with *me* tonight, Aleksandus," says the King, rising and gesturing for his valet, who was apparently lurking in the shadows of the Great Hall and watching Rah's performance before the barefoot King arrived.

"Excellent," responds the Amegan commander, turning back to the King as he might a junior officer, Rah still tucked under one arm.

"Jibril can eat with Rah also, Alek?" asks Rah, but Aleksandus merely takes his shoulders in a rough hug and gives him a good squeeze.

"Jibril can eat with the guards in the dungeon tonight, Rah. Tomorrow, if you insist, we will give you authority over him. A slave for a slave god. Only take good care to keep him happy, Amorite dog, else I will personally hack you into pieces and feed you to the palace lions."

"He shall be happy, Sir!" cries Jibril, who is even now being pulled away toward the dungeon.

CHAPTER 21

Kaspir is awakened in the Amorite camp of Iamhad by the sensation of a lump of bloodied meat hitting him square in the chest.

"Guh!" he cries out, like a man who has taken a punch to the midsection, and he grabs for the thing and hurls it from his breast. But his hand has come away sticky and his chest is wet. He throws himself against the tent wall behind his sleeping sack, blinking in the dark and searching wildly about for some clue as to whom or what has come for him in the night.

"Take heart, Captain," whispers Rush at his right ear like a lover. Kaspir feels the lump of warm meat being forced into his right hand. "Your Master is here to save you."

"Sa-a- save me from what, Sir?" is all Kaspir can manage. Rigid with fear he cannot maintain a grasp on the horror in his hand, and lets the thing slip into the folds of his nightshirt.

"From the fires of Tartarus, Captain. For even now they burn, can you not smell them? The camp is aflame, just as those burning believed my home to be aflame after they sent the plague to Amega in the blood of an ass. And you, Captain Kaspir, hold the heart of the man who set this army afire. For he as well as did so with his own torch when he dared to send a plague to the home of the Rush the Assassin. Now wake your fleas and flee, or roast along with the rest of these Amorite dogs."

Kaspir is wrenched to his feet and set on his legs.

"Take heart, Captain Kaspir, and do not lose it again or it shall be your own," says the black hell that is holding him upright. Once again, the heart of Iamhad is forced into his hand.

"Yes, Sir," responds Kaspir. But the assassin is gone. Kaspir stands in the center of the tent amongst his sleeping men, and now he hears the hysteria of what the assassin has accomplished all about in the darkness outside the tent. Men are coming awake in flames. The bright orange of a wall of fire lights the far wall of the tent and in the light Kaspir can see shadows running and falling. Men are screaming. Kaspir bends to awaken Marut and Wadin just as a triplet of horses crashes through the far wall of the tent, bringing down the poles and crushing underfoot the unfortunate men who had been sleeping on that side. The animals are screaming in terror. They fall, caught up in the tent. "Fire!" shouts Kaspir, kicking Marut in the head as he falls over Wadin. "Get up, you idiots! The man has torched the entire camp! We must flee! It is every man for himself now!"

Stumbling to his feet in a daze, Marut turns about, looking for his gear.

"Take your weapons belt and flee!" cries Wadin, grabbing his own and drawing Lar to his feet at the same instant.

"What of the horses?" Lar is shouting over the din now.

"Forget them! They will run down into the valley toward the river, as must we! Come! I will not meet that man again having failed to do as he has told me!"

Half an hour later the four spies have found their way down into the valley. They gather in a stand of trees, looking about for shelter.

"We will have to go west, meet up with the others," offers Wadin, throwing the pack he managed to salvage from the fire onto the ground to sit upon.

"To hell with that," responds Kaspir. "He will be here soon enough to claim us. Did I not tell you it was the assassin? He woke me moments before the tent caught fire. Handed me this..." he pulls the heart from the folds of his tunic. "Iamhad's heart."

The others are staring at the thing with stricken faces.

"Iam-m?" Lar points to the lump of muscle, no longer sticky with fresh blood but graying like a dried meat. "His heart?"

"His heart. Fancy looking for *that* in the afterlife for all eternity. "Kaspir holds the thing out for all to see.

"How can you carry that...?" Marut is pointing to his captain's chest, "so close to your own?"

"Have I a choice?" barks Kaspir, turning to drop his weapons belt in the dirt and slide to his knees with his pack. "He will find us, wherever we should go. If we attempt to return to our brothers, he will seek us out and kill us, I care not to think how. We have no choice but to wait for him to reclaim us and to give us our orders. We are his now, we are the chattel of the Great Wolf. Did you think you would escape him? We are fortunate to have been spared from the fire. We are no longer free men. Our lives are no longer our own."

"Well I for one would rather fight for the assassin than for Syria," pipes in Wadin. "Has he not proven he is unconquerable? We are soldiers for hire. What business is it of ours who feeds and clothes us?"

"I have family to think of," answers Kaspir, stuffing the grey wad of flesh into his pack. "A wife, sixteen young ones to feed. What will become of them? Or do you think he will allow me to return home to them?"

The silence that follows is broken by the familiar sound of horses, not thundering down upon them but strolling and blowing peacefully, as if led by the hand. The men jump to their feet, turn toward the noise, and are shortly confronted by the bizarre sight of the assassin himself leading six warhorses out of the maquis. The animals are quiet, even refreshed, as if they, too, understand that they were spared. One, a dun mare on the assassin's right, blows contentedly and runs her nostril up the man's brawny arm. Here is my master, she seems to say. Look how he has led me from danger. He is good and trustworthy. You are fools to run from him.

Rush looks about at the tattered group of men, then splits the leads, three and three, and gestures to Lar and Wadin. The men immediately approach to take the animals. One of them is carrying a large pack on its back which appears to have been tied in haste.

"There are bridles and pads," says Rush, nodding to the pack. "Tack them up. Who among you has ridden a warhorse?"

Wadin and Marut look at one another, then nod.

"And you?" Rush is sizing up Lar, who is the smallest among them.

"No, Sir. But I can ride," says Lar.

"Not well enough to know that riding a warhorse is another thing altogether, eh?" grimaces Rush. "Take the dun mare. She is gentle. Even so, put a hard leg on her and she will put you in a tree. Speak to her mouth as if it were the mouth of the woman you love."

"Then I should not touch it at all!" boasts Lar, whose lover is an Egyptian girl, taken as a slave by the Amorites when she was but a child. "For her mouth is as soft and as sweet as the petal of a lily," he lays a hand on his chest, his eyes misting.

"There you have it. Ride her thus," says Rush, "and give me the black." He gives Wadin a sharp look, lifts his chin to the pitch gelding he is holding on his left, and adds, "He is only recently cut, and is by the looks of his teeth a good seven summers old."

Wadin widens his eyes at the animal. "You are welcome to him, Sir," he says pursing his lip. "I do not care to have my back broke to be a hero."

"You will all be heroes before I am done with you," answers Rush, turning to snatch Kaspir's pack from his back and rummage through it. When he finds what he is looking for he takes the black from Wadin and mounts from the ground. The horse scoots forward, takes the bit, snorts and halts. Rush trots it forward, halts again, then suddenly spins the animal and launches a kick that would fell a half dozen men.

"A fine warrior," muses Rush then, trotting back toward the group of men and offering the black a single slap on the shoulder. "We will get along."

"Similar temperament," mutters Marut to Kaspir as the men mount their own animals.

Rush turns to the river and begins leading the group south and east.

"What is this?" Marut whispers to Kaspir. "Why do we return as we have come?" But the assassin has heard him. He whips his animal around to confront Marut, whose face pales.

"You are a big man with a bigger mouth, Marut," says the assassin, and the black paws and snorts as if awaiting his command to whirl and kick the fool who spoke.

Marut, somewhat astonished that the assassin has bothered to learn his name, makes no response. His horse trots backward tentatively, as if equally unnerved.

"I can make it bigger still," continues Rush, cocking his head at Marut to study his features.

"You will not hear from me again, Sir, I swear it," answers the other.

"Nor you from me. For I am not in the habit of giving my men my plans in advance, else when they are captured and tortured they give them to my enemy."

"Of course, Sir." It is Kaspir, who, giving Marut a harsh look, has brought his horse up to stand between Rush and Marut.

Instantly, two black, snarling giants break from the tree line and rush at Kaspir. Rush leans forward to grab the man's rein, keeping his horse from rearing and drawing him beside himself at the same time.

"Leave it!' he barks, and the wardogs drop to their bellies, wagging and smiling.

"With that horse and those dogs, you are an army, Sir," murmurs Kaspir, thankful of the assassin's intervention.

"I *am* an army, Captain," answers Rush, his lips nearing a smile. "Now hear me. You will take this mouth," he flicks a glance at Marut, "and continue south to meet Amega. Make a flag of surrender before you approach for the man who has been given leave to command my army is quick to loose a head. When he asks you for your rank, you are to tell him that you are Amorite spies who have been captured by his Master and sent to bring him a message. Say, 'the Wolf has burned the army of Iamhad in recompense for the plague he sent to Amega. He has saved our worthless hides for one reason only, that is, to inform Nikolaos of Cyrus, his ally, to remain on his southern flank, for an army is coming from Syria, one twice the size of that of Iamhad. They are tired and afraid for the Wolf has left his mark on their border. Yet they come, meaning to reach Hattusha in time to join with Iamhad and take the city. Now the Wolf will chase this Syrian flock of sheep into the Valley of the Gods for Amega to attack, plow through, and disperse across the countryside.' Say, 'Think not of their number, for two fools are worth less than one. You now command the best troops in all the Mediterranean world and you will defeat them or die at the Master's hand when he returns.'"

Kaspir looks to Marut, his expression grim. Marut makes no response, only kicks his horse forward to step beside that of his captain.

"We will do just as you say, Sir," says Kaspir. Then he takes his animal's reins, nods to Marut, and pushes his horse into the river, which is shallow here, to head south to meet Amega.

Lar and Wadin are looking at one another behind the assassin's back with dread.

"What do you frown at, little fleas?" says Rush without turning to glance at them. "Do you fear spending a night alone with me? Be encouraged. For now you, too, have orders. You will ride into Hattusha, present yourselves to my commander there, and tell him that the Master will be waiting for him in the Valley of the Gods. Tell him Iamhad's forces are dispersed, their camp burned in recompense for their plot against a King his Master had personally installed. Tell him he is to bring ten thousand of his best troops. Leave the rest to guard the city." Now Rush turns to give the two men a black look over his shoulder. "Tell him you are mine now, and should be branded as such."

"Brand-?" gulps Lar, unconsciously reaching to touch his cheek with nervous fingers.

"GO!" barks Rush, and the two whirl their animals about and take off at a gallop down the valley toward Hattusha.

In the evening of the same day, in a tent behind the forces of Amega, Mochlos turns to his assistant in the lamplight and sighs.

"Here it is then, enough poison to sicken an entire herd of cattle." He waves a hand over the bundle that lies on the trunk before him.

"But who is to feed it to them, Holiness?" asks the assistant nervously, for he is but a boy himself and surely not to be expected to sneak into an enemy's camp to accomplish the deed.

"I've no idea," responds the priest, stroking his open hand over his shaved pate in thought. "This Nikolaos may be as cold blooded as his Master, but he is clever. Too clever to send a priest or a priest's boy to do the job, of that I am sure. I only pray to the Goddess that I've the right plant, and that it will act the same on a cloven or uncloven creature, else my head be in a sack for the target practice of Amegan soldiers before the week is out."

Just then the flap of the priest's tent is pulled back and a man the size of a small buffalo, with a rough of hair cascading to his waist, blackens the doorway. He wears the Tears of the Bull on his cheek. The eye above is gone, taken, Mochlos suspects, in battle.

"The Lieutenant General wants you in his tent," barks the burly beast. "And bring your poison with you, priest." He spits at the high priest's feet, turns, disappears.

"Mother Goddess help me," whistles Mochlos into the still night air. "Let us go then. Go ahead, man. Take it up and follow me."

In the Captain's tent the air is heavy and dark. There is no lamp lit, and Mochlos stumbles over a furry beast as he enters. The animal offers him a low growl, barely perceptible and makes no effort to move out of his way.

"Come forward, priest." It is the voice of Nikolaos, coming from a far corner of the tent. But there is someone closer. Mochlos can hear the man's breath to his right. And another to his left. And more than one beast is breathing foul and meated air in his direction.

"What is this?" fires the priest into the thickening air. "Are we not safe enough to light a lamp amongst our own?"

And as suddenly as he has blurted the question, he hears the hiss of a flint, and then the spark of a lamp being lit. A lamp he would have as soon left dim, for all about him are the hulking shapes of the soldiers of Amega, their weapons glinting along their belts, their fierce faces framed by the wild hair of the Hatti warrior, and each sporting the Tears of the Bull just under their left eye socket.

"Merciful Goddess!" yelps Mochlos, looking about. Each man holds a monstrous black wardog on a leash at his feet. The dogs leer up at Mochlos, tongues lolling.

"Where is the poison you promised me, priest?" Nikolaos has come to his feet with the lamp. He steps forward, sets the light on a narrow table in the center of the tent.

"Here it is!" cries Mochlos, grabbing his terrified assistant by the arm and thrusting him forward with a package the size of a baby.

"Open it. Show me. How much for each animal?" asks the Lieutenant, looking down at the parcel curiously.

Mochlos makes quick work of unfolding the bundle. He takes a single sprig of the yew, holds it up for Nikolaos to see in the grim light.

"That is all," he answers smugly.

Nikolaos gives him a sharp look. "Impressive," he says, then nods to the man to his left. The man immediately steps forward, grabs the package and secures it, tucks it under his arm.

"Go, Peleshet," says Nikolaos. "You know what to do."

And the man is out the tent flap, his own dog, unleashed, at his heels. Several others follow him, clearing the tent but for the Lieutenant, the priest, and his assistant.

"We will see, priest, if you have a head in the morning."

The army of the King of the Amorites has reached the Valley of the Gods. They are camped and poised for their attack on Hattusha in the morning. They have been ordered to eat and rest tonight for they will not eat nor rest again until Hattusha is taken.

The men have doused their fires early and left a light guard on duty. In the stable area, a dozen sentries surround the chariot horse corral. Peleshet has counted another dozen keeping watch around a nearby tent, no doubt the army's store of hay and grain. But this is no obstacle for Peleshet. He has sent a man and dog team to take down the two sentries on the western edge of the corral. He has sent another team to take down the sentry at the southwest corner. He has split the contents of Mochlos' package between himself and four other men, and together they have distributed the yew in the dry and barren corral. Already, in the dark, he can hear the horses munching on the sprigs.

"That should do it," he hisses to the men following him out of the paddock. "If the priest is true, there will not be a chariot horse able for battle in the morning."

On a rise not half a mile away, Rush the Assassin sits astride a dangerous black warhorse, watching his men sabotage the Amorite roundup.

"Clever fox," he breaths through his muslin mask. "So you took the priest and his bag of tricks with you. With no horses to pull their chariots, they are but an army of frightened foot soldiers, numerous as cockroaches and just as fierce. Against my elite killers. And you have brought the dogs and their handlers. M-m-m, but will you strike at dawn, pup? Or take them in their beds. Let us weigh this measure heavily in our favor, and tuck their generals in for a good long sleep. You will have less to do in the morning."

With that he dismounts, tying the animal to a tree and leaving the dogs with the command to guard it, for he has grown fond of the spirited beast. He leaves his sack with the dogs as well, removing only one item from it before beginning his stealthy trek down the incline toward the Amorite camp. This time, I will make sport of you, you arrogant monkeys. This time I will leave my mark, so that you will awaken to the truth of all this-- that you were never in control, that Rush the Assassin has always had the upper hand. You challenge me, here in my own country where I am king. You believe you can teach Antaris a lesson in war. Well I will teach you instead, that I *am* War.

Rush moves through the night like the shadow of a carrion bird. He lands in the center of the camp, in the tent of the generals. Four men sleep in four sections of the tent, separated only by canvas drapes. The guards outside are sleeping, exhausted from their march into Anatolia.

Rush moves about the tent, easily soundless, peering in the dark at each sleeper until he finds the man he is looking for. Then he tugs the elaborately embroidered coverlet off his first victim. The man snorts, pulls at the blanket, turns onto his side. Rush perceives the braided beard of a top Amorite commander in the dark and takes hold of it. He has lifted the man from his bed by the hairs of his beard before he can come fully awake.

He pulls him close, close to his masked face, and hisses, "Kahla, we meet."

The man's eyes fly open in shock. He yanks his head away, tearing hairs from his own beard. He attempts to open his mouth to shout for his guards, but a thick finger has been shoved under his jaw, in that tender area just between the mandibles. Then, in the next instant, the surgically precise stab of a small, hooked blade severs the muscles there, leaving the man's jaw slack.

"You are done giving orders, Kahla," whispers Rush, before yanking the man from his bed, kneeing him in the groin and laying him out on the floor by his beard.

In another instant his hands are tied to his sides, his beard sliced off, and his mouth stopped with the dried ball of meat Rush has been carrying since he relieved Kaspir of the burden earlier that morning.

"Where were you when I invented war, Kahla?" muses Rush eerily as he trusses the man's legs, then pulls them back to tie his ankles to his hands. "Not in training that day?" he continues, rising to his feet. And the Amorite commander has a moment of relief, thinking that the black clad demon is leaving him, before the impact of a knee coming down hard on his chest knocks the air from his lungs. Then he is lost in a dreamy stupor, barely perceiving that the Tears of the Bull are being carved into his left cheek.

At the camp of the Army of the Assassin, Peleshet and his men have returned from their mission. Nikolaos has summoned the priest, Mochlos, back to his tent, this time with orders to instruct his dancers and the Rah's personal attendants to pack and ready for travel.

"I want you and your House far from danger when the battle begins. Peleshet and his men will take you into Hattusha. You will leave in an hour. It is two days journey on horseback."

Mochlos, relieved beyond words, can barely keep from throwing himself at the young Lieutenant's feet in gratitude, although he has never ridden a horse. But his words of praise for the man's wisdom are stopped as Nikolaos steps forward to take the front of his robe in his long fingers and whisper in his face, "See to it that the Rah is in good health and spirits when we meet again, Mochlos, for I am still uncertain if that head of yours is worth leaving in place. Might we not all be better off if you were to be relieved of the burden of it?"

When Mochlos is gone, Nikolaos mutters, "Calculating bastard. I wonder the Master suffers the man."

"He is a burden," answers Peleshet, looking to the tent flap out of which the man just fled. "Nevertheless, Sir, his magic is real. Before we had finished distributing the yew in the Amorite turnout, several of the beasts were already pawing the ground, a few rolling. It is a fast acting poison. I think that we will have few chariots to face in the morning."

"If that is so, and when the enemy sees how our dogs can attack and disarm a well-armed man, it may well be a short confrontation, though they be as numerous as wheat," answers Nikolaos. "I only wish that the Master were here to enjoy it."

In Hattusha, Wadin and Lar have been interrogated and released to join the army in the foothills. They have been branded with the Tears of the Bull, and to their surprise and relief, have been heartily accepted by their new peers as a result. Except for a few officers left in place by Aleksandus, they are the only men sporting the honored mark.

"It means that the Great Antaris has chosen you," remarks one man, a youth from the city only recently joined up himself. "It is a great honor. And the freshness of the wound," he takes a closer look, making little attempt to withhold his awe, "Makes it all the more admirable."

Aleksandus has left a guard along the western wall of the city and mobilized the ten thousand Rush has demanded. Within only a few hours of his receipt of his orders, Aleksandus and the ten thousand are marching toward the Valley of the Gods, ready to engage the enemy. Rah, and his new attendant, Jibril, have been left in the hands of the King and his palace guard. The palace steward has installed him in the wing opposing the Great Hall, a suite of rooms that is intended for the eventual Queen. But keeping Rah in a suite of rooms is not an easy task. Already he has bullied his guards with the threat of beheading should his Wolf return to find that he is not being cared for properly.

"Rah cannot stay here. Where dancers are? Where concubine for Rah? Rah need bath. Travel long time, no bath. You have bath master? Rah need special bath oil. Wolf come. He find Rah is no smell like Rah, he is take head! Put on stick! You see!"

"Obnoxious little demon," whispers the King's footman to the keeper of the royal bath, for there is no bath master in Hattusha, no royal dancers, no concubines here for Rah, only men in arms and nobility and servants of various rank. "He wants special oils for a bath. Says if he does not smell as he ought the Great Antaris himself will come and lop off some heads. Who knows what he is supposed to smell like?"

"We will do what we can," answers the keeper of the royal bath, who has not stopped staring into Rah's kaleidoscopic eyes since the boy raised them to him, pouting fiercely. "Leave him to me," and he waves the footman off.

"I cannot leave him anywhere, and that is my point," snaps the footman, who has already had more than enough of Rah in the hour the boy has been in his charge. "I am stuck with him, assigned to keep him out of trouble and happy until the man who owns him takes him off our hands."

"And who owns this?" responds the keeper of the royal bath, lifting a hand to sweep it over Rah's body from his bare, sun-browned feet to his emerald crowned head. "Is he not a slave god? Sent from Amega? Then he is the possession of the priesthood of Amega. No one is likely to come get him now, while there is a war on. Antaris has better things to do, I would imagine."

"Not this one," sneers the footman, turning to find a place to sit. "This one is the Wolf's favorite, and you have that from Commander Aleksandus. Mar a hair on that insufferable head of his and you will yourself be shaved and scalped. So good luck to you finding the right potion for him."

But the bath keeper is unperturbed by this information. He bows low to Rah, then invites him into a freshly poured bath. Round about, several servants watch with rapt attention, whispering behind their hands and pointing to the spectacle. For Rah has dropped his skirt and slipped into the water like a seal before the bath keeper can offer him assistance. He submerges his body, then jumps up in a splashing fit.

"Ayee! Too hot!" and he has thrown a leg over the rim to jump out.

"Not so fast, little god. You will get used to it," says the bath keeper, putting a gentle hand on Rah's shoulder and easing him back into the water. "Sit down now, slowly, go on. Itri will not scald you."

"You ought to scald the little rascal. Shut him up for a minute," says the footman. He has found himself a bench nearby and has relieved it of a pile of fresh towels with a single shove.

"Patience, Nasir, you need to learn it," responds the royal bath keeper. He has tossed a few figs into the bath with Rah and, as he suspected, the boy is distracted looking for them in the bottom of the basin. While he does so, Itri walks to a cabinet against a wall and begins opening bottles and sniffing the contents. "Ah, here now. What of this?" And he turns to put the top of the open bottle of myrrh oil under Rah's nose.

Rah's face brightens. He gives Itri a nod. "This good. This make Rah smell right for Wolf."

Itri pours a bit of the oil into the bath, then turns to return the bottle to the cabinet and poke about for something complementary.

The footman is looking from the bath keeper to Rah and back with some surprise.

"First time I heard him shut up all morning," he comments, punching a towel into a pillow and lying back on the bench for a well-deserved rest.

His siesta is interrupted by the sound of the King's valet pretending to clear his throat, for he is being followed by the King and his retinue.

The footman is on his feet and down on one knee in the time it takes the valet to step aside for the King's entry. Two house servants and a half dozen attendants accompany him.

"Ah, Itri, I see you are making our divine guest a proper bath. Excellent," says the King, waving for an attendant to bring him a stool to sit upon beside the basin Rah inhabits.

Itri has a second bottle of oil in his hand, this one oil of cherry wood. He is familiar enough with the King to make a simple bow only, then continue his ministrations to Rah. Rah has grabbed the neck of the bottle and sniffed, taking no notice of the King at all.

"This good!" he says, releasing the bottle so that Itri can pour the correct amount into his bath. "This like Tuma do."

"And who is Tuma, little god?" asks the King, who has seated himself on an opulent stool beside the basin so that he might better enjoy the vision of Rah bathing.

"Tuma is bath master in Knossos. House of Moon. Best bath master in all of Crete," confides Rah. "Where concubines is? Hattusha is no concubine for Rah? Wolf is take head," he slices his index finger across his own throat, just above his golden collar, to stress the seriousness of this offense.

"What else, little god? Hyssop no doubt, and lotus, for the deity. Here we are," says Itri, taking two more bottles from a shelf within the cabinet.

The King's valet has come to put a cushion under the King's feet. He kneels beside the basin, slipping the pillow beneath the royal slippers, and looks up as he rises to see that Rah has stood up as well in his bath and is staring at him with a black look in his feral eyes. A low burr has begun to hum in Rah's throat.

"He doesn't like you, Tarkim. He looks as if he will-" begins the King, but his sentence is shortened when Rah spits at the valet's feet.

"Spit," finishes the King.

The valet, in turn, has risen and is looking at Rah with bewilderment.

"Perhaps he does not care to share his pretty eyes with a simple valet," muses Itri, for Tarkim's eyes are as green as the emerald Rah wears between his brows.

"Where you from?" demands Rah. "You from north? Far north?" He is looking directly at the valet with little interest in anyone else in the room.

"He is from Kassara," answers the King. "He has never been further north than Hattusha. He is the child of my grandfather's favorite concubine. She had green eyes. An Egyptian slave. Why, little god, are they all green-eyed in the North?"

"Mmph," Rah pouts, frowning at Tarkim. "No more bath. Where Dashuri is? You take Rah to stable now." He is looking over his shoulder at the footman.

"Sir?" asks the footman, glancing at the King, then down at his feet.

"Horses, baths, concubines. You are quite a handful, Rah of Knossos. But will you dance again for the King before you go?" asks the King gently. How does the assassin tolerate this little minx? he thinks, rising from his stool so that the others may follow suit and grant Rah's demand.

Rah hops out of the basin, kicking the cushion from the valet's hands as he lands, then grabs the skirt Itri is offering him and does his best to storm off, although his bare feet make little noise on the cool tile floor.

"Rah need troupe for dance. You have troupe?" He raises his hands in the air dramatically. "No! Pah!" And he is gone, the footman chasing him, and the others are looking about at one another in awkward confusion.

"A dance troupe?" asks the valet, standing behind the King blinking, the cushion, which he has retrieved from the floor, clutched in his hands.

"Apparently, and anything else he can dream up, or remember from some long ago glory," muses the King, shaking his head. "Follow him, Tarkim. See what it is he desires. We must keep him happy, or else we will be explaining it in our beds one night whilst the Wolf of the Aegean rips out our hearts with his teeth."

Rah is already in the palace stable when Tarkim catches up to him. The valet, who has been following a good distance behind, quickly hides behind a stack of hay, content to spend the afternoon watching the strange creature from Amega in secret before making any attempt to speak with him. He watches as the golden-head disappears into a stall, then emerges with a fine boned black colt. He spies as Rah hops onto the animal's back with only a halter and a single lead rope to control it. He observes in silent amazement as the little god trots the animal out into the stable yard, then slowly lifts himself off the horse's back into a handstand on its withers, his feet pointing to the clouds above, his lean body curved in a perfect arch to match the rhythm and speed of the horse's gait.

"My gods," whispers Tarkim to himself, looking about for the footman, for if the Rah hurts himself it will surely be the footman who will pay the price. But the man is crouched in a corner of the tack room, lighting a pipe. Drugs, thinks the valet. Opium. He will be useless for the rest of the afternoon. Tarkim eases out from behind the hay bales and approaches the edge of the stable yard, careful not to startle the colt, or the strange creature on his back.

Rah has made a full circle around the yard, hand-standing on the horse's withers. Now he eases himself into a pike, until he is standing on the point of the hip. Two light hops to test Dashuri's nerve, and he has sprung himself into a double twist off the colt's back to land on the soft earth of the stable yard. Dashuri is quick to come to halt, turn, and walk casually over to snuffle the pockets of Rah's skirt.

Tarkim watches from the archway leading into the stable yard. He waits patiently for Rah to pay him some mind. But it is only after Dashuri has been given a treat, then patted and cooed to and kissed that Rah lifts his gaze to the youth.

Green eyes glare at green eyes in the soft winter sunlight. Rah turns his shoulder to the valet and moves off in the opposite direction, the horse following. Presently Tarkim becomes aware that he is building some type of obstacle in the center of the stable yard using stacks of hay.

My gods, thinks the valet. He is going to ride that animal bareback over a jump, standing on his croup! And here I stare, like a dim-witted lummox, watching him prepare to break his neck!

Tarkim walks out into the stable yard, unsure of what he will say when he is within earshot of the Assassin's favorite.

Rah is ignoring him with theatrical fastidiousness. He keeps his back to the valet, even when he is close enough to reach out and touch, and continues to march back and forth from the hay room to the center of the stable yard with bales of hay that are half his weight. But Tarkim will not be dissuaded from his task. He follows Rah to and fro, shadowing him like a dark alter, until at last Rah drops his third bale beside the others and whirls at him.

"What you follow Rah, heh? What you want. You want be like Rah? Only one Rah. You go, serve to King. Go!" And he gives Tarkim a shove that ought to send him to the ground.

But Tarkim only takes a few steps back and continues to stare at Rah.

"What you want!" shouts Rah, putting his fists on his hips for emphasis. Dashuri has come up behind him and now gives him a good nudge, pushing him forward so that he gracelessly falls into Tarkim's steadying hands.

Tarkim sets him back on his feet, then crosses his arms over his chest and waits.

Rah is warbling.

"I *am* serving the King, Rah," says Tarkim, "He has asked me to discover what will make you happy."

"Happy?" scoffs Rah. "Concubine make Rah happy. Dance make Rah happy. What kind city this is? No concubine for Rah. No dance troupe. Pah!" he throws his hand in the air dismissively and turns to the bales of hay.

"The only one in the palace who keeps concubines is the King himself," says Tarkim. "He has thirty-two of them, male and female, but rarely visits them. He is young," he shrugs, as if his own explanation makes little sense to him.

But his words have at last captured Rah's attention. He drops the bale he was hoisting atop another and turns to Tarkim, a single dimple beginning like the twinkling of the first star in a clear sky.

"What your name is?" he looks Tarkim over, giving him a thorough brush with his lashes and allowing himself the glimmer of a smile.

"I am Tarkim," says the valet. "Tarkim of Kassara."

"Tarkim of Kassara," repeats Rah, nodding, his hands back on his hips. "Good name for dancer. I like. Take me to King's concubine, Tarkim of Kassara. Maybe make Tarkim dancer too. City need to dance. Praise Rah with dance. Then have good war, good King, plenty rich. You see."

Tarkim is blinking at him nervously. How did this happen?

"I cannot take you to the King's harem, Rah. Only the eunuchs can enter the harem. I would be beheaded!"

"Pah. You take Rah to concubine or *Wolf* is beheaded you. Skin you first. Maybe eat heart too, I don't know. Better you take Rah see concubine. We see if can make dance."

Tarkim takes a deep breath, swallows. How did this happen, he thinks again, rubbing his bare stomach distractedly.

"Need to lose this," says Rah, patting Tarkim's belly as he puts an arm over the valet's shoulder and turns him toward the archway, for Tarkim is fond of sweets.

"I am a valet," responds Tarkim, putting Rah's hand away gently. "I am not meant to dance. I care for the King. Dress him, see that all of his personal needs are met." He turns to look over his shoulder at Dashuri. "What of him?"

"He eat hay. Is okay. Where King harem is, Tarkim?"

"It is as far from the smell of horses as it can be," chuckles the valet then. "For the King dislikes them. He was trampled by one as a child."

"Other side palace? We go," says Rah. "Come, come, Tarkim, you race Rah. This make you like Rah here," and he is gliding his palms down his sides. "Like dancer." But before Tarkim has fully accepted the insult,

Rah is on his toes and, in a flash, racing to the archway as only Rah can. He takes a few spins, then launches himself into the air and performs a set of springing handstands. Turning like a sprite at the arch, he gives Tarkim a mischievous look and disappears down the hall.

"Wait!" cries Tarkim. "You cannot enter the harem, Rah!" But he is already running, a thing he has not done since he became a junior valet to the King at the age of twelve summers, what now seems an eternity ago.

Behind him the footman has come to his feet in the grain room. Stupid with opium, he moves to the doorway and watches the valet disappear up a staircase at the end of the hall. "What the-?" he mutters to himself, then shaking his head, returns to his hiding place to sleep off his stupor. "Aggravating baggage," he grumbles, slumping to the floor. "Go get your heads removed, both of you, for all I care. Less trouble for me."

The King's harem occupies the entire east wing of the third floor of the palace, just above the King's own suite of rooms. The head concubine is Numira, old enough to be the King's mother, and mother of four of the harem girls. Numira is also the valet's mother, though she did not raise him. From birth he was taken by the Mistress of Children to be groomed for service to the King, a favor granted Numira by King Hattusilis himself.

Numira rules the harem, although a guard of ten eunuchs enforces her sovereignty. All answer to her, including the junior concubines, the harem dancers, male and female, the harem musicians, the harem seamstresses, hairdressers, cobblers, face painters and bath attendants (all eunuchs).

It is because of Numira that the King infrequently visits the harem. In short, he cannot tolerate her, nor she, him. Nevertheless, it is his duty to visit the harem at least once a month, during the mid-cycle of the moon, in order to generate royal offspring. For if the King dies before he has taken a queen and had sons to become princes, then a prince will be chosen from the offspring of his harem.

Today, Numira is teaching a new girl the skills required to entertain a king. Training a harem girl is a serious business and requires months of coaching. Today, the new girl is learning to play the santur. She is in the middle of a lesson with the Chief Minister of Music, a great, fat eunuch with a shaved head and body, whilst the head concubine watches with some distress. The girl cannot seem to keep the mallets between her fingers properly and is genuinely inept at music on the whole. She is a beautiful little thing, however, with a shapely body and a graceful manner. Numira knows the King's taste and expects this creature to be a favorite in short order, if only the child did not have a tin ear.

Numira is trying with all of her might to keep from grimacing as the girl attempts to shadow the tune the Chief Minister of Music is playing for her on his own santur. She forces a patient smile, an encouraging nod, knowing with all of the wisdom of a head concubine to a king that one can catch more bees with honey than with vinegar. But the girl is hopeless, each note more painfully sour than the last. She gives the Chief Minister of Music an apologetic shrug and turns to call one of the older girls for a tray of dainties, and perhaps a nice tea, the kind that stops headaches, when the sun bursts through the doors on bare feet and stops just short of falling into her lap.

"Oh!" cries Numira, skootching out of the way on her knees as Rah comes to an abrupt halt on his toes and gains his balance. "Arriniti, help us!"

Rah looks down at Numira, blinking with confusion at the second green-eyed Hattushan he has seen since his arrival, and then, looking about to realize he has found the harem, makes a dramatic spin with open arms as if to introduce himself to his audience. The stunned faces of the girl are quickly changed to modest hands covering giggling mouths, which only serve to make the painted eyes of the King's concubines more alluring. Blinking with the wide-eyed awe of a child in a pastry shop, Rah takes a moment to absorb the abundance of feminine loveliness that surrounds him before dropping like a puppet into his signature bow.

"Oh!" cries Numira again, this time rising to her jeweled sandals, her hand on her throat. Three husky guards have rushed into the room behind Rah. They lift him roughly off the floor and begin dragging him backward through the double doors.

"No!" yowls Rah, who has been lifted clear off his feet and has no purchase with which to struggle. "Must dance for King! I teach! Rah of Knossos is teach!"

"Oh, please Dimi, let him explain himself!" cries Numira, stepping forward with a pleading expression, her arms outstretched to Rah.

Perceiving instantly the presence of one who holds some rank as well as an inclination toward theatrics, Rah responds by letting his body slump in the guards' arms as if in a faint.

"Oh, see now Dimi, he has fainted!" scolds Numira, stepping forward with a mallet from the santur in her hand. She waves the little hammer at a plush divan that sits against a wall under a tapestry lively with belly-dancers in a garden setting. "Bring him here! Put him on this couch and let us minister to him!"

"But Madam-" begins the guard, who has nevertheless already lifted Rah into his arms and now holds him out like a bolt of cloth.

By now the Chief Minister of Music has managed to lumber to his feet to look down with unwarranted authority at the utterly lifeless body of Rah, hanging like so much linen in the guard's arms.

"What on earth is it?" says the Chief Minister of Music, unable to resist brushing Rah's curls from his forehead to get a better look at his face.

The answer to his question comes from the doorway, where Tarkim stands, out of breath and rather ashen.

"It is the Rah of Knossos," he says, flicking his hungry eyes about at the girls who have gathered around Rah, then dropping them. "An honored guest of the King, the favorite of the great Antaris of Amega. He is a god-slave from Minoa, rescued by the Terror himself just before the volcano exploded."

"Dimi, put him on this couch now, carefully, carefully!" says Numira, who is now more concerned with keeping her son's head on his shoulders than she is even of the scandal of allowing a young male stranger to enter the harem. And as the guard moves to place Rah on the couch, with the Chief Minister of Music hovering at his shoulder murmuring "Easy, easy!" she quickly shoves Tarkim back through the doorway. "Get out now, quickly! And say nothing to the King of this!" she whispers, shutting the doors behind him.

Turning to the crowd that has gathered around Rah, Numira claps her hands. "Shoo! All of you! Leave him to me now, go on!" She waves off the girls like so many flies. But Rah is coming to his senses on the chaise. He groans, draws an arm up to lay over his forehead and flutters his lashes.

"Aahh," he says, putting himself up onto his elbows. "Where Rah is?"

"Who is this, Rah?" asks the Minister of Music. "Is Rah not the Egyptian Sun god?"

"That is Ra, dear Minister," responds Numira diplomatically. "An easy enough error. But no, I believe he is referring to the Minoan Rah, the god of grain, fertility," and she strokes Rah's cheek with gentle fingers dreamily, for she has lost herself in his eyes. "Of pleasure and abundance."

"Yes!" says Rah, forgetting his faint. "She is have good head! Smart. What your name is? You see Rah dance? You are be in Knossos when Rah is win compete?"

"I have never been in Knossos, sweet one," says Numira, "Except in my imagination. But I have heard the stories." Numira smiles. "Many stories. Stories of the bull dancers, and of the glorious art and marvelous palaces there." She takes Rah's hand, leans toward him intimately. "I am Numira," she whispers softly. "I am the head concubine of the King's harem."

"Rah is come to Hattusha now, Numira. Come to bring what Hattusha need. But first must dance for King. This how Rah do in Knossos. Rah make grain and good wine in Knossos. Make priest rich. Same in Cyrus. Rah bring rain for wine when no rain many day. You see. Help Rah to dance for King. Rah make Hattusha happy."

Numira has been leaning on the couch with Rah. Now she takes his hands and brings him to his feet.

"And how can Numira help Rah?" she says, chuckling at his foolishness. "What would Rah have Numira do?"

"I show you," says Rah with dreadful seriousness. He releases Numira's hands and turns to look about the room. His eyes wander from girl to girl, each one giggling and hiding all but her eyes behind her hands as he does so. But Rah is not looking for a pretty face. He leaves Numira, moving with silent feet across the tile floors of the harem to examine one girl, then the other, with the possessive eyes of a prowling lion. He stalks about the room, moving from girl to girl, taking one by the hand and turning her about in a circle, the other by the chin to look deep into her eyes, the next by the waist to lie her back against his arm as he did Marta at the Palace of Cyrus when the little girl with no thumb thought she could not dance. The Chief Minister of Music watches, his expression turning from shock to captivation as the boy from Knossos begins to turn the harem into a theater. For it is impossible not to hear the music to which Rah moves.

Even the guards, the two burly eunuchs who had attempted to expel Rah from the harem, are watching with unchecked fascination.

At length, Rah makes his choice. He lifts the new girl from her knees, for she is kneeling before the santur. Her mouth opens in wonder as he guides her across the tile, turning her this way and that, leading her by the hips, by the wrists, and finally by example alone. Leaving her only to set another girl into motion, he moves back and forth between her and each of the other girls until the Music Minister has taken her place at the santur, the flautists have returned their flutes to their lips to accompany him, and the harem has become a pulsing ballet of sexual anticipation.

It is Numira herself who finally stops the thing that has taken control of her harem when, rousing herself from her own trance, she steps forward just as Rah is laying the new girl back on the very couch he 'fainted' on. There is little doubt what his plans are.

Numira steps forward and claps her hands, gesturing for the two guards. Chastised by the result of their earlier rough treatment of the Rah, this time they take him gently, almost reverently, by either arm and lift him off the girl.

But this is further opportunity for the expression of the dance. Rah begins to struggle against them, but his movements are still controlled by the music. He fights against their strength not with strength but with emotion. His face becomes a theatre of longing, his fingers reach, his taught belly heaves. One can almost hear his heart tearing as his bare chest strains against the captivity of the guards' hands.

The Chief Minister of Music stops playing, allowing his last note to linger in the air. He is looking at Rah as if for the first time, his face a study in confusion and then awe.

"He is the very soul of music," whispers the Chief Minister of Music. "This is a god-slave, certainly, for I can hear the harmonies of heaven in his mildest gestures."

"I tell you," says Rah confidently, looking from one guard to the other with mild annoyance until both have reluctantly released his arms. He stalks over to the Chief Minister of Music. "Rah come to bring all good thing to Hattusha. What you want? You want rain? Rah bring rain. You want good crop? Rah make all thing grow. How you say? Much, much everything."

"Abundance," offers Numira, nodding. "You mean to say that the god will bring Hattusha abundance in all things." She looks about the room at the King's concubines, male and female, the harem musicians, the harem seamstresses, hairdressers, cobblers, face painters and bath attendants. "But you must be allowed to dance for the King. And you must be allowed to teach the harem to dance an accompaniment to you. Is that not so, sweet Rah?"

"Must dance for King," nods Rah, looking about the room at all of the slaves and servants who make up the harem of the King of Hattusha with terrible gravity. "Rah must have concubine. Three. Must dance for King. Must sleep in chain. Can eat only white fish, egg from white chicken, milk, cheese from white goat," and lifting his hands to remind them of the deity he serves and hosts, "and all what come from Rah."

"We will lose our heads, Dimi," says one of the two guards who first took hold of Rah, and he shakes his own sadly at his friend.

"No lose head," assures Rah. "You see. I talk to Alek. Alek talk to King. You be okay."

But he has lost interest in their fears. He looks about the room, his eyes alighting on the new girl. "Maybe Rah take one concubine now." He gestures to her to come to him, and the girl rises instantly to go to his side.

"You cannot take a girl from the harem, sweet Rah," laughs Numira, moving forward to take the girl's arm and draw her back to herself. "She is the King's possession."

Rah gives Numira a frown, looking the girl over thoroughly. "I come back tomorrow. Then I take three," and he turns to go. At the beaded curtain he turns again. "Maybe six."

CHAPTER 22

It is a clear, cool morning in the Valley of the Gods when the Amorite camp awakens to the handiwork of Rush the Assassin. Hanging from a horizontal tent pole meant to dry wild meat, are the trussed corpses of Kahla and his four generals. Around the tent are fifteen dead guards, each one's throat cut neatly from ear to ear. In the commotion that has followed the discovery of the bodies the lesser officers are only just now learning that the chariot horses have been sabotaged. Although only one in twenty have succumbed to the yew, all but a few of the others are colicking and hundreds of charioteers are rushing from their tents to hand walk their animals in an attempt to keep them from rolling and twisting their guts.

Without their battalion of chariots, which is often terrifying enough to cause a city to surrender without a fight, the Amorites are forced to postpone their attack on Hattusha. They must stay in the valley, nursing the horses, burying their generals and choosing among the remaining superior officers their new leaders.

To the south the Army of Amega is in no such quandary. Captain Nikolaos has moved his forces into a semi-circle in the surrounding foothills where he commands an eagle's view of the disarray of the Amorite camp. From his vantage point he can see the chaos in front of the commanders' tent, which is easy enough to identify. It is located in the center of the encampment and is the largest except for the supply tents, which are conveniently set to the rear of the compound, closest to Amegan forces.

"Bring the dogs forward. Make ready for the attack!" barks Nikolaos to his messengers, who immediately race in opposite directions to inform the battalion leaders. Pulling his short Grecian sword from its sheath, Nikolaos fills his lungs and makes two slicing motions in front of himself. It has been a long time since he has been engaged in battle, unless one were to include the fight with the five Knossos palace guards in the City of the Dead.

They are confounded and at their weakest, thinks Nikolaos. We cannot allow them time to reorganize. I cannot wait for you much longer, Rush. I have followed your instructions until now and have remained on your flank, awaiting your order to attack. Only give me some sign that you are with me and I will drive these men into battle and bring your enemies to their knees, I swear it.

In the foothills north of the Amorite camp, Rush the Assassin has been watching the chaos from a different point of view. From where he sits astride a ferocious black warhorse, he has a commanding view of the camp, but can also see his own troops hidden in the tree line to the south. Far up the valley in the direction of Hattusha, the dust cloud of the King's ten thousand, led by Aleksandus, softens the otherwise crisp skyline.

Rush the Assassin smiles behind the muslin cloth of his hood. Using only his seat, he moves his mount forward into a clearing on the hillside, then hoists the flag of Amega above his head.

Less than a kilometer down the valley, hidden by a slow rise from the northern flank of the Amorite camp, Aleksandus has spotted the flag of his Master being raised on a hillside above the encampment and raises his own arm to bring his troops to halt.

Dressed in the breastplate and tall hat of a Hittite general, he, too, sits astride a seasoned warhorse. Stretched out to the left and the right of him, spanning the breadth of the valley, ten thousand Hatti warriors, many who served under Hattusilis, stand ready for his command to charge into battle.

Aleksandus raises the flag of the King of the Hatti, knowing full well that the man on the hillside has the eyes of a carrion bird and can see it as easily as he can find a throat to cut in the dark.

On the hillside, the hellish figure of the assassin raises his flag a second time, then makes a sweeping gesture across the valley floor.

Aleksandus nods to his messengers on either side and leads the charge into the valley toward the Amorite encampment.

In the Amorite encampment the thundering sound of the charging Hattushan cavalry has reached the commander's barracks. The officers next in line for command, who have been arguing as to who is to take charge now that their generals are dead, give up their debate and race back to their own tents for their weapons, shouting orders to their own junior officers. These in turn send their men to mount a defense along the northern edge of the camp. The charioteers, who have been ministering to their animals are now forced to abandon them and take up their quivers, their javelins and their shields and fall in behind the infantry. Despite the disarray, all except for those untrained for battle, the cooks and the cobblers, the supply carriers, stablemen and laborers, are assembled on the northern flank of the encampment in time to face Aleksandus.

On a treed ridge to the south, Nikolaos is squinting in disbelief at the scene below. Like a great storm cloud the Hittite army is charging into the valley, dead-on toward the Amorite camp. Across the valley, on a cliff side that is visible to the Hittite hoard but just out of view of the Amorite camp, is the assassin, sitting astride an animal as huge and fierce as he. He is wrapped in black from head to foot like a rotted thing from an Egyptian grave, and his right arm is raised. In his fist he is lifting the standard of Amega, a black and gold flag upon which is painted an eclipsed moon flanked by two crescent shaped blades. It is clear from where Nikolaos watches that it was he who gave the Hittite legion the signal, with his flag, to attack.

My gods, you have been here all along, thinks Nikolaos. It is your work they found in the commander's tent this morning. You who threw their camp into disarray, confounding their leadership. You who have cut off the head of this assault so that now they are on the defense, though they had been planning a surprise attack and a siege. And that must be Agrippa, or else Aleksandus, whom you sent into Hattusha disguised as yourself, no doubt, for you would keep your anonymity from your enemy, and perhaps also from your King.

Nikolaos of Cyrus mounts the horse that his man has been holding for him. He lifts his fist in the air, a sign of unanimity with the monster on the cliff across the valley, though the monster has disappeared from view. And the Wolves of Amega send up a battle cry and charge down the hill to launch an assault on the unguarded rear of the Amorite camp. Within minutes, the war dogs and their handlers are dispatching any men left to guard the supplies and the horses. Then they begin cutting off and killing deserters who are fleeing to the rear as the Hittite army plunges into their ranks from the north.

In the cliffs along the western flank of the city of Hattusha, Ammuna and the lesser portion of the Amorite army are fighting hard rain and hunger. They are dug in along the wall of mountains that face the western fortification of the city, and have been so for two weeks. Rain and mudslides have kept them from making any reasonably organized attack on the city and have made it equally impossible to retreat back down to the plains to find food. Supplies are dwindling and rations have been cut, and several of the regiments have deserted during the night.

For three days and three nights the top officers have been collecting around a fire in a cave situated in a cliff above the West Gate, arguing their positions on what should be done next. With no clear leadership and no central command, the arguing has come to blows in several instances and to a death in another. Until today, the fact that a son of the Great Hattusilis, who made his summer home in Hattusha, might have first-hand knowledge of the layout of the city and palace, had escaped them. But today, Ammuna himself has brought this information to the table and has proposed a daring plan. Though he holds no esteem among them, he has proposed he be given authority over a handful of their best killers, that they might breach the wall at dusk, using the cover of darkness and the rain to their advantage. Then he will lead them into the palace through secret passageways that he has been familiar with from his boyhood, to the very bedchamber of the King himself, in order that they might abduct him and take him back with them to the Amorite camp.

"And how can we be sure that you will not simply give them away, and escape into the city yourself, Ammuna? Or can an Amorite trust a Hittite further than he can throw his hacked off limbs in battle?"

"By now it should be as clear to you as it is to me that my nephew has no use for me," assures Ammuna carefully. "For did he not send me back to you to do with what you would? Is this the familial love you believe will save me? No. Give me what I need and I will bring you back this boy who has stolen my throne. Then if you desire an ally in Hattusha, put *me* in his place, an ally to the King of the Amorites and a servant of Babylon."

Several of the officers laugh at the proposition, but in the end no one can come up with a better plan. They will lose nothing if it fails but if they are successful the capture of the King of the Hatti could well bring Hattusha to surrender. Ammuna is warned that the men he will take into the city with him will kill him the instant they suspect him of any attempt at betrayal. And if he fails to produce the King as he has promised he will be executed upon his return.

Ammuna accepts the deal, confident that he has all the knowledge he needs to accomplish his goal. This single act of heroism will gain him not only the respect of the Amorites, but of the Amorite king, who will then certainly back his assumption of the throne.

That night, Ammuna is introduced to the seven men he will be leading into the palace. They are brought in from the rain, which has continued without ceasing for nearly a fortnight, and brought before the fire. They are a wretched group, dirty and wet, for their own tents have long since succumbed to the pounding deluge and collapsed. They are hungry and in low spirits. Even so, they are a frightening sight. Several of them sport gruesome scars across their faces from prior battles. These shine in the firelight like war paint. One man has lost an ear, another, most of his front teeth. The biggest man stands a full head taller than Ammuna himself, and the shortest is built like a boar, low and broad, with tusks for teeth and a split nose like a snout.

Ammuna is to call each only by the first letter of their family name, so that the big man is Ess. The boar, Aych, the man with no teeth, Zee. The men watch him with pitiless eyes, and Ammuna cannot help but imagine what this gang of Amorite dogs will do to him if he is unable to accomplish what he has promised.

"When?" he asks the officers, who watch him with curious eyes in the dim firelight.

"Tonight," says the one who has been doing most of the talking. "Tonight there is no moon. They will find an unguarded portion of the wall and take you over it. Then it will be up to you." And he looks to the big man, Ess, who watches Ammuna with the eyes of a snake.

"Agreed?"

"Agreed," grunts the giant, never taking his eyes from the prince. "But not like this," and he has stepped forward and grabbed Ammuna's tunic at the throat with no more respect than one might give a slave. "He must dress as we do. Put him in sackcloth. Cover his face with ash. Then we go."

"Fair enough," answers the officer, who seems a bit cowed himself by this band of henchmen, and happy to be rid of them. "Go with your new command now, prince. And do not return without the King."

Several hours later, Ammuna is heaved over the parapet on an isolated section of the western wall of the city. He has been dressed in filthy rags, a tunic he could barely don without choking from the stench and a cloak that already has him scratching for lice. Though it was he who suggested the men climb this part of the wall, which he knows to be lightly guarded, he has been shoved over first, to draw the eyes of an archer, should one spot him in the rainy gloom. But there are none, most of the men having taken refuge from the rain hours ago, when the sun went down.

He is nearly on his feet when he feels the impact of the others coming over the bulwark and landing on the wet stone beside him in the dark.

The next sound he hears is the sound of daggers being drawn all around him.

"Where to now, Princie?" grunts Ess, poking the tip of his weapon into Ammuna's back.

"We must find a rope ladder down the other side," answers the prince.

"Here's a door, here," hisses the hog-nosed Aych.

"No!" croaks Ammuna in a whisper. "The guards will have taken shelter from the rain within. We must find a ladder!"

He is propelled toward the opposite side of the parapet with a sharp shove from Ess. But as he feels his way along the wall, the hideous grimace of the toothless Zee startles him in the dark.

"Here's one," the man grins inches from his face. Then he is gone, hopping the bulkhead like a monkey and taking the rope ladder down to the top of a building below.

Before Ammuna can follow him, Aych has shoved him out of the way and followed his compatriot over the wall in the pounding rain. The prince is pulled back by the hood of his cloak into the bullish chest of Ess. Foul breath penetrates the rain to fill his lungs.

"You and me'll be last, Princie," he leers into Ammuna's face. "Let the others be cut down comin' over the wall. You and me is last till we find the King and start back." And he holds Ammuna by the scruff of his cloak while the four remaining men shove past to hop over the wall and begin their descent down the rope ladder.

Ammuna is not surprised, nor sorry, when the grunt of a man taking an arrow reaches his ears in the dark.

"Archers!" cries Aych from below, and there is a sound of scurrying for cover. Another grunt, then a gurgling cry from across the rooftop.

"There, that'll be Zee found the archer. Wait now," grunts Ess. And in another moment, a "p-s-s-s-t!" from below and he is shoving the prince over the wall.

At the bottom Ammuna steps over the bodies of two of the men who preceded him down the ladder. They are pierced through by the expert aim of a Hittite archer, a man whose quiver and bow is now in the hands of Zee. The man is looking the thing over and chuckling. He passes his dirty fingers over a palace insignia on the quiver and Ammuna recoils.

"Damn." The word has left his lips before he has realized he has made a sound. Just as suddenly the impact of a fist smashing into his face knocks him to the ground.

"Whose side you on, Princie, eh?" It is Ess hunching over him malevolently.

"I am the servant of the King of the Amorites," Ammuna responds, holding his jaw and drawing himself to his feet. He is quickly shoved along the roof behind the others, who have already crossed the open space for fear of more archers.

"Here," he says, pointing to an alley between this roof and the next. "We must follow this alley to the south wall and then take a passageway hidden within it. It will take us directly to the King's chamber."

"No tricks, eh, Princie?" whispers Ess in his ear as the others begin climbing down the wall.

"No tricks. I will lead you safely. But it may be time for you to realize that that Hattushan archer just took down two of you in the pitch darkness. Fortunate for you I took you to a section of the wall I knew to be sparsely guarded. You may do well to consider that without my leadership you will not make it out of this city alive."

That earns him no comment, but a kick in the head as he is descending the wall to the alley. The other men have already disappeared into shadow.

"Go on," grunts Ess as soon as his feet have touched the cobblestone street. Though too narrow to put a cart through, even this obscure alley is paved, giving him a new respect for the richness of the city he is about to rob of its sovereign. He gives Ammuna a shove and the prince turns to the right and heads for the south wall.

Although he cannot see a hand in front of him in the dark, Ammuna can hear the others following behind. He has no difficulty recalling the way, for the memory of his discovery of this secret route is becoming so strong that it burns in his heart like a hot coal. She was only thirteen then, thinks Ammuna, and I was fifteen summers. And even then, how she led me into darkness, and even so, how I loved her, and lusted after her as only a fifteen year old lad can. He draws in breath against the pain in his chest, stops to collect his wits, then turns back to the others as if he has lost his bearing, to cover his emotion.

Then, with renewed determination, he turns south again and continues feeling his way along the back walls of the outer buildings of the city to the passageway he remembers as if it were only yesterday.

CHAPTER 23

The two boys were the same age by any standard but those levied upon the sons of a King. Hammas, the elder by two minutes, was in fact the smaller of the two, and meeker in nature. But by virtue of his entry into the world of men two minutes ahead of his brother, he was treated as the clear second heir to the throne from birth, their elder brother being the first, and this was a custom that was so natural to the boys that Ammuna instinctively gave him precedence in all things and served him, as would any junior prince an elder brother.

And so it was that when they came to be young men, old enough even to govern should tragedy befall their father the King, it was perfectly normal for Hammas to demand that his younger brother give over to him the girl that he loved, and that every male in the palace lusted after.

She was the daughter of a lesser official in the court, and the product of a liaison unsanctioned by marriage. As such, she had some standing as a daughter of the court, but no means of elevating herself beyond that of playing the harlot to gain favor amongst the privileged. She would never marry, and at best would become the concubine of a wealthy nobleman. But none of this mattered to two boys of fifteen, boys that had watched her grow into a woman and a seductress at the palace before their very eyes, boys that would not and could not think of marriage for another decade.

Ammuna was the more handsome of the two, and at fifteen was already growing the beginnings of a beard. A rogue by nature, he loved to spar and to ride, was learning the chariot and had even made a name for himself amongst the officers as a clever cheat at dice. Hammas, the studious one, had little stomach for war, no innate skills in the games of combat, and hated horses. What was worse, he had no talent for leadership. He was more comfortable in the company of his tutors, who taught him the history of his country and of the ways of government, as well as the arts of poetry and music, astrology, and the skills of the scribe. He avoided most physical efforts, for which he had no natural talent, a flaw that was a constant embarrassment to the King. Only when it came to creatures of the opposite sex, were the boys in agreement. And so as puberty began to turn them into men, their eyes naturally turned to the girls of the court, who were available to them without restriction.

Sophina was one of these, and by the tender age of thirteen she had already learned her place in the world and turned her attention to the pleasuring of the older and more powerful men of the court. She was a proficient dancer, a favorite of tutors, and though she played no instrument she had a clean, perfectly tuned voice with which she favored only her most generous patrons. By the age of thirteen it was clear that as a woman she would possess an astonishingly beautiful body, full-breasted and narrow-waisted, delicately boned and refined of wrist and ankle, though her face already showed the insatiable hunger for power that she would know throughout her life.

It was not easy for a boy of fifteen, even a prince of Hattusha, to catch the attention of such a bird. But catch it Ammuna did. Lavishing gifts and favors on her as no other male could (their older brother was some ten years their senior and had been away at war for five of these) he soon convinced Sophina to become his concubine, much to the jealous misery of the shy and socially inept Hammas.

One day Hammas consulted the royal astrologer for advice.

"My brother has procured for himself the concubine that I desire. Tell me, what can I do to take her from him, or at least to have her once for myself?"

"Ah," said the astrologer, drawing lines in the sand and pointing from this constellation to that to justify his words. "It is in the heavens that your answer lies. For you will surely have the girl. Only this girl will leave you broken, and in the end she will leave your brother for one far greater than himself. But in the last days it will be your elder brother who will pay the highest price for her."

"What is your advice, then," frowned Hammas, who cared little for the details of this story but only for his part in it. Will I have her or not? And what must I do to have her, even if I cannot keep her for myself?"

"Are you not the second prince of the Great Hattusilis? Order your brother to give her over to you, and do what you please with her. But in the end, do not be infatuated by this woman. For not one but two of the princes of Hatti will be destroyed by her."

Not a little confused by this riddle, but determined to have what his brother had no right to keep from him, Hammas ordered Ammuna to give over the girl to him that very day.

"She will not have you, Hammas," responded Ammuna casually. "For she is in love with me."

But Ammuna was mistaken, for when Sophina was summoned by the second in line to the throne, she made no excuses to her lover.

"Am I to deny the second son of the Great Hattusilis? When your elder brother is at war and could so easily die in battle before he returns from your father's campaign against Syria? No, Ammuna. Though I am the daughter of a statesman I have little more rank than a slave. I cannot marry royalty. What is left for me but to go to the one with the most status? I must think of my future."

And Sophina was brought to the bed of Hammas that very night.

But this was no jeweled breastplate, no seat at table, no royal sight hound, not even a favored servant. This was the woman Ammuna loved, and his inherently forgiving heart was conflicted. This tore at the bonds that held him to the code of servitude to his elder brother he had always honored. This ripped at the chains that had bound him all of his life to give over to his brother what should have been his, things that his brother did not love, but took because he could take them. This he could not accept.

Each night that Sophina visited his brother, Ammuna paced the palace. He walked the halls outside his brother's chamber, he roved the passages past the royal harem above his father's bedroom, he paced the palace rooftops. And finally, one moon drenched night on the parapets high above Hammas' bedroom, and hearing the moans of the lovers below threaten to reach across the field just north of the palace where Keret and his men would one day demonstrate a three man chariot to his unborn nephew, Mursilis, Ammuna felt the heart within his breast tear like a man's limbs are torn from his body when drawn and quartered by bulls. And he realized, at last that he could not live forever in his brother's shadow, forever giving a lesser man what he loved for no better reason than the two minutes it had taken him to escape his mother's womb. And something like a door shut in his mind for once and for all. And he lifted his face and looked about at the city he would never rule though he was the better man, and he understood that he had been a fool for too long.

Why did you not push the runt out of your way, Ammuna, he said to himself. Why, and what did it ever gain you to be so passive? It is the same mistake you make, over and over. Will you make it again and again for the rest of your life, until there is nothing left for you that he not has robbed you of and defiled? Are you not a son of the Great Hattusilis? And what would your father have done? Would he not have wound his own cord about his brother's neck, there in the secret chambers of his mother's womb, so that the first child would have been born dead, so that the world would have known, right there at the start, that no one who sought to be ahead of him would ever live to enjoy their victory? No. From now on, the last shall be first, and the first last. From now on, Ammuna, you will be first.

That very night, pacing the length and breadth of the palace, Ammuna found the passageway that led from the roof above the harem down into the wardrobe of the King's chamber. It did not take his sharp mind long to realize why such a thing existed. This was not a servant's access nor a lover's getaway. One had to crawl up into an aperture above the King's wardrobe on a stool in order to access it. This was a well-guarded secret meant only to be used in times of extreme danger, a means of spiriting the King out of his city in case of siege! Putting the pieces of the puzzle together, Ammuna quickly calculated that there must be a way, then, to escape the city from the rooftop, without being seen. He returned to the roof, then made a careful search. There, in the south wall of the parapet was a small opening into which he slid, landing on his feet at the top of a narrow stairway leading to a tunnel in the south wall of the city.

The next night, under a full moon, Ammuna took a torch with him up to the rooftop. Sliding down the hole into the tiny stairwell he began what was to become a long and grueling search for the secret to the navigation of the tunnel. The thing was a labyrinth of paths leading nowhere, at the end of which he was to find more than one pile of human bones indicating the price it would cost him if he were to become lost. Night after night he returned to the tunnel, sweeping his torch across the walls for some clue as to how the channels were marked.

When he found what he was looking for, Ammuna knew that the noble and generous-hearted boy he had been was dead. And the man he would become was unafraid. Although the way was dark, sometimes so narrow that he could barely squeeze through between the stones, and filled with the eerie sounds of small, scurrying feet below and the squeak of bats above, he pressed on, following the sign of the king's seal marked above the threshold of each correct turn. He followed them clear across the city, behind the homes of the rich, to the western wall, where a doorway finally opened onto an alley. Then he climbed to the rooftops of a storage building and looked out over the mountains to the north and west and up into the domed starlit sky and knew that he would never be last again.

The next night, when Sophina was being led to his brother's bedchamber by her dresser and her nurse, Ammuna intercepted her and told her that he had made a dare with his brother, and that the two had agreed that whoever failed to complete the dare would forfeit her forever. Then he entered his brother's chamber without permission or escort and pulled the boy out of his bed by the hair. He struck him with all of the force of the pent up frustration that he had been harboring for fifteen years and sent him reeling, naked, to his knees, and he put a dagger to his throat and ordered him to exchange clothes with him, for he would never again dress in the garb of second prince.

"From now on, brother, you will precede me only as an ox precedes the farmer who goads it as it plows the field," smiled Ammuna when he was finished dressing in Hammas' finest tunic. Then, gagging him first with a sash, he shoved his brother up through the aperture above the wardrobe to the rooftop, across the parapet and down the stairwell into passageway that led to the maze of tunnels within the south wall.

When they had reached what Ammuna guessed was the half-way point, he doused the single oil lantern he carried.

"Where have you taken me, brother?" sobbed Hammas into the crypt-like darkness. "Why did you not tell me that she meant so much to you that you would take your own brother's life to have her? I would have given her back to you. Take me back to my bed, now, and I will never touch her again. I swear, I will say nothing of this, and never touch the girl again."

"Take you to your bed? And which bed is that, brother Hammas, the one with the coverlet encrusted in jewels depicting the crest of the second prince of Hattusha, the one in the chamber beside the first prince, overlooking the temple of the sun and the demonstration fields? Or do you speak of my chamber, the chamber of the third prince, which faces the common streets to the south, and whose bed is no more elegantly made than that of a valet? Oh, no, brother. I will not take you back to your bed, for your bed is mine now. Never again will I be your servant, and watch you take what is mine, simply because I allowed you to precede me out of our mother's womb by two measly minutes. Here you see? Do you recognize the darkness? I have recreated our birth. Here is our mother's womb and our birth canal. Find your way out first *this* time, brother Hammas, and I will play your second until the day I die. But if it is *I* who find the exit and return to the palace ahead of you, then I am first from this day forward."

And hardening his heart to the cries of his terrified brother, he slipped away in the darkness, careful to make no sound that Hammas could follow. He followed the corridor from which they had come until he knew that Hammas could not see the light of his lamp, and then he lit the lamp and careful to follow the marks that had guided him in, he made his way back to the roof above the harem. There he breathed deeply the fresh Anatolian evening before climbing back down the passageway into the King's wardrobe. That night, unable to sleep, he slipped out of the palace and down the darkened streets to the south wall. He climbed to the parapets and, careful to avoid the notice of the guards, walked the length of it by the light of a quarter moon, enjoying the knowledge that at some point he trod over his terrified brother's head.

And all the while, as he strode over the wall toward the mountains where he would someday plan a king's kidnapping, his heart threatened to burst from his chest in excitement and fear for what he had done, and he repeated to himself over and over, as if to give himself the courage to follow his plan through, "never again, never again, never again." When he finally returned to the palace to sleep in the bedchamber where he had only hours ago lain with Sophina, he ran his hand over the jeweled coverlet, sniffed the linen sheets for her sex, and finally bent to peer into his own reflection in the mirror over the prince's vanity in disbelief of what he had done. And the face in the mirror was not the face of a boy, but the face of a man. And he did not sleep until the wee hours of the morning.

In the morning the palace was in an uproar. For the story of the dare had circulated, and there was no question who had won the dare, for Ammuna lay in the bed of his brother.

A posse of palace guards was sent to scour the city in search of the prince to no avail and day turned into night. But no one questioned Ammuna, not even the King, who considered a dare between princes a fair enough determiner of leadership and bravery, and one that proved a prince's true place in line to the throne better than a few minutes of a woman's labor ever could. Indeed, it was three days before Ammuna himself returned to the passageway to find his brother, huddled in a heap of paralytic terror in much the same place as he had left him.

When he saw his brother approaching in the light of the oil lamp, Hammas jumped to his feet with joy and ran into his brother's arms.

"I knew you could not leave me to die here, Ammuna. I knew you would return for me." And he sank to his knees to kiss his brother's feet. "On my word and on my life, everything I have is yours. Only take me back to the palace."

"Everything you have, including your life, is already mine, Hammas, for I have taken it in your absence. Only remember, from now on the last is first, and the first, last, and so it will be to the end of our days."

"So be it, brother," wept Hammas, who was only too glad to be alive and would never again pretend to care for the things that a second prince should care for. Indeed, he was relieved as the years went by that this exchange had occurred, for never again was he pressed to take up the sword or the javelin, or to ride a horse or learn the chariot. He was allowed to study music and history and the stars, and to leave the art of war to his brothers. While Ammuna became bolder as time went on, using what he had learned that night to set the course of all of his dealings in life, Hammas became more and more timid, until he lived, quite contentedly, under the shadow of his younger brother's wing.

Even so, not a year later, when the first prince returned from war, Ammuna lost Sophina once again to an elder brother. And it was many more years before Rush the Assassin, by taking his eldest brother's life, unwittingly sent her to him once again. It was only then, because she was too old for the boy-king, Mursilis, that Sophina's lust for power sent her back into the arms of Ammuna on his promise that he would take Hattusha, gain the throne, and make her queen.

But now, all that was lost to him. Sophina was dead. And the assassin had killed her. That was clear, for it was the assassin who had sent her back to Amega on the plague animal. Sophina was dead, and even the throne was of little interest to him now. All of his boyhood goals had been wrecked like a Minoan ship, laden with treasured, torn asunder on an invisible reef. And so now I will take from you what is most dear to *you*, Rush, thinks Ammuna, as he leads the five surviving Amorite henchmen through a hidden door behind a mass of brambles at the end of the alleyway, then up a narrow stone stairway in the dark .

"No!" he barks at Aych, who has lit a torch behind him. "No torch until we leave the outer wall, else the archers on the rooftops see the light through the cracks in the mortar." And reluctantly the man with the split nose douses his torch in the mouse turds and guano they walk through, cursing under his breath.

"Filthy hole," grumbles Ess, and gives Ammuna a shove for good measure.

They have been crawling through the passage for an hour when Ammuna stops short, turns, and grabs the torch from Aych. He lifts it, looks about the place, expressionless. Then he hands the torch back to Aych, turning to his grizzly companions in the grim and airless dark.

"What's this, then, Princie? You lost or something?" whispers the toothless Zee, who seems to have lost some of his nerve and looks about at his companions worriedly.

"No. Not lost. This is it," answers Ammuna, turning to peruse the place once more.

"No time for nonsense Princie," barks Ess, but he too seems less the bully than he was before they entered the passageway.

"Remind you of anything, boys?" asks Ammuna, with a strange, challenging edge in his voice.

"That's enough, Prince," snaps Aych, pushing the torch at him as if he might light him with it. "Get us out of this hole before we all suffocate in here. My blood is pounding in my ears."

"How far down are we, anyway?" asks another, one of the two who have remained silent until now.

Ammuna gives an eerie chuckle. "Why, we are not down at all, Kah. In fact, we are one level up from the street. Not that that information will do you any good."

"What are you playing at, Princie? You want maybe we do you in right here and leave you for the rats to pick?" growls Ess, who steps forward but stops short of shoving Ammuna into a wall, and in the torchlight Ammuna can see the sweat beading on his simian brow.

"And then what? Can you find your way out without me? No. You are at my mercy now. Fools. Simple minded apes."

"But as soon as we have the King, and you have led us to back to the wall, you are a dead man!" Aych shouts nervously.

"Is that so?" snickers Ammuna, taking the torch easily from Aych's hand and waving it in front of the five henchmen. "And why would I do such a thing, Pig Face? When I am here in Hattusha, where I intend to stay?"

"You were here when they sent you back to us, Princie. Or have you forgotten your exile?" snaps Ess. "You are a man with no country. Now take us to the King, lead us out of this stinking hole and back to camp, and we will let you live."

"On your word, Ess? I think not. But on my own wit, yes. You may have my nephew, and good riddance to him. But you will find your own way back through the wall, once I am safely ensconced in the palace of my father. Then I will tell them a tale of how you tortured me for information, and how to save my own life I had no choice but to show you the way to the King's bed. Once I am rid of you and he, and I am the only heir left in the city, I care not if you ever make it back to your camp with him. So you had better pay careful attention to my directions out, when the time comes, or else you will be caught and killed yourselves, and I would not have my nephew returned to Hattusha prematurely. Now shut your holes and follow the only man among you with brain enough to lead you. And be glad that it fits my plans to have you take the King and leave Hattusha with him."

With that, Ammuna turns and leads the men on toward the King's chamber, using the marks he found in the walls a decade ago to guide him.

In a clearing in a farm field beneath a quarter moon, on the northern plains of Urgup, Rush the Assassin lies beneath a cold winter sky. He is alone and lies in silence but for the happy panting of his two exhausted dogs who flank him for warmth and the contented munch and tear of the teeth of the warhorse, who forages in a row of spelt grass not twenty feet from his bed. The animal no longer needs to be tied, and in fact will follow him like a puppy if he does not tether it to prevent this embarrassing display of affection.

Earlier that day, Rush disappeared from the hillside overlooking the camp of the Amorites, only to reappear like a great black wraith in their midst as they struggled to maintain ranks, crushed as they were between the oncoming Hattushan cavalry and the Army of Amega. Those men who had begun to fall back from the front were confronted with the very devil himself astride Iamhad's own battle horse. Those in the rear, who were only too ready to leave their posts guarding the supplies and rush toward the battle when the wardogs of Amega began tearing into them, found themselves running toward their worst nightmare: the man himself, the Black Wolf of the Hatti. Astride their own general's warhorse.

Had there been any chance for the Amorite army to withstand the onslaught of a two-sided attack before Rush arrived, there was none left when they found the Wolf of the Hatti himself in their midst, more horrible in the light of day because he was so out of place in it, there on the enormous snorting warhorse, his vicious hell dogs circling like eagles, ripping men's faces from their skulls, tearing throats open, protecting their master and repelling any who dared to approach that awful apparition. And the horse, pride like a fire burning in the whites of its eyes, felling seven men with one war kick while the assassin's battle ax lopped heads from shoulders so fast that they congregated together in groups on the ground as if taking comfort in their numbers. And they lost what was left of their courage and fled into the plains, to be hacked down by Hattushan horsemen and foot soldiers alike, and by the Amegan dog teams who hunted them like grouse in the fields until not a man among them remained standing.

He saw Nikolaos in battle that day, knew the man saw him as well, but he made no effort to find him when the battle was over. Rather, he slipped away as easily as he had appeared, like a dark smoke descending the hillside to slay all in its path. For he had long ago learned not to stand with any man in the fields of war.

That Nikolaos would search the battlefield for him until sundown once the enemy was routed and vanquished mattered little to him. But when the battle was clearly won he disappeared into the dust and chaos, knowing that another war lay ahead in Hattusha and eager to meet it. If he knew the man at all, he knew that Nikolaos would send the men of Amega back to his home with Aleksandus and lead the King's army back to Hattusha himself, not just to find Rush, but to find Rah.

CHAPTER 24

Mochlos is dreaming. He has been bouncing along in the back of a wagon on his way to the Palace of Knossos. He has six doves in a cage in his lap, and around him the colorful costumes of his fellow dancers sparkle and shimmer in the moonlight. The streets of Knossos are lit with oil lamps and the town is quiet. But he knows that the palace with be an uproar, a throng of admirers come to see him dance the Dance of the Doves before the King and his guests from Egypt.

Mochlos looks down into the cage he is carrying expecting to find his pets cooing and bobbing contentedly against one another. But the doves are gone. There is only one bird left in the cage and it is as big as a chicken. It is not white, but green, and scaled, like a turtle, and it has eaten its five companions. There are a few white feathers still in its beak, and when it looks up at him its eyes are the eyes of a lizard, double-lidded and vertically pupiled. But Mochlos is not concerned for the other five birds which have been eaten alive. He is not concerned that the thing in the cage is a monster that will eat the flesh of its kin. Somehow he knows that the beast is not concerned with him but only with eating its brothers. It is his failure to perform when the time is right that terrifies Mochlos. My goddess help me! For this will not do at all! How will I make this ugly creature fly when the time is right! And if it will not fly, and my dance is not satisfying, the King will fill my throat with emeralds and I will surely die!

Mochlos is awakened by the nudge of Mammut's javelin in his side.

"Wake, priest, we are here in Hattusha," says the man, as he slips easily from his mount and begins untying the cleric from his saddle, where he has spent most of the past two days jostling like a sack of cabbages on the animal's back.

"Hattusha?" murmurs Mochlos, rubbing his arms and legs where the ropes have bit into his flesh during the long and arduous journey. It is raining in sheets, a merciless downpour he has never experienced.

"The Storm God is angry, priest. You had better get to work." It is Peleshet, who has also dismounted from his animal. Several men are running toward them in the rain, and two take the animals and lead them off in another direction.

"Are we safe then?" asks Mochlos. One of the Hattushan guards has thrown a thick woolen blanket over his head and is now shoving him toward the black hole in the towering stone wall before him.

"The King has been kidnapped!" the man shouts through the deluge at Peleshet. "The City is in chaos!"

"How is this possible?" answers Peleshet, grabbing the man by the arm when they have reached the shelter of the archway in the wall.

"Ammuna was tortured, and forced to lead assassins into the city by way of a secret passageway in the wall. The passageway leads directly to the King's chamber. They took the King, and Ammuna has taken the throne!"

"Fool. He is a dead man walking," answers Peleshet, shoving the man out of his way. "The Master will hang him by his feet in the demonstration field and eviscerate him for all of Hattusha to see the gutless wonder that he is."

But the man, a palace guard, can only blink back in amazement and horror at the Amegan warrior's careless and open contempt for the new King of the Hatti. Still, the pitiless glare that slices though the rain at him like a blade from beneath Peleshet's brow causes him to step back and make a small nod of deference. These Amegans, he has learned in the past weeks, are not to be trifled with.

Peleshet has already stormed down the long tunnel that is the archway of the south gate of Hattusha, Mammut following briskly behind with Mochlos, who is winded and heaving by the time he has reached the interior opening of the tunnel into the streets of the city.

"Let us find this Ammuna, Mammut, and put him in the dungeon where he belongs, else we will be explaining why we did not to our Master."

"What of him, sir?" asks Mammut, nodding at Mochlos. The tunnel has opened to a wide cobblestoned avenue and even in the lashing rain and darkness the opulence of the homes here is evident. These are the houses of the assembly of the government of Hattusha, the nobles and courtiers, the palace physicians, scribes, merchants and tradesmen. Above their whitewashed domes the rear of the multi-leveled roofs of the palace can be seen gleaming in the hissing rain, gold and bronze. A detachment of palace guards is marching toward them from the end of the avenue, an important looking figure in fine garments at the head of it.

"We will give him to these palace poppets. We must find the god-slave first, and then, once we know that he is safe, install his priest in the palace to maintain his care. These are our orders. But beyond that, we had at best remove the coddled codpiece who has made himself king, and perhaps do something about finding the one the Assassin left in charge here."

"Halt!" It is the captain of the company of guards, who has marched up to Peleshet and planted his spear at his feet as if he is denying him entry into a palace hall. The man in the finery stands to his left, squinting in the rain at the three visitors with a mixture of worry and suspicion.

In an instant the man who has demonstrated his authority with the spear has had it snatched from his hands and broken over his own helmet. He is on the ground, holding his head and moaning. The rest of the guard is looking from him to Peleshet to the man in the finery, still as statues.

"Dare you give orders to one who comes in the name of the Wolf?" snarls Peleshet, kicking the man on the ground in the buttocks. "Get up, fool, and lead us immediately to the palace." But before he can do so, Peleshet has grabbed the man in the fine robes and pulled him out of the rain and back under the archway. He throws him against a wall and presses a blade, which seems to have materialized from thin air, to his neck. "Who are you, and why does this imbecile treat an Amegan warrior like an intruder?"

"I... I am the Minister of Palace Staff," blinks the man in the fine robes. "We, I and this detachment, have come on the orders of the King to escort you, under guard, to the palace."

"The *king*?" Peleshet squints at the man as if he has just grown another head. He looks over his shoulder at Mammut, who shakes his head sadly, and then turns and back-fists the man to the ground. The spearless captain of the guard, newly returned to his feet, makes a weak attempt to step forward to protect his superior but his company is unable to match his courage. They hop back a few paces, jostling against one another like a flock of spooked crows.

"There is no king but Mursilis," snarls Peleshet, "For it is he that the Master of Amega has set upon the throne. Call any other man 'king' and you will lose your tongue, Minister of Staff. Now," Peleshet gives the captain of the guard a moment to assist his superior to his feet. Then he gives them both a shove back into the rain, where Mochlos and Mammut are still standing. "This is Mochlos, High Priest of the Moon, and maker of the Rah."

Mochlos offers the man in the finery an apologetic nod. A fine way to be introduced to the chief of palace staff, he thinks.

"He is to be installed immediately in the palace," continues Peleshet, "to properly oversee the care of the Master's favorite. And you," he bats the captain of the guard's leather helmet from his head, "and your team of ear mites will escort us immediately to the new '*king*.'"

"As you say, sir," manages the Minister of Palace Staff, gesturing for Peleshet and Mammut to follow him back to the palace.

Half an hour later Peleshet is standing on the dais in the palace lyceum, staring with unbridled contempt down at Ammuna, whom he has just pulled by his beard from the ceremonial chair of state and tossed from the podium. Though surrounded by palace guards as well as an ever present crowd of royal sycophants, the newly self-appointed king had no defenders when the Amegan soldier leapt onto the dais and removed him from the royal chair. Nor do any come to his defense when Peleshet orders the palace guard to take him to the dungeon. In fact, the captain of the guard carries out the order himself.

"There will be no king in Hattusha until Mursilis has been found," barks Peleshet from the podium. "Ammuna is now the property of Amega, and he will remain in the dungeon until the Master himself determines his fate."

Down a hall and up an elaborately decorated stairway, Mochlos is being led by the Minister of Palace Staff and two guards to the chambers of the Rah. As he passes, servants and guards hurrying along on palace business step aside and tuck their chins, but Mochlos can feel their eyes wandering with unchecked curiosity over the golden threaded symbol of the Moon Goddess of the lost Isle of Crete on his back. As he continues up the stairs, the vault above which is twice the height of any he has ever seen and carved with battle scenes, he asks his companion, "Do they know of the destruction of my country, then?"

"Oh yes, we have all heard of the catastrophe that took Crete, and that Egypt as well has been darkened by ash and plague. They say that all the world is dark but where the Storm God of the Hittites and the strange and fickle god of the Hebrews maintain their power over the heavens of their people still. Nevertheless, there is rumor that it is the Hebrew god who brought about the cataclysm, for he was angry with Pharaoh, who would not release his people, though his prophet, Moses, demanded he do so and told him what would come of it if he did not. And so now Egypt is dying, choking on the dust cloud, and trade with most of our neighbors has come to a near halt." He shakes his head sadly, then nods to Mochlos to turn left, down a hall which has been completely paneled in cypress wood.

"This Hebrew god, I have heard of him. He is a strange one indeed," responds Mochlos, who is relieved to find that his companion is a refined man, like himself, and not another Hittite brute who cannot have a civilized conversation without threatening to cut off one's head. "I have heard that he will not tolerate the recognition of any other god by his people." He shakes his head. "How can you appease such a deity? When the world is full of them, can you ignore the rest and know only the one?"

The Minister of Palace Staff has stopped before an enormous double door with huge bronze handles, each as long as a man's forearm and shaped like the heads of lions.

"Is this where they are keeping him?" Mochlos swallows, blinking at the doors, which rise above his head to the height of two men.

The Minister purses his lips. He looks down the hall, sighs. "Well, not exactly. This is the royal harem."

"The harem!" exclaims Mochlos, splaying his hands against his chest as if this should astonish him.

"Yes, Holiness, I know it is not proper, no, not at all, that a foreign deity should be allowed to, well... mingle, with the ... women of the palace. But with the King taken, and Ammuna in his place..." he gives Mochlos a pleading look and shrugs. "Of course we have been quite cognizant of the fact that he has the great Antaris' favor and so he has been given everything he desires. Quite frankly, Holiness," and now the Minister of Staff moves close to Mochlos and takes his arm in confidence, "he has been quite a handful, I can tell you and I am not a little glad that you are here to take charge of his .... well, to take charge of him. I would not care to be in your sandals, sir, for he is quick to remind us all who it is who owns him and just what will happen to anyone who fails to meet his... rather peculiar and sometimes extraordinary demands."

At this, Mochlos can only bring his fingers to his lips to hide a small and self-satisfied smile. Oh yes, he thinks, nodding, he is a handful, alright, my little god-slave. But I still have a trick or two to hang over that golden head of his to keep him in line. That emerald, for instance. That magic emerald.

"Tell me, Minister of Palace Staff-" begins the priest, thinking only of the crown now.

"Oh please, Holiness, let us dispense with the formalities. I am Sopho. My mother was Greek, you know," he says proudly.

"Yes, yes, Sopho," smiles Mochlos, patting his host's arm. "Let us indeed dispense with formalities, you and I, for I can see that you are a sophisticated man and a man of the world, as am I. My given name is Mochlos. My mother, too, was Greek. From Pylos. My father, Minoan. Now tell me if you will, has the god-slave, Rah, taken any fits while here in the palace?"

"Fits? Why, no, Holiness, he has been sound as a judge! Why, he springs into the air like a little leopard! Spins and whirls and dances as if he had wing on his feet. No, no fits, only an occasional tantrum when he is not quite..." but here, the Minister of Staff stops short, thinking better of his loose tongue.

"When he is not quite coddled and pampered to his liking? You tell me nothing I do not already know in that, dear Minister. Do not expect chastisement from *me* for saying so. I fear I did spoil him in his making. But tell me, does he still wear the crown that the Assassin had especially made for him, with the fantastic Egyptian emerald that matches his eyes? For I can assure you, if he has lost the crown, heads will roll until it is found and replaced."

"Oh, no, sir! He wears the crown! Well it is woven into his hair, is it not? Why, when Royal Bath Maker, Itri, attempted to unbraid it so as to comb out that head of curls for him, he snapped at him just like a dog! Nearly took his finger!"

"Still snapping," murmurs Mochlos to himself, shaking his head. "Treat him like a prince's sight hound and he will nevertheless behave like a cur."

An uproar of laughter behind the great doors curtails their conversation. Looking to Mochlos with upraised eyebrows, Sopho collects his wits, makes a timid nod toward the door, and offers, "Shall we go in, then, Holiness?" Without waiting for an answer he raises his hand to take hold of the bell chain that is dangling above their heads. He gives it a good tug and the ringing of a dozen gay bells overhead is instantly answered by the arrival of a plump, shaven-headed guard at the door. Seeing the Minister of Staff, the guard quickly pushes the two great doors back against the exterior walls and makes a deep bow.

The scene inside takes Mochlos' breath.

The room is a gilded birdcage. Colorful tapestries and silks hang from the walls and domed ceilings. The intricate mosaic floor is decorated with marvelously patterned rugs upon which sit plush couches and settees in gold and silver embroidered fabric. The walls are cedar, inlaid with gold, the ceiling a domed and white-washed cathedral carved with scenes of scantily clad concubines dancing before a king who is flanked by an army of musicians playing santur and flute, cymbal and horn. About the room, which is the size of a small lyceum, an army of harem girls, all beautifully dressed in fine silken costumes, stand or lounge on couches while a dozen shaven-headed eunuchs, wearing white tunics and golden belts and sandals, sit cross-legged upon the rugs playing strange instruments.

But the most extraordinary thing in the room is Rah.

He is spinning in the center of a sunken wooden floor in the middle of the harem, surrounded by a cloud of dancers in yellow silks, male and female. The spin is impossible, Mochlos has never seen anything like it, until he looks down to the boy's feet to see that he is standing on a single toe, elongated by a shoe that can only be wooden. And as the spin slows, the dancers surrounding him draw back as if on cue, and the boy bends back like a thing without a spine, back and over so that he is nearly folded in two. Then, as suddenly as the spin stops, the boy is in the air, performing a series of outrageous handstands and backflips. The floor is a ravishing blonde parquet and has been polished to a brilliant gleam. Even so, it cannot compete with the explosion of golden motion that is Rah.

"My gods," says Mochlos, unthinking. "He is ... he is changed."

"How so, Holiness? Certainly he is well. Oh, certainly, quite in the peak of condition, I should think. Why I have never seen anything... no I am sure no one here in the palace has ever seen anything like him at all!"

But Mochlos can only stand and stare as his creation finishes his final leap with a spinning crescent kick, then falls to the floor on his knees, still spinning as if he were on ice and not a wooden dance floor at all, until inertia brings him to rest. Then, panting and spent, he rises to his feet with a smile so bright that even Mochlos' cool heart warms. His audience applauds wildly.

Rah makes a short, comic bow in each direction. Then, just as he is about to step up from the dance floor onto the tile, he spots his old master in the doorway.

It is not a smile, no, nor a frown, nor a look of haughty arrogance nor disregard which Rah gives Mochlos then. But a strange, dazed and innocent gaze, like a child who has found his mother in a crowded street after hours of being lost. And the look goes on, it continues, as if with its own voice, it remains on the golden brow of the Grain God of Knossos even as he rises from the sunken parquet floor to the tiles, even as he steps, deer soft and cat cautious, toward the priest.

The musicians have seen it, the dancers too. The music has slowed to a haunted melody of flute and string that lifts and holds as if on the clouded, incense-smoky air. The room is silent, as silent as the smoke.

"This my priest," says Rah at last, stopping in his tracks to look about the room while pointing to Mochlos with dramatic importance. "This is priest of Rah. This priest, he make Rah."

Everyone is looking back and forth between Mochlos and Rah, and at one another. What is to be done now? Now that the one who made the Rah is here? They look to Rah for instruction.

Rah steps back, as if to give the importance of his own motion room, then makes a soft open-armed bow to Mochlos.

To the priest's utter surprise, the entire room turns to the doorway and mimics Rah's greeting.

And then, as suddenly as it began, the theatrics are over. Everyone is laughing and chatting and pointing to Rah or the priest. The music livens and several male dancers take possession of the floor. A dozen harem girls are crowding around Rah to coo and pet and comb his curls back with their fingers. But Rah shoos them. "Leave Rah now. Rah is go to priest."

Mochlos lifts his shoulders. He straightens his back and brushes off the front of his robe self-importantly. I must act the part, he thinks. For here he comes, this wonder which I have created. I. A humble priest. From the simple tools of priesthood: a ceremony, a powder, a dance.

But as Rah strides toward him Mochlos loses some of his arrogance. My goddess, he has changed so, and yet how? What is really different about him? It is not his height, though he is a little taller. Not his form, though goddess knows, his physique is even more striking than before! Is it his stride? His bearing? So like a lion. He is no longer the fragile boy he was when first he came to me. Or is it that look he gives me, that cat-like focus, that confidence? Or is it that monstrous stone? This is the assassin's work, either way, and not mine. This is the assassin's favor that puts him above his proper station. I would have held him down, kept him humble. But it is too late for that now. I must learn to deal with him a different way.

"Dimi! You bring priest of Rah food. Priest is come long way to see Rah," says Rah, clapping his hands. At once a big eunuch, who has been standing by a pillar beside the dance floor, comes to attention. He looks about, then bows at Rah and struts past Mochlos and Sopho and out the door. Another man, almost identical to him, rushes out behind him.

"You treat them like slaves, Rah," says Mochlos when he is close enough for Rah to hear him over the din of the harem. "Is this wise? Is this not the King's harem you have stolen for yourself?"

"Rah is no steal. King is give to Rah. Rah say, 'Wolf is kill you, you no give Rah concubine. King say, 'Take them all!' Before he go." Rah shrugs. "Come and sit, priest. Must eat." And he leads the two men to a long, low table all around which are strewn silken-tasseled pillows of every shape and color.

"The King's table," murmurs Sopho in the priest's ear.

When they are seated, with Rah reclined on the long side and Mochlos and Sopho sitting upright on either end of the table, Rah raises one hand over his head and snaps his fingers. But a half dozen girls are already at work. One sets an amphora on the table, another three cups, a third a bowl of fruit and dainties. A fourth kneels behind Rah and begins to knead his shoulders like bread while two more settle behind the priest and the Minister of Staff to do the same.

After a moment Dimi returns with two men wearing cook's tunics. The first man sets a platter of sliced cheeses, pitas and meats wrapped like little packages in cabbage leaves in the center of the table. He bows and leaves. The next places a second platter, this one loaded with exotically prepared vegetable dishes, beside the first. A third man, wearing only a civilian tunic and a servant's apron, sets a soup tureen beside the platter of meats and another, carrying a trio of golden soup bowls and silver utensils, places one of each down before the diners.

Rah reaches for a pomegranate from the fruit bowl. Then, not bothering to peel it, he flicks his dazzling eyes at the priest and bites into the fruit. He regards Mochlos with a curious, catlike coolness. Red juice dribbles down his chin. He moves the fruit about in his mouth, spits the skin out into one hand, crunching on the seeds. A harem girl who has taken what is clearly an envied spot to his right, quickly dabs his chin with a fine linen napkin. He lifts his chin for her and the cat is gone. He is a little boy offering his face for his mother to wipe. The girl loses her bearing before the guests, melts to her hands to lick the juice from his lips. Rah giggles but makes no effort to return her affection.

My goddess, thinks Mochlos. He is extraordinary. Unable to concentrate on the meal before him, despite his hunger after the grueling trip, he smooths the front of his robe and folds his hands in his lap. A girl has come to kneel at his side. She begins preparing him a plate of food from the table.

"Well, they have been quite good to you here in Hattusha, Rah," the priest manages at last. "It is only the care of your divinity, through the prayers and ceremony of the Priesthood of the Moon that is lacking."

"Yes," agrees Rah, taking another bite of the pomegranate. "Rah need his priest. " He flicks his lashes at Mochlos again, and this time his lips are touched with the tiniest curl of a smile. The beauty of it threatens to knock Mochlos onto his back.

"I am honored," swallows Mochlos, barely able to believe what has just slipped so easily off his own tongue. But I am, he thinks. How has this happened? For did I not create you? What were you before I made you, but a pretty exotic who could dance? And yet behold. Do I owe myself credit for you? Or was this always what you were?

"Rah need Priest," says Rah a second time, looking into his old master's eyes with an unreadable expression. "But," and now he puts the pomegranate down and reaches for a square of cheese, "Priest need Rah also."

"All priests need their deity, Rah," answers Mochlos, offering Rah a bow with his hand to his breast.

Sopho has been looking from the priest to the god-slave with the expression of one who cannot reconcile that these two might have ever had anything to do with one another. Now, his appetite getting the best of him, he bends over the plate that his own server has filled with delicacies and comments, "We have done everything within the limits of the Kingdom to make the Rah as comfortable and as happy as he can be, I can assure you."

"Ah," says Rah, noticing Sopho as if for the first time. He reaches for a handful of shelled pistachios and drops half of them as he launches them into his open mouth, "but you lose King!" He shakes his head sadly, looking about the pillows he lounges on for the lost nuts. "You think Wolf is be happy you lose his King?"

Sopho looks from Rah to Mochlos, his eyes big with worry. "But it wasn't my fault!" he blurts.

"Is it true, Rah, that the King was kidnapped? Taken from his bed by Amorite assassins in the middle of the night?" asks Mochlos, eager to take the focus off his new ally. He reaches for the cup of wine that has just been poured for him.

"Is true," nods Rah, munching the nuts and continuing his search for the lost ones in his pillows. "This Ammuna, he say, Amorite men make him tell how to get King. Pah. How they know he is have way through wall, eh? I say, he tell them. He want to be king, so he come, bring men to take King." Rah shakes his head, his face suddenly a theater of sadness. "How can do like this to a king? This bad man."

"What is being done to find the King, Rah?" asks Mochlos, venturing finally to nibble at a few olives on his plate.

"Eat, priest. You no eat, you be sick. Priest sick. Rah sick, too."

At this, Mochlos must catch himself from giving away his delight that the god-slave still believes this bit of mythology. Ah, thinks Mochlos, I was quite clever to create this illusion. So I am of some value to him, even here in Hattusha, at least for the time being. Feigning obedience, Mochlos picks up a utensil and begins to sip at the soup, which is heady with the flavor of roasted lamb and delicate spices.

"The King, Rah," Mochlos tries again. "What is being done to find him?"

"King in wall," says Rah slurping soup. "Gah, Rah cannot eat!" he waves for a servant, who instantly removes the bowl he has filled. "No meat. Why you no remember? Only what come from Rah. Grain, vegetable. And milk and fish too. No meat!"

The servant hurries off with the bowl. Another is rushing to the table with a small tureen. The girl at his side jumps up to take it from him. She sets it before Rah, opens the lid. The pungent smell of roasted vegetables wafts toward Mochlos.

At first Mochlos is sure he has mistaken what he has heard. The boy's mouth has been full since he sat at table and he is difficult enough to understand when there is nothing in it but that crimped tongue. But as the words begin to come together in his head, Mochlos loses his poise. He drops his spoon into his soup bowl and stares across the table at Sopho, who is looking back at him in alarm.

"In the wall, Rah?" Mochlos leans toward Rah to whisper. "How can you know this?"

"Don't know," says Rah, shrugging. He reaches over the tureen to dip a pita into a saucer of yogurt. "Maybe is because god now. I see. See King in wall. Bad place. Like in Cyrus. B-r-r-r!" and he pretends to shake off a chill. "Like tomb." He stuffs the soggy pita in his mouth.

"Have you told this to anyone, Rah?" asks Sopho delicately.

"I tell Wolf when he come," says Rah through the mouthful of food. "He find King. Find king and men, too." He shakes his head. "Too bad for them, but King is be okay. Rah must dance for this king!"

"He speaks of the Wolf!" gasps Sopho, splaying his hand over his breast. "Of the Wolf's return! But how can he know…?"

"This is a new development, dear Mr. Minister of Staff. He seems to have developed some kind of sight… some kind of mystical sight, since I last saw him," responds Mochlos, watching Rah devour a plate full of bread and cheese, along with a bowl of pungently spiced chickpeas which a serving girl has just placed before him. "Tell me, Rah, for I am your priest and you are bound tell me all that affects you supernaturally, do you know these things for certain? Or are you guessing?"

"No guess," says Rah, leaning back to allow his attendant to pat his face again. "Rah can see." His docile posture soon leads to his attendant's collapse into his arms for another prolonged kiss which quickly threatens to turn into something far more lurid. But Mochlos' patience is at an end. He rises, claps his hands, and shoos the girl away.

"Enough of this. I must see this Ammuna. I must see him immediately. Come, sir, take me to the dungeon. There is no time to waste. If the boy is seeing the truth, if he has gained some kind of second sight from his divinity, then the King could be hours away from death. And if we had access to such information and did nothing, what do you suppose the Wolf would do to us, eh? He will have us for lunch."

"As you say, Holiness," says Sopho, lumbering to his feet, for he is a corpulent man. "I am instructed to give you access to anything you wish. I shall have the Rah's valet take you to the dungeon immediately."

"And perhaps you would do me the favor, Minister of Staff, of remaining yourself with my charge until I have returned," continues Mochlos, for his mischievous mind is racing now with opportunistic plans. "Indeed, I would be remiss to let him out of my sight without assigning someone with authority to minister to him."

"Again, as you say," responds Sopho, not a little relieved, for the interruption of a delectable meal in the company of the Wolf's favorite to visit the dungeon, a grizzly and depressing place on a good day, is not a thing he is burning with desire to accomplish.

Moments later, Jibril is leading the High Priest of the Moon down a wide, dark stair to a smoke filled chamber beneath the palace.

"It is an awful place, Sir. I myself spent a night here when I first came to Hattusha. But the Rah petitioned for my pardon and asked that I be made his attendant."

"How fortunate for you," responds Mochlos evenly, though he has barely heard what the man is saying for his mind is spinning with possibilities. Ammuna. I must learn more.

"This Ammuna, he is the uncle of the King?" he asks after a time. The passage is narrowing and the smoky light dimming. Even Mochlos has begun to feel a thread of apprehension pull in his spine as he draws back to consider what he is to say to the man he is about to meet.

"He is," answers Jibril. "It is he who challenged the King with a Syrian supported army. He was captured by the Great Wolf of the Hatti and put in the prison. But the King released him, and sent him back to us."

"Us?" is all Mochlos can think to say.

"Yes, Sir. I am an Amorite."

"And so he returns to Hattusha with a band of assassins to kidnap his own nephew, thinking he will then take his place, for surely, he believes he is the rightful king." Muses Mochlos, rubbing his chin.

"Here he is, Sir," says Jibril, stepping aside and sweeping a torch across a low wooden door with a narrow rectangular pass way at waist level. The door is barred from the outside.

"Will you open it for me?" asks Mochlos, a bit put off at the idea of seeing what is inside.

"The bolt is locked, sir. Only the Captain of the Guard can open it."

"And who is the Captain of the Guard?" asks Mochlos.

"I believe he has been beheaded by your man, Peleshet, Sir."

"Then he no longer has the key," swallows Mochlos, imagining Peleshet lopping off the head of a handsomely uniformed guard.

"No, I suppose it is in the assassin's man's hands now," nods Jibril, folding his arms over his chest and leaning back against a wall. "But you can speak to him through the pass way."

Frowning, Mochlos peeks into the rectangular hole. It is pitch inside and smells of excrement. He turns his head away quickly and coughs.

"Dear goddess," he says, bringing his hand to his face to cover his nose.

"He has been here several days, sir," remarks Jibril.

"We had no such thing on Crete. If a man sinned, he was put in the bull pit. But to bury a man alive like this…" his voice trails off. "Very well, give me a moment, would you? Under the circumstances, perhaps the poor man would like to speak to a priest in private."

"Yes, Sir," says Jibril, all too glad to leave Mochlos in the dark and return to the stair, which at least has some light issuing down from above.

"Ammuna!" shouts Mochlos into the hole when the valet is out of earshot. "I am Mochlos, a High Priest from Amega. I have come to speak to you about the King. Perhaps there is hope for you yet. Perhaps I can speak to the Master, Antaris, on your behalf, if you will but help me recover him."

"Go away!" cries a muffled voice from within the tomb-like cell. "Ammuna is no more!" And then a howl like the howl of a wild animal, the scuffling of feet, and a snarl from the other side of the aperture that sends Mochlos backward against a wall in fright.

"Goddess of the Moon, he is mad," whispers Mochlos to himself. "How then can I beseech him?"

"Ammuna, I tell you I can have you released! If only you will tell me how you entered the city, and by what route the thieves have taken the King! Think man, come to your senses. Where there is life there is yet hope!"

This entreaty is met by silence from the hole in the cell door. Cautiously, Mochlos approaches, keeping his body out of direct line of the hole, in case the man within should think to throw something vial at him. Moments pass, and Mochlos can hear the man breathing heavily, as if each breath is a labor. Finally, he answers.

"I am already dead. Death is not what you think, Priest. There is no oblivion, only suffering for one's sins."

And yet you speak to me, thinks Mochlos. And so you do not yet give up hope, for do the hopeless speak?

"Ammuna. You think that Mursilis is the darling of the Wolf of Amega. You are deceived. There is one whom the assassin would give five kings for. Ten!"

"What is this to me?" asks the voice in the hole, though Mochlos can hear that he has come to place his lips at the aperture to be better heard in secret. Ah, thinks Mochlos, I have you.

"Your very life, man. Tell me where the kidnappers are, and I will trade with them this information as ransom for the King."

"Even if there were such a one, what good would it do me?" asks Ammuna cautiously.

"Think, man. Think what the King of Babylon would give to have the Assassin's heart in his hands! And I tell you, this boy, has captured the man's heart!"

"A boy? You tell me a boy can be worth more than a King? More than my father's chosen heir?" wheezes Ammuna through the hole.

"A god-slave, from Crete. My very creation. A golden boy from the north who hosts the Minoan deity, Rah. God of abundance. God of fertility and prosperity. Of hope and fulfillment."

"A god, then? A King for a god?" Ammuna breathes heavily. "Yes, this is possible."

Mochlos waits. He can hear the man pacing back and forth behind the door, can imagine him rubbing his hands together greedily. And then the question.

"But why would you come to me? What is in it for you? You are the boy's priest, yes? Why give such a wonder away to rescue a King for a man who thinks less of the King than of the boy? No, you trick me, priest. You think my mind is addled, festering here in this hole. You look only for your own gain. To find the King for the Wolf of the Hatti and then leave me here to rot. Go away!"

"I would think the same," responds Mochlos carefully, leaning closer to the hole and lowering his voice even further. "What you do not understand, Ammuna, is that I wish to escape the beast myself. I myself am his captive, his slave. As long as he owns the boy. Do you think it has been easy? I am a civilized man. I am a Minoan. I have been kidnapped by a monster, a barbarous psychopathic killer. My life is hanging in the balance of his affections for the boy every day. Can you imagine what it is like for a man like myself? A cultured, educated man of delicate tastes, a man who spent his youth under the finest tutelage his wealthy parents could buy, who made a fortune as a businessman and high priest in the diamond of the Aegean, in Knossos? I wish to escape to Babylon with the boy. And I cannot do it without you, Ammuna."

Now the silence coming from the hole is palpable. Only the uneven breathing of the man in the chamber breaks it. He is sick, surely, thinks the priest, backing away from the aperture as the man coughs, sending a spray of spittle through the little window. He is infected with the-goddess-knows-what after lying in this filthy place. What must it be like for a man like this, a prince, to lie in a dungeon? He will take the bait, yes. Yes, he will.

"Get me out of here and I will show you the way," comes the answer at last.

"I cannot do it," answers the priest, honestly enough, though he has no intention of coming in any closer proximity to the wretch with whom he speaks. "The assassin's man has the key. And I cannot go and ask him for it, else he will wish to know why. If I tell him that I believe you know where the King is, that the boy has had a vision of him lost in the wall, he will come for you himself and torture the information out of you. And then I will lose my chance to be free of the assassin forever. This must be between us only, Ammuna. In secret. I will take the boy with me. I will exchange him for the King with his promise that for his freedom, he must release you upon his return."

"I have nothing but your word, then, upon which to base my faith," sneers Ammuna.

"You have said it," answers Mochlos. "You have nothing but my word. But it is your only hope. If you are responsible for saving the King he must release you. You are still a prince of Hatti."

"One who rots in a cell beneath his own palace," spits Ammuna viciously.

"That is the work of the assassin. Even if revenge were your only reason, would it not be perfect revenge, Ammuna, to take the one who owns the heart of the assassin and give him to Babylon? Give him to his enemy?"

"Revenge," murmurs Ammuna from the hole. "Yes! Revenge. You speak well, priest. For he took my heart from me when he sent my Sophina on a plague animal to Amega! It would be a perfect revenge. Yes. But," and now his breath begins to come more rapidly, as with excitement, "But how am I to know that this boy exists? Or that he does indeed have the Wolf of Hatti's heart?"

Mochlos can only chuckle. "Easy enough. I will bring him to you. You can see for yourself. And if he is what I say he is, then you will tell me what I need to know."

"Agreed," answers Ammuna, after which a fit of coughing silences him. Mochlos draws away, back to the stair where he finds Jibril waiting.

"He can tell us where the King is, Rah. You want the King to return, don't you? The Grain God must dance for the King."

Mochlos has been installed in an opulent room in the wing opposing the Great Hall, where Rah has been assigned a suite of rooms intended for the eventual Queen of Hattusha. Rah is in the company of several of the King's harem girls, who followed him back to his own chamber after his meal. Now they lounge with him, playing with his curls and the golden rings piercing his chest as he lies on his back on an enormous bed. Rah has one pinned against his side and is nuzzling her neck as the High Priest enters the room.

"Go away, priest. King can wait," he murmurs as he trails kisses down the girl's throat toward her bosom. The other girls giggle.

"No Rah. The King cannot wait. The King is trapped in the wall and he must be rescued. Must be rescued or he will die, do you understand? And Ammuna knows how to find him. But I must convince him that you are who I say you are. And that you are the assassin's favorite."

Rah lifts his head from the girl's breast. He looks at the priest warily.

"Why he have to know that?" he frowns at Mochlos.

"Because he believes I will trade you for the King."

"Tah, you trade Rah for King, you have no Rah. No Rah, no priest. Wolf is kill you." He turns back to the girl on the bed.

"Of course. But Ammuna doesn't understand this, Rah. He believes I will trade you for the King and then go with you to Babylon with the Amorites and be a rich man."

"Stupid," says Rah. "Cannot run from Wolf. I try. What Wolf want, Wolf take. He chase and chase Rah," he is looking at the girl he has been making love to. She nods, knowingly. "Cannot run from Wolf." He shakes his head at the girl, shrugs. "He want Rah. He take Rah." The other girls murmur amongst themselves, nodding and sighing in agreement. Rah looks over his shoulder at Mochlos. "He is kill you."

Mochlos is gritting his teeth. No, he thinks. Not if I am hidden in an Amorite army. Not if I am taken to Babylon. Not even the Wolf of the Aegean can breach Babylon.

"Yes, yes. Of course. I only said it to make Ammuna think I would do it and that for his release the King would in turn release *him*."

Rah sighs, pushing himself off the bed with a great show of exasperation for his female audience.

"Okay. I go. But only to dungeon. Show Ammuna Rah. Rah is no go into wall. Dark, bad smell, like death. Bad like in tomb. Like under palace of Cyrus…"

When Mochlos returns to the dungeon with Rah he does so without Jibril. Taking only a torch, he leads Rah down the same wide stairwell the Amorite took him, but at the bottom of the stair, as the walls narrow, Rah becomes agitated.

"No. Rah is no go down this place. Too much like Cyrus. Too much dark and close." He takes a step back up toward the light.

Mochlos grabs his arm. "Come now. We are not in Cyrus. We are in the dungeon of the palace of Hattusha. Your priest is with you, Rah. Nothing can harm you, you see? As long as I am with you. Now come along. Let us show the man what you are and get this thing accomplished." He leads Rah down, waving the torch before him to illuminate the stairs and then light his way through the darkness toward Ammuna's cell. Then he pushes Rah forward into the glow of the torch, several feet from the reach of the pass way in Ammuna's door and calls. "Ammuna! I have brought you the Rah of Knossos. The holy one. The favorite of the Wolf of the Aegean."

Instantly there is a scuttling noise in the cell as the man comes to his feet and then puts his nails against the doorframe as he peers out of the pass way. A hiss and suck, like the hiss and suck of a viper and then a low, ugly giggle. "Ahhh," is all that Mochlos can hear of his words.

"Are you satisfied then?" asks the priest after a moment.

Still there is no answer from the tomblike cell. Finally, a clawed hand stretches out from the narrow aperture, filthy fingers open and reaching.

"Let me touch him, then, so that I might know that he is not a magician's illusion. Let me see with my hand that he is indeed flesh and blood," wheedles Ammuna from within.

Rah has already stepped forward toward the hand. But Mochlos quickly snatches him back by the shoulder, even puts an arm across his chest as if shielding him from the sickness in the cell.

"No! You are ill, Ammuna, I can hear it. Your lungs are filled with water from your days in this damp hole. You will make him ill and then what good is he to anyone? Be content that you have seen him. He is not a conjuring."

"Give me a lock of that hair then," replies Ammuna, not missing a beat. "A locket of that hair. Yes. That I may show the Beast of the Aegean who it was who traded his heart to the Amorites for the King!"

At this Mochlos purses his lips in thought. He looks from the hole to Rah's head of golden curls, which glint like pearls in the torchlight. Without another thought he reaches out to snatch a lock from the nape of Rah's neck. The boy yelps and slaps a hand over the spot but the deed is done. Mochlos holds out the prize, a wisp of curls, about twenty hairs in all, but enough to catch the light and glimmer like threads of gossamer. Ammuna sighs, then reaches a filthy sleeve out of the aperture to grasp the ringlet.

"Yesss," he hisses. "This will do."

"Now tell me the secret of the wall," demands Mochlos, laying an arm across Rah's chest as the boy makes a grab for his stolen tress. "Stay back," he whispers at Rah. "If he can take hold of you he will not let you go. You will lose more than a curl, boy."

"The secret of the wall," murmurs Ammuna, pulling the curl back into his cell and the filthy dark. "The secret of the wall. How clever you are, priest."

"Time is wasting, Sir. I would not ransom the boy for a dead king."

"The entry is the King's chamber. A hole in the closet ceiling leads to the roof. From there, one need only follow the mark of the Kings."

"Mark of the Kings? And what is that, pray, tell?"

"One must follow the letters of the kings, from first to last: Amba, Pithana, Piyusti, Anitta, Tudhaliya, Sarruma, Labarna, Hattusili...And over again. Beginning with Amba. One must know the kings. How then, could an Amorite murderer ever find his way out? Ha-ha!"

"What are you saying? Are there marks along the walls then? Marks coinciding with the names of the kings of the Hatti? Damn you man, I do not know the succession of the Hatti kingship!"

"Then you must learn them. Amba, Pithana, Piyusti... be careful. For there are many false marks to lead you astray. You must know the names of the true kings."

"Amba, Pithana?"

"Amba, A-m-b-a. Pithana. P-i-t-h-a-n-a," begins Ammuna patiently, stroking the lock of hair he has captured as he whispers the words. And for the next hour, Mochlos sits beside the cell learning the line of the kings of the Hatti as if his very life depends upon it, for indeed it does.

CHAPTER 25

On their third day in the wall, Aych, Ess and Zee kill the two other henchmen. This was not in their plan, but with no water for three days, there was no other rational course of action. The King was still of value, should they ever find their way back to their camp, but the two extra men were becoming a burden, and their blood was sufficient to keep the others alive, though the King could not be persuaded to partake of it.

After Ammuna left them they had followed his direction to the letter. Two turns to the left, one to the right, down another narrow passageway, turn to the left, up a stairwell. At the top of the stairwell they came to a broken wall, nothing more.

"Must be a way through," said Zee then, looking about in the torch-lit dark.

"Idiot," spat Aych. "If we'd come through here on the way in, we'd remember, wouldn't we? We never been here. We gone the wrong way. I told you it was a right back there at the end of the passageway and not a left. We gotta go back."

"No," said Ess, looking about nervously. "No, we followed his directions, alright."

"What are you saying?" blurted Zee. "We aren't... he didn't..." he looked up at Ess, for a moment his toothless face the picture of wonder.

"Bastard deliberately gave us the wrong directions," muttered Ess, shoving past the other two, grabbing the trussed up king by the scruff of his neck and pushing him ahead of himself and back down the stairs. "We'll have to find our own way. How hard can it be? It's a damned wall, is all. Goes east west. We keep heading forward, we'll find the way out."

And so the others had followed him, followed him what seemed an eternity. Only it was impossible to continue forward. Each passage led to a dead end, or to a maze of other passages, ending sometimes in nothing more than holes leading down into the earth or else narrower and narrower channels until there was not enough room to squeeze a child, let alone a man. Gradually the band became increasingly disoriented until, in a burst of panic, and finding a larger channel which appeared similar to what they had passed through on their way in, they ran pell-mell into a wall of stone that seemed to reach from right to left beyond even the length and breadth of the exterior walls.

Terrified, Ess turned on the King then.

"Tell me the way out, boy, or I will cut you down right now, I swear it," he breathed into the young sovereign's face.

"I do not know it," answered the king. "I knew nothing of this passage until you pulled me through it. And if you were to let me go now, I would not be able to find my way back to my own bed."

Ess's eyes closed to slits then, and he peered at the young Mursilis with evil curiosity, lifting the king's beardless chin with the tip of his dagger to search his face for the lie.

"You are a queer one, aren't you?" he whispered into the boy's face, for Mursilis appeared neither winded nor frightened. He returned Ess's glare with an unreadable gaze of his own.

"I am my grandfather's heir. Would you have expected less?" he answered simply.

"S'more than that," answered Ess, poking the boy in his chest through his nightgown, for they had ripped him from his bed and given him no time to dress. "You got something up your sleeve. What is it? Tell me. Or we will have some fun with you before you die."

"The Wolf of the Hatti would not fit up my sleeves, not even if I were wearing the royal robes of my grandfather," answered Mursilis evenly. "And when he finds me missing, whether by then I be dead or alive, he will come for you, sir. He will come and even the score as only the Terror of the Aegean can. So think before you lay a hand on me again. What you do to me, he will do to you seven fold."

"Pah," answered Ess. "You think he will find us in this hole, when we cannot even find our own way out?"

"He could find a ruby in a field of poppies," answered the King. "And he will find you."

"We will continue," said Ess then, turning to ignore the king. "We will find our own way out, or die trying."

And so, on their third day in the wall, Aych, Ess and Zee kill the two other men for their blood. But the king will not partake, and he is near death when, only a few hours after the slaughter, the voice of Mochlos, shouting from a nearby tunnel, leads them back onto the only route out of the labyrinth.

Rush descends upon the city of Hattusha on the evening of the same day. Leaving his mount and his wardogs tethered outside of the city walls in an abandoned barn in the foothills he enters the city on foot through a little known passage in the wall, a passage which, ironically enough, by bisecting the wall north to south, formed the barrier that blocked the band of murderers retreat days earlier.

Once inside, Rush makes straight for the palace. He finds Rah first, sleeping in the King's chamber with two harem girls. His instinct is to toss the girls out and take his fury out on Rah, for the picture of the boy defying him, turning his back to him and mounting the colt and putting him into the river, flashes in his mind like lightening now that his fear of losing the little god is quenched. But the boy is a picture of innocence lying there on his face in the center of the opulent, gold-embroidered bedding, his mouth open and tongue lolling, his blond curls covering his eyes, one arm pinning a voluptuous beauty behind him, the other bracing a barely pubescent maiden against his belly.

Teeth clenched behind his mask, Rush fails to hear his own low growl of frustration as he storms out of the King's chamber and flies down a stairway to the guard's quarters on the first floor of the palace.

"Where is the King, Peleshet?" he whispers in his sleeping man's ear when he finds the captain's pallet.

"Kidnapped by assassins, Sir," answers Peleshet, rising to his knees to bow before his master. "Before we arrived he was already taken, and Ammuna had taken his place on the throne."

"And who sits on the throne now?" asks Rush, without any doubt of the answer.

"No one, Sir. I took the liberty of putting Ammuna in the dungeon, Sir."

"Did no one see this kidnapping then? A palace full of sycophants and guards and the King whisked away like a shadow in the night? The young King gone, and Ammuna suddenly appearing in his place?"

"He told a story of being forced to guide them into the city and through the palace," answers Peleshet, rising to his feet and grabbing his weapon's belt. "I will get him for you, Sir."

"No. Leave him where he is. He will tell me nothing. I know already more than he will tell me. That he did not walk into the fortress city of Hattusha with a band of stinking Amorite murderers and steal the King out from under the noses of a palace full of guards and staff. That he must have known of a secret passageway to the King's very chamber in order to avoid the prying eyes of every footman, valet and laundry maid. That he concocted this plan himself and sold it to the Amorites, a promise that he would lead them in safely and kidnap the King."

Rush has turned from Peleshet in the dark to stalk the barrack like a great wraith. "But how did he barter for his own freedom? He had nothing with which to barter, and so he did not. He tricked them. It matters not how. He tricked them, for he is a trickster and must play tricks as surely as a snake must slither, a scorpion must sting. He saw that the only way to have the throne was to remove the King from it, make him disappear. That with Mursilis gone, the people would look to the next likely heir, even if that heir was a traitor and a thief. Then I could do nothing to stop him."

"Must we return him to the throne, Lord?" asks Peleshet bitterly.

But Rush is already gone, for the realization that the King's chamber is vulnerable to the kidnappers, and that Rah now sleeps with his maidens there, readily available to any thief who might know his value, has dawned on him.

In the King's chamber the two maidens are awakened by the considerable noise of the three surviving Amorite bandits, the trussed and blindfolded King, and Mochlos, coming through the passage in the ceiling of the king's wardrobe. One of the girls is on her feet and has even made it to the door when Ess makes his entrance into the bedchamber, a huge and rank smelling bear with wild hair and a face so scarred by war that it is barely human. She stops to catch her breath at the sight and to scream for Rah to awaken, but her scream is stopped with a dagger, hurled from twenty paces away with such a force as to lodge in her abdomen to the hilt. The second girl is off the bed and cowering in a corner whimpering when Aych storms into the chamber behind Ess. The sight of him, more boar than man, sets her reeling, and by the time she has struck the ground Aych has opened her throat with his own dagger.

Rah remains on his belly on the bed, snoring softly into the silken bedding.

"I told you he would be easy enough to take. I have put him to sleep for you so that you wouldn't damage him. You need only carry him, now. He weighs nothing."

But the three murderers are dumb. They stand at the foot of the enormous bed, staring down at the creature that lies before them.

"Lots of jewelry there," says Zee finally. "A fortune I'll bet."

"He is worth more than a great hall full of such trinkets," snaps Mochlos. "I have told you what he is worth, and to whom he is worth it. Pick him up, carefully. Be quick! And do not mar him! We could be discovered at any moment. I know not where or from whence the Wolf is coming, but I know that he is coming."

That is enough to urge the men into action. Shoving the King down onto the bed, Ess grabs Rah by the ankles, then hoists him over a shoulder.

Zee makes quick work of tying Mursilis to the posts, while Aych moves to the door to bolt it from the inside. Mochlos has pulled a stool over to the wardrobe beneath the aperture.

"He is like a hollow reed," says Ess, shifting the boy's hip on his shoulder. "There is no weight to him at all."

A groan from Rah startles the killer. "Is he coming awake then?" he hisses, looking to the door. "He will give us away to the guard!"

"He will sleep long enough for us to slip out of the city with him. Then it will be up to you to hang on to him until we reach the Amorite camp."

At this Ess gives Mochlos a sly grin, saying nothing. He shoves the other two aside, steps to a basin beside the King's bed and takes a long drink from a full pitcher there, then finds the water gourd hanging from his belt and fills it. Aych and Zee need no prodding to do the same, but Mochlos merely tucks his hands into his sleeves.

Ess makes for the aperture in the wardrobe. "Come along, Priestie. Show us the way out of this gilded cage." He takes Mochlos roughly by the arm and shoves him toward the stool Zee has put beneath the opening. "Up you go."

Minutes later the door to the King's chamber crashes open, the bolt shattered. Rush stands in the opening, his eye scanning the scene. The King lies face down on the bed, trussed like a chicken and gagged. While Peleshet and Mammut rush to unbind him, Rush strides past them, straight into the wardrobe. He has shoved open the hidden door and hoisted himself into the ceiling before they realize he is gone.

A moment later the thud of his feet hitting the closet floor brings them to attention.

"We were lost in the wall," gasps Mursilis as Rush returns to stand at the foot of his bed. "For days. Starving. They killed two of their own men for blood."

"And yet they have returned you," murmurs Rush. "And the Rah is gone."

"The priest found us! He led us back. He convinced them that the boy was worth more than five kings and that he would lead them to him, and then out of the city, if they would return me to Hattusha and take them both to Babylon!"

"Fool priest," says Rush, turning back to the wardrobe. In an instant he is gone.

"Shall we follow you, Sir?" shouts Peleshet, rushing after him, but his question is left unanswered. A draft from the open ceiling lifts his beard as he peers into the darkened passage above.

"It is nothing more than a tunnel here, but somewhere above opens to the roof, thus the cool breeze," murmurs Peleshet.

"Will we follow him?" asks Mammut from below.

"We cannot. For he is already gone. I have the entire city searching for the King. If one could navigate this escape easily, we would have already caught them. I have heard of such labyrinths, built into palaces for the sake of concealing a king when the enemy has breached the wall, or else spiriting him out of the city to save the bloodline. They are treacherous and built to confound the enemy."

"What then of the Master?" asks Mammut.

"He will not go far, no further than his own recall back," answers Peleshet. Climbing down from his perch at the aperture he adds, "Unless he knows this passage already."

CHAPTER 26

In a tent at the site of the Amorite defeat, Nikolaos is pouring himself a cup of the Amegan spirit, from potatoes, that he found his officers drinking from water gourds after the fight.

"You will lead the Hattushan army back to the city in the morning, Aleksandus. And I am sending the army of Amega home to guard the fortress of the Master."

"As you say, Sir. And you?"

"I must fly to Hattusha ahead of you, Aleksandus, faster than a battle weary army can go. I must find the Rah and protect him."

"He was doing very well when I left him, Sir," answers Aleksandus.

"No doubt. But it does not take him long to find trouble, or for trouble to find him. He is more than a slave-god, Aleksandus. More than the agent of a Minoan fertility god. There is a power in his presence. I have seen it. Blessing and enriching everyone he meets, every land he inhabits. Some power that will not tolerate his abuse. What happened to Crete could happen here. He must be protected. And contained."

"You will travel alone then?" asks Aleksandus.

"I will take a few men from the rear as an escort," answers the Lieutenant. Turning to hand Aleksandus the cup he adds, "You have been fighting for the assassin for a while."

"Indeed Sir. Since he was sent to my company in Troy. I was his senior officer then."

Of course, thinks Nikolaos. He would have been a youth then, under your command, for you are good bit older than he. Pouring a small amount of the awful liquid in a second cup and raising it, he watches the seasoned commander drink his down in one gulp and look for him to do the same.

But Nikolaos can only smile and, lifting his cup to his lips tepidly, sip the brew with cautious distrust.

"Terrible stuff," he winces, putting the cup down on a makeshift table made of two bales of hay and a soldier's leather. "I wonder how you do not all go blind."

"It takes some practice, Sir," says Aleksandus

Two hours after spiriting the sleeping Rah out of the King's bedroom, Mochlos and the Amorite killers have reached the end of the tunnel.

"Here it is," says the high priest, waving an oil lamp he snatched from a table in the King's chamber at the back of the door leading into the alleyway. "There will be guards, no doubt, twice as many as before you kidnapped the King."

Through the cracks in the door they can see that it is dark outside. Ess moves toward it, peeks through a crack, Rah's body dangling limply from his massive shoulder. He steps back, waves to Aych and Zee to precede him.

"You and me last, Priestie," he growls at Mochlos, who is standing behind him now with the lamp. "Douse that," he adds, nodding to the light. "And keep close. Once we get outside we'll be moving fast."

"He will wake soon," responds the priest, nodding at Rah's limp body hanging over the big man's shoulder. "You had better tie his feet. If he sets them on the ground, you will never catch him. "

Outside, Zee and Aych have already climbed to the roof of the storehouse and disappeared. Above, on the parapet, the shadows of half a dozen guards can be seen moving to and fro along the western wall. Ess waits until most of the shadows have retreated behind a lookout post on the southwest corner, then makes a dash out the door, flattening himself against the storage building and moving along that way until he finds the ladder he is looking for. Mochlos takes a deep breath, says a quick prayer to the moon, and dashes out behind, making sure to close the door behind him. From the outside, it is nearly invisible.

As he climbs the ladder behind Ess, spitting debris that shakes loose from the big man's sandals each time he gains a rung, Mochlos hears a skirmish above. He flattens himself against the ladder, clinging for dear life, while Ess pauses on the rung above. Mochlos can see Rah's mop of golden curls hanging against the henchman's back in the moonlight and he suppresses an urge to pull the filthy skirt of the kidnapper's tunic up and over them to hide his treasure from the guards above. After a moment of hanging in terrified misery, he hears a voice overhead.

"Pssst! Up quick. There'll be more coming any minute!"

Mochlos follows Ess to the roof of the storehouse and across to the edge of the western wall of Hattusha. Three men in Hattushan military tunics and leather helmets lie where they fell on the parapet. "Mother Moon," breathes Mochlos, understanding with no uncertainty that his plan has caused the deaths of these three men. Somehow, the killing of royal guards had never figured into them.

Feeling as if he might vomit at the sight of their ignoble slaughter, for two have had their throats cut to the bone and the third is missing an arm, he scuttles across the top of the wall to follow Ess down the exterior ladder, utterly unaware that behind him the door of the hidden passageway has opened to release the shadow of the assassin into the alleyway.

In the camp of the Amorites a decision has been made. The kidnappers have not returned for some three days and it is more than likely that they have been caught and tortured for information. A counsel of officers has chosen a leader, Rim-Sin, who claims to be a descendant of the great Rim-Sin of Larsa. Rim-Sin is rich but wants to be richer. It is he who has held the Amorites in the mountains waiting for the return of the kidnappers with the King of Hattusha. But after three days, even Rim-Sin's appetite for riches is dimmed by the prospect that the men have given away their position and that even now an army is being mobilized to confront them. In this environment, so far from supplies, they are at a considerable disadvantage and could never withstand an onslaught by fresh troops from Hattusha. Rim-Sin determines to retreat early on the morning of the day of Rah's capture. The rain has stopped, making a retreat more realistic, and by the time Mochlos and the kidnappers have made it over the wall and escaped the city, he and the remaining Amorite troops are miles away, hoping to catch up with Iamhad's army and regroup.

Behind the kidnappers, Rush the Assassin follows with eerie stealth. He has no provisions and wears only his assassin's tunic, hood and leggings, and a pair of Amorite moccasins he discovered at the foot of Iamhad's bed the night he took the Amorite commander's heart. Unprepared to track a band of thieves into the mountains he nevertheless keeps pace with them, surprised at the speed they travel, and not a little amazed that the fool priest is keeping up. The climb is steep and sometimes sheer, still treacherously slippery from the rains, and even he has to be cautious of the footing. One misstep could send a man into a gorge or through the roof of a cave.

By day's end, the band of killers has reached the site of the Amorite camp and found it deserted. Exhausted from their three day ordeal in the wall and the hike up the mountains, far more strenuous than their journey down had been, they decide to camp there. At least there is a stream nearby where they can fill their gourds and drink, and garbage to pick through in hopes of finding food. Mochlos has brought along a sack of provisions but Ess is determined to ration it, unsure of how much of a lead the army has on them and how long they will need to stretch it. Aych finds a warped bow and a few arrows in an abandoned tent and goes off to hunt for rabbit.

Rah awakened shortly after their escape from Hattusha. Finding himself hanging over Ess' shoulder he immediately dug into the man's back with relentless teeth and nails. Ess screamed and threw him to the ground, murder in his eyes.

Looking about in confusion, Rah bared his teeth, growling low in his throat at Ess. His feet bound together, he could do little else.

Rush watched from his hiding place as the priest stepped between Ess and Rah, putting out a hand as if to shield the boy from the brute. "You will not vent your anger on him. He is priceless, and he will make us all rich men." He spoke authoritatively, calmly, patiently watching for Ess to fold, a clever merchant bartering with a fool.

"Pah," snorted Ess after a moment of glaring at the priest. "How am I to carry a wild animal across Anatolia?"

"He will come of his own accord," answered Mochlos. "Give me time to speak with him."

"Speak to that? That is not human. That is an animal. In the morning I will truss him like a goose and gag him. Then I will pick him up and we will move on."

After the killers have settled themselves for the night, Mochlos approaches Rah, who is sitting by the fire at the mouth of the cave the band has taken refuge within. When the priest squats beside him, Rah turns away, his only acknowledgement that he is aware of his presence a warning rumble in his throat.

"Listen to me, Rah. Hattusha is a warrior city. There is nothing here for us. Nothing here for the Rah. You saw it yourself. No temple dancers, no concubines devoted only to the god. But I have arranged for these men to take us safely to the most wondrous city in all the earth! To Babylon! Have you never heard of it? The streets are paved in gold! There are many, many priesthoods, many gods with which to compete! We will take it over, you and I, just as we did Knossos! Think! Do you want to be the assassin's pet? That is all you are now, all you can ever be in this land of bloodthirsty warriors. But in Babylon, there is art, there is culture, there are riches beyond your imagination! In Babylon, the Rah can truly be what he was made to be!"

Rah has stopped growling. He shoots the priest a curious look under his lashes.

"Babylon, big like Knossos? Many priest? Many dancer?"

"You could fit three cities of Knossos within the walls of Babylon, Rah. It is an awesome place, the very heart of the world! A place of peace, progress and prosperity. My dear boy, it is the center of civilization!"

"Who is king Babylon?" asks Rah.

"That is Samsu-Titana, a descendant of the great Hammurabi."

"How you know all this? You lie to Rah, priest. You are never go to Babylon. You are always live in Knossos. Tuma, he tell me."

"I have never been, no. But I have traded with Babylon. Why, the assassin himself has traded with Babylon, under the guise of Ameg the Merchant. Where do you think your silks came from?"

"Tiko say silk is come from China," says Rah, crossing his arms over his chest. But his prismatic eyes are twinkling with interest.

"From China, through Babylon, to Crete," responds the priest.

Rah bites his lip, glares at Mochlos, nods to his bound feet.

"You take off. No bind Rah like chicken. Rah is no chicken. No pet for Wolf. Rah must dance for King, save Ting Ya, save Josepha, save Hali from plague."

Mochlos raises his eyebrows. "The plague? Ah, you know about the plague then, boy, though you left Amega before the first signs of it?"

"Rah know. This why Rah leave. Must go to city of light. Dance for king."

Struggling to interpret this riddle, Mochlos makes a sudden connection. "Rah, you speak of Babylon, for Babylon is often referred to as the city of eternal light! Don't you see? You are being instructed by the god to go to Babylon with me, Babylon, city of light! To dance, as you did in Knossos, for the King!"

On the third day of their journey, the killers spy the Amorite army heading east over the plains. It is a dry day, oddly warm for this time of year due to the explosion of Thera, and they are descending into a valley when Aych points to a cloud of dust in the distance.

"There they are! We'll catch'em by nightfall if we double time." He is already jogging down the embankment with Zee when Mochlos takes Ess' arm and pulls him aside. Rah, delighted by the quickened movement, has passed Zee and Aych effortlessly and disappeared in a grove of trees below.

"Think what you are doing, man," cautions Mochlos. "Is it your intention to put our treasure into the hands of greedy men? Would you trust this treasure to a mercenary army?"

"He's ours and he'll stay ours," answers Ess, pulling his enormous arm from the priest's fingers.

"Oh, really? You are that marvelous a fighter that you can take on the entire legion we see ahead?" responds Mochlos.

"I got a reputation amongst them," answers Ess gruffly.

"No doubt! Though even so, I myself, were I a soldier of fortune, would want to smuggle this diamond into Babylon and present him to the King personally to claim the highest reward. But it is nothing to me what you chose to do with your share. Suit yourself," he gives Ess a shrug and begins down the slope. Ahead, a gleeful yelp followed by a splash indicates that Rah has found a stream to bathe in.

"Wait," says Ess, taking hold of the priest's sleeve with obvious restraint.

"Yes?"

"He's a greedy bastard, I'll give you that," says Ess, looking down the slope toward the sound of Rah's antics.

"He?"

"Rim-Sin. He'll be in charge by now, no doubt. Clever bastard, too. The rich always want to be richer."

"Well if you don't intend the others to run pell-mell into the army camp, you had better let them know your plans," Mochlos nods in the direction of Rah's giggles.

"No need," answers Ess enigmatically. He pushes past Mochlos and begins down the hill.

"The provisions I alone thought to bring will not last long, and they are hungry," continues Mochlos, following behind. "They expect that they will fare better when they rejoin their company."

"Army was out of food when the seven of us left. They're no better off now, 'cept for pillaging along the way," barks Ess.

When Mochlos reaches the bottom of the slope and rounds the grove of trees he finds Rah, wet and naked but for a loin cloth, standing in front of Zee and Aych with one fish in his teeth and another in his hand. He waves the larger fish over his head, taunting the two Amorites to take it from him. But each time one lunges for him he spins or flies backward out of their grasp, impossibly fast, giggling with mischief. Even with a live fish in his mouth he is dizzyingly beautiful, thinks Mochlos, who can only stand back and sigh, as if at the end of his patience, as the boy is ultimately tackled by the two hungry murderers.

Plying the larger fish out of Rah's left hand, which is still stretched over his head though he is now on his back, Zee shouts his victory. "Ha-hah! Got it! Got me a fish to eat!"

"You'll share that!" cries Aych, shoving Zee off the boy. "And be careful with him, you'll crush him, you fat oaf!"

"Me?" cries Zee, jumping to his feet. "You're the one who's sitting on him! Wonder he isn't suffocated. Tough little god, aren't you?" he makes an attempt to snatch the second fish from Rah's clenched teeth but has no luck. "Gimme that, little god, I'll cook'em for us."

By now Ess is towering over Aych. He grabs him by the rough and pulls him off Rah and to his feet. "Touch that boy again, I'll break your legs and leave you here to starve," he says, tossing Aych aside and reaching down for Rah with a strangely soft expression.

Rah looks up at Ess, subdued. He takes the fish from his mouth, offers it to the burley Amorite. "This one for Ess," he says. Ess ignores the fish, taking Rah's wrist instead and pulling him to his feet.

"You don't weigh nothing," he says, as if to himself, pulling the boy closer and looking into his face. Rah maintains his stare. "What the hell are you?" says Ess, snatching the fish and waving it in the boy's face. "This ain't human, catch'en fish with your teeth."

"No teeth," says Rah. "Hand. Fast." He makes a snatching gesture with his left hand, pecking Ess' midsection. He smiles up at the battle scarred face, turns over his hand and opens his fingers. There is a flint in his palm.

For a moment Mochlos, who has been watching this exchange from a few feet away, becomes alarmed. He makes a reaching motion toward Ess as if to protect Rah from a coming blow. But the big man only chuckles, takes the flint stone from Rah's hand and returns it to the hidden pocket of his tunic. Then he pops the boy on the head with the fish and turns to toss it to Aych.

"Go and fetch us a few more then," he nods at the stream, turning back to Rah. But the boy is already gone, a single explosion of water indicating that he has already determined to do just that.

"Strange creature," murmurs Ess, shooting the priest a glance. "Where'd he come from anyway? Fall to earth from a star?"

Mochlos is standing beside the burly giant, watching for the boy's head to break the water. "You could use a bath yourself," he says, ignoring Ess' question. "What sort of impression do you think we will make in Babylon, with you three smelling like a herd of billy goats?"

Ess has swung his head around with murder in his eyes. But the priest's laconic gaze defeats him.

"We ain't a pretty picture, Priestie, no matter what we smell like," he grumbles.

"Well," responds Mochlos, giving Ess a dismissive glance. "That will have to change. When we get to the city, we will purchase appropriate clothing for the three of you." He looks away when the big man raises his brows at him.

"And what do you expect we will pay with, Priest?" says Ess.

Mochlos looks up at the man with confident authority. "I think the King's seal ring will bring quite a handsome sum, don't you?" he answers coolly.

Ess' face darkens. "And you think I've stolen it?"

"One of you has it. It was not on Mursilis' finger when we redeposited him in his chamber."

"You're a clever bastard, Priestie," is all Ess answers, after a moment of silence. Rah is trotting back up onto the beach with two more fish. Ess gives him a bemused look and nods at the boy. "That's quite a catch there," he smirks at Mochlos, then moves off to collect some branches for the fire. Mochlos' eyes trail after him, uncertain if the man was referring to the fish or to the boy.

Half a mile away, Rush is collecting a feisty grouse from a snare he had set in the brush the night before. He has seen the remnants of the Amorite army moving east through the valley a half day ahead of the kidnappers and the priest. He has watched Mochlos play the biggest of them like a fiddle on the strings of his greed and he is no longer concerned for Rah's immediate wellbeing. After breakfast he will head back to the place where he tied Iamhad's warhorse and his own dogs. He will fetch them, then catch up with Rim-Sin and the rest of the enemy horde by nightfall. But this time he will not be so kind as he was to Iamhad's men. These men will not be allowed to die honorably, in battle. These men will pay for their decision to kidnap the King of the Hatti.

On a ridge overlooking the valley, Aleksandus, accompanied by the ten thousand victorious, and highly energized, Hittite troops, has spotted the Amorites making their way east. They are yet a dark speck in the distance, a stain on the landscape of Anatolia, but their presence in his country is a thing so abhorrent to the Amegan commander that he has all he can do to keep himself from leading a second charge down into the valley to meet them head on. Instead, he holds his hand up, halting his troops, and turns to face his officers.

"We will camp here for the night," he informs his lieutenant, who draws his horse up beside him and stares down the valley toward the cloud of darkness that is the Amorite hoard like a falcon who, from above, has seen a flock of crows converging on its nest.

"And let them escape while we are asleep?" he turns to Aleksandus with a look of genuine pain.

"Our men need rest. They, too, will need to rest. They are in a strange land and have no doubt exhausted their provisions. Nor will they move at night, and it is nearing dusk. They will camp in the valley, where there is water and a chance to find food. In the morning, before the dawn, we will attack."

Nikolaos has reached Hattusha. Riding his animal to exhaustion, he has had to make the last miles on foot. He has not slept, and has long since lost the men he chose to accompany him. Now he enters the city by the south gate to be greeted by Peleshet and a company of newly retrained Hattushan troops. They come to halt in a neat formation, eyes forward, shoulders back, hands on hilts and chin's up as Peleshet rushes forward to drop to his knees in a military bow to the Lieutenant General of Amega.

"Where is Rah, Peleshet?" are the first words to come from the man's mouth.

"Kidnapped, Sir," answers Peleshet, rising. "And the Master has gone after him."

"Gone after him? He is in pursuit of the kidnappers? Then there is nothing to fear," responds Nikolaos, exhaling a breath he feels he has been holding since he left Amega.

"There may well be, Sir, even so," answers Peleshet carefully. "Amorites, Sir, entered the city by way of a secret passage in the wall, led by Ammuna, the exiled heir. He took them to the King's chamber and traded places with the sovereign. By the time I had arrived he was on the throne, and these bureaucrat fools who run the palace were taking orders from him."

"He is a traitor then?" asks Nikolaos innocently enough.

"It was the Master who installed Mursilis on the throne, Sir, for that was the wish of the late Hattusilis. Mursilis is grandson to the late king. Ammuna and Hammas were estranged from their father when he died."

"And where is this Ammuna now, Peleshet? I trust he is no longer on the throne," responds the Lieutenant.

"He is in the dungeon, Sir. But the Priest, Mochlos, must have learned of his deed and discovered the secret to the passageway from him, else he would not have known of its existence."

"And how do we know he knew of its existence, Peleshet?" asks Nikolaos, still struggling to understand.

"The Rah had taken to sleeping in the King's chamber after Mursilis' disappearance three days ago," answers Peleshet, a look not unlike an apology crossing his face. "He was almost always in the company of one or more harem girls once he discovered the King's harem."

"This is no surprise," frowns Nikolaos, shaking his head.

"When the Master arrived and learned what had happened to the King, he went immediately to see that the Rah was safe. We found two harem girls, their throats cut, the King bound and near death. The Rah was missing."

"Of course," breathes Nikolaos, putting a hand to his brow.

"The Master must have deduced the truth instantly, for he immediately looked for and quickly discovered the hidden passage in the King's wardrobe and he disappeared into it, we assume in pursuit of the kidnappers. We could not follow, for the place is a death trap, a labyrinth of tunnels leading nowhere, and without knowledge of it one will become lost and die there. One of the girls had yet enough breath left in her body before she died to tell us that the priest and three filthy Amorites had burst in upon them as they slept in the King's bed. They attacked the girls before they could run and alert the palace, deposited the King, trussed and gagged, on his bed, and took the Rah."

"The priest? Are you sure?"   And it was I who sent him ahead! thinks Nikolaos, squinting in pain.

"Yes, Sir."

"But why? What possible good could it do him to exchange Rah for the King when the Rah is worth more than twenty kings to the assassin?" murmurs Nikolaos, almost to himself.

"Perhaps Ammuna knows the answer to that, Sir. For why would Ammuna give the secret of the passage away except for some gain, or promise of freedom?"

"Take me to the dungeon," says Nikolaos, his grey eyes darkening.

"Sir." Peleshet makes a curt bow from the waist and turns on his heels. The troops split instantly to form two lines at attention, and Peleshet leads the Lieutenant General of Amega toward the palace at a near run.

In the dungeons of Hattusha, what is left of Ammuna's mind is spinning with delightful thoughts of retribution against the assassin. As he paces his cell, though it is pitch dark within, he holds the lock of Rah's hair to his cheek and strokes it with filthy fingers, humming a tune he learned as a boy in the days before his brother took Sophina and twisted his psyche forever.

There is no light in the dank and putrid smelling hole in which he lives, and there is no one in the dungeon with which to share his victory but for a pair of murderers who killed a man in a brothel brawl seven years ago. But he can see the silvery golden strands in his mind's eye, and he speaks to them like a woman speaks to her favorite child. You and I will tear the assassin's heart from his chest, he whispers to the lock, stroking it with patient, even reverent fingers. It is our turn, our turn, our turn.

So deep is he into his reverie with the curl from the Rah's golden head that when Nikolaos and a dozen soldiers come storming down the stairs with torches that he does not notice them until they are at his door and the door is being unbolted.

He is here! thinks Ammuna then, and a wave of manic glee shudders through him as he is grabbed by either arm and dragged out of the cell.

"Careful, fools!" he gasps, clutching the curl in his right hand. "See here what I have in my hand, Antaris! It is your heart!" And yanking his arm from the soldier's grasp he holds his fist high in the air in the light of the torches so that the gossamer strands might catch it.

"What is in his hand?" snaps the tallest of them. He steps briskly forward to catch the man's wrist and examine the wisp.

"It is your heart, Antaris!" hisses Ammuna, blinking in the harsh light. "Put back those torches, you blind me."

"My gods, it is hair! It is hair.... golden..." Nikolaos chokes. "It is the Rah!"

"Yes, Antaris. You're heart," wheezes Ammuna, turning his shoulder at Nikolaos and hunching over the curl protectively.

"Who has taken him? Where?" Nikolaos has grabbed Ammuna's arm and flung him against the wall of his cell with such force that the crack of his bones is audible. The prince slumps to the ground.

"You're heart..." he murmurs, holding up the curl. "I have your heart, Antaris," he chokes, spitting blood.

Nikolaos is on his knees, both hand on the prince's throat. Ammuna's face goes crimson, then blue. It is Peleshet who puts a hand on Nikolaos' shoulder, bringing him back to sanity.

"He is no good to us dead, Sir," offers Peleshet, bending to speak into Nikolaos' ear.

The color returning to Ammuna's face belies the Lieutenant's grip relaxing.

"Who has him, Ammuna," says the Lieutenant.

"I have nothing left to lose and nothing to gain," answers the prince, gasping but smiling still. "I have already lost everything, because of you. You sent my Sophina into your own nest on the Amorite plague animal. But I have learned that you have a heart, Antaris, and that that golden boy," and he holds the curl up to Nikolaos' face, "is the key to it. And so I have ransomed my nephew with your heart! Is the boy gone, Antaris? Then the killers have taken him and by now they are far away, no doubt in the clutches of the Amorite army. No doubt Rim-Sin is retreating to regroup with Iamhad. He is out of your grasp, Antaris. He is gone. The priest is taking him to Babylon to present to the Amorite King!"

He has no sooner said this than Nikolaos has his sword at his throat. But again Peleshet sets his hand on the young commander's arm. "Had we not had better leave his fate to the Master, Sir?" he cautions.

A vision flashes through Nikolaos' mind, then, of the assassin, freshly returned from gutting and hanging two renegade palace guards by their feet, his tunic darkened with blood, his mask tucked in his belt, a grouse hanging by a snare in his left hand. "What did you do with them, Captain? I was not finished with them," and then, "Do you know what a Hittite commander does to a junior officer who fails to discipline his men appropriately, Captain?"

A shudder runs through Nikolaos bowels. "I know what the Greeks do," he says aloud to no one, withdrawing his sword from Ammuna's throat.

"Sir?"

Nikolaos rises to his feet. "Leave him here to rot, Peleshet. We must follow them."

"To Babylon, Sir?" whispers Peleshet, incredulous.

"To Babylon," answers the lieutenant general, turning to lead the men out to the stables.

CHAPTER 27

Rim-Sin is bathing in a stream when Rush finds him.

It is a strangely warm day and the Amorite commander is taking advantage of it. He has stationed a handful of guards further up the stream, then allowed his body to drift down toward an overhang of vegetation so that he might satisfy his personal needs in private. The water is chill but the air is tepid and he is oddly comfortable with the contrast. He is accustomed to bathing in icy waters, and always takes advantage of an opportunity to refresh himself. He is a man whose life has always been about taking advantage of opportunities.

Rim-Sin has no illusions about the effectiveness of the guards he has posted, nor about their loyalty to him. In this army of mercenaries every man is, in the end, for himself, and no one is going to lay down his life for him. He is not disturbed by this fact. It is the way of the mercenary, and it is the way of the businessman. But he has paid the six men well to keep watch and they are some of the brawniest of the bunch. On top of that, they believe he is the progeny of the great Rim-Sin of Larsa.

Rim-Sin also believes he is a descendant of the great Rim-Sin I. He believes this because his mother told him stories as a child of his link to the illustrious legend. According to her, his father's mother was from Uruk, where two hundred years earlier Rim-Sin I had sacked the city, sparing its inhabitants. This made him a beloved figure in Uruk. More than one family claimed that their ancestor was impregnated by the great warrior, who had a healthy appetite for the spoils of his conquests and frequently chose the prettiest virgin daughter of the king of the city he conquered to keep as a concubine. Rim-Sin's mother claimed that his father's ancestor was one such virgin, and that he was the result of that liaison.

The fact that Rim-Sin's mother was a whore who could only guess at who her youngest son's father was did not dim Rim-Sin's certainty that he was a descendant of the great conqueror, later defeated by the illustrious Hammurabi himself. Rim-Sin was named after the monarch and that was enough for him. Besides, it made him quite popular with the ladies.

It also had a peculiar effect on his superiors when he was first forced into military service to King Samsu-Titana. It seemed to strike a chord of awe with his betters, and it wasn't long before he found he was being promoted again and again based on little else. Apparently it never occurred to them that a whore might have the audacity to name her son whatever struck her fancy.

He learned quickly to take advantage of every opportunity his name afforded him, and until now, his name had served him well.

But finding himself now leading an army of half-starved mercenary soldiers in the land of the Wolf of the Hatti was no advantage, as far as he could see. Except in that he had every intention of leading them straight back to Babylon, where he could return to his life as a rug merchant without losing his head.

Refreshed from his icy bath, Rim-Sin shakes the water out of his ears and climbs up the bank of the stream to fetch his garments, which he has hung in a tree so that they are not pissed upon by some animal wandering by who takes the rank smell of many weeks of soil as a proclamation of territorial dominance.

He steps up onto the shore and stands, arms out and legs wide to allow a breeze to dry his body before he dons his tunic, taking a moment to enjoying the feel of an unusually warm winter sun on his skin. He closes his eyes and lifts his face with an "Mmmmm," and is smiling like a fool when the blow of a catapult ball strikes his midsection, forcing the air from his lungs in a loud grunt and sending him back onto his bare bottom on the gritty beach.

"You are the leader."

Unable for a moment to inhale, Rim-Sin rolls over onto his face, clutching his stomach. Is this how I am to die then? he thinks. And not even see the face of the one who is killing me?

And then the delirious relief of taking air into his lungs. Not yet! I am not dead yet. But he has barely had a chance to turn his head. Something huge and black there, dressed in rags like a swaddled corpse. And then a tree falls on his back between his shoulder blades and he hears his rib crack.

Despite the jolt of pain he is unable to do more than grunt. Nor is there time, for he is being turned over and pinned to the ground under an almost unendurable weight on his chest. He gulps for breath as a massive palm presses his forehead into the grit. A great black thing looms over him, more hideous even than the legends it has inspired amongst his people.

A head made of black rags, one furious obsidian eye exposed, and a gleaming gold and silver dagger with a tip like a needle, a blade as thin as the edge of a feather, a base as wide as a man's palm, is coming toward his left eye.

Rim-Sin manages an "Uugh" as the needle sharp point takes a pearl of flesh from his cheek. The monster holds the bit of flesh at the end of the blade for him to see, an inch from his eye, then flips it casually off the blade to be lost among the pebbles.

And he is being hauled to his feet by his hair and tossed like so much laundry against the tree upon which his garments no longer hang.

"Name," says Rush, and it is a moment before Rim-Sin realizes that this is a question.

"Rim-Sin," answers Rim-Sin hopefully. Surely he will recognize the greatness of the name and consider his actions carefully.

"Put them on, Rim-Sin." A wad of cloth is thrown in his face. "You are mine now."

Rim-Sin grabs at the clothing and instinctively covers his naked genitals. Blood is running down his cheek into his mouth and he licks at it, afraid to raise his hands to his face for fear that the ghoul may think it a gesture of non-compliance. He stands holding his clothing over his shriveled sex and looks at the thing before him like a child who has finally laid eyes upon the monster he has always known was hiding under his bed.

The man is towering, a good head taller than he, but it is not his height that strikes awe in Rim-Sin's heart so much as the murderous energy that comes from him like a heat. It is like a catapult ball of rage and it strikes him full in the chest, taking his air.

All of his fanciful dreams of his glorious origins drain into his feet with his blood. His knees obey his instincts and bend, nay, crumple like broken pillars and he falls upon them, and then puts his face into the sand as well.

"Lord Antaris. Do not kill me. I am your servant," he breathes, shielding his head with his forearms.

His garments fall on his hands.

"Then obey me. Put them on," comes the voice of doom above his head. "And that is the last order I will ever repeat to you, Rim-Sin."

"Master! I am honored to-"

Another blow catapults Rim-Sin onto his naked buttocks just as he is coming to his feet to offer his utmost loyalty, his devotion and, yes, even affection, to the illustrious Wolf of the Hatti and Master of Amega.

"Speak when you are spoken to, imbecile," growls Rush, settling his hands on his hips as he watches the Amorite leader crawl to his feet and hastily pull on his tunic and moccasins.

"Follow," grumbles Rush, turning to slip into the vegetation like a black ghost. It is all Rim-Sin can do to keep sight of him, let alone match his stride. Soon enough he realizes that they are headed straight for the soldiers he posted further up the stream.

Ah, thinks Rim-Sin. He is walking straight into my guard! Could it be that I, Rim-Sin, will be the man who captures the Wolf of the Hatti?

Rim-Sin's head is spinning with dreams of fame and glory as he follows the black beast up the beach into denser foliage. Presently the sound of the forest around him dims as a disturbing chorus of guttural moaning reaches his ears. At first Rim-Sin thinks this is the breeze pushing the limbs of the cork oak to and fro, but when he stumbles into a clearing and sees the first man hanging by his feet from the broadest limbs of a particularly lovely specimen, his belly sliced open, his entrails in his hands, he cries out.

All six have been trussed, hung and gutted in the same manner, and all but one is still alive.

"Rim-Sin, Amorite dog, take note," says Rush, stopping short to plant his feet apart and admire his work. When the Amorite leader fails to step forward he looks back at him, the brow over his exposed eye arched, then grabs the man by the throat and pitches him forward to his knees.

"See here," continues Rush, folding his arms over his chest and nodding at the butchery. "The best an Amorite who crosses my borders can hope for. They have yet a few hours, perhaps as much as a day, to live. As long as they keep their bellies from spilling onto the ground, where predators will surely find them and gorge themselves on their living flesh. As it is, they have only the birds to concern themselves with." Rush has wandered over to the closest man to give him a push, causing the man to spin on the rope he hangs from.

Rim-Sin falls yet again to his knees. He puts his face to the dirt and cries, "Master, spare me their fate! I am your ally!"

"Slave soldiers to Amega," says Rush, turning to offer Rim-Sin a smile beneath his hideous hood.

"Master?" the fallen leader whimpers, looking up between his fingers.

"Slave soldiers, Rim-Sin. Yes. A new concept in war. Why not? Am I not the author of war? You will lead them south and surrender them to the Hattushan army. They will be taken under guard back to Amega. Fair payment for the damage done by the plague animal. A burned out apartment and grain room. And Ghedi. I liked Ghedi," he shakes his head sadly.

If he could move at all, Rim-Sin would have to laugh at the picture, a sad, wingless gargoyle, hands on hips, head bowed, mourning his lost servant.

"Master, there are several thousand men in the King's service-"

"None in the King's service," answers Rush, lifting his head to consider another of the moaning, gutted guards. Casually he steps beneath the man, then lifts his dagger to poke at the entrails spilling though his fingers. The man screams and faints. "All slave soldiers to Amega now, all mine. Under your command of course," says Rush, giving the unconscious man a spin.

"Dear Inanna!" breathes Rim-Sin into his hands. "How am I to convince four thousand mercenaries to walk themselves into the Wolf's den to become slaves?" He is not addressing Rush, but speaking to his hands, as if the goddess lodged in the creases of his palms.

"I do not know, little Amorite dog," answers Rush, clearly enjoying himself. "But you shall. Man is a resourceful creature, and you are more resourceful than most. It takes some imagination to pass a rug merchant off as the descendant of one of the greatest warriors in history. And so you will take your lying, imposter's brain and shake it until it rattles. And an idea will fall out. For if you do not," he moves to the third gutted guard and gives him a good spin so that the man loses his grip on his guts and they fall in impossibly long ropes nearly to the ground.

"Uuughhh!" cries Rim-Sin, in unison with the man in the tree.

"As you see," says Rush, lifting his dagger to gesture proudly at his work. "It is an art, this thing so callously called 'assassination'. I am no dumb brute, no savage." He lifts his arms, gesturing to the carnage he has created. "I am an artist."

Rim-Sin is whimpering into his hands. Suddenly he is lifted to his feet by his beard to face the wolf's hot breath on his face. "And you are my brush, Rim-Sin."

"You wish for me to lead them into an ambush then? To spare my own life? To offer up thousands as slaves, for the sake of one?" whispers Rim-Sin, looking up into the assassin's single exposed eye. It is a terrible eye, cold and predaceous. It is the eye of a shark.

Rush releases the Amorite leader, folding his arms over his chest as if considering the complaint.

"A better man would not do it," he muses, then stoops to holster his dagger. "No. A better man, a man who had a name he did not steal, would not. But you," and as suddenly as the words have hit the air, two crescent shaped blades are pressed to Rim-Sin's temples. "You will do it. You will lose face before your men," and that rapacious eye winks, "or lose your face altogether."

Rim-Sim feels himself swoon. But if I fall, he will cut me. He will do what he says. He is fast in his work, this I know. This is the legend. They say in some countries he is also called Rush. Rush the Assassin. His blades are terrible and swift. I would not make it to the ground without being parted from my face.

And so Rim-Sin stays on his feet, staring at that single black eye that seems to glitter with mischief, perhaps even mirth. His mouth is dry and he cannot speak, nor is he able even to lower his gaze in deferment. His eyes are fixed on the assassin's. He waits, forgetting even to breathe.

Presently the monster removes the blades. "Tongues are a nuisance, are they not? They frequently wag when they should be still, and are still when they should wag." He gives Rim-Sin another moment to speak. When he does not, the assassin takes a heavy breath and holsters his blades.

"Very well, I will interpret, for your cowardice speaks for you. You are indebted to me for sparing you the continuation of your miserable, counterfeit existence as a descendant of a man whose lineage took a darker turn than even you have imagined. You are, in fact, no longer a counterfeit man. You are not a man at all. You are now the genuine Amorite slave-dog of a true descendant of Rim-Sin I. You will bark when I say speak, and you will bite when I say attack, and you will lie on your belly and wag your tail when I say down. And so here is your master's first command. You will return to your troops. Our little meeting, a secret. Speak of it to a single soul, even that of a camel, and you will awaken the next morning with your own face lying on your pillow beside you. Understood?"

Rim-Sin's head is still reeling from the assassin's admission of true filiation with the man he has been claiming for his own ancestor. I am a dead man, he thinks. It takes him a moment to nod his head, though he is certain now that it will do him no good.

"You will send one man ahead, taking the road south from Hattusha to warn my general and his troops. The man will surrender, and tell my commander that he is to take as many men as will not fight to the death," Rush pauses, considering, "That should be all of them." He gives Rim-Sin a shove and then a boot to his buttocks. "Now off with you. I have business elsewhere."

"But we are heading west, back to Babylon! How can I convince thousands of starving troops to follow me south, toward the Valley of the Gods, when they hope to catch Iamhad's army and share his supplies?"

Rush has turned to take a last look at his handiwork hanging in the cork oak. His broad back blocks the sun, except for the two triangles of light created when he plants his knuckles on his hips.

"Were Iamhad's army still an army, they would be eating their own horses by now, for my men would have surrounded them and pinned them down on the plains. But as it is, Iamhad's army is no more." He turns to bat the black lashes of that shark-like eye at Rim-Sin.

"No --- no more?" whispers Rim-Sin, struggling to understand. "How can that be, when there were half as many more as we? And chariots as well! Many hundreds of them."

"No, my little slave dog," Rush has snatched his throat in one bear claw with such speedy that Rim-Sin would be punched back off his feet if he were not being held by his own trachea. "My little imposter." His face is so close to Rim Sin's that the cloth of his hood tickles the Amorite leader's nose. "I took Iamhad's heart from his chest while he yet lay in his own bed, amongst his generals, deep within the safety of his own forces. And in the morning his charioteers awoke to find their horses collicking, and his confounded troops facing adversaries on two sides. The ten thousand of Hattusha, led by my own Aleksandus, on their front and the Wolves of Amega tearing at their rear guard. They are slaughtered, Rim-Sin. Slaughtered like the dogs they were, who thought that they would breach my border, lay Hattusha under siege, and take my King."

Rush released Rim-Sin's throat in time for him to take a breath before he passes out. Rim-Sin gasps for air, but finds his trachea swelling from the abuse. He wheezes and chokes, panicking.

"Now," continues Rush, unperturbed by the interruption, "With no Iamhad to betray me to, where will you flee, little dog, when I release you? Will you attempt to take your troops home? Aleksandus will drive you onto the Table, then starve you out and cut you down, another stack of headless Amorites to add to my collection. Or will you lie to them and lead them into slavery, h-m-m? Will you play the imposter? It is your calling, Rim-Sin. It is your nature. You were never much of an officer, where you? You look more of a merchant to me. A rug salesman perhaps."

The assassin's breath is steaming though his muslin mask in little puffs despite the mildness of the morning air. He is a volcano, thinks Rim-Sin. Hotter than heat. Deadlier than death. He is not a man, but a god of the underworld. He can read my thoughts. I must appease him. All gods demand appeasement. I must sacrifice the army of Samsu-Titana, which is in my command, to this god.

Rim-Sim slides to his knees. He makes a fist of his right hand and thumps his heart, head bowed. Blood from the new wound on his cheek has coagulated, creating a scarlet tear that runs to the corner of his mouth. He is a sad clown.

"I am your servant," he squeaks through his bruised trachea.

"Indeed," responds Rush. He gives Rim-Sin a shove back onto his buttocks. By the time Rim-Sin has righted himself, the black apparition is gone, no trace of him remaining but for the gently swaying bodies moaning in the trees. Rim-Sin considers cutting their throats as an act of mercy to his own countrymen, but reconsiders the idea. Perhaps the assassin, whose eyes have somehow grown roots in his own brain and clearly sees all he sees, would consider it a gesture of insolence or disobedience. He backs away from the men, mumbling, "I'm sorry," before he turns to run like a child from the gruesome scene.

"Bring him here to me," barks Aleksandus, jumping down from his mount and handing his reins to a foot soldier. "What are you saying man. Your commander is laying down a challenge then?"

"Sir," answers the messenger, panting, for he has been running for hours. "These are his words exactly: 'Tell Aleksandus that Rim-Sin leads the remaining army of Samsu-Titana, King of Babylon. Tell him Rim-Sin has been visited by the prince of the underworld himself. Tell him he knows my name and the hour of my death. Tell him that he has ordered me to lead the troops to the Amegan general's doorstep. Tell him that he is to take as many troops as will not fight to the death.'"

Aleksandus has turned away from the man to grab his lieutenant by the arm and draw him aside. "This is most peculiar, is it not Hazar? To send a messenger thus, to give me advanced warning? And a challenge? What say you?"

"Is it possible, Commander, that he has sent us a coded message?" answers the lieutenant, who is in fact Aleksandus' brother by marriage.

"A code, Hazar? For what purpose?" answers the commander, looking back at the heaving messenger. He is a youth of sixteen or so, of African lineage and tall as a sapling. "He could be Ghedi's boy," he murmurs.

"Indeed, Sir. There is a strong resemblance," answers Hazar, looking back at the winded boy and then taking Aleksandus' arm to draw him further out of earshot. "Perhaps Rim-Sin did not want this boy, nor his own troops, to know what he was saying. Perhaps he has had a ... an encounter... with the Assassin."

Aleksandus regards his brother-in-law with surprise. Then his face brightens, as much as the face of an eagle can brighten, and he claps Hazar on the back.

"Hah! 'The Prince of the Underworld. Knows my name and the hour of my death.' Hah!"

"He is surrendering his men to the Master, without their knowledge," continues Hazar, not a little amazed.

"Well, not without a fight, brother," responds Aleksandus, his mirth dissolving. "He said I am to 'take as many troops as will not fight to the death.'" He turns to the messenger, who is being held at sword point several yards away. "Boy, what is your name?"

"I am Akintunde, Sir. My father is of the tribe of Ta-Antyu of Punt. He was taken as a slave and traded to Babylon as a boy."

"The Ta-Antyu of Punt?" cries Aleksandus. "But this is our Ghedi's tribe also! It may be that you are a relative!"

"Ghedi is the name of my father's oldest brother, Sir. He was sold in Egypt also, to a fine man, a kind and rich merchant who traded all along the Great Sea."

Aleksandus flashes Hazar a keen look. "A great merchant, you say? By what name, do you recall. Tell me the truth boy, and you will be amply rewarded."

"His name was Ameg. He was a young man then. He would be in his middle age now, if he lives."

"Your uncle was in turn sold to the Master of Amega, Akintunde. He was in the Master's employ until his death only a month ago. He was a fine horseman, one of the finest, and beloved by all in Amega. He was struck by plague, smuggled in by means of an ass. Let us say an ass on an ass. It was the Amorites who killed your uncle, Akintunde. The murdering Amorites. The same Amorites you serve. But they are about to get their come-uppance."

"Rim-Sin instructed me to return with your answer, Commander," responds the youth bitterly. "But I would stay here with you and fight them, if you would have me."

"You are a boy, Akintunde, unskilled in battle. I would not lose the nephew of our Ghedi to an Amorite axe. But any army needs a swift messenger. You are welcome to come with us. Only if you have made any friendships among the Amorites, hide your eyes for the next twenty-four hours, for only the best will be left standing, and those will become the property of the Master of Amega."

At sundown, Rah and Mochlos and the Amorite kidnappers have reached a familiar bend in the stream.

"This where I find Dashuri!" cries Rah, excitedly. "Maybe we find more horse. Can ride to Babylon."

"Who is this Dashuri, little god," asks Zee, who has taken to walking along with Rah ahead of the others.

"Dashuri my horse. Find here," Rah gestures to the river, "by water. Wolf is catch me. He find me at Table of God. Rah is crazy. Many ghost. Rah hear them march, march," he pantomimes the marching men. "No head. They look, can no find. Wolf, he is take head, far away. Ghost come for Rah. Maybe eat Rah. But Wolf, he come, he scare them away." Rah shrugs. "He scare everybody. He save Rah. Always save Rah. Then he kill -" he hesitates, then turns to Zee and makes a sudden batting motion at his head, snarling. Zee puts out a shielding arm and grabs for his dagger.

"Leopard, maybe? There's leopards on these plains," offers Aych, looking to Ess for confirmation.

"Yah, this," says Rah, making his snarling cat face and raising his hands to claw into the air. Then his face sweetens, distracted by an enormous yellow butterfly that is floating amongst the milkweed beside the stream. He is Rah again. "He kill her."

Ess looks at Mochlos. "What's all this about a wolf?"

"Rah is mad," Rah continues, turning to walk backward so that he might better address his audience. "Spit at Wolf. Pah! Then, here," "he points to some brush along the bank, "here is come Dashuri. Right here. Rah is think, 'Hah! Look here is come horse just for Rah. Now Rah can go Hattusha, dance for King. Save Hali, save Ting Ya, save everybody. Don't need Wolf. I talk to horse. Tell Dashuri, Rah is good rider, strong, big heart for horse. You let Rah ride, pretty boy, we go to Hattusha. Dashuri he say 'Okay Rah, you ride me. We go Hattusha.'" He turns to look at Aych, who is lumbering along with the priest several yards behind. "Dashuri know way," he explains. "Maybe he born there."

"So you found a horse down here by the river," chuckles Mochlos, "Some poor man's warhorse, no doubt, and hopped aboard whilst the assassin watched. That must have sat well with him," he pats his breast. "And that is how you ended up in Hattusha ahead of the beast."

"Ya," says Rah. "This how."

"Assassin? What assassin?" Ess has grabbed Mochlos by the collar of his robe.

"Did I not tell you he was a treasure beyond reckoning? Beloved of the Master of Amega? Of the great Antaris? Rush? Rush the wolf of the Aegean? Do you know nothing but killing and bullying, you ignoramus?" Mochlos' words are bitter but there is a lethal sneer on his lips.

"The Wolf? The Wolf of the Hatti?" stutters Ess, releasing the priest's garment. He looks to his companions, who are standing like clods of dung, mouths open, staring at Mochlos.

"Are there two? Two such men?" responds Mochlos scornfully.

"You said nothing of Antaris of Amega. You said he would be prized beyond measure in Babylon. That he was worth a hundred kings," says Ess, wiping his brow.

"Well there you have it," answers Mochlos, nodding to Rah. "What is worth a hundred kings, numbskull, but the heart of the Assassin?"

"Taru help us. We are dead men." Ess closes his eyes. "What sort of madman are you, priest, to hatch such a scheme? How can you imagine we could outrun the Wolf of the Hatti, and here in his own country no less? We are doomed."

He has no sooner said it than Zee, turning to find that Rah has disappeared, hisses at him, "Look!" He points to the far side of the stream, where Rah is approaching a quartet of horses in full tack.

"Well, I'll be staked," whispers Ess, blinking at the vision. "Those are Amorite ponies. Look at the saddles!"

"They're ours, alright," nods Aych. "And he's got the one."

Across the stream, Rah is refitting the dun mare's saddle, which has loosened and fallen down onto her side. After a few minutes of soothing and patting, he hops easily into it and nudges her toward the water.

"He's bringing them over," whispers Zee. "Maybe the others'll follow 'er."

As they splash into the shallow water the two other ponies tip-toe down the bank, considering their options. Rah turns in the saddle and makes a purring sound. Then he turns forward, ignoring them, and takes the mare to the opposite side.

The two other ponies leap into the stream and fly across if they were trotting over hot coals.

"She is nice, no?" Rah pats the mares shoulder. "Even have pack still. Maybe food." He turns to uncinch the pack and tosses it at Zee.

"You take him," Rah nods to the brown gelding who is crowding the mare. "You take him," he points to Ess and then to a big grey. "This one good for you," he grabs the rein of a flaxen-tailed filly who is nudging his mare with her muzzle. He hands the reins down to Aych. "Priest, he can ride with Rah. She carry both."

"Have you named them also, Rah?" chuckles the priest.

"I can name. This Ono. Dias. Pekla. Far." He points at the horses in the order in which he has assigned their riders. "Ono, she good girl." He pats the mare's shoulder again. "She keep other safe until Rah find. She say, I want go home now, Rah. Go to Babylon. I take you. Now we go Babylon fast, fast."

Ess is standing with his hands resting on his hips, shaking his head with incredulity. Zee and Aych have already mounted their animals and Mochlos is making a sad attempt at climbing onto Ono's back behind Rah. After a few failed attempts, he is shoved by Ess over the horse's croup. He scrambles onto his seat and takes Rah gingerly around the waist.

"You hold tight, priest. Rah ride fast," says Rah.

"Very well," responds the priest, attempting to settle himself as comfortably as possible behind the saddle. "But do not take offense to my hands and turn and bite me, Rah."

Rah laughs. "Rah is no bite priest," he chuckles. Then he turns about to offer Mochlos a whisper. "Better for priest ride with Rah, smell good. You be bad, I make you ride him," he nods at Ess, who is climbing onto the big grey.

"I appreciate your thoughtfulness, Rah," Mochlos whispers back, looking at Ess with distain. "I will see to it that you are well taken care of in Babylon."

"Ta-hah," says Rah, kicking his mount into a trot. "It be Rah is take care of priest, in Babylon. Wolf is come. He is always chase Rah. When he find, he is kill priest if priest no good to Rah. Wolf he is come for Rah. You see."

Not to Babylon, thinks the priest, he cannot enter Babylon, but the grim chill that skates down his spine is the first of many he will fight to ignore as the band makes their way in seeming peace to the borders of King Samsu-Titana's kingdom.

CHAPTER 28

Four days out from Hattusha the band of kidnappers, now making considerable time on horseback, clears a rise to look down on the Valley of the Gods and witness the capture of Rim-Sin's army.

It is the scream of horses, forced to charge into a battle they do not understand, a battle that is made by men, for men, and won or lost by men, that finds the crack in Rah's mind and opens it. Then the reckless insanity of men at war, the fear of the horses and the stench of blood and death rising from the valley splits his psyche, and he is plummeted into his animal world again.

Rah releases an inhuman howl and lets go his reins to put his hands against his ears. Ono, sensing that she is free of her rider and that her rider has lost his mind to panic, panics also. But war is what she knows. The screams of the battle horses call to her. She can only go forward, down into the melee to join her sisters. Rah clings to her back, a cat's instinct to stay aright, but has no control of her charge. Behind him, Mochlos loses his grip on the boy and falls like a sack of flour to the ground.

"Rah! It is battle! You will be killed!" cries the priest from the ground. And then he is lifted up by the great, brutish arm of Ess and thrown behind him aboard Pekla to hang on for his life as the trio of murderers gallop down the hill into the fray.

"I'll not lose him!" booms Ess. "He's mine and he'll stay mine!" but Mochlos can only cling to the big man's back and pray to the Moon that he does not fall again.

"What in Tartarus?" Hazar and Aleksandus are watching the Hittite legion clean up the last of the Amorites. The first charge felled the half of them, and what was left soon broke and ran. Most of the stragglers were cut down attempting to flee, and there are no more than a few hundred who had the sense to drop their weapons and surrender.

"Taru, God of War, it is the Rah!" cries Aleksandus, raising his hand to signal a triplet of mounted officers who have been watching the clean-up.

"You see the horseman charging down the hill? Go and catch him before he is harmed!"

"Who is it, Commander?" asks the nearest man.

"It is the Rah of Knossos! The Master's favorite!" and the men have charged off before he has had time to shake his head and mutter, "Though what in hell's name he is doing here is beyond me."

"Aleksandus, look! There are others! Amorites! Perhaps they have kidnapped him and, seeing his friends, he races to us for safety!"

"Indeed. Three follow him. And race after him as if they know his value. Well, he is in good hands now. As for them, my officers will make short work of them."

But when the Amegan riders reach Rah, Ono, sensing their intention to seize her, spins and delivers a merciless kick to the closest man. He screams, his leg shattered, as Ono spins again, ready to deliver another blow. The immediate violence brings Rah to present. He takes up his reins and drives her into them, using the energy of the impending kick to spring forward into a gallop, east and away from the madness.

"Follow him!" cries the man with the broken leg, who is the ranking officer. "Do not let him cross the border!" But Rah is already diminishing into the distance.

From behind the injured rider, the humongous shape of Ess, whose stench is evident even at this distance, gallops past at full speed on a horse of equal scale. Fastened to his back, and dwarfed by the monster he clings to, is a man wearing the robe of a Philistine priest, on the back of which is embroidered the tripled moon, in gold.

"By the gods, it is the priest, Mochlos," murmurs the officer to himself, squinting at the pair in pain and confusion.

"Halt! He is the property of Amega!" he shouts, but his words are lost in a southern breeze that draws them up and away on a current of arid air above the battlefield.

Rush has been riding for two days without more than a few hours' sleep when he reaches the camp of the combined armies of Hattusha and Amega on the southern flank of the Valley of the Gods. It is midnight and the moon is new, but the black-wrapped, one-eyed beast on the back of a sweat-drenched warhorse is instantly recognized by the Amegan guards who hear his animal skid to a halt only yards from them before they can make out his outline in the faint starlight. His dogs instantly come to his side as he leaps off his mount.

"Take him," Rush snarls, passing the reins to one of the men. "Hup!" he commands the dogs, and the threesome disappear into camp before the guards have had time to drop to their knees to greet their sovereign properly.

Aleksandus is engaged in a game of dice with Hazar when he hears the unmistakable silence that is the Master's approach. "Listen!" he hisses to Hazar, then scrambles to his feet as the shadow of the assassin fills the doorway.

"Lord." Aleksandus bows his head, striking his breast with his fist. Hazar does the same on his knees.

"I have come from Hattusha," Rush drops his pack and pulls off his hood. He looks about the tent, then strides past Aleksandus to take a wineskin hanging against the wall of the tent. He lifts it to his lips and takes a long draught. "Where I found that the King had been kidnapped by Amorite bandits hiding in the mountains. By the time I arrived, the priest had traded himself and the Rah for the King, no doubt expecting to be taken to Babylon, where he might be safe from me and carry on as he did on Caphtor."

Aleksandus nods, too well acquainted with Rush to add or subtract at this juncture.

"I have tracked them to yesterday's battle." Rush has been pacing. Now he stops, takes another swig of wine from the skin, and turns to give Aleksandus an unreadable look. "A good job, Alek."

"Thank you, Sir," responds the commander evenly.

"Two were captured," Rush continues, "And, I trust, reserved for me here. But the others escaped eastward."

Aleksandus allows Rush a moment to continue. When he does not, the commander answers the unasked question.

"The Rah, Lord. He has fled on horseback, east. One of the Amorite kidnappers has taken the priest and gone after him. The other two are in our possession. I have sent a team out in hopes of catching the boy before he crosses the border."

"Hah." Rush shakes his head. "The Rah on horseback? You will not catch him. Nor will the thief."

"I am sorry, Sir," murmurs Aleksandus after a pregnant pause.

"Sorrow is no use to a soldier," murmurs Rush, turning to offer his commander his broad black-swathed back. In the lamp-light it is monstrous, his shadow casting a mountain range on the tent wall. "And yet the thief took the priest with him. Why? Why share the prize? Unless he understands that the boy needs his priest. And what might have convinced him of that?"

"Perhaps the boy himself, Sir," responds Aleksandus.

"Yes, Alek. I believe you are right. My little cat has done it again."

"Done what, Sir?" asks Aleksandus, looking down at Hazar, who shrugs and shakes his head.

"He has seduced another monster," answers Rush before he pads out the door on silent feet.

Late the following day Ess and Mochlos reach the Syrian border. Rah and Ono have long since disappeared from their sight, Ono being the far lighter and swifter steed, and Rah being the far lighter and fitter rider. Ess, nevertheless, continued his pursuit, convinced that the Amorite pony would take the Minoan god slave straight into Babylon, or at least to the borders of the city kingdom, where she would have been bred. The unlikely duo have spent the past twenty-four hour in near silence, their only conversation occurring when Ess offered the priest a portion of the rabbit he had snared and skewered whole over a flame. Mochlos looked at the desiccated hare, its fur singed but not removed from the carcass, its eyes expelled from its skull by the heat, brought his hands up as if to shield himself from the sight of it, and moved off to sit by himself and nibble on dried fruit and nuts from his own stash of provisions.

"I will not eat like the beasts," he muttered, wrapping himself in the sleeves of his robes, for the night was chill.

"Pah," chuckled Ess, tearing and spitting out chunks of the rabbit's hide to get to the meat beneath, "Dainty, civilized Mochlos, the Minoan priest. You don't fool me. I seen a tiger lurking behind all that camouflage." He has ripped a hind leg off the hair and is gnawing at the bone, watching Mochlos over the licking firelight, his eyes half closed, peering. Mochlos shifts on the rock he is using for a stool, putting his shoulder to the brute.

Presently, Ess whispers in an eerie growl, "What was it like to have that beauty all to yourself back in Caphtor, eh? Yours to do with as you pleased? Man like you, he has certain leanings, does he not? I'd take you fer a man who likes to inflict a bit of pain now and then, maybe a flogger. Mmmm. Did you leave all that sweetness to itself, Priestie? Or did you long to dirty him, eh? Bring him down to your level. Make him beg, like you was better 'n he. Like you was his god or something."

Mochlos shoots Ess a brittle look. "How charming. A soldier of fortune, and a fortune teller as well!"

Ess chuckles, but the chuckle is low and lewd. There is no more conversation that night.

Now the pair sit astride Pekla, the priest clinging to the mercenary's back, looking out across the lush agricultural fields that mark out the boundaries of the Babylonian kingdom. They are on a road leading through acres of barley, beyond which a cluster of buildings suggest the comforting possibility of a night's rest under a roof. A puff of smoke issues from a corner of the main building. Ess nudges Pekla forward at a trot.

"Will we be welcome?" asks Mochlos, wondering to himself if there must be more bloodshed before this is over.

"We're in my country now, Priestie. I'm a servant of the King. I've a right to anything in that home."

"This Babylon, Ono!" Rah and the mare have reached the walls of the city by noon of the same day. He stopped for an hour to rest and to graze the mare in the barley fields that Ess and Mochlos would pass later that day, then watered her at an irrigation ditch and rubbed down her legs. Satisfied that she was fit to continue, he mounted her, promising her grain and Syrian pears when they found the King.

"He will give my Ono a soft bed of straw in the palace stable," he coos to her in his native tongue. "Rah will dance for him. And he will be good to Ono. And all of Babylon will love Rah and prosper. And Hali and Ting Ya will be saved from the plague."

Now, as he approaches the great glittering limestone wall of the city, a handful of palace guards, riding fine boned Egyptian horses, trot through the gate. They wear red tunics and elaborate breastplates, and their heads are covered in leather helmets. Behind them, a litter, decked in silks and festooned with colorful flags, is carried by several footmen. Rah pats Ono's shoulder. "Hah, this maybe King, no?" he says in Hittite. "Good for Rah. Meet him now."

Rah hops from Ono's back with a panther's lightness. He steps forward, blocking the road. Ono blows behind him, encouraging.

The horsemen pay him no mind, only continue trotting in a parade rhythm out of the gates. They slowly close the distance between them.

Perturbed at their failure to take notice of him, Rah takes another step forward. Deliberately and with great drama, he unties his cloak from around his neck, swirls it about his head, then drops it into the dust at his feet. It is more than drama. It is a dare.

The two lead riders break their stride and look at one another. What is this nonsense? Their horses come to parade halt, one snorts, the other blows. This is unusual, says the one. I like him, says the other. He smells of grain.

Now there is a commotion beside the litter. Rah waits, small and trim and golden in the arid air, a myth, an illusion. Something brought about by light playing in the bits of feldspar mingled amongst the pebbles in the road. Unreal and beautiful.

A ray of morning light, streaming over the shoulders of the guards from the east, like the fingertips of Ting Ya's sun goddess, strikes the magnificent emerald on his forehead and explodes, a kaleidoscope of colors. The two lead horsemen put their hands up to shield their eyes.

Something is happening in the litter. It is rocking. And the horseman who has been walking beside it is looking about in alarm at the other men. Now he jumps from his steed, passing the reins off to a footman, and falls to his knees.

A second footman, an older man with gentle eyes and a long face, has stepped up to draw the curtain back. He offers his hand, and slim, jewel-bedecked fingers reach for it from within the litter.

Rah blinks, confused. This is not the King. He waits, fighting his instinct to fall to his face in a slave's bow.

She steps to the ground and turns to face him.

Above a silk veil her eyes are smiling. She is beautiful.

Rah pauses, allows her to take him in.

"What loveliness is this?" Her voice is the song of a desert bird, assured and gentle. Full of mystery. It hits his ear and sends him to his knee and into his finest Minoan bow.

"Careful, Majesty. He could be a spy. He could be dangerous! Let us-"

She walks forward. She is but a girl, no more than Rah's age. They dare not allow her to reach him, yet dare not touch her to prevent it. Two guards jump from their horses and rush past her to take hold of Rah. He is hanging in their hands before she has closed the distance.

"Oh!" She has put one, jewel laden hand over her mouth. Amber eyes sparkle with delight above the hand. "Oh he is so beautiful! Look at his eyes, Mefali! Look here!" She is pointing, but not with arrogance. She has stretched out a strong yet delicately long-fingered hand to his chin to lift it for the old guard's approval.

Mefali is at her side, the only guard with the courage, or perhaps the authority, to place a hand on her shoulder and draw her back. Her hand slips away as Mefali leans forward, peering into Rah's face as if it were a fine piece of pottery.

Rah, however, has not taken his eyes off the princess.

Another guard, a large man with fire in his black eyes and five daggers along his belt, storms up and barks, "Lower your eyes, fool!"

Rah gives the man a scowl. He lifts his lip, exposing a single incisor. A burr is collecting in his throat.

"OH!" and now she is laughing with delight, both hands over her mouth. "Oh he is a cat! Hear him! He growls at you, Petuk! He is like my ocelot!"

"I'll give him something to growl about!" snarls Petuk, raising his arm.

But when the princess places herself between his open hand and Rah he lowers it, and his eyes as well.

She turns to Rah. Her face is veiled but for her eyes, which are almond shaped, like his, tip-tilted and twinkling with mischief. They are the color of fine pine resin, or of the rich golden beer made of a certain root in Tarsa. Her eyes alone reveal her beauty, for such eyes cannot be found in any but a beautiful face. The high forehead is evident, and the cheekbones. A small, perfect nose hides behind the wisp of silk covering it, and a heart-shaped and delicate jaw.

"Do you speak, little cat?" she says in Hittite.

Rah blinks. It is the first time anyone but the assassin has called him by that name.

"Rah speak," he says. "Speak Greek, Illyrian, little Minoan. Little Hatti." He finds himself attempting to back away as she reaches out a finger toward his mouth, but the strong arms of the guards prevent him.

"Is your tongue hurt, little cat? You speak as if you've only half a tongue. Poor thing. Did they cut it?" She is stepping forward again, her hand outstretched as if she would pry his mouth open to explore it.

"Rah is no hurt. I bite. I am baby. Always this way."

There is a moment of silence, silence but for the soft breeze that is blowing the silks about her face and lifting Rah's curls. Silence but for the tinkling of the horses tack, and their occasional stomp and blow.

"Majesty-" begins Mefali.

"I want him," she says, giving him a dismissive look. "Never mind our outing, Mefali. Let us take him to Papa and see if we may keep him."

Then she turns to offer the old guard her hand, and allow him to escort her back to the litter. Over her head Mefali shoots Petuk an irritated look. Petuk nods.

"Put him back on his horse," he barks at the two men holding Rah. Then he lowers his voice and leans toward the closer man so that he might whisper in his ear. "And be careful with him, if you want to keep your hands today."

THE WOLF

We can run, and we can run. But the wolf will find us. He is never far away.

And so it is with Rah. Rah who believes that it is *his* magic that will save Amega, save Josepha and Ting Ya, save Hali and all of his horses. But it is not, has never been, *his* love that saves.

It is the wolf's love. The terrible wolf, who thirsts after us, longing, but unable to satisfy that longing. It is the wolf's terrible love that destroyed Crete, and it is the wolf's terrible love that nailed the plague up and burnt it before it could take Amega.

And it is the wolf's love that chases Rah into Babylon.

The historians say that in 1595 B.C. the Hittites, who until then despite their fantastic fighting skills and despite their rise and reign in the region, after years of failed attempts, suddenly took Babylon from the Amorites.

Took it, held it for a brief period in time, and then, mysteriously, lost it.

Or gave it back.

Historians like to make history up as they go, proving their own theories by finding only what they are looking for and ignoring the rest.

They do not know why the great civilization of the Hittites, that in history has been pushed off their table of speculation like so many bread crumbs to the favor of the more talkative Greeks and Egyptians, a civilization that was both fierce and fair, one that invaded, then embraced, the cultures it found, one that, perhaps more than any before or since, would have been the most likely to preserved Babylon for us as it truly was, did not keep the fairest city of all. Babylon the Great.

Because they have overlooked one thing.

One very dark thing.

The wolf.

Perhaps the Hittites, perhaps *one* Hittite, gave Babylon back for the very reason that he took it.

Perhaps he recovered what he'd lost there.

To be continued....

ABOUT THE AUTHOR

Susan Shepherd is a retired law enforcement officer who has spent most of her career interviewing criminals and writing reports for the Court. She lives on the North Fork of Long Island, New York with her husband, three horses and four cats.

www.ingramcontent.com/pod-product-compliance
Lightning Source LLC
Chambersburg PA
CBHW070642180626
46817CB00006B/2211